THE VINES OF YARRABEE

by Dorothy Eden

Dorothy Eden

THE VINES
OF
YARRABEE

COWARD-McCANN, Inc.
NEW YORK

FEDE

FIRST AMERICAN EDITION 1969

Copyright © 1969 by Dorothy Eden

Library of Congress Catalog
Card Number: 69-11054

Third Impression

PRINTED IN THE UNITED STATES OF AMERICA

Acknowledgments

I wish to acknowledge the great help given me in research by Darli McCourt, who suggested the background for this novel, and also by Jim Sare, both of Hodder & Stoughton, Sydney. And for the actual knowledge of Australia as a country, I wish to thank my sister and brother-in-law, Win and Bernie Hampton, of Hunter's Hill, Sydney.

c. 1

Prologue

WHEN the rapidly spreading district of Parramatta, in the Australian state of New South Wales, had exceeded ten miles from the old church and cemetery, it threatened the existence of the big house called Yarrabee, a historic dwelling built in the late 1820's. There could be no question of its being pulled down to make way for the new housing estate. It was an authentic piece of Australian history and, as such, must be preserved.

A notice was put on the rusted iron gates: YARRABEE, THE FORMER HOME OF THE EARLY PIONEERS GILBERT AND EUGENIA MASSINGHAM AND THE SITE OF ONE OF THE FIRST VINEYARDS IN AUSTRALIA. CIRCA 1827-1864.

The house itself was opened to the public. Lovers of architecture could admire the verandaed colonial style with the honeysuckle (cuttings from the original plants) twining around the veranda posts. The garden had been famous and was still a source of delight and wonder. The familiar jacaranda, oleander, waratah, and wattle made a background for a most comprehensive selection of English flowers and shrubs, including a profusion of white climbing roses that cascaded over an ancient trellis, like snow in the blazing Australian sun. A lily pool held a few inches of dark-green scummy water. It was still possible to decipher the words on the sundial: "Every hour shortens life."

Indoors, the furnishings were true to the period. Visitors might admire the faded Chinese wallpaper in the drawing room or more particularly the charming portrait hanging above the fireplace. It was of a slender, long-necked young woman holding a rosy-cheeked little boy on her lap, a hat with green ribbons dangling from her wrist, and a white cockatoo in a cage at her side. The small brass plate read: EUGENIA MASSINGHAM AND HER SON, CHRISTOPHER, WITH PARROT. PAINTED BY COLM O'CONNOR, IRISH EXILE.

There was a story that the house was haunted by a lady dressed in lavender carrying a parasol. No one knew whether this was true, but one of the dresses in the glass case was lavender in color, and there was an ancient parasol, furled and faded.

A Sheraton writing desk with a not very craftsmanlike mend in one leg stood in the little room called Eugenia Massingham's sitting room. Across the hall, in the high-ceilinged dining room, there was a long oak table set for dinner with old English silver and a sophisticated number of wineglasses, four at each place setting. It was well known that guests were invited to drink Riesling, claret, champagne, and port, all of Yarrabee vintage.

Upstairs in the main bedroom an elaborately carved bed bore an inscription stating that this bed in the French Empire style had been part of the dowry Eugenia Massingham had brought with her from England.

Another plaque claimed that Governor Sir Charles Fitzroy and Lady Mary Fitzroy had slept in one of the large bedrooms facing south.

On the grounds there was a winery with concrete walls eight feet thick. It contained an ancient press and vats that still held a faint sour odor. This was the only evidence that a flourishing vineyard had existed on the sunny slopes beyond the house. There was not even a gnarled vine left. They had all been destroyed long ago when the devastating disease phylloxera, that had mysteriously crossed fifteen thousand miles of ocean from the vineyards of Europe, had ravaged the vineyards of Australia.

If one wanted more evidence of the vanished family, one had to go to the old cemetery and find the large ornate headstone with the inscription GILBERT MASSINGHAM, FORMERLY OF SUFFOLK, ENGLAND, LATE OF YARRABEE, FAMOUS VIGNERON, AND

EUGENIA, HIS DEARLY BELOVED WIFE. Nearby was a small sandstone angel, badly eroded, on which the lettering could just be deciphered. VICTORIA, BELOVED INFANT DAUGHTER OF GILBERT AND EUGENIA MASSINGHAM OF YARRABEE.

And a little farther off, for the cemetery must have been getting crowded by then, LUCY MASSINGHAM, YOUNGEST DAUGHTER OF THE LATE GILBERT AND EUGENIA MASSINGHAM OF YARRABEE.

Not many people noticed the simple cross that read MOLLY JARVIS, FORMER NATIVE OF ENGLAND, but then no one was likely to connect her with the occupants of the big house on the edge of the town.

Chapter 1

EUGENIA could see him at last. She had been gripping the side of the small rowing boat, straining her eyes shoreward, ever since she had clambered down the ladder of the *Caroline,* leaving that three-month-long home anchored in the blue waters of Sydney Cove. Mrs. Ashburton was perched on the narrow plank beside her, taking up the room of two with her ample girth and billowing skirts. She was exclaiming petulantly as the wind tore at her bonnet. The brisk breeze had also nearly snatched Eugenia's parasol from her hand. She had had to furl it and let the sun beat on her unprotected face.

Sun and wind and water, wooded slopes with rocky outcrops, glistening honey-colored sand and patches of pale-red earth, primitive rows of buildings clustering around the little jetty. The town of Sydney in Botany Bay, or New South Wales as this part of Australia was now being called.

When Eugenia at last caught sight of Gilbert, she thought that he was the color of Australia with his red hair and sideburns, his sunburned skin, and strong blue eyes.

He was waving wildly.

"Eugenia!" She could hear his voice above the clatter and confusion of the boat being tied up at the jetty.

He cupped his hands to his mouth and bellowed, "Welcome to Australia! Have you brought my vine cuttings?"

Mrs. Ashburton gave Eugenia a nudge and began to laugh in her jolly fashion.

"Well, that's a fine welcome, miss! Which is more important to this young man, his intended wife or his vine cuttings?"

Mrs. Ashburton, a family friend who had providentially been traveling to Australia to join her son, and who had agreed to chaperon Eugenia, had proved a great trial on the long voyage. She was garrulous, tetchy, unpredictable, and had an irritating habit of constantly losing her possessions. The voyage had been spent in a search for a mislaid fan, or lorgnette, or shawl, or smelling salts, or any of a dozen other objects. But she was kind. And at this moment Eugenia's only friend.

All the same her ribald remark gave Eugenia a flutter of uncertainty. She knew Gilbert's dedication to his vineyard, but she had not imagined it would take precedence to her in this first moment of encounter.

She had met Gilbert three years ago at her uncle's château in Burgundy. Her mother was of French descent, and her Uncle Henri was a noted viticulturist with a château and vineyard. It happened that the young Englishman Gilbert Massingham, who had already spent five years in Australia and had seen its possibilities as a wine-growing country, was visiting France at the same time as Eugenia, for the purpose of collecting vine cuttings. He had been traveling in Málaga, Portugal, and the wine-growing areas of the Rhine for the same purpose.

On her first evening Eugenia had seen the way he had looked at her Uncle Henri's wife, who was a very beautiful woman, still young and graceful, and a gifted hostess. Indeed, she had been convinced that he had been interested in no one but Aunt Honoria, until she realized that he saw her aunt as an essential complement to the dinner table, the silver and fine crystal, the epergne full of roses, the good food. And the wine. A chilled white burgundy in long-stemmed, shallow glasses with the fish and later, with the pheasant, a full-bodied claret. Eugenia watched the young man raise his glass and silently toast Aunt Honoria. Then, with a speculative look in his eyes, he had turned to Eugenia and raised his glass with a curious deliberation.

It would, of course, have been rude to ignore her, the only

other woman at the table. But his subsequent attention to her, in the drawing room and afterward strolling on the terrace, had nothing to do with wine.

Or had it?

It certainly hadn't seemed to when he had followed her to England and asked permission to call on her parents.

They were in London for the end of the season. Jessica, the eldest daughter, had been presented. Eugenia must wait until the following year, since she was scarcely eighteen, and money was a little short. There were three younger sisters also, so it was important that Jessica and Eugenia find husbands before too long. A certain younger son of an earl had been particularly attentive to Jessica, and now, it seemed, Eugenia had her Australian.

But he was *not* an Australian, Eugenia emphasized. He had merely spent five years in the colony and, being of an adventurous and ambitious nature, had decided that it was the country of the future. Orphaned at an early age, he had been brought up by a maiden aunt, whose modest fortune he had eventually inherited. With no family and a comfortable amount of money, he could afford to indulge in the adventure of sailing across the world and discovering the country for which he was to develop such a passion. He had already acquired a thousand acres of land near Parramatta, a settlement some distance from the already overcrowded town of Sydney. On this land he proposed erecting a house suitable to bring a wife.

But more important than the house was the frail beginning of his future profession as a viticulturist.

His whole visage changed when he spoke of his infant vineyard. Some men saw Australia in terms of sheep or cattle, some in trading; some were already prospecting for gold. But soon after his arrival, Gilbert had visited a small thriving vineyard at vintage time, and his imagination had been instantly fired. The challenge of such a life exactly appealed to him. Not for him the dusty sheep or the cattle dying in a drought. He much preferred the luscious grapes, the satisfying red wine, and the hazards and uncertainties and triumphs attendant on the beginning of an industry that could become world-famous. This was something worthy of dedicating his life to.

After Australia, Gilbert went on, England was small, confined, limited. The skies were too diffused a blue, the weather too cold, the cities too crowded. There was too much poverty, squalor, crime. When Eugenia's father pointed out that on the contrary Australia was little more than an outdoor prison, a miserable dumping ground for the dishonest trash and riffraff of the British Isles, Gilbert vigorously denied such a thing.

That state of affairs had existed only in the time of the first fleet and the second fleet, nearly half a century ago. Now explorers were making exciting discoveries: the country was large beyond imagining and could hold unbelievable riches. Responsible settlers were wanted, hardworking, healthy, adventurous young men. And women to marry them. The convicts, only a fraction of the population, were an asset in their own way since they represented a constant supply of cheap labor.

Gilbert himself could never hope to build the house he planned without the use of convict labor.

He would begin it on his return. When it was finished, could he anticipate the arrival of his bride?

Yes, yes, Eugenia wanted to cry, because she was in love with Gilbert Massingham's vitality and persuasiveness. But afterward, because she had a strong streak of caution and common sense, she was glad her father had stipulated that she should wait until she was of age. Three years would give both of them time to be sure of their feelings. Gilbert would return to Australia and build his house and establish his vineyard (if such a thing were possible), and Eugenia would remain at Lichfield Court, the old red-brick manor house in Wiltshire which had belonged to her father's family for two hundred years.

Gilbert was anxious that she should spend the three years continuing her study of music, painting, and other ladylike pursuits, none of which, he assured her, would be wasted in the new colony. He took the greatest pleasure in listening to her fluent French, although it was a language he spoke very little himself. His own education had been practical, rather than classical. He seemed to think that possessing a wife who spoke French was somehow an asset to be compared with an appreciation of good wine. Everything, Eugenia reflected, came back to wine.

But her devotion to her lessons was not to exclude time for writing letters. Eugenia was a dedicated letter writer. She assured Mr. Massingham that addressing a correspondence to him would give her the greatest pleasure.

That was when the reality of her rather perplexing courtship by the redheaded young man from the colonies turned into the dream.

He lived for her on paper. She had almost forgotten what he looked like. He was the black-scrawled handwriting that began "My dearest Eugenia" and ended "With devoted thoughts," and if the matter in between was largely concerned with plain facts about housebuilding and the problems of establishing healthy grapevines in alien soil, she scarcely noticed. She loved to be called dearest and to have someone dreaming devoted thoughts of her.

In the flurried weeks preceding her departure, Sarah, the sister who was only eleven months younger than she and who had always been like her twin, had constantly burst into tears and begged Eugenia to assure her that she was happy. It was such a tremendous thing to do, to travel by sailing ship fifteen thousand miles to marry a man whose features she could scarcely remember.

By that time the matter had gone too far, and Eugenia was too proud to admit her own misgivings. In any case, what else was there for her? Jessica had married her Honorable, and little Elizabeth, younger than both Eugenia and Sarah, was engaged to marry a curate with very moderate means. That left only Sarah and Milly. Milly was still a schoolgirl, and Sarah herself said that she would never marry. She meant to stay at Lichfield Court with Mamma and Papa, to comfort them in their old age. She was a born spinster.

But Eugenia was not. And her excitement was real enough.

It was the greatest fun gathering together a very complete trousseau, because it was unlikely that she would be able to buy wearable gowns or decent bonnets or good materials in Australia. The formal dozen of everything must be two dozen, and in addition, she must take out a great many household goods. Gilbert had written asking her to bring various pieces of good furniture, a massive oak dining table, chairs, and sideboard, a bed and bedroom furniture, which she was please to choose for herself, since he trusted her good taste entirely. She was also to find some good drawing room pieces, but not a carpet, as he had already ordered fine carpets from China. And pictures and knickknacks, of course. A Waterford crystal chandelier, for instance, would look good, and some good wall mirrors in the Chippendale style.

The rest of the house could be adequately furnished with materials at hand. He had come across an ex-convict carpenter, who was making pieces for the spare bedrooms and the kitchen. Bamboo and cane furniture was practical for the climate. In the summer a great deal of time would be spent on the veranda.

Lastly, and most important, he wanted her to bring the selection of vine cuttings her Uncle Henri had promised him. She was to send someone to France to get them. If no one was available whom she could trust, she must go herself. And she must see that the cuttings were correctly dipped in the solution that would preserve life in them during the long voyage. He had arranged with Charles Worthington at Kew Gardens to advise her in this respect. He would like at least a hundred cuttings, since some would undoubtedly die. He would then have a good number of varieties of grapes, for white and red wine, for sherries, and for drying into raisins. His crop this year had unfortunately been badly affected by a long drought, but some grapes had survived. The vintage would be small.

After reading and discussing this letter, more than half of which concerned Gilbert's grapes, Sarah commented that she felt drunk from wine already.

"Don't, I beg you, become a drunkard," she entreated.

Eugenia laughed merrily. "What a very unlikely prospect!"

"Gilbert seems obsessed by the subject."

"Any man who is to succeed in life must be obsessed by his chosen career," Eugenia said a little pedantically.

"Yes, I know, but this career requires so much tasting of the product, doesn't it? You know the ritual that goes on at Uncle Henri's at vintage time."

"Yes, and I have never noticed that Uncle Henri became the worse for wine," Eugenia retorted. "Anyway, I hear that rum is the drink in Australia. And I assure you I will not be tasting that."

It was exciting making the trip to London to look for the furniture Gilbert asked for. He had put five hundred pounds at Eugenia's disposal. That seemed a fortune, although when she began choosing the quality furniture Gilbert wanted, it soon disappeared. Eventually her grandmother suggested giving her a four-poster bed as a wedding gift. It was in the French Empire style, painted pale gray and decorated with gilded cupids and love knots.

Her treasured piano, which had also been a gift from her grandmother on her eighteenth birthday, could not be left behind. There were many more personal articles of furniture among her baggage, her writing desk, her favorite watercolor, rugs, quilted bedspreads, a Dresden dinner and tea service, silverware, household linen. All these things were intended to make her feel civilized in a rough, wild country.

But now, in this heart-shattering moment three months later, while Gilbert shouted anxious inquiries about his vines, she could think only that the lovely French bed was going to be too fragile for his big frame.

Chapter 2

"THE sun has caught your nose. It's as red as a bottlebrush."

Gilbert roared with laughter. To tell the truth, he was a little shy of the young woman who stood in front of him. He had forgotten how aristocratic she looked. Women in this country, even the more gently bred who may have contrived to keep their peaches-and-cream complexion during the long voyage from England, soon acquired peeling, sunburned skins and freckles. It surprised him that he suddenly cared passionately that this should not happen to his wife.

"What is a bottlebrush?" she was asking in her soft, well-bred voice.

"It's a shrub that grows here. It's vivid scarlet. I'm uncommonly happy to see you, red nose and all." He wanted to take her in his arms and hug the breath out of her. But he had an instinct that she would not care for so public an embrace and that he must restrain his ardor until they were alone. He satisfied himself with a chaste kiss on her cheek and a murmured, "Welcome, my love," and Mrs. Ashburton, who had had the delicacy to move a little distance away to permit the lovers a moment of privacy, came forward, her plump hand held out, her expression unabashedly inquisitive.

"Well, Mr. Massingham, aren't you going to thank me for delivering your bride safely to you?"

Eugenia performed the necessary introduction.

"Gilbert, this is Mrs. Ashburton, who has been in charge of

me. Or I in charge of her, I don't know which. But here we both are safely."

"I'm happy to meet you, ma'am. I understand you have a son in Sydney."

"Yes, my only child. But he doesn't appear to have much feeling for his mother, or he would be here to meet me." She continued to study Gilbert and presently nodded approvingly, saying to Eugenia, "You are a fortunate young woman, I believe. I could wish I were forty years younger myself." She nudged Gilbert, laughing coyly. Then she exclaimed, "Why, there I see my son! Don't let us bother with introductions at present. You two are anxious to be off. We will all meet again shortly."

"At our wedding, ma'am," said Gilbert, "if not before."

"Certainly at your wedding. I have no intention of missing that."

Mrs. Ashburton took her departure, thrusting her way through the crowd to reach her son. Gilbert turned to Eugenia.

"I have arranged for you to stay with good friends of mine, Edmund and Bess Kelly. Your Mrs. Ashburton is quite a personality, isn't she?"

"A rather overpowering one at times," Eugenia admitted. "Who are Edmund and Bess Kelly?"

"Edmund is a land agent. He was an officer in the navy but abandoned it to settle here when he saw the money to be made with so much land for sale. He brought his wife out from England. They have a house in King Street. You may find it a bit cramped, but I promise you won't be able to make that criticism about Yarrabee."

"Yarrabee?"

"Yes. That's the name I decided on. In the native language it means a gum forest, and that's exactly what my land was when it was granted to me. I spent a year clearing enough acreage to get my vineyard started. I had to build terraces on the hillsides and put in brush fences for windbreaks on the flat. But now I have four hundred acres under cultivation and cattle wandering on the rest. I need the cattle for manure for the vines. Tell me, did you bring all the vine cuttings I asked for? How did they travel?"

"I believe they were not affected by the motion of the ship, as all the rest of us were."

Gilbert had the grace to look a little abashed.

"Forgive me. I should first have inquired how you fared on the journey. I do sometimes think of things beside my vines, even if you find that difficult to believe. Come!" He took her arm. "I'll take you to the Kellys and attend to the baggage later."

At last Eugenia smiled, and the dimple Gilbert remembered appeared in her right cheek. He understood that she must feel strange and homesick at first. When he had arrived for the first time in Australia, he had been overwhelmed by its size, its brawling vitality and primitiveness. It was only when he had recognized its challenge that he had begun to develop an obsessive love for its harsh heat-ridden, lonely spaces. Now he felt cramped when he returned to Europe.

For a woman, the initial shock would be even more startling. He must sympathize with that.

But he could hardly control his exultation at the sight of her with her proud neck, her delicate features, her luxuriant dark hair. He thought that she was like the black swans that came to the lake on Yarrabee.

As towns, or cities, went, for it was said that Sydney would be an important city one day, the place had an air of ramshackle impermanence. Governor Lachlan Macquarie had left his mark in well-planned streets and a number of fine, simple sandstone buildings designed by a convict architect, but the general impression was one of roaring, untidy life. Inns with creaking signs stood at far too frequent intervals and also too frequently spilled out their staggering customers. The streets were unpaved, so that a fine red dust hung permanently in the air. This was stirred into a cloud when a coach dashed by or a laborious bullock team toiled up the hill. Shops shaded by veranda fronts displayed many wares besides the necessities of life, outlandish souvenirs brought back by sailors, beads, native clubs and spears, gaudy-colored parrots in cages, fringed cashmere shawls, pottery, and red-lacquered chests from the Orient.

The houses, even the smallest, had verandas to provide a little shade and wooden fences to separate them from the street: There were many flowering shrubs and creepers, whose names Eugenia did not yet know. Above the unpleasant odor of garbage and manure and the prickling dust she caught the heavy sweet scent of some blossom.

She noticed, as she walked along on Gilbert's arm, that people turned to stare. Perhaps she walked a little unsteadily, for the wide street had an uncanny tendency to tilt, as if it were the deck of the *Caroline*. Horses, noses in feeding bags, tails switching at flies, were tethered outside public houses. Tangle-haired, barefooted urchins gaped at Eugenia fastidiously holding her neat brown traveling skirt out of the dust. A thin mongrel dog sniffed at their heels.

Suddenly Eugenia stepped aside in dismay from what seemed to be a bundle of rags lying in the dust of the gutter.

"Rum," Gilbert said contemptuously. "It's a scourge here. They drink it, good, bad, or indifferent. Convicts make it illicitly. Heaven knows what they put in it. I shall educate them to drink wine."

Eugenia thought it wiser not to comment that that human relic in the gutter scarcely looked educable as far as wine was concerned. One could hardly imagine that dirty hand lovingly holding the stem of a wineglass. But it would be pleasant if it could be done, of course. She agreed with Gilbert on the principle of his argument.

A moment later she was diverted from that sordid spectacle by an infinitely more distressing one, a line of men shuffling along the street with chains clanking. They were dressed in shabby gray clothes liberally daubed with arrows. Most of them kept their eyes on the ground, but one looked straight at Eugenia. No, not at her, through her, for the strange, melancholy light eyes were seeing nothing but some unrealizable dream.

In spite of the heat, a violent shiver went over her. Her fingers tightened on Gilbert's arm.

"A chain gang," Gilbert said briefly, answering her unspoken question. "They're on their way to the stone quarries."

"How perfectly dreadful!"

"It's a sight you will have to get used to, my dear. You must remember that these men have all committed some crime."

"But surely not one to merit that treatment!" She had turned to look back at the shuffling line, the drooping heads, the unkempt hair, the general air of degradation. Her dismay was intense. She had never been able to bear witnessing the humiliation of a human being, but this was much worse than humiliation: It was barbarism.

"There are cases of injustice, I agree," Gilbert said judicially. "But usually in those the man's natural honesty allows him to rehabilitate himself when he gets his freedom. There are plenty of ex-convicts in the colony leading honest lives. Come, my love, don't look so shocked. If one is ill, one takes a dose of medicine and recovers. That's what those fellows are doing."

"Medicine doesn't always cure."

"No, I admit some cases are irreclaimable. They become permanently degraded."

"And what about their keepers?"

Gilbert looked at her with suddenly sharp eyes.

"You think administering punishment is debasing?"

"I am sure it could be."

"Do I look debased? I have several convicts in my employ. I often have to administer punishment. But I think I remain a decent enough fellow."

"What sort of punishment?" Eugenia asked apprehensively.

"The lash. A couple of dozen strokes. That's light punishment compared to what the courts mete out. I don't care for it, but order must be kept. I narrowly avoided a mutiny last summer. You get one bad element among these fellows, and then there's trouble."

"You—do this—yourself?"

"My love, it's nothing you must worry your head about. Of course, it must be a shock to you at first. You've lived a sheltered life. I hope to go on keeping it sheltered and protected. But this is a phase of colonial existence which you will have to accept."

"You would expect me to accept seeing a man whipped!" Eugenia said incredulously.

"You don't have to witness it. Heaven forbid! But you must accept it as a necessary part of our society at present. When England stops treating us as a dumping ground for human rubbish, then we will have other laws."

"But you said in England that you found the convicts a blessing," Eugenia said stubbornly. "Or words to that effect."

"For cheap labor. Yarrabee could not have been built without them."

Yarrabee. The walls rising as the men in the arrow-daubed clothes built stone on stone. The men with the hate-filled minds, the despairing eyes, the scarred backs.

I am not going to be able to bear to live in it, Eugenia thought. It is going to be a house haunted by these ragged, unhappy ghosts . . .

Gilbert pressed her arm against his side. He said tolerantly, "At your age I also was shocked. One learns to accept. The present system is deplorable, but until it is altered, we must make it as workable as possible. I promise you I am a fair employer. I keep on every man who wants to stay when he becomes free. Except for the utterly depraved, of course. And that reminds me, you will want a good maid. Was there anyone on the ship who took your fancy?"

"I shared Mrs. Ashburton's maid, Jane King. She wasn't getting on very well with Mrs. Ashburton; she could never seem to please her. I think she would like to come to me. Of course, this would have to be with Mrs. Ashburton's consent. Jane is a rather forlorn creature. She's an orphan and needs someone to be kind to her."

"And that person is you? So it seems as if both Jane and I need you. I am an orphan, too."

"I know," Eugenia murmured, but looking at him sideways, she thought that he was an altogether different case from Jane with her timid eyes and skimmed-milk complexion. She, poor thing, was ready to fly to anyone who would give her affection. But not this man with the sure lift of his chin, with his keen blue eyes and crest of flaming hair. He had learned to hide or disclaim his hurts. Privately she believed that he was a man to whom ambition came first and a woman second. But even believing this, she had decided to marry him. She was so certain that beneath his strength there would be great tenderness. To tell the truth, she found the situation challenging and exciting. But also a little alarming, for now she kept seeing a tiny figure in her mind, a black shape no bigger than a fly, with its arm rising and falling as the lash was administered to tortured skin.

Chapter 3

"And what did your mother say, love, when you told her you were coming all this way to be married?"

Bess Kelly was a homely woman with a big bosom and light, fluffy hair that escaped its pins and hung in damp tendrils on her brow and around her plump neck. Eugenia had perceived at once that she would not have been society in England. But standards out here were different. Obviously, if a woman were honest and respectable, she would be accepted in most houses in this country.

Eugenia found the attic bedroom to which Bess had shown her very small and dreadfully hot. The sun struck through the iron roof so that one seemed to have been put inside a stove, preparatory to being cooked.

All the same the room was to be hers alone, for there was only one bed. This was bliss, after enduring three months of Mrs. Ashburton's talkative company in a none too comfortable ship's cabin. There were sprigged muslin curtains at the slanting windows; the bed and dressing table had pretty chintz covers. Mrs. Kelly pointed to a bowl of cream-colored flowers floating in water and said the children had put them there. They were called frangipani and smelled nice. You needed sweet smells because the drains in the summer and the slops thrown out by the public houses and sluttish housewives brought less pleasant odors, not to mention flies.

"Didn't it break your mother's heart, my dear, you coming so far? Of course, she'd be wheedled by Gilbert Massingham. If ever there was a man who knew how to get his own way, it's Gilbert. You're going to have all the unmarried young ladies envying you, I can tell you that. Ever since Gilbert came back three years ago and announced he was bringing a bride out, there have been tears and pouts. But we all knew there was no one good enough for Gilbert in this ragbag of a colony. He intended to have the best. The same as his wines. He's going to make the best wine in Australia and, what's more, make people drink it. Well, I've been here ten years, and I say it will be something near a miracle if the rum and beer drinkers can be turned to wine. But if there's a man who can use his persuasions, it's Gilbert Massingham."

Eugenia found there was no need to say anything at all. She thought that Mrs. Kelly could have few people to talk to, for she was behaving like someone who had been denied conversation for a long time.

She could hear rustles and whispers on the stairs. It must be the Kelly children, wanting to have a peep at the new arrival. The children who had thoughtfully put the frangipani on her dressing table.

But the sweet smell and the heat were making her feel a little suffocated. The day had already held too much. She had a scarcely formed thought that if the first sight of Gilbert had filled her with unmitigated joy, she would not have been so aware of the other things. The sickening glare of the sun, the dust, the rawness of the town, the ragged children, that shattering glimpse of a chain gang.

On her first day she had hoped and expected to be aware of nothing but the pleasure of her reunion with Gilbert.

Letters and absence, she realized, were dangerous things. They led to dreams that were too euphoric and unrealistic. She simply hadn't expected Gilbert to have taken on the color of his surroundings the way he had.

"You're a very fortunate young lady, do you know that?" Mrs. Kelly was saying. "No bride ever had more preparations made for her. Have you brought a wonderful wedding gown?"

Eugenia shook her head. "No, it's very simple. I thought a

too elaborate one would be out of place." She tried to sound gay and excited, since this friendly woman obviously expected her to. "But I have a veil of Brussels lace that my grandmother and then my mother and last year my sister Jessica wore. I have to send it back for my sister Sarah, though I am not so sure she will marry; she's very serious and studious. But there's still Elizabeth and Milly to come after her."

"Five girls! My, your mother must be pleased to find husbands for you, even if you had to come all the way to Australia."

There was no "had to" about it, Eugenia thought indignantly. But she remembered being surprised that Mamma and Papa had agreed so readily when Gilbert had made his request. She had thought they might have protested about this impetuous young man, of whom they knew very little, planning to carry their daughter off to such an impossible place. But they had emphasized how much they had liked his vitality and his ambitiousness.

She herself had always known that in Gilbert's mind she was inextricably associated with the dinner party at Uncle Henri's château. He had seen her through the euphoria produced by her uncle's vintage wine. She was part of a set piece and, therefore, an essential figure in his ambition. She had wanted to be this, and still did, in spite of their somewhat uneasy meeting today. But she had to smile a little, for if she had been secretly dismayed by his sunburned, earthy appearance, what had he thought of her, windblown, semispeechless, with a sunburned nose? That was not the elegant, poised young woman of the French dinner party. Had he been disappointed?

If so, he had gallantly hidden his feelings. That was kind and thoughtful of him and prognosticated well for the future. When her bags had arrived, and she had bathed and changed and rested and perhaps begun a letter to Sarah, she would feel more composed. The letter writing to Gilbert in a far-off country which had been a balm and a release would now have to be done in reverse, with her dearly loved sister Sarah as the recipient.

Mrs. Kelly did finally leave her, though not before three

bashful children had been brought to meet her. They were plain, sunburned, freckled children, the youngest a toddler, and a fourth, said Mrs. Kelly, lying in the graveyard. The summer heat was hard on little ones.

As always, Eugenia's spirit calmed when she took up her pen.

SYDNEY, JUNE 18, 1830

DEAREST SARAH,

I am supposed to be resting before dinner, but I am talking to you so busily in my head that I might just as well put my remarks on paper.

I have arrived and safely disembarked from the *Caroline.* Strange as it may seem, I was sorry to leave the ship as I had grown quite fond of it (though *not* of Mrs. Ashburton, who was the most indefatigable talker I have *ever* met).

I have not time now to regale you with my impressions of this town and of Australia generally. Anyway, I know you must be longing to hear of only one thing, my meeting with my affianced husband. These comments are for your eyes only, for I must tell you that he seems rather uncomfortably a stranger. He has grown so weathered-looking: his skin is the color of the burnt umber in our paint boxes, a rather hard, unbecoming color caused by the climate here. He is broader, too, and looks very strong and healthy. You remember how quiet and observant he seemed to be when he came to Lichfield Court. Now he is brisk and confident and more hearty in manner. I was amused that he seemed more concerned to know that his vines, rather than I, had traveled well. However, he could see immediately that I had, so there was no need to inquire. And how do I know that if he seemed a stranger to me, I did not seem even more of one to him? I have been sitting here trying to reassure myself by going over my good points. I count my hair, my eyes, my neck, my waist, and my hands as good. But my funny, crooked nose has caught the sun. I am too thin because I could eat so little of the food on board ship. I really look half-starved, with hollows under my cheekbones. I could see Mrs. Kelly looking at my small bosom. Really, how can I be critical of my dear Gilbert's colonial look, when I am such an inauspicious example of an English gentlewoman!

"Miss Lichfield! Eugenia!"

That was Mrs. Kelly's voice calling up the stairs. Eugenia laid down her pen and went to the door.

"You will allow me to be friendly and call you Eugenia, won't you, love? The children are in bed, and we're about to sit down to supper. Are you ready? Edmund is waiting to meet you, and you have an impatient bridegroom here."

The burbling voice faded away. Eugenia hastily smoothed her hair, looking in the little dressing-table mirror. The swift antipodean dusk had begun not ten minutes ago, but now it was almost dark. She could scarcely see herself in the mirror, enough only to confirm what she had just written to Sarah about her appearance.

At least it was a little cooler now, and some color had come back to her cheeks. She had tried to look her best, putting on the muslin gown that Mrs. Kelly had whisked away to iron with a flatiron in the kitchen. She said she could not trust the maid to do it; she was only a child who had come straight from the fleet prison. The important thing with a convict maid, Mrs. Kelly had added, was to take the woman immediately on her arrival. If she were allowed to go live in the female prisoners' barracks, she would become debauched and depraved in no time at all.

A light shone in the little front parlor. It was from there that the sound of voices came.

A sixth sense told Eugenia that she was being discussed. The voices were deliberately lowered. She heard only part of Mrs. Kelly's remark. ". . . looks delicate . . ." And Gilbert's denial. Or it seemed to be a denial since it was made in a quick low murmur at some length. Then there was a burst of laughter, and Gilbert said in a normal voice, "This is a time-honored custom in wine-growing countries. The wine laid down at the birth of a son is drunk at his wedding."

A strange voice said, "That may be so, but this is Australia, and you haven't proved yet that you can keep wine in a bottle for twenty or thirty years. The cork may blow out and hit the ceiling."

"I'll keep it," said Gilbert. "And it will be as good a vintage as any in France or Portugal. In the meantime we're going to drink one of the bottles I brought with me today. It's a very young wine, I admit. Only bottled two years. But I'll guarantee it will make a decent drink."

"That sour stuff," complained Bess. "The last you brought tasted like vinegar and no mistake."

"I agree. The grapes got too much rain at the wrong time. There wasn't enough sugar in them. That's a hazard I have to contend with."

So they were not talking about her after all, but grapes, wines, vintages. She made her mouth lift at the corners, in a pleasant expression, and went into the room.

Gilbert sprang up to greet her. He introduced her to Edmund Kelly, a plain man with leathery-brown skin, whom she immediately liked. Gilbert said that all her baggage was now ashore, but the furniture stored in the hold would not be unloaded until the next day. He proposed having it loaded onto wagons and taken to Yarrabee, a distance of about thirty miles. They would follow it in a week or so, after she had become his wife.

He intended to arrange for a simple ceremony in the new church in Macquarie Street on Wednesday next, if that suited her convenience.

He took her hand to press it to his lips. All she could do was nod silently. She was thinking of the wine to be laid down on the birth of their first son. Her heart was beating uncomfortably. Things were too direct in this country.

Next Wednesday. It was too soon to marry a man who had become such a stranger.

"No point in keeping him waiting," said Mr. Kelly.

She flushed, knowing that one person at least had read her thoughts.

Gilbert took her arm.

"Come, my love. Bess wants us to sit down to dinner."

His voice was gentle. She believed that he might be feeling

strange and ill at ease, too. She must think of that and stop being so intense about her own sensations.

The table was lit by candles that quickly became uncomfortably hot in the small room. Bess explained that she had had to prepare roast beef because this was what Gilbert had asked for. His red wine must be drunk with meat. Now if he had simply had a mug of beer with his meal, they could have had a cut off a cold joint and remained much cooler.

But Eugenia had to admit that the wine Gilbert so lovingly poured into the glass tumblers had a very good color. It compared favorably with Uncle Henri's. When she held it up to the light, it had a beautiful rich glow. She saw Gilbert watching her and was pleased that his eyes were tender. Though this may have been for the merits of his wine, rather than for her action.

She sipped and restrained a grimace. Little as she knew about wines, she could tell that this was too raw, too young.

"It's very pleasant, Gilbert," she said loyally.

Gilbert rolled it around his mouth, swallowed, and shook his head disappointedly.

"No. It's not good enough. But it's better than last year. Isn't it, Edmund?"

"That was vinegar. Yes, this is an improvement. But you won't convert the rum drinkers on it."

"This is made from the vines I brought from the Douro. I believe I'll have better luck with my new ones. They looked in good shape, I'm glad to say. I'll begin planting immediately after the next good rain." He raised his glass across the table to Eugenia. "I'm sure you will have brought me luck, my dear."

"The man's got no conversation about anything but his vineyard," Bess said. "Tell Eugenia something about the colony. When are you going to present her to society?"

"Society?" Eugenia inquired.

"Such as it is," said Mr. Kelly with a touch of irony. "To be a socially presentable person here, you must be a successful lawyer or a rich landowner or an important civil servant or the governor himself. We have plenty of colonial magnates who think they own the country. No ticket-of-leave men need apply."

"I should think not," said Bess. "Imagine it!"

"Ticket-of-leave?" Eugenia asked.

"Convicts who have been rewarded for good behavior. Before their sentence expires, they may have the privilege of choosing their master. Or even of pursuing their own trade. Later they will be freemen. And I swear you can't tell the difference between them and me."

"Edmund," Bess chided.

Gilbert laughed, enjoying what should have been a joke. Catching Edmund's eye, Eugenia realized that it was not one. But only she and he seemed aware of that.

"I have several ticket-of-leave men on Yarrabee," Gilbert said. "Most of them are Irish rebels. I've still to be convinced that it's a crime to fight for one's country. Though I admit not every Englishman has sympathy for a wild Irishman."

"Begorra!" said Edmund. "You don't mean to tell me you have Irishmen tending your vines! Surely they'd think it was poison you were brewing."

Gilbert roared with laughter.

"At that they're not beyond having a sup. I caught one fellow spitting it out. I very nearly ordered him a dozen lashes. Edmund, let me fill your glass. I've sent a dozen bottles of this vintage to Government House. Do you think Darling will enjoy it?"

"He'll commend you for it, but I doubt that it'll convert him from his imported port."

"And are these men ever repatriated?" Eugenia asked.

Bess looked at her, her plump face flushed in the candlelight. Gilbert said politely, "What men are you speaking of, my love?"

"These Irishmen who are not guilty of a crime."

She saw the quick frown that drew Gilbert's brows together.

"When they get their freedom, they may do as they please. This is not a subject that must trouble you, my love."

"If it is under my nose . . ." Eugenia began, saw the frown deepen, and desisted.

Bess broke in. "My dear Miss Lichfield, you'll be too busy with babies and household affairs. You'll be like all of us, complaining about your latest maid, who is lazy or dishonest or dirty or drunken. You have lived a protected life, I can see. You had better be good to her, Gilbert."

"Good to her!" said Gilbert. "Why, she's going to be the most pampered woman in the whole of Australia!"

Chapter 4

THE stars were low in a perfectly black sky when Gilbert left the Kellys' house and set off to walk back to his own lodgings. He had a room at the Castle Inn, a hotel near the Botanic Gardens, where he meant to make an inquiry about the safe arrival of his vine cuttings. He had said his good nights early because Eugenia had looked tired and more than a little dazed.

But she had not disappointed him. The look of elegance and poise was more pronounced than he remembered it. She was not a beauty of the china blue eyes and well-rounded bosom type. Some men would not have considered her beautiful at all. But Gilbert found the unevenness of her features fascinating and utterly charming. Every movement she made was graceful. He could have sat until midnight watching the thoughtful, deliberate way she turned her head on her long neck. In spite of her weariness, she had made a fastidious toilette. He had imported a rare creature, he thought.

That he scarcely knew her did not worry him. He had chosen her for her background, her upbringing, and her appearance. He had been overjoyed when consent had been given to his suit. Of course, he had known the family was not overstuffed with money, a fact in his favor. He also knew that he was a personable young man, even though he had chosen to live in such a far-off colony, inhabited by convicts and snakes. He had relied on his powers of persuasion and on his intuition that Eugenia would have a sufficiently adventurous spirit.

He didn't deny that he had had occasional misgivings during

the three years that he had waited for her. Her letters, for instance, arriving with monotonous regularity on each sailing ship from Tilbury or Southampton had bored him. He had never practiced the art of letter writing, and the fact that his affianced bride possessed it to such a devastating degree was slightly alarming.

All that information about life at Lichfield Court! The visiting aunts and bishops and local gentry. It was impossible to reply in the same vein. He could hardly report that the cook, a blowsy Cockney, had stolen all the money out of his wallet while he was sleeping and had run off with one of his carpenters for a night in town and that both of them were convicts on tickets-of-leave. Nor could he say that her replacement was an aboriginal woman, hideously ugly, and the mistress of his foreman. He had caught them together after vintage one hot night. They were both tipsy from raw wine. He had prodded them to their feet with the toe of his boot and told them to be more discreet in future. He had never had a fancy for the dark-skinned lubras himself.

Of course, that aspect of life was to be kept hidden from Eugenia. When he had engaged a suitable staff, he intended that she should live the life of a lady, busying herself with her music, her painting, her sewing—in short, all the occupations which young ladies of her station pursued. He planned to have house parties, such as was the custom in England, the company riding or driving from Sydney on Friday afternoon and staying over Sunday and Monday. It was important to invite the right people so that the name of his wines, Yarrabee Burgundy, Yarrabee Claret, and Yarrabee Sauterne, would become known and eventually famous, not only in Australia but in London and the English great houses.

He had taken some early bottles on his last visit to England. The opinion pronounced on it by discriminating men and professional wine tasters had been favorable on the whole. It was a plucky beginning, they had said. At present his product was as raw as the new colony, but it might have a future provided it could be transported such an overwhelmingly long distance.

If it could not be, and this was likely, since traveling upset good wine, Mr. Massingham would be well advised to turn his attention to converting his fellow countrymen to the delights of a more civilized drink than rum or beer.

Gilbert strode along, preoccupied with his thoughts. His way lay through the infamous Rocks district where people lived in the small shacks put up by the first settlers, wattle-and-daub erections that had never been intended to stand for more than a few years. The walls caved in; the roofs caught fire from faulty chimneys; the tiny windows let in little light, let alone fresh air.

It was a reeking sordid area occupied by prostitutes, female convicts who had been granted their freedom, but whose will and ambition had been broken by the long misery of their imprisonment, and by a few honest people whom fate or laziness or lack of ability kept perpetually poor.

An occasional oil lamp cast a circle of light for a circumference of a few yards, making the darkness between these oases all the more impenetrable.

Not that such darkness was unwelcome to the pickpocket or the drunkard lurching home in happy anonymity. It was far from welcome to the servant girl running a last errand for a demanding mistress or to anyone going about innocent business. It was a curious fact of human nature, Gilbert reflected, that even a community as new as this one was, vice could be so well established. He had no intention of allowing Eugenia to observe this aspect of antipodean life, any more than he intended her to witness the necessary punishment of his more incorrigible servants. The innocent gaze of her gray-blue eyes—what did they resemble? English bluebells or the smoky blue of the unfolding passionflower?

A passionflower? Eugenia?

His lips quirked doubtfully. His musing was abruptly shattered by a disturbance. Running footsteps came behind him; there was the sound of distressed, panting breathing. He stopped, and a shape, petticoats flying, fled past him. He saw the woman briefly beneath the lamp on the corner, fair hair tumbling down and skirts held up. Then she disappeared around the corner, and presently two men, walking with long strides, passed him.

They turned the same corner. If they were pursuing the woman, they were not in any great haste. They probably knew where she lived. She must be a prostitute or a ticket-of-leave woman if she had lodgings in this area, Gilbert reflected. It was none of his business that she had seemed scared out of her wits. He had no wish to get involved in an unsavory incident virtually on his wedding eve.

He did not turn the corner beneath the streetlight, but walked on. He was fifty yards away when the shot rang out, followed instantly by a scream.

Those were sounds he could not ignore. He turned on his heel and began retracing his steps, running. Another person— or persons—was running, but in the opposite direction. If he was not mistaken, it was the two men who had been making a joke as they turned the corner. He could hear their footsteps fading in the distance.

A feeble shaft of light shone on the street from the open door of one of the deplorable shacks. Gilbert could see a woman kneeling in the doorway and something lying half in the passage, half on the dusty path.

At first he thought it was a dog. More accurately, he hoped it was a dog, though that was a wild hope. The shape turned faceward to the night sky was that of a gray-haired man, and he appeared to be dead.

Gilbert pushed the kneeling woman out of the way and felt inside the man's jacket. His fingers came away wet and sticky. He put his ear to the man's breast.

"Fetch a light," he said.

With a small gasp the woman rose and went inside. She came back in a moment with a lighted candle. Gilbert moved the frail flame across the upturned face and observed unemotionally that it was exactly the same color as the tallow candle.

He had seen enough dead men. This one looked as if he would not have been far from his natural end in any event. He was as thin as a starving dingo.

He stood up slowly, giving the candle back to the woman.

"What happened?"

She was not crying, he observed with detachment. Although still breathing too fast, she told him quite lucidly that she had been coming home from the public house where she worked in the kitchen when two men had followed her. They had thought she was a street woman. When she had refused to stop, they had shouted abuse at her and had begun to pursue her. She had thought she was safely home. She had wrenched open the door, calling to her husband, and he had come at once.

He had stood in the open doorway, shielding her. He was only a thin, small man, as Gilbert could see. And one of the men had taken out a pistol and shot him. Just like that. The man, both the men, had been drunk. Though not so drunk that they couldn't run off like weasels.

"This is your husband?" said Gilbert. He was surprised. Her father, more likely, he would have thought.

"Yes," said the woman. "He's been through a lot. Seven years in Van Diemen's Land. It's aged him. He's only forty-six. Was," she added belatedly. For the first time her voice trembled. "Is he really dead, sir?"

"I fear so. But we'll get a doctor."

"A doctor! In these parts at this time of night!" The woman's voice was stiff with contempt. "Why, there hasn't been even a door opened to see what the noise was about."

"Have you any decent neighbors?"

"Oh, yes. They only don't want to stick their noses into trouble. There's Mrs. Murphy in there."

She pointed, and Gilbert stepped over the rickety fence that divided the two houses.

"I'll rouse her. You can stay with her while I go for a doctor. And I promise you one will come."

The woman's head went down, and the tumbling hair fell

around her face. She was crying, though silently. Only her heaving shoulders indicated it.

Gilbert patted her shoulder perfunctorily.

"You've been splendid. Don't give in now. I'll be back soon."

He had to rouse his friend Dr. Philip Noakes, who had just gone to bed after attending a dinner party.

"Did your host offer you a decent wine?" Gilbert asked. "Don't answer. I can see it by your bleary eye."

"Port. It went around too deuced many times. What's up? Did your bride arrive? She's not ill, is she?"

"Eugenia is in the best of health, I am glad to say. No, this is a poor wretch shot in the Rocks district. Dead, I think. Be a good fellow and come along."

"To rouse the dead? That's a wasted journey. What happened?" Dr. Noakes squinted forward at Gilbert. "You're not involved, are you?"

"Good God, no. I was only passing."

"That's a blessing. I don't suppose your bride would take kindly to that sort of thing on the night of her arrival. Well, I suppose I must come. Though what you're doing playing good Samaritan I can't imagine. It isn't exactly a role that fits you like a glove."

Philip Noakes was one of Gilbert's best friends. He had been a ship's surgeon before settling in Australia permanently. Gilbert would have taken Eugenia to the Noakes in preference to the Kellys, except for Marion Noakes. She was a disgruntled, outspoken Englishwoman, who had hated the country from the moment of her arrival. Gilbert did not intend having his wife exposed to that sort of acid faultfinding on her first day in Sydney.

But Phil was one of the best. He drank hard and worked hard. He was plainspoken, honest, and a dedicated fighter for the rights of the convicts. More than once he had made himself unpopular for exposing sadistic masters. There had been an unpleasant scandal about the death of a laborer subsequent to a flogging. The employer who had administered the punishment was one of the newly rich landholders, a man with influential friends. For a few days it had been a toss-up who would emerge with his character in shreds, the man who had wielded the cat-o'-nine-tails or Phil Noakes, the convict lover as he was beginning to be called. Fortunately the newspaper *The Australian* had taken up the case and had made a fervent plea for justice and the simple facts of humanity. Where did fair punishment end and murder begin?

The guilty landholder left the colony, and Dr. Noakes was called on to work harder than ever among a long and diverse list of patients to justify his defense of what he called the ragtag and bobtail victims of an unfair social system. This pleased his wife even less than her forced residence in such a crude country.

There was nothing he could do, when he reached the scene of the tragedy, but pronounce death from a gunshot wound and suggest that the bereaved wife come down to the barracks and tell her story to the officer on duty.

She agreed quietly. She had regained her composure. She smoothed her hair and put on a bonnet. The door of the humble cottage was closed on the dead man, and with Gilbert and the doctor on each side of her, she walked down the street to the barracks.

On Dr. Noakes' questioning, she said that her name was Molly Jarvis; she had been married to Harry Jarvis, the dead man, only six months. He had had bad lungs and probably hadn't long to live, but he had thought that marriage might give her a little protection. There was no other kind for a woman in her position, was there?

Yes, she said defiantly, she had come out on a convict ship eight years ago and had only recently got her freedom. She was the cook at the Seven Bells, a bad enough place to work, but she had never gone on the streets. Those men tonight had thought she was a prostitute and had been furious when they found she was not. No, she had never seen them before and couldn't describe them since it was too dark and she hadn't seen their faces. They would escape scot-free while poor Harry lay dead. Men always escaped, didn't they?

This was said without bitterness, merely as a statement of fact.

"Not necessarily," said Dr. Noakes dryly, and Gilbert looked at the young woman, trying to see her face beneath the prim black bonnet. Her voice intrigued him. It was not altogether a lady's, but neither was it a servant's. His guess was that she had worked in some place where she had learned to improve her speech. But what he liked most was her self-discipline. Whatever rage and grief were burning inside her, she was able to speak quietly and logically.

So she had a grudge against men, had she? Well, that was common enough among women in her situation. It was her quietness that was uncommon. She didn't indulge in hysterics or vituperation. She was a rare one, indeed. Both he and Philip agreed on this when they left her in the care of a sleepy sergeant of police.

Dr. Noakes was dead tired, he had begun the day at five with a confinement, and Gilbert was remembering his original destination, a call on the curator of the Botanic Gardens.

It was after midnight now. Too late to do anything but go to bed.

Yet he couldn't sleep because he began to wonder what crime had led to Molly Jarvis' transportation. Not that it should concern him. Nevertheless, speculation about it and the shock of the crime he had witnessed gave him a restless night.

The morning was utterly lovely, without a breath of wind stirring, and the sun radiant over the blue waters of the harbor. Heat would follow. But now everything glistened. Birds screeched and warbled—the noisy parrakeets, the bell-like notes of the black currawongs, an aggressive contemptuous cacophony from a flock of kookaburras.

Gilbert hoped Eugenia was listening, enchanted with her first Australian morning. He imagined her at the open window in her nightgown, her loosened hair falling about her face.

Then, without any bridging thought, he was seeing, abruptly and shockingly, Molly Jarvis sitting by her dead husband.

But she wouldn't be doing that, would she? She would have spent the night with the neighbor, Mrs. Murphy.

All the same it wouldn't come amiss if he were to pay her a visit and see what had been the outcome of the night's affray, what arrangements had been made for the burial of her husband, for instance. An ex-convict's funeral was a furtive affair at best. He might be able to arrange for a decent coffin which the widow could follow to the cemetery. It was a pity that he didn't have an influential friend among the clergy, as he had among the medical profession.

He felt bursting with vigor and optimism himself on this sparkling morning. It seemed unfair that other people were in trouble. He would call on Molly Jarvis and then present himself at the Kellys for breakfast and another meeting with a rested and refreshed Eugenia. Later he would supervise the bringing ashore of the crates of furniture and china, and have them set off by bullock wagons to Yarrabee. It was going to be a busy day, a fine, successful, invigorating day.

But Molly Jarvis first.

He found her in the cottage, which was even more wretched by the light of day. She answered his knock and stood in the doorway staring at him.

Her eyes were a warm chestnut brown. Her pale hair was brushed back neatly and pinned in a luxuriant knot at the base of her neck. Her lips were curved and full. The drab dress she wore showed a charming rounded figure. By George, she was a beauty. But not a friendly one. Her voice was inimical and suspicious as she asked who he was.

"Where are your eyes, Mrs. Jarvis?" Gilbert said in amusement. "I was here last night. I brought the doctor."

"Oh, you're the gentleman." Her voice remained suspicious. "What do you want?"

"I came to see if I could be of any more help. You were in bad trouble. What did the sergeant say?"

"The same as me. That you might as well look for a needle in a haystack as find those two murderers."

"They'll make inquiries about who was drinking in the Seven Bells last night. They should be able to narrow things down."

"But those men weren't drinking there. They were just passing as I happened to come out to go home."

"That does make it difficult, I agree. Apart from that—what about the funeral?"

Mrs. Jarvis pointed over her shoulder. "He's in there, if that's what you're wondering."

"You spent the night here?"

"Why not? I'm not afraid of a dead man. Especially my own. The authorities will bury him. He won't mind that. He would say that he was entitled to it, anyway, for all they did to him."

"And you, Mrs. Jarvis? What will you do now? Go back to the Seven Bells?"

Her lips tightened. She half-nodded, but there was a flicker of fear in her eyes. She must have been aware of it and was ashamed of it, for she said aggressively, "What else?"

"I have a property at Parramatta. I need servants."

The words were out before he knew that he had intended to speak them. But no, that was not entirely truthful. The vague thought had been in his mind ever since he had left her last night.

What he didn't expect was that Molly Jarvis should shrink back from him into the dark passageway.

"What sort of servants, sir?"

"Why, a cook and housemaids. My name's Massingham. I've just built a house for my wife. I've waited for her arrival before engaging an indoor staff. I thought it only fair that she should see and approve of them. How good a cook are you?"

The brown eyes, enormous, were looking at him out of the gloom.

"You're married, sir?"

"No, but I'm about to be. My bride, Miss Lichfield, only arrived yesterday. And you would oblige me, Mrs. Jarvis, if you wouldn't behave as if I am not to be trusted. I am making you a perfectly honest offer, and if you must know why, it is because I like your appearance, and I admired the dignified way you behaved last night. Also, I need some good servants."

"Your wife—how will she like an ex-convict?"

"My wife will have to grow accustomed to the way of life in this country. But I've already told you—if she doesn't approve of you, there will be no question of your coming to Yarrabee. I am making only a tentative offer."

Gilbert smiled, knowing how persuasive his smile could be. Besides, he was speaking the entire truth. Meritorious as Mrs. Jarvis appeared to be, he would not dream of employing her if Eugenia objected.

Or would he?

"Come in," she said abruptly. She disappeared into the gloom of the windowless passage. Following her, Gilbert saw her at the door of a lean-to kitchen.

"My husband's in there," she said, nodding to her left. "And the other room's the bedroom. I hope you don't mind the kitchen. Or we could sit with Harry. He won't hear."

Was that a macabre joke? No, it wasn't, for the serious brown eyes looked at him with their devastating desolation.

Suddenly he was wishing that he had met Molly Jarvis six months before Eugenia's arrival. He might have succeeded in changing her mind about men.

Anyway, here they were in the tiny, already hot kitchen, which must be a furnace by midday, and on the other side of the flimsy wall a dead man's nose pointed at the ceiling.

"If I accept your offer, Mr. Massingham, you must know what I was transported for."

"Naturally. Although I can't believe it to be a serious crime."

"It wasn't one at all!" Molly Jarvis said with sudden violence. "It was a made-up story. I was a lady's maid, and my lady's husband wanted me. He even offered to set me up in my own place. When I refused, he turned nasty and trumped up this story about me stealing his wife's diamond brooch. It was found in my box, where I kept my little bits of treasure. No one believed I hadn't stolen it. Why should they? I was only a servant. So I had to stand trial and was sentenced to transportation for five years. After we got to Botany Bay, I was sentenced to another three years for attacking an officer. I kicked his shins and gave him a black eye. I was only defending myself." Her mouth twisted. "Poor Harry was the only bit of good I found in eight years."

"Eight years? You must have been a child when you were sentenced."

"I'm twenty-six now, sir, and if you're really offering me a position, you'll have to hear the rest. I'm going to have a baby."

That was something unexpected. Unwelcome.

"When?"

"In six months or thereabouts."

Gilbert looked down at the pale, intense face. It bore marks of strain and weariness now, but he found himself wondering how it would look if Molly Jarvis were laughing. If she ever laughed. And he couldn't believe that she didn't because of the way her mouth tilted upward.

All the same, it was a devilish nuisance that she was pregnant. He hardly knew how Eugenia would take that. He must explain that good servants were extremely hard to come by and Mrs. Jarvis looked like a pearl.

He didn't doubt for a moment that she had told him the truth about herself. She would hardly lie, with those dead ears in the next room listening. He almost believed himself that the unfortunate Harry Jarvis was listening to his entirely genuine proposal to make his poor widow's life easier and happier. She could do the cooking and have a room to herself and manage the other servants. It would be a load off Eugenia's shoulders.

"I expect the child can be accommodated," he said. "Yarrabee is big enough. I have a small vineyard. But I intend it to be a bigger one before I'm much older. One day it will be famous."

He must have looked optimistic and confident, for suddenly, at last, Molly Jarvis smiled. Her lips curved back over strong white teeth, and her eyes softened to warm velvet.

A tingle went down Gilbert's spine. He thought of Eugenia in her immaculate morning toilette, waiting for him, and said hastily, "I must be off. Tomorrow, or the next day, will you present yourself at Mr. Edmund Kelly's in King Street. My fiancée will want to interview you. I will have told her the whole story, so there's no need to be nervous."

Nervous? Not this woman with her warm, straight gaze.

Vin ordinaire, Gilbert was thinking.

If Eugenia was champagne, this woman was the satisfying robust wine to be drunk with bread and cheese.

What a fancy! And he wasn't really sure what he had done, what he had got himself involved in. He was certain only of one thing, that Molly Jarvis would be an asset to Yarrabee.

Chapter 5

ALREADY they had had a disagreement. It was about the woman, Molly Jarvis. Eugenia had no objection to Mrs. Jarvis as a woman. It was her history and the circumstances under which Gilbert had made her acquaintance that gave Eugenia a feeling of distaste which she could not overcome.

Imagine, at Lichfield Court, engaging a woman who had been not only in Newgate Prison but a passenger on one of those terrible convict ships. Eugenia reiterated that she was perfectly prepared to believe Mrs. Jarvis' story of her innocence. But nothing would take away the fact that the poor woman's character must have been affected by living for so long in conditions of such depravity. What was more, she was to have a posthumous child fathered by a convict. Well, an ex-convict, then, though she failed to see the difference. Besides, what about Jane King, with whose services Mrs. Ashburton had proved perfectly happy to dispense? She cried too much from homesickness and forgot her duties. Eugenia was more than welcome to her.

And now here was Gilbert saying generously, but with a lack of sympathy that annoyed her, "By all means have the King girl if you can put up with her sniffles. I daresay she will make herself useful, though you had better prepare her for the fact that Yarrabee is isolated and lonely. A woman like Mrs. Jarvis won't mind that. These are important things to take into consideration when you engage servants in this country."

"You didn't tell me these things yesterday."

"No, my love. I apologize. I should have done so."

Gilbert's face was the same as it had been yesterday, but now she couldn't look at it without thinking of those dark, horrifying doings of the previous night and wondering why no shadow showed. If anything, his blue eyes were brighter, as if stimulated by the excitement. She had thought the stars so peaceful when she had looked at them before falling asleep, and when she had awakened to the brilliantly sunny morning, she had experienced a surge of happiness and excitement.

But now the heat of midafternoon was beating on the roof. Mrs. Kelly had drawn the blinds to shut out the glare. The resulting dimness, instead of being cool, was airless. A constant harsh uproar from the cicadas in the garden was exacerbating to the nerves. Eugenia had to mop her damp brow. The scrap of lace handkerchief crumpled in her palm was damp and inadequate.

And Gilbert, with that implacable look on his face, was disturbing. He had told her once that he always meant to get what he wanted. Now, for some reason, no doubt a perfectly sensible and valid one, he wanted a convict woman in his house.

She had to admit to herself that had she heard about Mrs. Jarvis in other circumstances, she, too, would have had sympathy for the woman's misfortune.

The story of the amorous employer was entirely believable. One often enough heard such stories. In the past Eugenia and her sisters had always sympathized strongly with the unfortunate maidservants.

So why now was she being so unreasonable? It surely couldn't be that she was jealous of Gilbert's sudden enthusiasm for this unfortunate woman!

"But there's to be a baby!" she protested.

"Do you not care for children?"

That was not the point. Eugenia looked at Gilbert indignantly.

"Of course I like children. But there are certain circumstances where they are not so welcome."

"Mrs. Jarvis' was conceived in wedlock. Even if it hadn't been, there are conditions in this country that make an illegitimate child forgivable. This is not England. Or I should say it isn't the England you know."

Eugenia's eyes flashed.

"You don't need to remind me that I am fortunate in my birth and upbringing."

"But perhaps I do need to remind you of exactly that. So that you will have more sympathy for others less fortunate. Now let's have done with the matter."

Eugenia's voice grew as chilly as Gilbert's. "If the matter has already been decided, why do you ask me to interview this woman?"

"Because I had hoped I would find you completely in accord with my own feelings. I had hoped to see pity in your eyes."

"You think I am heartless!"

"Not in the least. But if you could take up the cudgels for plain Jane, why not for someone in far greater need?"

"I suppose because she is your protégée, not mine," Eugenia retorted, and then wished she had not said such an irrational, impulsive thing. For Gilbert's annoyance had vanished in a flash, and his eyes were twinkling with good humor.

"My darling, I love your honesty. Were you afraid I wasn't going to let you run your own house? Of course I am. You are in complete charge. I have only asked you to interview this woman. If you dislike her, no more will be said, I promise. Now we are to dine with my old friend William Wentworth at Vaucluse this evening, so I want you to take that frown off your face and look your prettiest. Talk to Mrs. Wentworth and the other ladies about their experiences with servants. You'll find that by standards here, Molly Jarvis is a pearl."

As it happened, the women at dinner that night were less interested in servants than in fashions. Every item of Eugenia's toilette was discussed. Were her leg-o'-mutton sleeves the latest thing in London? What were the new season's bonnets like? Had those chilly muslins with the high bustline ever come back? They had been downright shocking with their transparent appearance. One of the ladies remembered an aunt, her mother's younger sister, coming down to dinner in one such gown; it had been pretty, too, with rosebuds sprinkled on the gauzy material. But her shape beneath had been all too visible, and the curate, who was visiting, had abruptly left the room and never returned.

If it hadn't been for the close heat and the everlasting sound of cicadas in the warm night, Eugenia could have imagined she was at a party in England. There had been a four-poster bed with chintz hangings in the bedroom where the ladies had left their wraps. The winding staircase and hall were hung with large oil paintings; the drawing room was completely English in style, with striped wallpaper, gilt-framed mirrors, heavy, comfortable furniture. Everything was much more grand than she had thought it could be. The dining table was laid with silver and crystal and a beautiful porcelain dinner service.

It was reassuring. Life could be civilized here, after all. She was glad now that her grandmother had persuaded her to take with her the elaborate French bed and other bric-a-brac that had seemed to her unsuitable and foolish. She would make the house Gilbert had built as beautiful as this one. They would have parties, too, pretending for a little while that the wilderness outside did not exist. The thought made her look toward Gilbert and catch his eye. When he responded to her small secret smile, her heart fluttered a little. She recognized a lover's glance. She believed she was in love, after all.

Mr. Wentworth, of whose tempestuous career she had heard little, except that he was a controversial person in Sydney and not welcomed everywhere, was gallant toward her. He was handsome, with his high, aristocratic forehead, and thick, glossy hair brushed smoothly back and curling on his neck. But he was autocratic and opinionated. When the subject turned to Gilbert's wine, Mr. Wentworth said that he believed Gilbert was making a mistake putting all his eggs in one basket. "You've heard what the governor said in his speech in the House yesterday—that our wool is our wealth, that colonists must have sheep if they want to continue to be wealthy."

"I never have been wealthy," Gilbert said mildly.

"No, and you may never be if you don't run sheep. You have

plenty of land. Wasn't your grant a thousand acres? You can't plant all that in vines?"

"True. I have a herd of cattle and a few sheep for killing for mutton, but otherwise," he said stubbornly, "I intend to put all my energies into my vineyard. It is the only way to succeed, to have a single aim."

"Well, I wish you luck," Wentworth said dryly. He signaled to a servant to open another bottle of the Yarrabee wine which Gilbert had presented to him and said to the table at large, "We must drink all we can to maintain our friend's prosperity."

After dinner Mr. Wentworth wanted to show Eugenia his treasures. He had bought Vaucluse at a public auction, and although the legal title was still in doubt and the subject of litigation in the court of claims, he had gone ahead making additions and improvements. He intended the house to be one of the best in the colony.

"But I understand, Miss Lichfield, that you will be living in a very fine one at Parramatta?"

"Yes, I haven't seen it yet. Mr. Massingham has only described it to me."

"Then allow me to say that it could not be too fine for its new mistress."

Eugenia lowered her eyes. The man's admiration was a little blatant. Bess Kelly had told her that he was an illegitimate son. His father had been a fine young scoundrel, who, after a forced arrival in Botany Bay, had acquired a fortune very quickly. This had enabled him to have his son educated in England. But William Wentworth himself was one of that new race, a man who had actually been born in the colony and who had its interests at heart. He would make his mark. He was a man to know, Gilbert had said. For it was at tables such as his that Australians would acquire the civilized habit of wine drinking.

Nevertheless, the good taste of Vaucluse had reassured Eugenia, and she was happy that Gilbert was pleased with her tonight. She was learning quickly. The quality that would be of most importance in this country was tolerance. Accordingly she set herself to be charming to her host, admiring his furniture purchased in Venice and Berlin, the grand oil paintings and Italian marble fireplaces, the French clocks, and costly porcelain. She almost forgot the unhappy subject of convicts and poverty.

Someone asked her if she sang or played the piano. When she assented, everyone begged for a song. It really was like a pleasant social evening at Lichfield Court. She could almost have believed Sarah sat in the shadows, listening to her, waiting to applaud. Eugenia had a pleasant, light, tuneful voice, and even without Sarah, there was plenty of applause. Eugenia heard Gilbert saying, "Yes, she sings very well," and when Mrs. Wentworth asked him if it was her voice he had fallen in love with, he answered, "It is a distinct asset, don't you agree?"

She touched his arm with her fan a little later, when he was standing a moment alone.

"Do you give me marks for my assets?" she asked playfully. "So many for my singing voice, so many for my ability to dance or to paint or sew, so many for my taste in dress? And later, of course, when I am more knowledgeable, so many for my ability to recognize a good wine?"

Her voice was light and teasing. She really was enjoying the evening immensely, and at this moment it didn't matter that Gilbert might have totted up marks in his mind. So long as she came near the maximum for a desirable wife, she was content. Wasn't this how the most successful marriages were made? Even if that warm, spontaneous flash she had caught in Gilbert's eyes across the dinner table had meant more to her than a cool tally of her worth.

Gilbert did not respond to her teasing manner but said seriously, "Everyone likes you. You are doing very well."

"I am not as pretty as they expected." She had noticed the other women looking at her assessingly.

"You have a good color tonight. It becomes you." He smiled, patted her hand, led her across the room to speak to someone else.

A good color, she thought. Like one of his wines. If he could, he would hold her up to the light and study her for possible flaws. But he was pleased with her tonight. She remembered again that look in his eye at dinner . . . She was sorry the evening was over so quickly.

"Miss Lichfield, do tell us what you are to wear at your wedding. Or is it a deep secret?"

In the privacy of the bedroom upstairs, the ladies gathered around her again. With the journey home and everyday life to face, they forgot their party manners and began to speak more plainly. Eugenia found herself abruptly back in a strange country where servants could not be trusted, where children got unaccountable illnesses that carried them off with savage suddenness, where decent clothes, water, even sometimes food, were scarce. Where an escaped convict or a party of roaming blacks with spears could terrorize lonely country farms, where a bush fire might rage over thousands of acres in a day or the terrible summer heat turn the small cottages into ovens.

Above all, there was the violence of the criminal classes. That case last night, for instance. Everyone was talking about it. The woman whose husband had been shot protested innocence, but of course, no one believed her. She was obviously a street woman; otherwise why had she lured the two men on? The truth was that she hadn't expected her husband, elderly and sick, to put up any opposition. Probably she had hoped to creep into the house with her followers, without waking him. Who knew how often she had done such a thing before?

When Eugenia was engaging servants, she must be especially careful. Mind you, it was difficult to get a woman who hadn't a criminal record, but some were anxious to redeem themselves and could be kept honest, if constantly watched. The younger the girl, the better. Once in her twenties, the creature had become hardened.

There was nothing for it but to tell them. They would hear soon enough. She had known all the time that she had had no real intention of opposing Gilbert on this first issue between them; neither had she the slightest intention of making excuses for him or being put in the position of having to defend him.

She said calmly, "Mr. Massingham and I have already engaged the two servants we will take with us. One is the young woman who accompanied my chaperone and myself on the voyage, and the other is the very woman you are talking about, Mrs. Jarvis. Isn't that a coincidence!"

She laughed merrily, looking at the circle of bonneted and shawled ladies.

Very ordinary faces, she thought. Bess Kelly's was endearing, but too fat and not well bred. Dr. Noakes' wife, Marion, had all the marks of breeding, but hers was a pale, sour face, discontent in her sharp eyes and the downward turn of her lips. The rest were flushed from the gaiety of the evening. Some were pleasant, some plain. All had one look in common, astonishment.

"You must have heard the part Mr. Massingham played in the affair," she went on serenely. "He almost witnessed the crime."

A flash in Marion Noakes' eye and a quick lowering of her eyelids gave Eugenia the smallest pause. Mrs. Noakes suspected Gilbert of being more than a passerby! Had he that kind of reputation? And did they know already that Mrs. Jarvis was expecting a child? She lifted her chin a little higher.

"Mr. Massingham and I were both impressed by Mrs. Jarvis' honesty and her truly unfortunate circumstances." (But she hadn't set eyes on the woman, as no doubt her audience very well knew.) "I expect this kind of thing happens all too often out here," she rattled on.

"Not precisely that kind of thing," Mrs. Noakes said repressively, and kind Bess Kelly came quickly to Eugenia's aid.

"I think it's a very fine and Christian thing to do. Eugenia is setting an example to us already."

"Christian perhaps, but let us hope wise," someone murmured.

"Miss Lichfield is very new here. We all make mistakes when we first arrive," said Mrs. Wentworth, surely meaning to be tactful.

"But husbands make edicts that wives must follow." Marion

Noakes had the last acid word as she briskly gathered up her wraps and prepared to depart.

Bess Kelly tucked her arm in Eugenia's, hanging back as the other ladies made their way downstairs. "Did you really like Molly Jarvis?" she whispered.

"How could I admit I haven't seen her yet?" Eugenia whispered back in mortification, and Bess began to giggle.

"Oh, that's too amusing. And you were behaving like a duchess. All the same—"

"All the same, what?"

Bess seemed to regret what she had been about to say. She said instead, "I did admire the way you stood up to them. You must know that everyone has speculated for months what Gilbert Massingham's bride would be like." She giggled again. "Now they know."

"What do they know?"

"Why, that you're a lady," said Bess comfortably.

The nagging doubt that perhaps a lady was not truly what Gilbert wanted, if he were to be honest about it, was reasonably allayed by Gilbert's affection on the drive home.

He told her that she had done very well and he was proud of her. She had made all the other women look like colonials.

"Wentworth was bowled over by you. So were the others. You're very ornamental, my dear. And you sing charmingly. What did you think of your first colonial dinner party?"

"It was very pleasant. I was particularly interested in Mr. Wentworth's explorations. Is there really so much still to be discovered?"

"There is, indeed. But we'll be content with Yarrabee and our vineyards. Our sons can do the exploring. I make a guess that it will take the rest of the century to discover Australia entirely."

Bumping over the rough road, Eugenia was thrown from her seat in the buggy against Gilbert. He instantly put his arm around her.

"Our eldest son must learn viticulture, but the next can be an explorer, if he wishes. Will that please you?"

"It seems that husbands make all the decisions," Eugenia murmured into the silk of his cravat. "Do you mean, in our marriage, ever to ask my opinion?"

"Oho, I believe you are thinking of Mrs. Jarvis again."

"The subject came up this evening while we were upstairs. I informed the ladies of our decision."

Gilbert gave a little snort of laughter, a pleased sound. Then he let her waist go to take the reins in both hands and whip up the horse, so that they were flying down the bumpy road.

"Wentworth wanted to drink his French wines this evening, but I persuaded him to try Yarrabee White Burgundy with the fish. I don't think it was from mere politeness that everyone pronounced on it favorably, do you? I noticed that Phil Noakes had his glass refilled. After vintage this year we'll give a party. So don't wear out all your pretty London gowns. And keep up your singing practice."

The wind, no longer bearing the savage heat of midday, was pleasant and refreshing. It carried a faint smell of smoke and gum leaves and dried grass. The road that led back to the center of the already sprawling town wound around the bay, giving glimpses of moon-washed sea. Far out the riding light of the *Caroline* swayed gently, a friendly star. The stars in the velvety darkness of the sky seemed not too unfamiliar. The horse clip-clopped briskly along, and Gilbert's arm came back around her waist.

Tomorrow she would continue her letter to Sarah, saying that she already had discovered that marriage necessitated an outward show of unity even though privately one might be in disagreement. But to please her dear Gilbert with loyalty would make her own sacrifice worthwhile. She would try to abide by that always.

But would she? Already she was realizing the impossibility of such a resolution, as her head came up.

"Gilbert."

"Yes, my love."

"Can you swear to me that the child Mrs. Jarvis is expecting is not"—her tongue stumbled as she realized the enormity of her words—"is not yours?"

There was a long moment of silence. She peered at Gilbert nervously. Was he furious with her? Was he wondering how to admit his guilt?

He was not angry. He was amused. If the shout of laughter he suddenly gave was amusement.

"What have those confounded gossiping women been saying to you? I declare women should never be allowed to retire upstairs together. There must be more time spent talking scandal in bedrooms than there ever was in sleeping."

"Oh, no, Gilbert, nothing like that was said."

"Only by innuendo? Well, perhaps I am a fair target. I have led a free enough bachelor life. But I assure you that I had never set eyes on Mrs. Jarvis until last night. Do you believe me?"

She did, of course. She was quite certain he would not lie to her about so important a matter.

But he still did not say that he would find a more suitable servant. In his eyes, Mrs. Jarvis obviously was a suitable servant. If he had met her only so recently as last night, she had clearly made a very strong impression on him.

Eugenia began to be curious to meet the woman herself.

Chapter 6

THE past was the past. Molly had told herself a thousand times to accept it and forget it. Even what had happened yesterday was now in the past. The grave dug in the dusty earth and the poor rough box that contained Harry Jarvis were only a memory. She doubted if she would ever visit it. The crackling gum leaves would lie on it, and the wind would stir the mounded dust until it was flattened and all trace of the grave had gone. Not that she hadn't had an affection for Harry. She would remember him every time she looked at his child. She was grateful to him for having given her a refuge, poor as it had been, and she was still bitterly angry about his unnecessary death. He had only just begun to be happy, poor wretch. He had called Molly his dear wife and his bonny girl. His terrible experiences had left him unbrutalized. There were permanent scars from irons around his thin wrists and ankles, but he had not forgotten how to have tenderness.

And now he lay in the bone-dry earth, and she, feeling slightly queasy from her pregnancy—or was it nervousness?—sat in Mrs. Kelly's little parlor opposite the young woman who was to be her mistress.

She had thought she had long got past feeling nervous about any situation. In ten years of humiliation and misery she had never failed to hold her head up. Her mother had taught her that from childhood. She was the eldest of a large family. They had lived in a picturesque, but damp and insanitary, cottage in Buckinghamshire, her father working as a farm laborer. His wages were a pittance, but there had always been eggs and milk from the farm, and fresh vegetables grown in their little plot of land, and plenty of home-baked bread.

Molly's mother, who had been a housemaid in the squire's house before her marriage, had, if anything, been overambitious for her children. In the manor she had had a glimpse of a fine style of living, and if her young ones could not hope to achieve that, they could at least better their lot. So they all were taught to read and write, to have pride in their persons, to be honest and obedient, but not servile. Molly went to her first position as a lively rosy-cheeked country girl, with what she thought was the whole world before her.

Her world had been before her, certainly. Fifteen thousand miles of it, across endless seas, in squalid misery. She had heard, years later, that her mother had died soon after hearing of her daughter's sentence of transportation. She had cried in desperate sorrow, but she still refused to be entirely cynical or entirely crushed. How could she allow herself to be, with Mam in heaven watching and telling her to mind her manners and keep her pride? There was nothing she didn't know about men, beginning with the master in London and continuing with that terrible four-month-long sea journey. After the first attempted rape in the night, in a fetid corner of the hold, when she had fought like an animal and had finally overcome the skinny, odorous creature, who had eventually wept at her feet, she had learned, in a strange way, to accept even that. These wretched men were as miserable as herself. As long as she had sufficient strength, she wouldn't be taken in that way, but neither would she hate too much. She had seen the women who hated and who grew into sharp-tongued, evil-eyed viragoes.

She herself became bitterly hated for being different. She was called vain, stuck-up, ambitious. She was looking to catch the eye of one of the officers, that was it. Why did she think she was so much better than the rest of them?

At Botany Bay, when at last they arrived, she was in further trouble for resisting the advances of one of those officers. Dressed in her gown of harsh Parramatta cloth, issued only to convicts (for what poorest free person would wear it?), she made an attempt to be neat and modest and inconspicuous. The difficulties of her position, it seemed, were insuperable. Her ticket-of-leave was postponed for three years because of the trouble with that persistent lieutenant. She lost the position she had in a house with a decent, but narrow-minded, mistress, and almost starved, rather than go on the streets as many of her fellow convicts did. Inevitably, the day came when she encountered a man too strong to fight. She remembered that there had been a thornbush on the ground where she was flung. Afterward she hadn't been able to tell which had hurt the most, the thorns or that brutal animal attack on her. So this was the act of love, she had thought incredulously.

And at the same time a cool part of her mind, which had somehow contrived to let this storm pass over it, remembered the peacefulness of her childhood home and the quiet devotion with which her parents had looked at each other.

So love could not always be bad. There must be two kinds, this nightmare of pain and humiliation from her unknown assailant (who had swaggered off, leaving her to try to arrange her torn clothing), and the other kind, the gentle, familiar loving of her parents that put a new baby in the cradle each year.

One day she would find that kind.

She had not expected it of Harry Jarvis. He was weakened by disease, and his hungry grasping of her had been pathetic. It was gratitude only that prevented her from wincing from him. She owed him this. And when she knew there was to be a child, she was glad for his sake. She resolved that her baby should know the kind of peaceful home that she had known, because it was the memory of that only which had enabled her to survive, without permanent scars, that other violent assault.

But now Harry was gone, and her unborn child's secure home gone. Once more she had to face the unknown.

Yarrabee—the country place with the musical name. She had never been in the country, never seen more than the heat-hazed hills on the other side of the harbor, and wondered what lay beyond them.

Yarrabee, and the redheaded stranger who had been kind without the motives she had come to expect from men. Or if the motives had been there, they had not been apparent. Molly was so unused to either kindness or sympathy that she thought this must be why Gilbert Massingham's remained so vividly in her mind. She remembered the liveliness of his blue eyes, his quick smile, his look of virility. He was not overhandsome (she would have mistrusted that), but he had a strong, stubborn look that she liked. He was a part of that unknown country that lay beyond the harbor hills. Her heart beat more quickly when she thought of it. Was this what she had kept her optimism for, for so long?

But the slight young woman sitting opposite her, very upright in an immaculately starched and ironed muslin gown, and asking questions in a cultured voice was another thing. She looked so freshly out of a well-ordered London drawing room that Molly was already anxious for her. And envious, too. Homesickness could surely be faced with equanimity if one had someone like Mr. Massingham at one's side, to cherish and protect one.

Cherish and protect. What lovely words, representing something completely alien to her.

"Please answer me, Mrs. Jarvis."

"I'm sorry, ma'am. I was wool-gathering."

"What were you wool-gathering about?"

"I was thinking how long it was since I was in a nice room like this."

The young woman looked about the room in some disbelief. Of course, it wasn't grand, but if Miss Lichfield only knew what other kinds of rooms existed in this country, she would appreciate the luxury of the rugs and polished furniture and starched lace curtains.

"It was a long time ago, ma'am. I was only eighteen."

"That was your age when you were—when you left England?"

"When I was accused and sentenced quite wrongly, ma'am. But I expect your husband will have told you about that."

"He is not my husband yet, Mrs. Jarvis. We are to be married next week. But we are talking of you, not of me. Mr. Massingham tells me that you are an accomplished cook. Is that by English standards or by those in the colony?"

"I wasn't trained as a cook, ma'am. But my mother taught me good plain cooking when I was a child. I was the eldest of nine, so I had to be useful. I never learned fancy dishes, but I can do everything else necessary."

"Well, that should not be a problem." The young lady had a very pleasant face when she smiled, not pretty, but lovely and gay, with light shining in her lavender-gray eyes. "I have a large household companion book that my mother insisted I should bring. I am sure it contains all we will need to know." She pressed her lips together as if she had realized she was too quickly accepting a woman with so doubtful a past. She sat up straighter and said primly, "Since Mr. Massingham has engaged you, I don't imagine you expect to be cross-examined. I have been here only two days, but already I have seen that there is a great deal of misery in the colony. I don't wish to make any judgment on your past. It is your future that concerns us. I hope you appreciate that Mr. Massingham and I are offering you an opportunity to completely rehabilitate yourself, and I only ask you not to abuse our trust."

"Oh, I would never do that, ma'am," Molly said earnestly.

"I believe you are in a certain condition."

"Yes, ma'am."

Miss Lichfield regarded her intently. Then she said in a suddenly gentle, sympathetic voice, "Mr. Massingham assures me there is a great deal of room at Yarrabee. Accommodating the child should be no problem. I think that is all, Mrs. Jarvis. Mr. Massingham will be telling you how the journey to Yarrabee is to be accomplished. I believe he and I are to drive in the buggy, and you and my maid, Jane King, are to follow in another conveyance with the baggage. The heavy furniture that came out on the *Caroline* is being sent on ahead by bullock wagon. It will await our arrival at Yarrabee. We will have a busy time sorting everything out. I imagine you are used to the country and the bush?"

"No, ma'am, I have never been beyond Sydney. I have always wanted the opportunity."

"Well, now you have it. It must be fate. That is what my sister Sarah would say."

She was so young. Not as young as Molly had been when she had been thrust so rudely and miserably into this hostile country. But young in experience and the ways of the world. Under that poise which she wore like another dress, she was probably nervous about a great many things, including her marriage. Well, lucky for you, you delicate young thing, you won't be thrown mercilessly into a patch of scrub, and suffer for weeks afterward with thorn scars, as well as the other scar on your mind. You'll have a soft bed, clean sheets, and a gentle lover— if that redheaded man knows how to be gentle . . .

As she curtsied before leaving, Miss Lichfield stopped her with a movement of her hand. "Oh, dear, I am forgetting. Mr. Massingham instructed me to tell you that your wages would be seven pounds a year, and I was to give you this"—she took five sovereigns out of a little leather purse—"to purchase material and make suitable clothes. Can you sew?"

"Yes, ma'am."

"Good. I think one plain dress—I see you are already wearing a neat one, but you will require a warmer one for the winter. And I would like you to have three plain caps and aprons and what underclothing you require. Will that amount be sufficient?"

"Ample, thank you, ma'am."

"Then anything you have left—you will require baby linen —I leave it to your discretion, Mrs. Jarvis."

"I managed very well in employing my first servant," Eugenia wrote to Sarah that evening. "You will be shocked to hear that she has been a convict, but she seems to have been unfairly accused of a quite petty crime, and Gilbert absolutely vouches for her honesty. She seems a pleasant and capable woman who deserves another chance in life. But I confess I cannot get used to a country so full of felons. I have to force myself to walk past a chain gang in the street. The poor wretches make me feel sick with pity. Gilbert says I will soon accept this state of affairs as natural. Natural! It will never be so to me."

The Kelly children were highly excited at having a bride dressed for her wedding in their house. One face after another peeped around the door until at last Eugenia asked that they be allowed to come in.

"Very well, you may come in if you sit quietly," Bess said. "Annie, mind Tom. Don't have him putting grubby fingers on things. Sit quietly on the bed, the three of you."

Eugenia revolved slowly for the children's benefit. "Well, how do I look?"

"Like a bride," Annie said, awestruck with admiration.

"Polly?" Eugenia bent over the younger girl, who hung her head bashfully.

Tom, the toddler, pointed a masterful finger. "I'll marry 'oo."

This precocious remark set the little girls off into fits of giggles, and the awed silence had vanished.

"Little boys don't get married, do they, Mamma?"

"Mamma, will I look like Miss Lichfield when I'm a bride?"

"Miss Lichfield, can I touch your veil? My finger's very clean."

"When will Mr. Massingham put the ring on your finger, Miss Lichfield? Will you have to keep it there until you die?"

"Hush, hush!" cried Bess. "If you can't be quiet, you'll have to go out. Eugenia, does your veil need another pin? The wind could snatch it off your head as you get out of the carriage."

This remark renewed the children's giggles. It was very hot in the little room. Already Eugenia's clothes were sticking to her, and her veil, securely pinned by Bess, dragged at her hair. But the children's gaiety was infectious. She adored them, sitting there in their best clothes, their plain faces shining with innocence.

"Come on then," she said, taking Tom by the hand and making him stand beside her. "If you are going to marry me, you must do so quickly, before Mr. Massingham arrives. This is how it is done. You must put a ring on my finger. Bess, lend me your ring. Soon I will have my own, but that will be too late for Tom."

This was too much for Annie and Polly, who shrieked with laughter until tears ran down their freckled cheeks. Real tears stood in Bess' eyes. She impulsively kissed Eugenia's cheek and said, "Oh, I do hope you will be happy. It's so different from the way it would have been in your own home."

"I like this way very much indeed," Eugenia answered serenely. "I couldn't have a more appreciative audience. Tom, now we are married. You must go back to your sisters and begin to grow up."

"Oh, the carriage!" Bess cried, flying to look out of the little window. "Quick, children, take a peep at the white ribbons the driver has tied to his whip. Here's Edmund come for you, Eugenia. Your gloves! Are you sure your veil is secure? Oh, and your flowers! Bless you, deary, you look a real treat."

In many ways, the getting ready was the nicest part of her wedding, for the heavy, airless atmosphere in the church made Eugenia feel a little faint. The minister surreptitiously mopped his brow, the ladies fanned themselves, and the men, wearing uncomfortable collars and starched shirts, were red-faced and perspiring. Gilbert's color was high also, but Eugenia knew she must look as pale as her dress. Bess Kelly had pinned her veil too tight, after all, and it was dragging painfully. Her white silk tight-waisted wedding gown trimmed with Brussels lace felt as hot as if it had been made of thick wool. She was damp all over with perspiration. She could hardly remove her glove for Gilbert to place the ring on her finger, and when he clasped her hand firmly and lovingly, they became welded together with sticky heat. It was only in that moment that Eugenia re-

alized she was married. She had been striving so determinedly
against her faintness that she hadn't taken in a word of the
wedding service.

"You must sign your name, my love," Gilbert was saying.

The pen shook in her fingers. In her endeavor to keep her
hand steady, a blot fell off the nib. It spread in a tiny black
pool at the end of her new name, Eugenia Massingham. The
minister blotted it up. Gilbert took the pen and signed his own
name with a flourish. When he looked at his bride there was
pride and excitement in his eyes. He didn't seem to notice her
pallor. He tucked her hand firmly in the crook of his arm and
began to walk down the aisle. It wasn't so much a walk as a
swagger. Eugenia felt touched that he was so pleased to be
showing her off and relieved that he hadn't noticed her distress. He wouldn't have cared to have a swooning bride on his
hands.

In the very back of the small church, among a little cluster
of uninvited spectators, she noticed Mrs. Jarvis. She was neatly
dressed, but she looked pale and sad. Poor thing, she had just
buried her own husband.

A sharp spasm of feeling came back to Eugenia, and her fingers tightened on Gilbert's arm. He responded immediately
with a quick smile. My husband, as of the past ten minutes, is
very much alive, she thought gratefully, and at last the faintness left her, and she felt happy and optimistic and eager for
the future.

She had a rival, however, at the wedding breakfast. Gilbert's
interest was divided with a nice discretion between his new
bride and his new wine.

The guests were persuaded to drink Yarrabee Claret, or, for
the ladies who preferred a sweeter taste, Yarrabee Sauterne.

"I laid this claret down when I came back from England after
my engagement," Gilbert said, rolling the wine critically in
his mouth before swallowing. "It will improve with keeping.
But it isn't bad. What do you think, sir?" He hoped Eugenia
was flattered by the presence of the governor, Lieutenant General Ralph Darling, at her wedding. To Gilbert's gratification,

he pronounced the wine excellent, though he agreed that it would improve with keeping.

"It will be better for my son's christening," Gilbert said.

There was much laughter, although Gilbert had not meant his remark to be a joke.

Eugenia looked at the red liquid in her glass and tried to imagine its being drunk by the phantom young man who was to be her son. Suppose she did not have a son. Would Gilbert be able to forgive her?

"I hope you are going to be able to share your husband's ambition," said the dry, grudging voice of Marion Noakes.

"To have a son?" Eugenia said, startled.

"No, no, I meant Gilbert's obsession with his vineyard. How is he to convert the sort of riffraff who live in this country to drinking wine? My husband says he will end by being ruined." Mrs. Noakes took a drink from her glass, savoring it. "But I must say this is moderately good. Well, I share my husband with his patients, which I suppose is no worse than sharing him with a vineyard and a winery."

"Doesn't a wife always share a husband with his profession?"

Mrs. Noakes gave her ironic laugh. "But not to extinction, my dear. Not if you're clever. And pay no attention to me. I have a macabre mind, Philip tells me." Under her breath she added, "If we had children, it would be better."

"You are not able to?"

"We had one who died. The same thing might have happened in England, I am told. My husband calls my attitude in blaming this country stupid prejudice. But take no notice of me, Mrs. Massingham. You are a beautiful bride, a treat for disillusioned eyes. And sometimes I deserve to be silenced in some effective way."

"My love!" Gilbert's hand was on Eugenia's arm. His face was flushed; his eyes were bright. He looked as if he had swallowed a good deal of his wine. "What is this old crow saying to you?"

"Now, Gilbert Massingham, it is quite unnecessary to call me something that I realize perfectly already."

Gilbert roared with laughter, but Eugenia, looking into the long, melancholy face, the sad, quizzical eyes, found herself suddenly liking Marion Noakes. Or at least being in sympathy with her. There was no opportunity to talk more, for Gilbert wanted to carry her off, if he could induce the guests to part with her. They were all in raptures about her. So elegant, so pretty. But now it was time for her to return to Bess Kelly's to change and to have her wedding gown packed into a separate box, which her maid Jane could take charge of.

Eugenia was just tying her bonnet strings and hoping that her traveling dress would not be too hot on the long, dusty drive when the alarming news came.

A dangerous convict had escaped from Cockatoo Island after seriously wounding one of the guards. He had made for Lane Cove and the hills beyond. He would be hiding out in the bush. More alarming, he had a gun and ammunition, which he had stolen from the injured guard. It was unlikely that he would venture near the road, unless he planned a holdup for the purpose of stealing money or food. Eugenia must not be nervous, but it was better to be prepared than unprepared. Had Gilbert got his rifle?

Gilbert did not seem at all perturbed by the news. He said that he never traveled without a rifle, and when Eugenia inquired why, he answered that no one traveled far into the country unarmed. They might be marooned by accident and require to shoot game for food. Or they might encounter a party of hostile blacks, although that rarely happened in these comparatively civilized days.

"Not on a well-known road like this one," he added, noticing his wife's face. "I meant farther into the interior, where there are no roadside inns. But don't be alarmed. This fellow will keep clear of habitation for his own good."

Gilbert was in the highest spirits. He almost seemed to enjoy the prospect of an encounter with a dangerous criminal.

"Where will he go?" Eugenia persisted.

"Into the Blue Mountains or beyond, I expect. There are plenty of escaped convicts who go into hiding and are never found again. They live with the blacks, if they aren't assassinated by them."

It appeared that the convict had been sentenced to transportation for forgery. He had been an educated man, with a sensitive mind, which the brutalities of his confinement had tipped into insanity. If he were encountered, it would be wise to treat him with respect.

Jane King had begun to sob. Mrs. Jarvis brusquely told her to calm herself. A frightened man running for his life had only one object, and that was to remain out of sight. Who better to know than Mrs. Jarvis? Eugenia reassured herself. She must have had enough experience of desperate men. There was the driver of the bullock wagon, too, Will Murphy, a convict who had obtained his freedom and now worked for Gilbert as a groom and stableboy. He was a rugged-looking fellow, who looked as if he could be trusted.

But Eugenia's sudden heavy feeling of apprehension was not only of the escaped convict, but also of those long, heat-hazed distances that were going to take her farther and farther away from civilization. Of the strange, harsh bird cries, the endless whirring of the cicadas, the unholy brightness of the sun that made the parched landscape so strangely melancholy. All the week she had tried not to think of this moment of departure. All that morning she had preserved her determined gaiety and had even been happy. As, of course, she was still, beneath this sudden cowardliness.

Mrs. Ashburton, wearing an enormous lavender-colored bonnet, her face beneath it purple with heat, fussed to the last.

"Eugenia, have you your smelling salts handy? Where is your parasol? What would your mother say to me if I allowed you to get sunstroke? Will you take my fan? It will help you keep cool." The elaborate lace fan was pressed generously into Eugenia's hands. "Now remember, when you are settled, I intend to pay you a visit. A few desperate convicts won't worry me. I will simply brandish my parasol in their faces and tell them to behave themselves. Come, my dear girl. Kiss me good-bye."

Eugenia had thought she would be so glad to escape that perpetual voice, as persistent as the cicadas. But now she clung to her, and then to Bess, whose small, hot, stuffy house seemed a haven. "I should really have married Tom," she said, in a last forlorn attempt at a joke.

Gilbert, not disguising his impatience, asked her to be so good as to climb into the buggy. It was time they were off. Farewells must not last forever.

The little group in the street waved and shouted good wishes. The children danced and screamed. The men flourished their tophats. A shower of rice hit the buggy. Then Gilbert whipped up the horse, and they were off. When Eugenia looked back, there was nothing but a cloud of pale-red dust.

And her married life had begun . . .

Chapter 7

A BRISK trot, Gilbert said, would bring them to Parramatta by dark. There he had arranged for them to spend the night in a comfortable hotel and wait for the bullock wagon to catch up with them the next day. After that, an easy drive of ten miles would take them to Yarrabee.

Mike Hansen, the hotel proprietor, was expecting them and was keeping his best room. There was a shortage of water after the dry summer, but he had faithfully promised Eugenia a bath.

Gilbert told her this when he noticed that even her veil did not keep the powdery dust off her face. As for her gown, chosen so carefully and made with such care so long ago in London, it was ruined. It didn't matter; she had plenty more. What was a mere dress, so long as this rough, jolting journey was soon safely over. Although she smiled cheerfully, Eugenia's secret apprehension failed to leave her. She particularly disliked the patches of bush, where although the shade was welcome, there was too much concealment for a fugitive. She preferred the open country in spite of the heat. The parched soil grew little but thornbushes and the everlasting eucalyptus trees. Crows circled over the landscape, black shadows with black croaking voices. Or a small gathering of kookaburras gave their maniacal laughter. But once Eugenia had to cry aloud in delight as a cloud of gray cockatoos with rosy pink breasts rose and swept across their vision, like a sudden sunset.

"What are they, Gilbert? They're so pretty."

"Galahs. You'll see plenty of them at Yarrabee. They haunt the gum trees. Make a devil of a noise."

It was just after this pleasing incident that the disaster occurred. The horse stumbled in a pothole and went lame.

Gilbert leaped out of the buggy, cursing as he examined the horse's left fetlock. Then he remembered the presence of his bride and apologized.

"But this is the devil of a fix. We'll have to wait for the bullock wagon. I'm desperately sorry. I've done this journey a dozen times with this mare. She's never failed me before."

Eugenia climbed out of the buggy to look at the trembling mare.

"Is it a serious injury?"

"It will be if we try to continue our journey. She'll have to rest. And so, I am afraid, will we."

The spot was open. There was a little shade under a clump of young gum trees, with their pleasant scent, and, blessedly, very little cover anywhere for an assassin. Eugenia summoned up her good spirits.

"Then we might as well make ourselves as comfortable as possible. Let us spread the rug under these trees. We can pretend we are having a picnic. It's such a relief to take this hot veil off."

"Yes, I like that better. Now I can see your face. What a pity we didn't bring a bottle of wine with us!"

"I would much prefer some cold water," Eugenia said honestly. "Is the sun always so hot?"

"Don't complain about it. It's ripening my grapes. Well, we do look like a pair of fools, I must say. I'm afraid there's no chance of our reaching Parramatta this evening. We'll have to put up at the nearest inn. Will you mind?"

"Is there one?"

"Yes, about six miles on. It's not much of a place, but it will be a roof over our heads. The devil take it, what a wedding night!"

Eugenia began to giggle at the absurdity of it all. What a

story this would make to write to Sarah! Seeing her mirth, Gilbert laughed, too, and pulled her toward him to kiss her.

"Bless you, my love, for taking it so well."

"I had always expected some hardships in this country," she said. But her laughter had gone as she became aware again not only of the oppressive loneliness, but of the possible nearness of a desperate fugitive, who might think to turn their plight to his advantage.

"What will happen to him when he is caught?" she couldn't help asking.

"Your mind is on that convict again? He'll be sent to a penal settlement. If he isn't hanged, he'll be kept in irons."

"He must have had a bad master."

"Quite probably. There are plenty of those. But this isn't a subject for our wedding day. Enjoy the quiet and the rest. We shouldn't have too long to wait."

The sun, however, was sinking in a great flame and the gum trees had turned black in a lonely haunted landscape when at last the wagon creaked up to them and came to a halt.

Jane tumbled out, crying, "Oh, ma'am, are you all right? Oh, isn't it all awful!"

Mrs. Jarvis said quietly, "Be quiet, you silly girl. The mistress isn't hurt, as you can see."

"No, I am not hurt. I am only tired and thirsty and covered in dust. Our horse went lame. It was the worst possible luck." She began to laugh in sheer relief. "I am so glad to see you. We are to go to an inn which is quite close, my husband says."

There were no longer mistress and maids, but three women isolated in the enormous wilderness. They kept close together as Gilbert and Murphy transferred the luggage from the buggy to the wagon and tied the lame horse behind.

"Now get in, all of you," Gilbert said. "If you don't want to be lost in the dark."

There was light from a window, a swinging sign that said MULDOONEY'S, and a dog barking. A woman with straggling hair and wearing a dirty apron came to the door, looked at the wagon and the weary travelers, said, "You want accommodation? You'd better come in," and they had found their night's refuge.

A narrow passage led to a stairway. On one side an open door showed a bar at which several bearded men were making a great babel.

"Rum drinkers," said Gilbert to Eugenia, in a tone of disgust.

"Come along in and shut the door," said the woman, who was now holding a lighted lamp. "There's a prisoner at large. We don't want to wake up with our throats cut. Which is your wife, sir?"

Gilbert took Eugenia's arm.

The woman's eyes rested briefly on Eugenia's fashionable gown. "You'll want to get that off. The heat must be killing you. I can give you the front bedroom, but the other ladies will have to make do with the small one at the back."

Eugenia asked, "Have you heard about the prisoner already?"

"We have. The troopers have been out. They've told us to put the bars up tonight. It's months since we had a holdup and I don't want another. You new here, missis?"

"She arrived only last week," Gilbert said stiffly, resenting the familiar tone.

The woman gave a short laugh. "She'll get used to it. Or go mad. Won't you, dear? I'll show you your room. Do you want to eat?"

Gilbert was about to acquiesce, but Eugenia's hand was on his arm. "I'm not hungry, Gilbert. I will go upstairs at once."

The room, she supposed, could have been worse. There were rag mats on the floor, a double bed with a clean cotton spread, two upright wooden chairs, and a table, on which stood a jug and basin. No wardrobe, no mirror, no *chambre de toilette*, which meant braving the terrors of the backyard. Her wedding night. It was going to be memorable, to say the least.

Somehow she managed to smile at their slatternly hostess. "Thank you. This will do very well."

The woman gave her caustic hoot of laughter.

"You don't need to give me your grand lady manners. I can see this isn't what you're used to. But it's better than the bush." Some not quite forgotten dignity came to her, and she added, "Sleep well, my lady," and withdrew.

"My lady!" said Eugenia, stretching her arms behind her head and yawning. "I confess I never felt less like a 'my lady.'"

"My poor darling, how can I tell you how sorry I am?" Gilbert wanted to take her in his arms. She moved away. She was sticky with heat.

"It isn't your fault. I blame no one but Providence. Do you think we will be eaten alive by mosquitoes if we have the window open?"

"I fear so."

"Then we will have to die of suffocation instead. Anyway, that window looks as if it would fall out if it were tampered with." Eugenia sank down on the bed. She really was so fatigued she could scarcely stand. "Do please stop looking at me in that anxious way. All I require is a jug of water and the small wicker bag that contains my night things. When I have those, you are free to do as you please. You may even join the gentlemen at the bar and persuade them to drink your wine."

Gilbert gave a half laugh, looking at her with tenderness and admiration.

"Shall I send Jane to you? Or Mrs. Jarvis, who looked the better for wear, I must say."

"Neither. Just make sure they are comfortable for the night. Or as comfortable as can be."

"Very well, my love." Then he did come to take her in his arms, putting his cheek against hers. "You have my greatest admiration. You have behaved wonderfully. But pray don't regard this as our wedding night. You are much too tired, and these are hardly the surroundings in which to show you how much I love you. Get into bed and sleep. I'm going to see to the horse and the baggage. I promise not to wake you when I join you."

The water, when it came, was red from the rusty soil. But

it was cold, and somehow she had to conquer her distaste and wash gingerly in it. Mrs. Jarvis had brought it, as well as Eugenia's wicker bag.

She had asked if there was anything else the mistress wanted. Jane, she explained, was in a state of collapse. The lonely country had frightened her.

"Then she must either get used to it or go back to Sydney," Eugenia said briskly. "No, thank you, Mrs. Jarvis. I don't require anything more. I mean only to unpack my night things and go to bed." She thought that there was a glint of admiration in Mrs. Jarvis' eyes, too. But it had taken all her ingenuity to keep up this bold front. The truth was that she was a feeble creature, utterly dismayed by the night's events. When the necessity for a journey down the dark back garden became evident, she was filled with nervous terror.

Should she call Mrs. Jarvis back? She rejected the impulse immediately. How ridiculously helpless that would make her! As if she could not find the way alone.

The stairs and the narrow passage were lighted by an oil lamp. The door, bolted with a rough wooden latch, opened easily enough. There was even sufficient light from a window (obviously belonging to the kitchen, for there was a strong odor of stale fat) to show her the dusty path to the odorous privy.

It was as she was leaving this unpleasant refuge that she had her first fright. A thin shape leaped at her ankles and began weaving about them, mewing loudly.

A cat! Eugenia said aloud, "You wretched little creature! Such a fright you gave me! Why, you poor thing"—she had bent down to touch the quivering body—"you're nothing but a bag of bones. You're starving. Doesn't anyone here feed you?"

The cat mewed again, with a pitiful note of supplication. Eugenia remembered the hard, narrow, mean face of the woman who had admitted them. She remembered, too, the smell of fat from the kitchen and was reasonably certain there would be the remains of a joint of mutton somewhere. She could not abide people who were unkind to animals. They deserved to be stolen from.

"Come, kitty, come," she said, picking up her skirts and running, with the cat at her heels, to the kitchen door. When she found that it was slightly ajar, one part of her mind was elated; the other recorded that it was strange for the passage door to be bolted and this one open.

There was a lamp turned low on the table. In the gloom someone moved.

"Mrs. Muldooney?" said Eugenia tentatively. "Your cat seems to be starving. Is there a little spare food?"

The shadowy form took a quick step nearer.

"If it is your cat—" Eugenia went on, and the next moment a hand was clapped over her mouth; an arm like iron held her still. Her nostrils were filled with an intolerable stink of dirty clothes, unwashed flesh, foul breath. In the dim light she saw the bearded face, the glint of wild eyes.

"Hush up!" a voice growled. "If you yell when I take my hand away, I'll shoot you. Now, where's the food?"

It seemed as if the cat, probably familiar with kicks, had had the good sense not to come into this treacherous room. Eugenia could hear its howls retreating down the garden. From farther off, laughter came from the distant bar. Gilbert was in there, no doubt washing the day's dust out of his throat and talking about his vineyard. His wife was alone with an escaped convict.

For who else could this desperado be?

The nauseating hand was moved tentatively. When no scream came, the man loosed his grip, nodding approvingly.

"Food," he demanded again in his rasping voice.

"Then turn up the lamp so that I can see what I'm doing," Eugenia said. Was that her voice, so cool and composed?

The dirty hand came out to obey. As the light bloomed, she looked round swiftly. The ragged figure stood menacingly between her and the door. He held a pistol. Another door into what looked like a pantry was on the opposite side of the room. She pointed instinctively.

"In there. The joint left from supper."

Her wrist was seized, and she was dragged to the door. Dear heaven, suppose it was not the pantry! It was so dark neither of them could see what was within. But the smell of cooked meat was plain enough.

The grip on her wrist tightened. The bony fingers cut into her flesh. Skeleton fingers. The man was more starved than that pitiful cat.

"Where's the food?"

"On the shelf. Can't you smell it?"

Again she had acted from instinct, not realizing that his hunger would drive him into carelessness. For with a groaning intake of breath, he let her go and groped with both hands for the tantalizingly invisible joint of meat.

In a flash she was able to shut the door and press against it with all her might, at the same time screaming in a voice that could never have been her own.

"Help! Gilbert, Gilbert! Help!"

The door rattled violently behind her. She heard the cursing voice. "You slut! You bitch! I'll kill you!"

She screamed again, piercingly loud, and then the whole world exploded behind her.

He had fired his pistol, she realized. She could not have been hit, for she was still on her feet pressing against the rickety door, as it inexorably opened behind her. It burst open at the precise moment that another door burst open and the room was suddenly full of people. And the stench of gunpowder and that unforgettable sour jail smell.

Someone was carrying a lantern. All at once the light was too brilliant, too cruel.

For the fugitive she had trapped, held now between two burly men, was like that starved cat in the backyard. A little scarecrow of a man with a tangled black beard and blazing, defeated eyes. He didn't look at her. He looked beyond everyone into some unreachable distance. He had the expression of the men she had seen in the chain gang in Sydney, wild, forlorn, unbearably hopeless.

She felt suddenly terribly sick. She hardly realized that Gilbert had his arm around her and that his face was alight with pride and admiration.

"So the little bride caught him!" Mrs. Muldooney was exclaiming. "Trapped him in my pantry. Got some nerve, ain't she? Never would have thought it!"

"Dearest, you aren't hurt, are you?" Gilbert was looking with concern at her white face.

She shook her head dazedly.

"We heard the pistol shot. Look at that!" Gilbert whistled in horror. "The bullet went through the door not six inches above your head." He gripped her to him so tightly that she felt swimmingly faint. Yet her eyes stayed stubbornly open as she watched the prisoner's bony wrists being tied with cord. Tightly, cruelly. Didn't they realize they were cutting him to the bone?

"What's that, love?" Gilbert bent his head to hers as the scarecrow in the ragged clothes was hustled outside.

"I was asking if they would give him some food. He's starving."

"He'll soon find there are worse things than being hungry," Gilbert said grimly.

"Are there?"

"Of course there are. I'd prefer not to mention them to your pretty ears."

"Have you ever been hungry as he is? He was so hungry he forgot to be careful. That's how—I caught him."

"And were the bravest woman in the world," Gilbert declared, proudly, entirely failing to understand what she was trying to say.

"She deserves a pint," someone shouted. "Give her a pint. She's a regular heroine."

But Eugenia begged to go upstairs. She was not a heroine. What she had done had been perfectly simple. She had suffered no damage but a bruised wrist.

"You can't make light of it in that way," Gilbert said. She saw that his eyes were very bright and that now his first shock

was over, he looked as if he were enjoying the excitement. "Mrs.
Jarvis will take you upstairs. I'll be up when I have assured myself that our prisoner is safely secured. We'll have to mount a
guard over him until the troopers arrive."

Upstairs, in the small bedroom from which she had seemed
to be away for an age, Eugenia asked, "Where will they put
him, Mrs. Jarvis?"

"They'll have to tie him to a tree. I've seen that done more
than once."

"A tree! Like a dog!"

"None of those rotten old sheds would hold him. That
pantry door wouldn't have held him a minute longer, would it?"

Eugenia shivered violently.

"He put his hand over my mouth. I must wash. I can still
smell his smell."

"You were very brave, ma'am." Mrs. Jarvis' eyes were warm
with admiration. "Can I get something to soothe you? You're
all of a tremble. Some milk with a dash of brandy?"

"I wish I'd let him go," Eugenia whispered.

"What did you say, ma'am?"

"I wouldn't have been so frightened if I had known how
small and thin he was."

"But he had a gun. He was dangerous. Don't you be wasting
your sympathy on him."

It was quite some time before Gilbert came upstairs. Eugenia had obediently drunk the milk lavishly laced with brandy
that Mrs. Jarvis had brought. Since she had scarcely eaten all
day, the mixture had immediately gone to her head. In a daze,
she had allowed Mrs. Jarvis to undress her, put on her nightgown, and settle her in bed. Her head spinning, her eyes smart-
ing and burning, she had lain listening to this terrible night's
unfamiliar sounds. A dog barking incessantly, men's voices,
Mrs. Muldooney shouting something in her harsh tones, a horse
galloping off. She thought she heard someone crying, too. But
the brandy that had made her head spin must have distorted
her hearing. That deep, uneven breathing, like caught sobs, was

the intermittent rustle of wind in the metallic leaves of the gum tree near the window.

The tree to which the prisoner was tied, the cord cutting into his thin wrists?

When Gilbert came in quietly, he leaned over the bed to see if she was sleeping. At first she pretended to, not wanting to look at him in case that wild excitement was still in his eyes. She had once seen one of her father's gamekeepers look like that when he had caught a weasel in a trap and had found that the animal was still alive.

Men had this overpowering pleasure in hunting down a dangerous quarry. It was perfectly natural and right. Murderous felons, as well as weasels, must be destroyed.

"Eugenia! Are you asleep?"

Her lashes trembled. "Mrs. Jarvis made me drink—quite half a pint—of brandy."

"Splendid." He was laughing softly. "Exactly what you needed. I can't tell you how proud I was of you tonight." He was taking off his clothes, dropping them in a great hurry on the floor. "I didn't intend you to have such an initiation to this country, but you have passed your first test magnificently. I am almost glad it happened so that I could see your mettle. Which I knew you would have, of course."

The blankets were tossed back, and he had lain down heavily beside her, his hands dragging at her nightgown, his face almost smothering her.

"Gilbert, you said—"

"What did I say? Something I've since regretted." His breath smelled heavily of wine; one of his arms was around her neck like an iron bar. Her head swimming with brandy and shock and exhaustion, she recognized a horrifyingly familiar sensation, the grip of the convict's bony arm making her prisoner, the feeling of suffocation when his hard hand had held her mouth.

Crazy! This was her husband kissing her, murmuring endearments.

"I meant to leave you to rest tonight. But I can't resist you. That's the simple truth. You're so lovely. You don't want me to resist you, do you, my darling?"

She started up tensely.

"What's that noise?"

"Only a dingo howling."

"Dingo?"

"A wild dog. They roam around." His voice was impatient. He had no ears for anything outside the confines of this room. He playfully loosened her hair and pulled it over her ears to deaden sound. Then, smiling, his lips came down on hers, his hands pulled at her nightgown again. She could no longer even protest. She was not permitted the breath. And the melancholy howl, half-human (could it really be what she fantastically imagined it was, that miserable wretch tied to the tree howling for mercy?), came again, and later again, echoing her own sudden, startled cry of pain.

The room went black. She was only half-conscious, struggling with the fantasy that it was the thin, savage face of the convict above her and his body performing this unbelievable intimacy.

She fought the darkness, opening her eyes wide to stare at the flickering candlelight, telling herself that it was her own loved husband whose body, slippery with sweat, was sliding off hers. There was his familiar red hair, his loving eyes, his voice murmuring inaudible endearments.

When she said nothing, he settled down beside her, one hand entangled in her hair. Almost at once he was asleep, and she, too exhausted to move, too feeble even to loosen his hold on her hair, thought that she was as much a prisoner as the man tied to the tree.

In the end, her exhaustion was a blessing, for it made her sleep. She awoke to a tremendous cacophony of noise as kookaburras in a gum tree outside her window saluted the morning. She was alone. Gilbert's rising had not disturbed her, but the harsh, uncanny laughter from the squat kingfisherlike birds was something she was sure she would never grow used to. It had a primeval sound, just as the animals here were primeval. In what civilized country would one find a creature as awkwardly shaped as the kangaroo, for instance? Or the giant lizards that looked a million years old. She must remember to tell Sarah about the lizard she had encountered on the stairs at Bess Kelly's, both of them so frightened that neither could move.

But nothing of last night must be recorded.

It was better to pretend that it had never been, shutting out the shocking, painful memory. The dog had stopped barking; the convict was no longer howling for mercy; the dark, secret pain between her legs had gone. There were dishes rattling in the kitchen and loud, cheerful voices. A smell of frying bacon drifted upstairs. The sunlight lying across the floor was already hot.

She must get up and groom herself as well as possible. Daylight made the rust-colored water in the jug look even more distasteful. But the sooner she was dressed, the sooner they could leave this horrible place.

She noticed, as she got out of bed, that the gown she had worn yesterday had been neatly laid over a chair. All trace of the dust that had smeared it had gone. Her underthings were also laid out.

Jane was proving more capable than one would have expected her to be, after her prostrate state last evening. She must have been surprisingly quiet, too, since her movements in the room had not disturbed Eugenia.

There was a tap at the door.

"Is that you, Jane? Come in."

"It's Mrs. Jarvis, ma'am." The door opened. Mrs. Jarvis, dressed in the gray cotton dress in which she had traveled yesterday, but which also had been cleansed of travel stains, stood there.

"Jane is poorly still, ma'am. So I've come to see if there's anything I can do."

Eugenia's first impulse was to send her away; those warm brown eyes saw too much. But this was nonsense. The woman seemed to be a good servant; that was the important thing.

Much better that composed face than Jane's sickly, hysterical one bending over her. Besides, she found she rather badly wanted the company of a woman; otherwise, that terrible combination of homesickness and fear that lay just beneath her consciousness would rise and burst over her in a flood.

"Thank you, Mrs. Jarvis, you can help me dress and pack my night things."

"Very well, ma'am. Can I brush your hair for you, too? There's no mirror, and the water they expect you to wash in isn't fit for a pig. But I expect we can manage one way and another."

The hair brushing was soothing. Mrs. Jarvis had a nice rhythmic style. She twisted the heavy locks into a respectable coil, pinned it up securely, and then helped Eugenia into her dress. Since there was no mirror, Eugenia had no way of knowing what her face looked like, and she didn't intend to ask Mrs. Jarvis. The quiet eyes were observing enough already.

"I am stiff all over from that jolting in the wagon yesterday," she said, and at last found that she could talk about the previous night. "What has happened to the convict?"

"Two troopers came for him. He was taken away before dawn."

"What will happen to him?"

"He'll be hanged," said Mrs. Jarvis quietly. "I have to tell you the truth."

Eugenia shivered.

"How have you not been brutalized, Mrs. Jarvis? You must have seen so many dreadful things."

"It's my nature not to be, I expect, ma'am."

"And you don't want to go back to England?"

"What would there be for me there? I belong here now. My child will belong here."

And so will yours, those too-perceptive eyes said.

Eugenia pressed her hands to her stomach, wondering fleetingly if there was the seed of a child there already. She saw that Mrs. Jarvis had noticed the movement and hastily smoothed down her skirt.

"Did you hear the dog barking all night, Mrs. Jarvis?"

"It was a dingo. There, ma'am. You look very well after such a long journey yesterday."

"It was a long journey for you, too, in your condition."

"I'm a strong woman. And I'm used to the climate."

"Yes, you seem to be, I must say. Then I will be obliged if you will bring me my breakfast. Just some tea and a little bread and butter. Then I must go see how Jane is. If she is still so poorly, she had better ride in the buggy with Mr. Massingham and me."

Though her motives, she admitted privately, were not entirely concern for Jane. The girl's presence would serve to postpone the moment when she had to be alone with her husband.

Chapter 8

THE house was such a surprise that as the buggy stopped and Gilbert leaped out, Eugenia fell spontaneously into his arms.

They had turned off the road at a sign YARRABEE painted on a post in rough black letters and had driven more than a mile over a bumpy track that seemed to lead nowhere. Then suddenly the graceful sand-colored house, on a slope that led down to green willows and a glint of water, was like a mirage in the parched landscape. It had two stories, a veranda running around the lower one, and balconies at the upper windows. The doors and window frames and veranda posts were painted a pristine, glistening white. The whole impression was of cool, shady comfort.

"Oh, Gilbert, I couldn't imagine it would have been like this," Eugenia exclaimed in delight.

Gilbert looked pleased and proud. He looked a suitable part of the landscape, too, with his sky-blue eyes, his pale-red thatch of hair. Seeing him like this against the background of his fine new house, Eugenia could almost forget the hot, slippery body that had slid off hers last night. She intended to forget it, at least in that particular context. Here was her new home, and it was much much better than she had dreamed it could be. Even in England she would have been proud of it.

Only in England it would not have been built by unhappy, suffering men detained at His Majesty's pleasure.

"I treated the men well." Gilbert was getting rather too clever at reading her expression. "They were sorry when the house was finished and they had to leave. But come in, and see it properly. Your furniture has been arranged, but you may care to dispose it differently later. When you've seen the house, I want you to see my winery and vineyard. I expect you not to be too tired for that."

On the ground floor the dining room, the drawing room, the library (as yet empty of books), the sitting room, each opening onto the veranda, a china room, a linen room, and across a paved courtyard the kitchen, the dairy, and the servants' rooms. Upstairs six bedrooms, a nursery, a schoolroom, two bathrooms with enormous baths mounted on pedestals. It was all just as Gilbert had told her it would be, three years ago, in England. He had kept his word about everything.

In her mind, Eugenia was planning wallpapers, curtains, rugs. She would like a yellow bedroom and a blue bedroom, as there were at Lichfield Court. She could hardly wait to get at her boxes and crates and begin unpacking the smaller items she had brought with her. The French four-poster bed, already arranged in the largest bedroom, looked wonderful. The high ceiling and the long windows onto the balcony set it off perfectly. There was a Turkish rug that she would put in the sitting room which faced south, the direction that got the most shade in this upside-down country.

Gilbert enjoyed her exclamations of pleasure, but he hadn't too much time to waste on the house. He was impatient to show her his prized possession, his vineyard.

Jane, still a greenish color beneath her crumpled bonnet, but looking more cheerful, had crept into the downstairs hall. She had sat, a silent third, in the back of the buggy, more like a miserable little animal than a human being. But now her eyes had brightened a little, and she was timidly asking for instructions.

"Take the smaller bags upstairs and begin unpacking," Eugenia said, enjoying giving her first order in her new home. "We will decide later where things are to be put. But I would like my white muslin aired and ironed. Gilbert, is there someone to prepare a midday meal for us?"

"Yella will do that. To the best of her ability."

"Yella?"

"A native woman. Now don't look alarmed, my love. That's the very reason that we have brought Mrs. Jarvis. Because I didn't think you would care for Yella's very amateur skill. Besides, she hasn't the most advanced ideas on hygiene. Well, come. I've waited long enough to show you the most important part of the estate."

On the far side of the courtyard, beyond the kitchen buildings, there were stables, cowsheds, and a row of huts. Where the outside staff lived, Gilbert said briefly. The stableboys and the laborers who tended the vines.

"Convicts?" Eugenia asked, trying not to let her distaste show.

"Ticket-of-leave men and two ex-convicts who have elected to stay at Yarrabee. They work well, for the most part. They get drunk at vintage, of course. One has to allow that. And one has to see they go to church on Sundays. That is a law."

The sun was growing unbearably hot. Eugenia was glad to step into the cool winery, with its immensely thick stone walls situated a little distance beyond the stables. It was full of casks and had a pervading sour smell that she found nauseating. The odor strengthened as she followed Gilbert, who carried a lighted lantern downstairs into a long, cool, dark cellar.

Here were more casks, which Gilbert explained were filled with wine ready for bottling. In another room, bottles lying in neat rows on racks were labeled with vintage dates. The huge vats, empty now, would be scoured and made ready for pressing the new season's grapes in just over a month, if this hot weather kept up.

Gilbert went on to describe the pressing, the great piles of grapes squeezed until the juice, or must, ran into the vat to await fermentation. He explained how the bloom on the grapes carried its own fermenting property, how the temperature of the cellar must be exactly right, and the hope that the fruit would have had the most beneficial amount of rain during its swelling on the vine. Too little affected the flavor, too much produced a woolly fungus.

After fermentation, the bottling was a skill in itself. Sufficient space must be left between cork and wine to allow ullage; the bottle must lie on its side—

"Are you following me, Eugenia?"

"I am afraid some of the words you use are unfamiliar."

"They will soon be familiar to you. Is something the matter? You look a little pale."

"There's a very strong odor down here."

"You'll get used to that. You'll grow to like it. Wait until vintage, when the baskets of grapes begin coming in. Murphy and Tom Sloan and I do the pressing. It's hard work. We don't use our feet as the Portuguese do; we use wooden presses, which are just as effective and more civilized to my way of thinking."

"Gilbert, I'm sorry, a little fresh air—"

She managed not to vomit. She rested on an empty cask in the storeroom above and saw Gilbert's cool, disdainful gaze. Was it disdainful? Or just disappointed? Was he going to be sorry that he had married a woman who couldn't stand the smell of sour wine? She was furious with herself.

"I will get used to it," she said determinedly.

"Of course. I expect you're still suffering from the shock of last night. I should have realized that. Shall we return to the house? I can take you up to the terraces later."

She would have preferred the terraces, where the sun shone on rows and rows of ripening grapes, to the dark winy cellar. She was sure she would have been able to express enthusiasm there and have felt her sense of adventure returning.

But Gilbert, leading her back to the house, seemed to have overlooked the fact that she had not expressed enthusiasm. He was explaining that he had laid out his entire capital on the house and its contents and the vineyards. It was important that this year's harvest be a good one. The portents were excellent. The vines were bearing well; there hadn't been late spring frosts, the little blight he had noticed on the Malaga vines hadn't reached the red Bordeaux or the Epernay. If it would only rain a little in the next few days, he would begin planting out the new clippings. It was best to put them in after a heavy shower. He had had men preparing new terraces all the winter and spring.

"We'll give a housewarming after vintage. You can dress the house up by then, can't you? I have enough money left to make the place civilized."

"The garden?" Eugenia asked. For there had been none, only dusty, dried grass and a few recently planted shrubs, struggling to survive.

"That's your province, too. I'll let you have Peabody. He says he was a gardener at a royal palace, though I doubt if he's telling the truth. He lives in a realm of fantasy. But it was he who planted the shrubs. He said coming straight from England, you would be homesick for a bit of green. You can buy plants from a nursery in Parramatta, rosebushes, geraniums, plenty of English flowers to stop you feeling homesick."

Eugenia evaded his searching look and asked how such plants could grow in the parched soil. The shrubs didn't appear to be very happy.

"They need to be kept watered. You can even have a lawn if you water it. Luckily water is one commodity we aren't short of. I've sunk a very good well. And when it rains, that little creek down the slope overflows its banks. There's a lake five miles away where the black swans nest. You'll find it charming. Well, my dear? Are you satisfied with your new home?"

As convincingly as he could wish, Eugenia replied that she found it quite astonishing, out here in the wilderness.

His look of gratification made her smile. She was touched that he had wanted so much to please her.

"We'll make it famous. We're the aristocracy in this country, because we've come of our own free will. That makes us the true inheritors. Do you see what I mean?"

She could hardly tell him that at this particular moment she was reluctant to accept her inheritance. The dusty, dry land—would it ever grow roses? Would she ever be able to walk bareheaded in the blazing sun or get used to the wild, melancholy, uncanny bird calls or the enormous sky? Or the captive men who sometimes howled like dogs. She gave a little shudder that Gilbert took for physical discomfort.

"You haven't brought your parasol. It's my fault, I should have insisted. I never want to see you out without it when the sun's as hot as this. You have an English skin. I want it preserved. I don't want a burned-up, sallow wife."

"Very well, Gilbert," she answered meekly. If carrying a parasol pleased him, it was a simple enough thing to do.

She held the parasol over her head when she took a walk down to the creek later in the afternoon. Still suffering from that miserable inertia, the aftermath of last night's unnerving experience, she had felt too languid to do anything but consent when Gilbert had suggested that the arrangements in the house be left until the arrival of the bullock dray with Mrs. Jarvis and the remainder of the baggage. It had become too hot even in the shade of the veranda, where a rocking chair had been set out. Gilbert had said the creek was dry, but she thought she could see the shine of water. It looked cool.

Strolling down the half-mile slope was a small diversion in the boredom of the afternoon. For immediately after the midday meal Gilbert had gone off to his vineyard, leaving her alone. He hadn't bothered to conceal his impatience to get there.

She was glad to see him go, yet when he had done so, she felt unbearably lonely. Jane, who had cheered up considerably now she saw that she had not come to a hovel, was busy washing and ironing the clothes they had worn on the journey. Yella, the native woman, who looked at least a hundred years old but who must have been reasonably young since she was undoubtedly pregnant, had served an almost uneatable meal of tough cold mutton, pickles, and stale homemade bread. Eugenia had had to take herself sternly to task for feeling queasy at the thought of those brown hands touching the food. But she had eaten only a mouthful or two of the mutton. Poor Gilbert, if this had been his daily fare. Tomorrow she would take the servant problem in hand. There must be young white girls in the town of Parramatta who would come out here to learn to be housemaids.

Yella could remain, of course. Eugenia had no intention of being unkind, but in the future the woman must have nothing to do with the actual cooking. She could prepare vegetables, under Mrs. Jarvis' instructions, wash dishes, sweep the floor. She would no doubt be happy enough. She looked like a lazy creature. How unattractive the Australian natives were, with their low brows and deep-set animal eyes! But they were friendly and harmless if they were treated kindly. One didn't need to fear a spear in one's back. They had a musical language, too. Yarrabee. That was one of their words.

This property had been part of their hunting grounds. They were disturbed that white settlers were destroying the game, kangaroos and wallabies, emus, wombats, and the giant lizards called goannas. Or so Gilbert had told her. In the past raiding parties of blacks had sometimes attacked small farms. But that time was over. All was peaceful now in these parts.

And if there had once been a gum forest here, there was still plenty of the tall, graceful eucalyptus trees, some with white trunks, some mottled, some a pale pearly pink, like human flesh. There was also boxwood, tea tree, wattles, and the fascinating blue-gray smoke trees. And down at the creek the willows drooping in the heat.

If there was no water, how did the willows survive?

Actually, there was the tiniest trickle of water surrounded by cracked yellow clay. And on the opposite side of this miserable stream in the shadow of one of the tired willows, a small cross. Two sticks nailed together and tilting sideways.

Surely it wasn't a grave!

Catching her breath, Eugenia stepped across the tiny rivulet of water.

Unmistakably the mound, covered in dusty weeds and thistles, was a grave. A very small one which must belong to a child. What innocent little creature had breathed her last in this lonely, unhallowed spot?

Bending down, Eugenia could decipher letters scratched with a burned stick on the homemade cross. PRUDENCE.

In the distance white cockatoos, like overblown peonies, screeched in the gum trees. A little wind stirred the heat. A trickle of perspiration ran down Eugenia's forehead. She caught the long-ago grief that had hung around the lonely little grave and was filled with a sense of desolation.

What a strange, haunted country this was, and how utterly alien she felt!

Chapter 9

It had been a good, satisfying day, Gilbert reflected. At eight o'clock the swift dusk had come down. Now they sat dining by candlelight.

It was exactly as he had imagined it would be when he had returned from England and begun to plan his home. The pleasant, civilized evenings spent with his wife after the toil of the day, the occasional conversation, though not too much of that because he didn't care for chitter-chatter all the time. Nevertheless, this evening Eugenia had been a little too quiet.

She had asked some questions about a child's grave down at the creek. He had had to make an effort to remember the circumstances. Mrs. Jarvis was waiting on the table. Eugenia would have to make other arrangements about that. He had hired the woman to cook, not to wait on table. He found her quiet movements curiously distracting. She must have been well trained in her youth. Her downcast eyes and expressionless face were faultless. But her neat dress accentuated, rather than concealed, a certain voluptuousness of figure, which perhaps accounted for his distraction.

"What were you saying, my love? A child's grave? Yes, I do remember the circumstances. A family on their way west by bullock wagon had camped down at the creek. It was vintage time, my first vintage. We were pretty busy. A man came up for help. He said his little girl was sick with a fever. He wanted to borrow a horse to go to Parramatta for a doctor. But the child died in the night, before the doctor arrived. So they asked permission to dig a grave by the creek and buried her there. Someone said prayers. Then they packed up and went on."

"Leaving her?" Eugenia said distressfully.

"What else could they do? This kind of thing happens out here."

"Was the mother very upset?"

"I never saw her. I gave the father a glass of wine. But it was pretty raw and sour, and he was in a distressed state. It only made him vomit."

Eugenia winced.

"How old was the little girl?"

"I don't know. I don't believe I asked. She was the eldest of four. I suppose she was six or seven."

Eugenia's face in the candlelight looked very pale. Her eyes were intense. She might have been the bereaved mother herself.

"I told you to keep out of the sun. You shouldn't have walked down to the creek in the afternoon heat."

"I thought I could see water. It looked cool. But the leaves of the willows were dropping off."

"I'm afraid we're in for a drought. My vines are ripening too fast. The grapes haven't enough flavor. At this rate we'll have to start picking in two or three weeks."

Eugenia stirred her food with her fork. She exerted herself to make polite conversation.

"Was everything well since you had been away?"

"Comparatively. I have a good overseer, Tom Sloan. There have been no fights, which is saying something. One man was caught stealing. He had a bottle of wine under his coat. Meaning to drink it secretly, I expect. Have you given any thought to the garden, my dear?"

"Did he have to be punished?"

That too-intense look in her eyes again. But he liked her sensitivity.

"The fellow stealing the wine? I let him off with a reprimand. Since I had just brought my bride home. He can count himself lucky. He owes his reprieve to you."

"Otherwise what would his punishment have been?"

"A dozen lashes. Now why do you look at me like that? I don't enjoy administering punishment any more than the poor wretch who gets it. But you must understand that these men are felons. Look at what happened last night."

Eugenia pushed damp hair off her brow.

"I would rather not talk about that. I have been trying to forget it. Could we have our coffee on the veranda?"

"Of course. Splendid idea."

They rocked gently in their rocking chairs in the warm darkness. Gilbert pointed out the Southern Cross and other constellations, then, when Eugenia was silent, fell silent himself. He could see the pale blur of her face, her quiet figure. He wanted to move nearer and take her hand in his, but desisted. Tonight she was too remote, wrapped in private thoughts. He intended to be very gentle later. He had had an occasional fleeting feeling of anxiety that he had allowed his desire to get out of hand last night. He had been so excited and stimulated by the sight of his bride trapping a felon that he had been unable to control himself. He had hoped Eugenia had understood his passion.

She had been so quiet all day that he had been forced to have those vague feelings of remorse. But tonight, in their own home in that elegant French bed which had made him laugh with a distinctly sensual pleasure when he had seen it, he would make amends. If amends were required.

"I will plant honeysuckle to climb up the veranda posts," Eugenia said at last, dreamily. "Do you remember the honeysuckle over the summerhouse at Lichfield? It used to scent the mornings and evenings."

"It will remind you of home," Gilbert said.

"Yes. Do you object to that?"

"By no means. Plant all the things that make you happy. Rose beds, perennial borders, yew trees, whatever you can persuade to grow."

"I will make a beautiful garden. A lily pool, a sundial, a yew walk, climbing roses for shade." She sighed. "But it will take a lifetime."

"Growth is quick here. Anyway, we have a lifetime."

Now he did reach over and take her hand. She didn't resist. Her own, small and warm and dry, lay within his. His heart began to beat faster. He tried to check his rising excitement, remembering, as he hadn't done last night, that this delicately bred woman would have to be taught, patiently and gently, to return passion. But on the whole he liked that. He wouldn't have it any other way. Even if she never did . . . But she would, of course. At least she would always welcome him into her arms.

As if she read his thoughts, she stirred and said that she would go upstairs. Would he be late coming to bed?

Was there eagerness in her voice? He would have liked to think so. When she had talked about the garden, she had sounded animated, though there had been a febrile edge to her voice that had made him think of someone whistling in the dark to keep his spirits up.

It would be different when all those plants she talked of were growing and she could watch them every day. And perhaps a seed would be growing inside her. A child would be the thing to make her settle down happily.

Yarrabee, his vineyard, this tremendous country he loved and with which he now absolutely identified himself. And this fragile, elegant, exciting woman. Would heaven strike because he had too much?

When he went upstairs half an hour later, Eugenia, in a white lawn nightgown with lace at the high neck and wrists, was sitting up in bed, her fine dark hair loose and shining. She had obviously made every effort to be as attractive for him as was possible. A light, flowery scent hung in the air. A blue silk bed robe hung over a chair. The curtains were drawn, and the room looked dim and mysterious in the candlelight, with the big bed and its quiet, almost ghostly occupant.

This was more like a wedding night, Gilbert thought with

pleasure. This was different from that hot, squalid room last night and the lumpy bed and the lovemaking he had not intended.

The only thing wrong, he realized, as he came closer, was his bride's face. It was tense with apprehension.

He made himself delay a hasty undressing and instead sat on the edge of the bed and talked.

"We must write and thank your grandmother for such a splendid wedding present. I shouldn't think there's a finer bed in Australia."

"It's French."

"I know, you told me so, and I can see it for myself. That elaborate headboard. I remember nothing but solid mahogany beds and heavy curtains in England. Very somber. This is delightfully foreign."

"My parents thought it a little frivolous. All those garlands and cupids. I hardly knew how you would like it."

"I like it immensely. It will be a feature of Yarrabee. Like the Venetian wineglasses and the Chinese silk wallpaper."

"I haven't heard anything of either of those."

"Neither had I until this minute. You have inspired me to these ideas. My wine will require the glasses, and my wife the setting of a beautiful room. I know a sea captain who goes regularly to the East. He will get the silk for the walls, and silk for dresses, too, if you want it. And I know how to get the wineglasses, through an importer in Sydney. You must have realized we weren't living in the wilderness after seeing Vaucluse. There are other homes in New South Wales that are just as fine."

She was catching his mood.

"I have brought family silver. It's in the packing cases that haven't yet been opened. And a lot of other things. Pictures, ornaments, rugs. A sampler I made when I was a child. A rocking horse." She laughed a little, but her laughter trembled. "Mamma said I should bring that, although it seemed—well, how does one know?"

Gilbert sprang up.

"Venetian goblets or not, we still have glasses out of which to drink wine. Where's your maid? No, I'll get them myself."

"Get what? Why?"

"Only a glass of Madeira to make you sleep. It's not even of my own brewing."

He thought this was an inspiration. Only Mrs. Jarvis saw him return upstairs with the silver tray holding the bottle and glasses. She paused, then went quickly out into the courtyard as if she might have thought she was witnessing something private.

It was private, too, the fact that he had to make his wife relax and look loving. But not unusual. Far from it. Though it would have been better if he had had this aphrodisiac last night.

"This is Spanish wine," he explained as he poured the ruby liquid into the long-stemmed glasses. "I brought over a supply to carry me through until my own wines were ready. I still have a couple of dozen bottles. Now savor it, and tell me what difference you can detect between this and the Yarrabee claret we had at dinner."

Eugenia sipped obediently, holding the glass in her narrow white hands. She was intent on trying to give an answer that would be intelligent enough to please him.

"Does it taste more smoothly on one's tongue?"

"You're perfectly right," he exclaimed triumphantly. "That's because it has been bottled for several years. The flavor improves. The rawness disappears. And the color—" He held up his glass, fascinated as always by the rich color of red wine. There was nothing in the world like it. "Drink it up, my love. After a couple of glasses of this the world looks as rosy as the wine."

"Isn't that—d-dangerous?"

Her tongue was already tripping delightfully over her words. The color was coming into her cheeks.

She frowned a little. "I can hear people singing."

"That's the servants. They'll have had their rum issue."

"Rum?"

"Unfortunately their tastes have been corrupted. Rum has been the drink that has saved their reason. Or so they think. But I intend to educate them differently. Let me quote from another Australian who brought some of the first vine cuttings here. Mr. James Busby said, 'Now I think it is extremely likely that if each farmhouse possessed its vineyard and produced a sufficiency of wine to supply the wants of all the laborers employed on the farm, as well as the farmer's own family, a deadly blow would be given the ruinous habit of the farmer himself indulging daily in the excessive use of spirits and his free laborer running every time he received his wages to the nearest public house.' "

He paused. "How does that seem to you, as the farmer's wife?"

"I hadn't heard of your ruinous habits, my love. But as an exercise in memory, you have done very well."

Her dry voice and the gleam in her eyes pleased him. Another glass, and he would begin to undress.

"But I shall never like the taste," she said presently, putting her glass down.

"What, not even in France, at your uncle's château?"

"I pretended," she admitted, showing a dimple in her cheek.

Now he had to undress quickly and blow the candles out. His self-discipline had come to an end. He wanted her nightgown over her head and that slight body in his arms. And gently . . . Gently, if he could . . .

So gently that she gave only one small cry . . .

From the beginning Eugenia had seen through Gilbert's careful plan. She had had her own plans, the nightgown she and Sarah had made with such loving care, the brushing she had asked Jane to give her hair, a hundred strokes, and then ten more for good measure, the perfume, the welcoming picture she had made sitting up in bed when Gilbert had come in. She had even allowed her head to get dizzy with the wine, commending Gilbert's good sense, for when he had pinched out the candles and she had lain down in the darkness, she had felt as if she were floating as lightly as a cloud.

But it had all been of no use at all. For as soon as he lay beside her and touched her, the walls began to close in. She was suffocating. She wanted to scream. The darkness was black and terrifying, and when she felt the weight of his body and his now-familiar wine-smelling breath in her face, the nightmare of the previous night began all over again. Except that this time, instead of the melancholy howls of a man driven to lunacy, the sound she heard was a sick child crying. And the grave under the willows was open and black . . .

She was overtired, overstrained. The tremendous events in her life, the heat, the inevitable homesickness, that dreadful experience last night, followed too quickly by her initiation into marriage, had created a mental state that must surely pass. It was not essential that she should enjoy her husband's caresses, but at least they did not need to induce this revulsion in her.

She would get over it. She must.

There was no one she could talk to. She could only sit at her familiar writing desk, taken out of its packing case and placed at the window in the little sitting room, and write to Sarah.

But what could she tell Sarah, so far away and a spinster?

> All my belongings are now unpacked, and seeing my familiar things about me has made me weep a little from homesickness. We have put the Turkish rug in my sitting room, together with my desk, and the low chair with the tapestry back that you worked. My piano is in the drawing room, which is a large, light, handsome room.
>
> I have hung your watercolor of Lichfield Court over the mantelpiece, and I spend a great deal of time looking at it and thinking of you within those dear walls. Yarrabee is going to be a fine place, too, but I cannot be expected to love it yet! There is so much still to be done inside, and the windows open onto a veritable wilderness. I close my eyes and dream

of smooth lawns and tinkling fountains, and open them to the acres of coarse brown grass and blinding sunlight.

Everything gets green in the spring, I am told, so that is when I will have the lawns laid down. Gilbert has allowed me to have one of his workmen as a gardener. Peabody, who is nearly sixty and whose weather-beaten appearance makes him look more (he is like a crooked stick, with lizard eyes), says he has been a gardener all his life. He hints at grand employers in England, before he got washed up on these shores— and one hesitates to ask *how* he got washed up. But he is an admirable worker, if a little gloomy in temperament, and insists on calling me "my lady." Already we have made great progress in planning the garden. The rose beds have been dug and left to lie fallow. The cuttings must be planted early in the winter, Peabody tells us.

Winter! It seems unimaginable in this ovenlike heat. In a month it will be vintage, and after that Gilbert wants to begin entertaining, so I have simply a thousand things to do, including engaging satisfactory staff.

Jane King who came to me from Mrs. Ashburton has too nervous a disposition, I have discovered. She admires the house but is finding the country lonely. Mrs. Jarvis, on the other hand, is proving excellent. She is a very good plain cook and, more important, a good organizer. Already I find I turn to her for advice. She has what Nurse would have called an old head on young shoulders.

But she is a widow, and it would surprise me if she did not marry again, even though she will be burdened with a fatherless child. Then I suppose Gilbert and I would lose her . . .

Eugenia laid down her pen, thinking how ironic it was that after her reluctance to engage Mrs. Jarvis, she was now afraid of the day when she might leave Yarrabee.

She read through the pages of neat, upright writing, a little scrawled here and there when all the things she had to pour out to Sarah had run away with her.

Yet the matters that weighed on her most—her new and entirely irrational fear of the dark, the long nights when she kept waking to find herself listening for any unfamiliar sound, her reluctance to retire to bed, and the way she kept Jane with her until the girl was dropping asleep on her feet, then, although she dreaded to be alone, her catch of apprehension when she heard her husband's footsteps on the stairs—these were things she could not put down in a letter, nor even tell Sarah if she were here in the room with her.

They were foolish, nervous fancies of which she was thoroughly ashamed.

Once during their lovemaking Gilbert had asked her if he hurt her, for she had seemed to wince from him.

She had quickly buried her face in his shoulder, whispering no, she loved him, of course.

She had added afterward, when he was almost asleep, that the night was full of strange noises that alarmed her. If he were ever away, she would keep the candle burning all night.

"Good gracious, you are a strange creature!" His voice was indulgent, although it held a tinge of impatience. She had roused him on the edge of sleep, and he was tired.

So she didn't go on to confess that she still thought of that miserable convict. Sometimes a bearded desperate face came into her dreams.

She had so much to do and yet so little. She could decide where to hang pictures, where to put furniture, give orders about what food should be prepared, but she must not actually do these things herself. She had servants, Gilbert pointed out. Make them work; keep them out of mischief. He didn't wish her to soil her hands with anything at all. She must occupy herself as she had done at Lichfield Court. With her music, her embroidery, her watercolors, a morning walk before the sun got too hot. He also encouraged her to drive the buggy. He wanted her to pay calls in Parramatta, though there were few enough people to constitute the kind of society she had been used to.

However, the governor and his wife spent the greater part of the year at Government House, a plain two-story building, the first of its kind to be built in the colony in 1799. Apart from them there were other people whom it was desirable to meet, politicians, bankers, merchants, sheep station holders, who called themselves the aristocracy and who came to town for ceremonial occasions.

These were the potential customers for Gilbert's wine. Cultivating them was a necessity, if not always a pleasure.

It would be better, Eugenia thought, when vintage was over. As the days grew shorter and the nights chilly enough to light a fire, they could spend companionable evenings together, she stitching at her embroidery and Gilbert doing his accounts, which had to be neglected in the busy season. Then, she told herself, it would be like being at home in England.

Now she scarcely saw her husband. He was up at daybreak and off outdoors, often not to make another appearance until dinner at night. He apologized for not always joining her for the midday meal. He was too hot and sweaty, he said; he would offend her. He preferred to eat a cold lunch with the men in the fields. This was how he had been used to living. He could not change his working schedule for a wife. But he could bathe and change in the evening and eat in the dining room in a civilized manner. And there were always Sundays.

Sarah would be interested in their Sundays.

> We go to church in Parramatta for the morning service. Gilbert and I drive in the buggy, the house servants, Mrs. Jarvis, Jane, and a young girl, Phoebe, whose parents have a bakers' shop in Parramatta, follow in the dray, driven by Tom Sloan, Gilbert's overseer. Murphy and Peabody also ride in this vehicle.
>
> The rest have to travel the distance on foot. Gilbert says this keeps them out of mischief since the Sabbath is regarded as far as possible as a holiday. And of course, as I have told you previously, all these men are convicts on ticket-of-leave, and it is an obligation on our part to see that they attend divine service.
>
> They put on their Sunday best, such as it is, and some of them actually seem to enjoy the service. If their lusty singing is anything to go by. But I confess I can never get used to their poor sad faces, although to be truthful not all are sad;

some are low and cunning, and one at least has a look of boyish innocence. But all of them are too thin and show signs of their past ordeal. Gilbert does not care for me to show curiosity about them and indeed has asked me not to go near their living quarters. So all I see of them is this weekly attendance at church, and only God knows whether the minister's words make any impression on them.

We come home from church to a cold collation set out by Yella, who really is the most ill-favored human being I have ever seen, and how my poor Gilbert survived when she did the cooking is beyond me. I, or Mrs. Jarvis, have always to inspect the table hastily and set knives and forks to rights. I imagine Yella wonders what barbarian instruments they are.

After our meal Gilbert dozes in his chair on the veranda, and I read or stroll in what will one day, with hard work and faith, be my garden. I have one great hardship, and that is that there is so little to read. Would you send me a set of Miss Austen's novels, as these will always bear rereading, and anything else that you think I would enjoy rereading a dozen times? Otherwise, I have only a treatise by a Mr. James Busby on the cultivation of vines and the making of wine, and the Bible. I have long ago exhausted all I brought with me . . .

Eugenia found the new maid, Phoebe, willing but quite ignorant of such refinements as polishing furniture and silver, brushing carpets, and making beds correctly. She was a clumsy girl and made a constant clatter. At Lichfield Court she would not have lasted a week. But this was Australia, where one had to be less critical or one would find oneself servantless. Besides, poor child, she was almost as ignorant as Yella. Eugenia had found her one day tracing the scrolled flowers and garlands on the French bed with the tip of a none-too-clean finger.

"Have you never seen anything like that, Phoebe?"

"Oh, no, mum, where would I have the chance?"

"Ma'am, Phoebe, not mum."

"Yes, mum, you've told me that. I can't get me tongue round ma'am, that's the truth."

"You must try. It isn't very difficult. And don't waste time in here. You haven't begun on the stairs yet."

There was so much dust. Windows had to be open to allow a current of air to circulate, and with the air came the red dust that lifted off the dry earth in small whirlwinds and deposited itself on floors, furniture, windowsills. It even settled on one's tongue, with a gritty taste, and irritated one's eyes. Indoors, Eugenia kept her hair covered with a light muslin cap, and outdoors, she wore her large floppy garden hat tied beneath her chin with ribbons. This kept the dust out of her hair, but Gilbert, who was less careful, came in at night with his hair powdered with the clinging stuff. He washed it when he washed the grime and perspiration off himself before coming down to dinner, and then it clung to his head in a neat dark-red cap that made him, Eugenia said amusedly, look villainous.

This irritation of dust would go with the first autumn rains, he told Eugenia. But he was privately enjoying it, because it was part of the excitement of the ripening grapes and the approach of vintage. His blue eyes had a clear compelling sparkle; he could scarcely sit down for five minutes to rest; he had to be watching over his vines. Even at night he would go outdoors to see that the stars were shining and that the fine weather would last. Nothing, Eugenia was convinced, was more permanent than the iron band of heat around the earth. But Gilbert had stories about hailstorms and great gusts of wind that could strip the fruit from the vines in one destructive hour.

Or a marauding herd of kangaroos might trample through the vineyard. Or the worst scourge of the summer, a bush fire, great tongues of flame flung from tree to tree, might blacken and desolate the countryside.

She was sure she could never be in love with this last month of tension before harvest in the way Gilbert was. She could hear his laugh, with its undercurrent of excitement, all over the house. He talked a great deal; he made jokes to the maids: he asked her to play for him on the piano after dinner and then got up restlessly and left the room before she had played more than a few bars. He had a quick temper, as Eugenia discovered the day he lost it over a trifling episode with Mrs. Jarvis.

Yella had disappeared. She had been absent a whole day, and

when, the following morning, there was still no sign of her, Mrs. Jarvis had sent for one of the convicts who had been seen, at times, in conversation with the black woman. He was a scrawny little Irishman from County Down, inclined to melancholy.

When he came to the kitchen door, he had looked like such a poor, wizened, unhappy creature that Mrs. Jarvis had spontaneously asked him into the kitchen and offered him a glass of milk.

Unfortunately, the master had walked in just as the wretched man was half through his glass of milk. He had gone up and dashed it out of the man's hands onto the floor and ordered him out of the house.

Then he had turned on Mrs. Jarvis.

Eugenia, in the linen room which was just across the courtyard, could not help hearing the commotion.

"And what, Mrs. Jarvis, do you think you are doing, giving hospitality to a man like that in my house?"

"I only wanted to ask him about Yella, sir." Mrs. Jarvis was clearly distressed. "Mr. Sloan said she used to talk to him—"

"And the nourishment was to encourage him to talk more?"

"Oh, no, sir, it's only that he looked half-starved."

"Are you suggesting I starve my servants?"

"He only looked so miserable, sir. He reminded me of my poor husband, to tell the truth."

"He's a felon."

"So was my husband. So was I, according to the law. But we're still human beings."

"And haven't I treated you like one? Reid—you see, I am actually human enough to remember his name—will be treated properly if he works properly. If it's his nature to look sick and miserable, that I can't help. But understand"—there was a sharp rap on the table—"I won't have these men in the kitchen of my house. If I catch one of them here again, he'll be flogged, and you'll be able to thank yourself for his punishment. Well?"

Poor Mrs. Jarvis must by this time be in tears, Eugenia thought. But her answer came steadily. "If these are your orders, sir, they will be obeyed. I was only wanting to inquire about Yella, in the first place."

"Oh, damn that black woman and all her kind. Let her go to the devil."

Yet when Gilbert came into the house half an hour later, he was all sunny good temper.

"You're looking very well, my love. I like that dress. Have I seen it before?"

"No, I think not. Jane and I are still unpacking boxes."

"And you have more pleasant surprises for me? Some elegant things to make all the other ladies jealous?"

"What other ladies?"

"Why, our guests from Sydney. Can we put up a dozen people, do you think? Some double rooms and two or three single for the bachelors. Now why are you looking so surprised? We have talked of this before."

Eugenia couldn't help clapping her hands with delight. "I hadn't known you were serious. You didn't seem to have any time to spare from your grapes. Oh, I would so dearly like to see some people, Bess and Marion, even Mrs. Ashburton."

"Even Mrs. Ashburton!" he mocked, good-naturedly. "You make it sound as if you have been serving a solitary prison sentence. Come and kiss me."

"Now!"

"I adore you when you pout like that. Your eyes are sparkling." He gave her a light kiss and laughed as she adroitly spun away from him. "We'll send off invitations for the first weekend in March. If this weather holds, vintage will be over, and I'll have a cellarful of casks of good wine. We must make this an annual celebration, as they do in France and Spain."

"Twelve people!" Eugenia exclaimed. "But we haven't nearly enough help."

"Get some in from Parramatta. Ask Mrs. Jarvis to arrange it. I don't want you to exert yourself too much in this heat. Mrs. Jarvis is a capable woman."

"But this morning—I heard you—I couldn't help overhearing—"

The sunny blue eyes looked down at her.

"Giving Mrs. Jarvis a lecture? Well, I suppose that's not quite the way it's done in England. I haven't all the niceties. I sometimes lose my temper."

"Mrs. Jarvis only wanted to know about Yella."

"She knows my rules. No convicts in the house."

"But Mrs. Jarvis herself was a convict. Aren't you being illogical?"

Although a deep frown suddenly cut down the center of his forehead, Gilbert spoke quite mildly. "I don't understand your long words. I didn't have your education. Will you ring for luncheon to be served? And please sit nearer to me. The end of the table is so far away. I like that lavender color of your dress. It matches your eyes."

Yella came back that afternoon carrying a tiny dark-pink baby in her arms.

No one knew where or how she had contrived to give birth without assistance. But that she had done so without being too discommoded was obvious from her wide grin and the proud gleam in her deep-set eyes. She wanted the white women to admire her baby. It was a girl, and she was going to call it Ginny.

This was to be interpreted as a gesture of admiration and loyalty toward the mistress. Eugenia took it as such and was amused and delighted. She took the baby, wrapped in a scrap of grayish cloth that was obviously part of Yella's skirt, and held the funny, little, snuffling black-haired creature in her arms. A great longing stirred in her. She, too, would like a baby.

Yella grinned from ear to ear. Mrs. Jarvis stood quietly with her hands resting on her stomach, an acknowledgment of her own condition. Jane, with her skimmed-milk face, registered disgust for the dark tinge of the baby's skin, so different from a white child. She thought it exactly like a monkey. And Phoebe, the Australian, had a practiced eye, although she was only sixteen. She had seen enough native babies to recognize that this one had a white father.

"Have you any baby clothes, Yella?" Eugenia asked.

Yella shook her head.

"Then I will see that you get some," she said eagerly. "Jane, we must quickly make some long dresses and bonnets."

"Native babies don't wear long dresses, mum—ma'am," Phoebe pointed out.

"Then this one will be an exception."

Eugenia thought that this was the most heartwarming thing that had happened to her since she had come to Yarrabee. She realized that she had been walking about like an automaton in her dainty, immaculate clothes, with her absurd parasol, a slender ghost in a heat-scarred wilderness, always secretly afraid of the night. But now there was Yella's baby, later there would be Mrs. Jarvis', and later still . . .

It wasn't to be like that. It appeared that Gilbert had strong objections. Once he wouldn't have turned a hair if a native woman had raised a brood of a dozen bastards on his property. But now the house had a fastidious and sensitive mistress, and it just wouldn't do. Especially taking into consideration the fact that the child was a half-caste. Even more embarrassing, he was well aware who its father was, and he had no intention of losing a good overseer because he conducted a liaison with a native woman.

Yella must be moved to Parramatta, and Tom Sloan could visit her there if he found he wanted to continue the disreputable affair. He wouldn't, of course. Yella had merely been available, when there had been no other woman around. He would get himself a white wife now that more women were coming out from England, and Yella would be well advised to find one of her own kind.

Perhaps if Gilbert had explained all this to Eugenia, she would have been more sympathetic to his point of view. But how did he tell a well-bred young woman that good, reliable, honest Tom Sloan, an indentured employee whom he had brought out from his native Gloucestershire, had this desire for a native woman who was as ugly as sin?

Unaware of the true facts, Eugenia was full of indignation.

"Yella is to go because she has a baby! But how unkind! How callous! I won't hear of it. I refuse to allow her to be turned out to starve."

"She is not being turned out to starve. I explained that I would see she found another place. There are plenty of small farmers or innkeepers who want a cook and can't afford to be too fussy. Anyway, natives don't starve. They have all kinds of disgusting ways of feeding themselves. On grubs, for instance. They eat a kind of caterpillar called a witchetty grub."

Eugenia looked, if anything, more offended.

"You can't prejudice me by telling me things like that. Yella has been of use to you, she has given birth to a baby on your property, and that baby has a white father. Phoebe told me. So your obligation toward her is even stronger."

"My obligation will be discharged by seeing the woman placed somewhere else. You must trust me to know what is best in these matters. You are very new to colonial ways, after all."

"Then what about Mrs. Jarvis? Is she also to be treated in this summary way when her baby is born?"

Gilbert repressed his rising temper. He had already lost it once that day to his regret.

"Mrs. Jarvis is an entirely different matter. For one thing, she is widowed. For another, her child will be white. And for still another, we were both aware of her condition when we engaged her."

"When *you* engaged her," Eugenia flashed back.

"Very well, when I engaged her. But you have since admitted to me that you are entirely satisfied with her. So was my decision at fault?"

"Not about that," Eugenia admitted reluctantly.

"Then trust me in this matter. Yella is a slut. You will find you have a hideously ugly baby on your doorstep once a year, without fail, if she stays here. Now let us talk of something else."

Eugenia bit her lip.

"I thought the baby so sweet."

"Well, that's natural enough. I like a woman to be sentimental over babies. But preferably her own."

That made her flush and lower her eyes. He found himself remembering the flashing fire of Mrs. Jarvis' gaze that morning. He knew she would have liked to strike him. A shaft of intolerable excitement had run through him, and he had had to raise his voice and shout at her, simply to keep that fire in her face.

But Eugenia was a gentle creature who withdrew into herself. He thought regretfully that he could scarcely hope for any more warmth in her embrace tonight. It would have been a satisfying way to make up a quarrel.

A quarrel? Scarcely that, although he found his wife hastily trying to remove traces of tears when he joined her in their bedroom later.

"My love! Surely you're not wasting tears on that worthless slut!"

"N-no."

"Then what is it?"

Forced to answer, because he had put his hand under her chin and lifted her face up to him, she said with her gentle dignity, "I confess I was thinking about Lichfield Court and how green it always was in summer. My sisters and I used to feed the birds that came to the garden. There were so many, finches and wrens and robins and blackbirds. There was one robin that actually sat on my finger. It came year after year."

"Not always the same one?" said Gilbert, humoring her.

"Perhaps not. But it seemed to be. Gilbert, you have never asked me if I am happy here!"

The sudden outburst startled him.

"But you are, surely?"

"There, you see, you say it as if there could be no other answer. Why, do you think that in a few weeks I can begin to love all this desolation?"

Desolation! What a word to describe his beloved Yarrabee! To him it was entirely beautiful. It astonished him that she did not find it so. His terraces of vines bending with their burden of ripening fruit, his fine house, the great, free, unconfining, shadowless spaces—and she was fretting for the rains and mists of England!

Naturally she missed her parents, her old nurse, all those sisters to chatter with. If he hadn't been so busy he would have realized this. He *should* have realized it, since it wasn't to be expected that she could yet share his excitement about approaching vintage. By this time next year she would be as totally committed as he was himself; of that he was sure.

He took her in his arms very gently, kissed her flushed cheeks and forehead, and began to talk to her in a patient and loving voice, at the same time undoing the hundred and one tiny buttons of her bodice that exasperated his clumsy fingers.

And after all, it proved his point, that this was a satisfying way of making up a quarrel, for she clung to him crying urgently, "Let us have a baby, Gilbert! Give me a baby!" He congratulated himself, as he turned sleepily into his pillow, on his patience and gentleness. At last things were going better, even if he didn't delude himself that this display of emotion was passion for him. Eugenia had got sentimental after holding that ugly half-caste baby in her arms. That, he feared, was the answer. But it was a step in the right direction.

Molly Jarvis, walking outdoors because she couldn't sleep, saw the light in the upstairs bedroom go out. She gathered her wrap more closely about her and told herself she had no right to be out here where she could watch the master's bedroom. She hadn't meant to watch it. It was unavoidable simply because this was the only window showing a light. When it went out, it was like the moon going behind a cloud, leaving the night very dark.

She, too, had been upset about Yella's dismissal, although she had lived in this country long enough to understand Mr. Massingham's reason. He wanted to set the highest standards of living for his wife. She was to be protected as much as possible from the rawness of life in a convict colony. She was to remain an English lady. And she was up there now in his loving arms. And what would that be like, Molly wondered, beginning to shiver violently. She would never forget Mr. Massingham's splendor that morning when he had stood in the kitchen, legs apart, eyes blazing, bawling at her for having that poor harmless convict in the house.

She knew that his temper had been half pretense. He had shouted at her to make her look at him.

If only he knew how she had to use every bit of her willpower to keep her eyes off him. She would watch him as he walked across the courtyard, admiring his broad shoulders, his narrow hips, his confident swagger. One day she was afraid he would read her feelings in her eyes.

She had repressed all her natural loving instincts for so long. When the baby came, it would be better. She could pour out all her emotion on it.

Because she must never behave in a way that would make her have to leave Yarrabee. It was the nearest thing to paradise here. She loved the great sky and the distances. The wind crackling in the gum trees, the lonely voices of the crows and pewits, the dazzling light over a drought-stricken landscape, all meant freedom to her. She did not intend to lose it.

But she wished it was not so difficult to sleep on these hot nights.

In the morning Gilbert himself took Yella and her baby to Parramatta. He drove off in the buggy at a spanking pace, Yella crouched fearfully in the back, clutching the baby as if they both were riding on one of those sudden spirals of dust and whirling leaves that the natives called a willy-willy.

When Gilbert returned at midday, he called loudly for Eugenia.

"Where are you, my love?" His voice could be heard all over the house.

Eugenia came to the top of the stairs, wondering what new problem had occurred.

"I've brought you a present," he said, holding up a large birdcage. "Fellow in Parramatta catches them and sells them.

They make fine pets. Talk, too. So be careful of what you say if you don't want it repeated."

The bird in the cage was a white cockatoo with a yellow crest. It edged along its perch and regarded its surroundings with a bright, appraising eye.

"You said you were missing the birds you used to feed at home. So I brought you this one."

Eugenia came flying down the stairs, laughing with pleasure. "Oh, he's beautiful, Gilbert! Look at his knowing expression. Oh, how delightful of you!"

Spontaneously she flung her arms around him, lifting her lips to be kissed.

"But if you imagine I am going to play with this instead of Yella's baby—"

"You are, of course. Anyway, I got Yella settled with George Harris at the local hotel. He wanted a domesticated black to fetch and carry. Didn't mind the baby. So all's well."

A new home for Yella, a plaything for her. Eugenia lifted a thoughtful eyebrow. Gilbert was exceedingly pleased with himself, thinking he was so astute and clever at arranging their lives happily without giving way on any point himself.

But it was true that she was delighted with the white cockatoo, and it was ungrateful of her to be critical. In marriage the man was the master. What woman would want any other arrangement? She had complained last night that Gilbert had never inquired if she were happy, and now here was evidence of his thought for her.

This was an occasion in her marriage she would always remember, for it was the moment when she became firmly determined to be happy.

Chapter 10

Vintage . . . The pickers had been arriving since dawn. Two dozen or so men and women of varying ages had walked or ridden in ramshackle conveyances from Parramatta. They gathered in the courtyard for cups of hot strong tea and the plates of freshly made bread and scones that Mrs. Jarvis had been up at four o'clock to bake.

It was a tradition at Yarrabee that the grape pickers were well fed and well cared for. Enormous baskets of cold provisions would be carried up to the terraces at midday, and in the evening another meal would be provided, with plenty of *vin ordinaire* from last year's brewing. For those who couldn't stand the taste of wine there would be more of the strong sweet tea. But no beer or rum.

Gilbert Massingham of Yarrabee was regarded as an eccentric in this respect. But he was an honest employer; he paid good wages and was well liked. So even the most hardened rum drinkers, who winced at the sour taste of the wine, drank it for want of something better. The women watered it down to quench their thirst.

What they liked even better was that Mr. Massingham shared their impromptu breakfast with them, striding around, laughing and talking, treating them as old friends—as indeed some of them were. One was an elderly woman, gray-haired and stoop-shouldered, who gave a merry, toothless grin and lifted up her skirts and danced a jig when a tow-haired youth produced a fiddle and began to play.

Watching from the doorway, Eugenia clapped her hands, enjoying the lighthearted scene. The youth bowed with a deep flourish, and the old woman executed a sketchy curtsy. Vintage at Yarrabee had an added spice this year since there was a new mistress of whom to catch glimpses.

Not that they were to see much of her. Gilbert had ordered Eugenia to stay indoors out of the hot sun. Paying no attention to her indignant protest, he said that he didn't want her doing anything so foolish or beneath her dignity as donning old clothes and joining the merry throng laden with their long baskets. When the sun went down, she could come observe from a distance, if she pleased.

So the day, which had begun in such a lively manner, resolved itself into just another long, idle expanse of hours. Doing a little sewing, playing the piano, beginning a letter to Sarah, bitterly resenting being shut out of all the fun. She couldn't even have her customary chat with Peabody digging up thistles and thornbushes in what was already called the garden because he, too, had joined the pickers. After midday the house was further depleted. Mrs. Jarvis had prepared a mammoth lunch of bread, cheese, and cold sausage. Phoebe had helped her carry the baskets of food to the workers, and without a by-your-leave, both of them had remained on the terraces.

There was only Jane, with her pale, plain face, left in the house. When Eugenia asked, with a slight edge to her voice, if she, too, did not want to join in the excitement, Jane replied emphatically that she did not.

"I couldn't stand the heat, ma'am. I don't know how Molly does. She must have a skin like leather."

"Molly?"

"Mrs. Jarvis, ma'am. I beg your pardon. She said to call her Molly; it was more friendly. She's only a year older than me, after all. Only twenty-six and all that's happened to her. It would have killed me."

"I expect it would," Eugenia commented dryly. Jane's milk and water nature was beginning to irritate her severely. But who was she to criticize? Mrs. Jarvis' harsh experiences would probably have killed her, too.

All the same, she found it intolerable remaining indoors like a prisoner when so much was going on, and after lunch, defying Gilbert's instructions, she put on her wide-brimmed hat, opened her parasol, and picked her way up the dusty track to watch the animated scene from a suitable distance.

One man had a red handkerchief tied over his head, another a blue. Gilbert scorned a head covering. Eugenia saw his red head as he moved up and down the rows of vines, observing, admonishing. There was a great deal of merry chatter, sometimes snatches of a song. The sky was blue, the hillside brown and olive green, the grapes black with a dusty silver bloom. It would make an interesting watercolor which she could send home to Sarah. Tomorrow she would bring her easel and box of paints. Perhaps Gilbert would consider that a ladylike enough occupation for her. But her loneliness still rankled.

That evening at dinner she pushed away her plate, the food scarcely touched. She considered the slices of mutton uneatable.

Gilbert looked up. "What is it? Not hungry?" He had cleaned his own plate, tough meat, gristle and all.

"Not now." She rang the little silver bell at her right hand, and when Mrs. Jarvis came, she said in a cool, reflective voice, "I don't think you can do two tasks satisfactorily, Mrs. Jarvis. You either do the cooking or pick grapes, but not both."

Mrs. Jarvis, neat as always, in her white cap and apron, only the curve of her throat showing the hot red of sunburn, looked quickly at Gilbert, then back to Eugenia, and lowered her eyes.

"I'm sorry, ma'am. I thought I might be useful on the terraces; the grapes seem so ripe and need picking quickly."

"Do you understand viticulture?"

"No, ma'am, but it's easy enough to see when fruit is ripe."

"Well, I, at this moment, can only see that the dinner is uneatable. Clear the table, and bring some fruit—if you can find anything apart from grapes."

"That was unfair," Gilbert said as Mrs. Jarvis withdrew. "I found my portion perfectly edible."

"Because you didn't taste it," said Eugenia. "You're still in your vineyard. And I hope you won't uphold Mrs. Jarvis' behavior. I didn't give her permission to stay on the terraces."

"Well, drop the matter, my love. She was interested and wanted to share in the fun. She worked hard."

"It isn't the kind of work a woman in her condition should be doing. Any more than you consider it the kind of work for your wife."

Gilbert's eyebrows went up exasperatedly.

"So that's what it is. Your nose is out of joint."

Eugenia pouted. "It was such a long day, all alone except for Jane, and she's poor company."

"Then keep Mrs. Jarvis in the house and see that you get a good dinner tomorrow night. But accept the fact that I will never allow you to work outdoors. Having the skin peeling off your nose." He got up to drop a placatory kiss on it. "It's much too pretty. Now will you excuse me? I have a lot of things to see to."

Eugenia thought that Mrs. Jarvis looked at her with pity as she sat alone at the table in the lamplight. But the woman didn't say anything, just put the bowl of peaches and apples down, and went out. A moment later Eugenia heard her laughing in the courtyard. Or someone was laughing, and someone was singing. The scraping of the fiddle came distantly to her ears, and the sound of dancing feet on cobblestones.

Was none of those people tired from the long day?

Even the white cockatoo stirred his feathers and squawked softly in his cage, as if he had caught the prevailing excitement. Eugenia could have sworn she could smell the raw sour smell of new wine on the warm air.

But that was impossible. It would be at least twenty-four hours before fermentation of the must in the scoured dark vats began.

There would be three or four more days like this one before the vines had been stripped, the grapes pressed, the wine casks filled, and vintage over.

Next year Eugenia resolved that she would not feel like such an outsider. She would not need to vent petty irritation on Mrs. Jarvis to disguise her loneliness.

Although Gilbert would not permit her on the terraces in the hot sun, he did, at the end of the second day, ask her to come into the cool winery. He was excited. He came hurrying into the house, calling for her, and when she came, he took her arm and said she positively must see what was happening.

It was always, to him, a miracle. Fermentation had begun. The juice of the pressed grapes was moving. It seethed and hissed and bubbled like some sort of black porridge, the mat of grapeskins twisting constantly as the gas bubbles broke through.

The winery reeked with the tingling sour smell of fermentation. Eugenia longed to hold her handkerchief to her face. But this, she sensed, would have offended Gilbert and all the red-faced, sweating men who were operating the press over another vat.

"It seems to be alive," she exclaimed.

Gilbert laughed aloud. He was intoxicated without having touched a drop of his half-brewed wine.

"The bloom on the grape makes a kind of yeast, and this begins fermentation. The secret is to know when to run the wine off into casks. For a sauterne, to keep the sugar content, fermentation has to be brief. For the dry reds it's a much longer process. This vat will produce the best Yarrabee Claret—from your uncle's vine cuttings, gathered the day we first met." He took her hand, and she caught his excitement, smiling up at him warmly, in spite of the fact that the sour smell of the cellar was again making her feel nauseated. She didn't think she would ever get used to it. She secretly didn't consider that seething witches' caldron a very romantic thing to have come out of their first meeting in France.

"Is it being a good vintage?" she asked. She was glad that Gilbert was giving her this chance to make amends for her childishness the previous evening.

"Excellent. You have brought me luck."

"My dear Sarah," she wrote several days later:

For the first time I am alone, except for the servants. My dear husband has set out for Sydney with a consignment of wine bottled two years ago. This is to make room in the cellars for the present vintage and also to bring in some money. The wine will be bought by hotels and clubs and private individuals in Sydney, and a small selection of it is, I believe, to be sent to London, with the aim of establishing the fame of Australia as a wine-growing country. We hear that the other vignerons in the Hunter River Valley may have a preferable situation to us, as it is more sheltered from the burning summer winds and winter frosts.

But Gilbert has created Yarrabee with such pride and so much hard work that I know he will never leave here. I am glad because we have the little town of Parramatta not too far away. In the Hunter Valley the vineyards are much too isolated from civilization.

It is my first time without Gilbert, and I got a great fright early this morning when there was a crashing noise, and three kangaroos came leaping past the house, over Peabody's newly dug garden. They are such strange awkward creatures. They seem to have springs attached to their hind feet. It appeared that a herd had got into the vineyard and trampled the vines badly. We are so thankful it happened after and not before vintage. But this is one of the hazards an Australian vigneron faces.

My white cockatoo—I have called him Erasmus because he looks so wise—screeched with alarm, or it may have been with approval, when this disturbance happened. He seemed very pleased with himself, and after all his squawking he quite clearly enunciated one word which he must have learned from me. It was "Mercy!" He said it with such a quaint inflection, all the time cocking a bright eye at me as if he knew he had amused me. And indeed he had. I laughed so much that Mrs. Jarvis came in to see what was the matter.

We tried our best to persuade Erasmus to show off his cleverness again, but he refused to do so. He only hung upside down by one claw. He really is an endearing clown of a bird.

When Gilbert returns, he will be bringing with him our first weekend guests, Bess and Edmund Kelly, dear fussy old

Mrs. Ashburton, whom I long to see again, Dr. and Mrs.
Noakes, the Wentworths, and another winegrower, a Mr.
Blaxland, who is also an explorer and reputed to be an inter-
esting character.

Our guest rooms will be in use for the first time. So you
can imagine how busy we women are . . .

The weather was cooler at last. It was possible to walk in the
sun and actually to enjoy it. And Eugenia, with her inescapable
honesty, had to admit that she was enjoying having her husband absent for a little while. When he returned, they would
meet like old friends. That slight uneasiness between them, a
reserve on her part that she had been unable to overcome and a
perplexity on his, would vanish. Or so she hoped.

There was little time to brood on problems, for the house
was in the kind of upheaval that she had always enjoyed when
it had happened at Lichfield Court. Rooms were scoured, beds
made, stores of food checked, menus discussed with Mrs. Jarvis,
Peabody supervised in the garden.

There had been a series of heavy thunderstorms, which made
the ground easy to work. A haze of green was spreading over it
from the seeded summer grass. The rose cuttings, acquired by
Peabody from various sources in Parramatta, were planted, also
honeysuckle to climb up the veranda posts, various native
shrubs, poinsettias, hibiscus, and wattle which Peabody promised would be a fluffy golden glory in the spring. At the point
which divided the garden from the horse paddock Peabody
planted a line of weeping willows. These Eugenia was not so
happy about. They reminded her of the child's grave by the
creek. She had never liked going back to that sad place, even
when the black swans came. She had stood at a distance, thinking that the swans had looked like mourners.

But the willows would have to stay because Peabody was a
stubborn creature whose eccentricity had to be humored.

Once, when Eugenia had ventured to criticize his choice of a
spot for planting a shrub, he had thrown down his spade and
walked away. He had come back later, muttering to himself and

casting suspicious glances toward the house. The shrub had eventually been planted exactly one foot away from the original spot. No doubt that was the best Peabody could do in the way of an apology.

The birdbath which Eugenia had found at the blacksmith's in Parramatta—it had been discarded by emigrants whose dray was already overloaded—was just tolerated by Peabody.

"For them blasted crows!" he said.

"No, when the garden has grown, the small birds will come. I have seen them in the garden at Government House. Wrens and fantails and finches with wonderful colors."

"You'll get them big greedy wood pigeons, too," Peabody said gloomily. "And kookaburras and galahs deafening you."

Eugenia ignored his pessimism, saying dreamily, "I can hardly imagine when all this will be a bower of flowers and trees and birds."

Then the immense lonely distances would be hidden, she thought privately. But all Peabody could say was that it would take too long for everything to grow the way she imagined it.

"You're like the master," Peabody grumbled. "Always talking of his wines maturing. He's going to live to drink his fifty-year-old brandy, he says. Laid down his first year at Yarrabee. That's a long time to wait. And you waiting for your garden to look like an English one."

The shut-in look came over the leathery face.

"Blasted country," he said, shuffling away.

That was when the foolish, surly fellow distressed Eugenia. He constantly struck that sad, lonely chord in her own self. But she would overcome her homesickness. She was determined to.

Chapter 11

Mrs. Ashburton had lost a shawl and a small tapestry bag containing various necessities such as rice powder, gloves, handkerchiefs, and smelling salts, and two fans.

She couldn't imagine where she had mislaid these articles, but Eugenia was not to allow this misfortune to upset the weekend. The only problem was that Mrs. Ashburton could not possibly go down to dinner without carrying a fan or venture outdoors without gloves. She was also inclined to grow faint if she knew there were no smelling salts available. And if one could only see her complexion without the aid of a little clever disguise in the way of a touch of rouge and powder!

It was the history of the journey from England to Australia all over again. But now Eugenia found it endearing, rather than irritating. She was so happy to have the house full of people. It was immensely exciting, her first house party. She said eagerly, "I am sure your bag will be recovered. In the meantime, I can provide you with all the missing articles. Do tell me if you like your room. I don't believe you have looked at a thing."

"Oh, yes, I've seen that you have a grand house. And this room is very nice. Very nice." The lady's agitated gaze was turned perfunctorily on the room. She didn't appear to notice Eugenia's prettiest patchwork quilt on the bed or the meticulous equipment of the dressing table from silver-backed mirror to pincushion. "Which way does the window face? I can't endure to be awakened by the early morning sun." Then she real-

ized her rudeness and gave one of her wide, warm smiles.
"Come give me a kiss, Eugenia, bless your heart. I think you
have a lovely home, and you're looking quite bonny. You have
a good color."

Folded to Mrs. Ashburton's ample crackling bosom, Eugenia
protested. "That's only because I'm so excited. I usually go pale
in the heat. I look like a peeled potato. But now it's cooler, and
I'm in excellent health. And *so* happy to have you here."

"I'm happy to see you, too, my dear. I've missed you. What's
more, my son is finding his old mother a trouble and a bore. I
declare it's too bad. All he can say is that he wants to go exploring into the interior. And this may be for a matter of months or
even years. I have no patience with him. Bringing me on this
long journey to live all by myself in Sydney. I could have done
that in Cheltenham, and much more happily, I tell him. Well,
that's the thoughtlessness of youth. And I must say it's a pity no
one told us of the prevalence of flies in this country. A very persistent insect."

"Mrs. Ashburton, I must go look after my other guests. Will
you rest for an hour? I'll tell Mrs. Jarvis to bring your tea upstairs. We don't dine until eight."

"Mrs. Jarvis? Is that woman still here?"

"Indeed she is. She is an excellent servant. I couldn't do
without her. Are you prejudiced because she was a convict?"

"I declare, Eugenia Massingham! That might have been
your husband talking. No, I am not prejudiced because she was
a convict. I merely thought she might find country life too tedious."

"If you are implying she is pining for the life of the streets,
you are very much mistaken. She is an agreeable and refined
woman."

Mrs. Ashburton pouted and puffed and patted at her wadded
gray hair.

"Well, well, I daresay. You are so young and innocent, Eugenia. I expect you are going to be one of these good women
who help fallen women. For my part, I find them simply tiresome and would happily leave them lying in the gutter."

Eugenia laughed merrily. "Dear Mrs. Ashburton! I really have missed you so much."

"That's nice, my dear. But why? With your good-looking husband I scarcely thought you would have time for a thought for your friends."

The airiness of Mrs. Ashburton's voice was not to be misunderstood. She had a clever way of prying into people's secrets. Eugenia answered with perfect good humor.

"Gilbert insists on my leading such a lady's life that I have a great deal of time for my friends. I sometimes wonder how time went by so quickly in England when I did no more than I do now. But I warn you, I have a great many activities planned for this weekend. We are going to play cards and have music after dinner this evening. Tomorrow we are to have a picnic at the lake. It's five miles away, and I haven't yet been there. But there are the famous black swans to be seen, and it will be cool by the water. The gentlemen will take their fishing rods. Then on Sunday we will all go to church, and in the evening some friends from Parramatta are coming out for a cold supper. On Monday my husband wants to show the men over his property. They will take their guns and hope to shoot some kangaroos that raided the vineyard the other morning. So we women will sit on the veranda and sew and talk, and in the evening I thought it would be amusing to roll back the rugs in the drawing room and dance a little. You remember how we used to do this on board ship?"

She paused and said anxiously, "How does all this sound to you? I do want to be a good hostess."

Mrs. Ashburton said in her dry manner, "Don't worry, my lamb, you'll please your husband."

There were just a few minutes to see that Bess and Marion were comfortably settled before it was time to dress for dinner.

While Eugenia was doing so, Gilbert came in.

Apart from a formal greeting, in front of the newly arrived guests, they had not spoken since Gilbert's return.

Now he was anxious to kiss her lovingly and comment on her appearance. He seemed to be in the highest spirits.

"How have you been while I have been away? Dull?"

"I have hardly had time. We've all been so busy preparing for this weekend. Oh, I engaged another maid temporarily. She will wait on table so that Mrs. Jarvis is free to remain in the kitchen. Her name is Ellen and she seems brighter than Phoebe."

"Splendid. Keep her permanently, if she suits."

"Gilbert, you are too generous to me. Isn't that extravagant?"

"Don't worry about extravagance. I had a successful trip with more orders than I could fill. Next year, with more vines bearing, I'll be able to increase output. I must get Yarrabee wine established before those fellows on the Hunter River get ahead of me. But I didn't come back to talk business to my wife. Where's Jane? Isn't she helping you dress?"

"I've sent her to Mrs. Ashburton. She has already unpacked for the other ladies."

Gilbert laid his lips on the back of her neck.

"Then you must allow your husband to help you."

"You putting up my hair!" She had to laugh merrily, the thought was so amusing, but she wished he would leave her to dress quietly. The pleasant spacious room always seemed too small when he was in it.

"You're charming when you laugh," he said. "Is it true that you didn't miss me at all?"

"Why, of course I did."

"And you were not too afraid at nights?"

"Oh, I have got over that silly childish nervousness. I am sure you will be glad to hear it."

"Yes, I am glad to hear it. But not altogether. I like protecting you."

Eugenia looked at his too-bright eyes.

"Gilbert, have you been sampling the wine for dinner?"

"Do I seem intoxicated? Then it must be your effect on me. Suppose I were to help you undress, instead of dress?"

She took a step backward.

"Oh, no! There isn't time."

"There should always be time for love."

"But at six o'clock in the evening when we have a houseful of guests! Truly, you are absurd."

She had kept her voice light and friendly, so that it was unreasonable that the fire should go out of his eyes in that way. As if he could have expected her to be tumbled on the bed at such an inconvenient time.

She tried to make amends.

"I had intended to wear this gown. What do you think?"

He looked at the pale-gray silk abstractedly and then told her to put it on, so that he could judge better. When she had done this and pinned up her heavy dark hair, he ordered her to walk in front of him, then to sit down with the wide skirt spreading gracefully about her.

Now he was no longer looking at her as a lover, but critically, as if she were to walk onto a stage before an audience.

"Yes. I like that," he said at last. "I must buy you some jewelry."

"Oh, no, Gilbert. Get your vineyard established first. I have my pearls and my little fob watch. That's enough."

"It's far from enough. Besides, I would like you to wear my jewels. But in the meantime you look very well."

The waist of the silk dress seemed to have grown a little too tight. It was uncomfortable. She wondered if she could sit through dinner in it, maintaining the elegance Gilbert so admired. She had a feeling of despair as she realized that she preferred this discomfort to the time later tonight when she unhooked and unbuttoned herself and waited for that overbrilliant look to come back to her husband's eyes.

It was cooler tonight. There was even a hint of frost in the air which seemed to be a minor miracle. The dining table, set with silver and crystal which gleamed in the candlelight, would have done credit to a fine London dining room. Mr. Wentworth looked particularly handsome in his dinner jacket. His friend, Mr. Blaxland, had a stubborn, weather-beaten face that did not lend itself to meticulous dressing. Dr. Noakes wore a jacket that was unashamedly shiny with age, but Edmund Kelly was natty, and Gilbert looked smoothed down and unfamiliar in his formal clothes.

The ladies had put on a brave show, especially Mrs. Ashburton in a lavender gown with many layers of lace and her usual slipping cashmere shawl. Mrs. Wentworth was elegant but unobtrusive, Marion Noakes just on the verge of dowdiness, and dear Bess Kelly too plump for her bright-blue satin.

The conversation was animated. At first it was entirely congratulatory as the appointments of Yarrabee were discussed. An oasis, a miracle, a remarkable piece of admirable extravagance.

"Even if you are running before you can walk, Massingham," said Mr. Wentworth, "I maintain you have done right. This kind of thing will encourage the better type of settler to Australia. I hope you are writing letters to England describing your home, Mrs. Massingham."

"Writing letters! She never stops. Do you, my love?"

"I miss my sisters, I confess," Eugenia said. "And there is so much to tell them. Sarah wants to know about houses and clothes, and Milly, who is still in the schoolroom, about the strange animals. Papa about the social system—"

"You mean the convicts?" said Marion Noakes in her caustic voice.

"Not at all," Gilbert replied quickly. "Eugenia has nothing whatever to do with that unfortunate side of the colony."

"A side that is scarcely unfortunate for you, my dear fellow." Mr. Wentworth's voice was bland. "Where would Yarrabee be without them?"

"I agree. I merely meant that as far as my wife is concerned, they don't exist. I have asked her never to go near their quarters. Especially after her experience on our wedding night."

"We heard all about that, Eugenia," Bess Kelly said admiringly. "I declare I could never have done what you did. Gilbert said you were nearly killed."

"And to think we worried about her being such a novice." Eugenia had noticed lately that Marion Noakes' cynicism was softened when directed at her. "There was no need to. Was there, Gilbert? You got a wife with steel in her."

"Shouldn't expect Gilbert to choose any other kind. You ought to know him better than that, my dear." Philip Noakes raised his glass. "Vintage or nothing, eh, Massingham? Let's drink to our hostess."

Eugenia was embarrassed that her lips trembled when she tried to smile. She was delighted and flattered that these, her new friends, all approved of her. They must never know, no one must ever know, of her foolish nervousness of the dark and her terrible divided emotions about the convicts, one part of her hating and resenting the element of danger they represented, the other full of a profound pity for them.

For this reason she had obeyed Gilbert and had not gone near their quarters.

But now Marion was saying, "By keeping away from them, can you really pretend they aren't there?"

"No. Not altogether," she answered. "But they are well treated here." It was true. There had never been any outcry or disturbance in that forbidden area beyond the stables and cowsheds. At least, not to her knowledge. Only the spilled glass of milk when one of them had dared to set foot in the kitchen.

"Better treated than they deserve to be, the brutes," Mrs. Ashburton said comfortably. "Eugenia, can you possibly tell me how this syllabub is made, or must I seek information from the kitchen?"

"From the kitchen, I am afraid. I am quite useless as a cook."

"My wife has more important things to do," Gilbert interposed, "such as entertaining us to some music after dinner."

"Lor'!" said plain Bess Kelly admiringly. "I wish someone would say that to me. I have nothing but squalling children at my apron strings all the time." She spoke with a contentment that completely lacked smugness.

Mrs. Wentworth said, "I had my children's portraits painted recently by a very clever Irishman. I recommend him to you, Mrs. Kelly, if you want likenesses of your children. His name is

Colm O'Connor. He also paints studies of native birds and flowers. He is making a book of them for a London publisher."

"What interesting people you meet in Sydney!" Eugenia said, rising. "Shall we leave the gentlemen to their port? I can see that they are longing to talk politics."

"But seriously," Mrs. Wentworth continued, when the ladies were in the drawing room. "Mr. O'Connor is, in my opinion, a most gifted artist."

"I have nothing for him to paint but my parrot," Eugenia said, laughing. "Shall I invite him to Yarrabee for that reason?"

"Perhaps next year?" Mrs. Wentworth said tentatively, and Eugenia laughed again.

"You mean when I have a child? I confess I am longing for one. But in the meantime, if Mr. O'Connor passes this way, he will have to make do with Erasmus, who is a very paintable subject." The wine, first the dry red claret, then the sweet sauterne, had made her feel gay. She was enjoying the evening and the company. "Actually, I consider myself a reasonably accomplished artist and intend to begin sketching seriously now that the weather is cooler. There are flocks of galahs that gather in the gum trees and are quite lovely. But why are we standing here? Who will be the first to sing or play the piano? The rest of us are permitted to sit comfortably and do nothing more strenuous than pay attention."

Mrs. Wentworth sang quite pleasantly, but the other ladies refused to open their mouths.

"My dear, if one has a voice like a frog, one keeps it quiet," Marion Noakes said. "You must be the next to perform, Eugenia."

"But how disappointing! Does no one else sing? Then when the gentlemen come in, we will get out the cards. Oh, here they are now. Gilbert, none of the ladies except Mrs. Wentworth—"

Eugenia's light prattle was rudely interrupted by a hoarse shout from the passage.

"Mr. Massingham, sir! Mutiny!"

Mrs. Ashburton gave a dramatic scream. Gilbert stiffened in the doorway, then abruptly wheeled around and went out, quickly followed by the other men. Their footsteps sounded across the courtyard and died away.

Eugenia hurried to the long windows leading onto the veranda and flung them open. In the chilly night air, she and the four ladies stood shivering and listening to the distant sounds of shouts and angry voices.

"A mutiny?" Mrs. Ashburton said apprehensively. "The convicts?"

"It isn't uncommon," said Marion Noakes.

"Eugenia, aren't you alarmed?" Mrs. Ashburton was clutching at Eugenia's arm.

Eugenia nodded without speaking. She was filled with that too-familiar indescribable dread. The night was dark, alien, violent, the cozy drawing room behind the French doors a myth.

"It's probably only a small disturbance," Bess Kelly said with brisk good sense. "The men will soon have it under control. I really don't see why we should all die of cold out here."

"Yes, let us go in," said Eugenia with an immense effort.

She thought the voices were growing calmer. A horse whinnied in its stable. A light flickered, as if someone were carrying a carriage lamp.

A hand plucked at her sleeve. She turned to see Mrs. Jarvis in her white cap and apron in the doorway.

"Excuse me, ma'am, but I thought you'd like to know it's nothing to get upset about. One of the men has got into the wine cellar and run off a pint of raw wine out of a cask and got drunk. He's been making a lot of noise. That's all it is. There's no mutiny."

Eugenia gave a deep sigh. She was grateful that the full, stiff folds of her skirt hid her trembling knees.

"Thank you, Mrs. Jarvis. I am so glad it's nothing more serious."

"Then what was all that shouting of mutiny?" Mrs. Ashburton wanted to know.

"It was only that the drunken fellow was making a speech to incite the rest," Mrs. Jarvis answered. "I've seen enough of that kind to know they're all brave words and nothing more."

"Yes, that's true," Eugenia said emphatically to the other ladies. "My husband would never employ a dangerous felon. Let us go in. It's chilly. I believe I hear the men returning."

When they came in, the men were animated and excited.

"A black Irishman from Killarney—never heard his name, did you, Wentworth?"

"Paddy Donovan. He was roaring drunk; that was all that was the matter. He had quite a turn of eloquence, however."

"The Irish always have. They talk themselves into trouble; that's why they've landed in Botany Bay."

"Wanted to form a company armed with sticks and stones and charge the house, Mrs. Massingham, if you can imagine such a harebrained scheme," said Mr. Blaxland. "Your husband will be well advised to keep his cellar more securely locked in future."

Mr. Wentworth laughed in amusement. "He's getting the wrong converts to wine drinking. It's amusing when you come to think of it. Though I doubt if the fellow would have touched wine if he could have laid his hands on a bottle of rum."

"Where is Gilbert?" Eugenia asked, her fingers digging into the palms of her hands.

The men exchanged a quick glance at one another. Edmund Kelly rubbed his hands together. Mr. Blaxland tilted his chin to the ceiling, saying casually, "He'll be here shortly. These disturbances happen, Mrs. Massingham. You mustn't let them upset you. I declare, you're as white as a sheet."

"This would be the time when I lose my smelling salts," Mrs. Ashburton fussed.

"I don't require smelling salts," Eugenia heard herself saying with cool contempt.

"Perhaps not. You're a heroine, they say. But I'm a coward, and I don't mind admitting I was scared out of my wits."

"Mrs. Jarvis," said Eugenia, "will make you a soothing tisane. I'll go tell her."

"Can't you ring for her? She was here a moment ago."

"It's a special recipe," Eugenia said vaguely. "I must give her the exact directions."

She was out of the room and in the hall. She had enough command of her senses to go first to the kitchen and give the order for the tisane before carrying out her real intention.

She felt cold to the center of her bones, but a compulsion was driving her on, making her walk swiftly down the dark path that led beyond the stables. A path she had never gone down by daylight, because she had never before suffered from this terrible compulsion that overcame even fear.

In front of the row of huts there was a stretch of bare ground and clustered at the end of it a small group of men. One of them was holding a lantern aloft. Its yellow light shone on something that looked like a large dog.

But it wasn't a dog. Eugenia drew in her breath as she realized that the crouching form was a man bent across a wooden bench. She saw also that the upper part of his body was naked and that his hands were tied behind his back.

Someone had just moved into the shaft of lantern light to stand over him. A tall man in black trousers and a white ruffled shirt who was raising his arm to strike.

"Stand back!" Sickness rose in Eugenia's throat. She had known the man was Gilbert. She hadn't needed his hard, abrupt voice to tell her so. She was about to witness what he had blithely called "administering a little punishment." That was what this torture scene under the high black sky was, with the men shuffling back, the lantern dipping and swaying, and the upraised arm in its immaculate white sleeve coming down, followed immediately by the unendurable sound of lashed flesh.

One stroke, two strokes, three, four . . . The prisoner began to moan. Held rigid by her deadly hypnotized fascination, Eugenia saw the dark welts coming out on the pale skin. Then the man screamed, suddenly and shatteringly, and Eugenia recovered her mobility.

She flew across the intervening ground, sobbing, "Stop! Stop! Stop! Gilbert, stop, for the love of God!"

Hands held her, bruising her arms. The lantern, swung into her face, dazzled her.

She heard Gilbert exclaim, "Good God, Eugenia!" and she caught a glimpse of his highly flushed face and disheveled hair. A last fragment of her consciousness told her that the prisoner was stirring and lifting his head out of the dust. Then everything of the nightmare scene had gone. The slowly gathering darkness was blissful.

Chapter 12

SHE was in bed; the lamplight was shining on her face. She turned her face away, and someone came forward to move the lamp.

"Are you feeling better, ma'am?"

It was Mrs. Jarvis, her face calm behind the yellow glow of the lamp.

"Did I faint? I felt so ill."

"You gave everyone a fright, ma'am. Particularly the master. He carried you upstairs himself."

In those strong arms that had just ceased wielding the lash?

"Why aren't you in the kitchen, Mrs. Jarvis?"

"Because that silly girl Jane is having the vapors, and I thought I could be of more use to you."

Eugenia put her hand out, clutching at Mrs. Jarvis' hand.

"My husband was—" The very word brought back her sickness. Mrs. Jarvis calmly supplied it for her.

"Flogging the prisoner, ma'am? It was necessary."

"There was blood."

"Some bleed easily."

Eugenia winced, closing her eyes. Her feeling of nausea had come back. She wondered if she were ill, as well as shocked and repelled by what she had witnessed.

"I know it's not my place to say this, ma'am, but what sort of discipline would there be here if the master didn't keep the upper hand? You have to remember you did so yourself with that dangerous convict at the inn. It was his life or yours or other innocent lives. I've thought of these men as like a hive of angry bees. If they get out of control, they sting, and they're poisonous. That's all the master was doing, keeping them in control. Think of it in that way, and if I may suggest it, ma'am, keep away from places where you might see these sights. Now I'm going to make you a nice cup of tea."

Tea. The panacea. Even for a hive of stinging bees. But he hadn't looked dangerous, that boy with his head hanging in the dust.

"I won't be kept in a hothouse," Eugenia said stubbornly.

The calm brown eyes surveyed her speculatively, and Eugenia thought again what an extraordinary person this woman was. She seemed to know everything, and nothing ruffled her.

"Well, sometimes I think that would be a nice place to be," Mrs. Jarvis answered. "Anyway, rest now. That was what the doctor said."

"Doctor?"

"Dr. Noakes, ma'am. Don't you remember?"

Eugenia started up. "My guests! I should be looking after them. What are they doing?"

"The last I heard, they were playing cards. But it's eleven o'clock, and I expect they'll soon be retiring."

"Here I am, in fact," came Gilbert's voice from the doorway. He advanced into the light and stood over Eugenia, an immense shadow, his head almost touching the ceiling.

"My dearest girl, I can see you are feeling better. Noakes said you were to be left to rest, but I was anxious about you."

"What's happened to that man?"

"The prisoner? Just put him out of your mind. He'll go back to work tomorrow congratulating himself that he escaped so lightly. Now let us say no more about it. I'll save my lecture until you're better."

Eugenia struggled up. "But I'm not ill." She wondered why Gilbert had that small, half-amused smile on his lips.

"No, you're not ill, but I want Phil Noakes to take a closer look at you. He seems to think you might be in a certain condition."

Eugenia's heart jumped. The baby she longed for making its presence known at such an inauspicious moment? Her eyes were dark with remembered horror.

"Not *now*, Gilbert!" she begged. "Not like this."

"How do you mean?" he said in the gentle, teasing voice that usually she enjoyed. "What other way is there?"

He hadn't begun to understand the complexity of her thought. Why should he? He didn't know her private nightmare. He really didn't know very much about her at all. Nor she about him. They must really set about mending that situation. Just now she only longed for physical comfort, to be held in loving arms, to have soothing words whispered to her.

But Gilbert hadn't changed his shirt. There was a small dark splash of blood on its ruffle. She couldn't let him touch her. She lay back, closing her eyes, waiting for him to go.

"Eugenia, I'll send Phil up. He'll give you a sleeping draft."

She could make no criticism of Dr. Noakes because she liked his plain, blunt manner, his sensitive hands. She could almost have confided her nightmare to him; only he didn't give her the opportunity. He merely confirmed his suspicion, though he promised no absolute certainty for another two or three weeks.

"Take things easy," he said.

"But I always do. Gilbert won't allow me to exert myself."

"There are different forms of exertion, my dear. An overactive mind is one of them. Do you miss your family, your home?"

"Of course I do, Doctor. Terribly."

"And Yarrabee?"

"It's a beautiful house. Don't you think so? When my garden is made—"

"Of course. You can't be expected to settle down in a week, or a year if it comes to that. My wife still hasn't settled down entirely. But it would be different if her child had lived. You're going to be lucky."

Gilbert must have been waiting in the passage, for when Dr. Noakes went out, she couldn't help overhearing voices.

Gilbert's was eager and impatient. "Well, am I going to have a son?"

"I can't speak for the sex of the infant, my dear fellow."

"Eugenia?"

"She'll be all right. She's talking about her garden. You might do well to think of her in that way yourself. When you transplant a delicate bloom to unfamiliar soil, you must take care of it."

"I like that analogy," Gilbert said in a pleased voice. "You can be sure I will protect her. I wish she hadn't seen that episode tonight, but when my wife determines to have her own way, she has it. Not that I'd like her to be different. She has spirit." The voices were farther off. Eugenia heard Gilbert saying, "When I've attended to a little unfinished business—" and Dr. Noakes protesting, "Must you? Why not let the fellow off with what he's already had?"

"You don't understand, Phil. I can't risk losing my authority. If I did, I could have my throat cut or my house set on fire at any time. Even the quietest of these species isn't to be trusted. They've had too long brooding over their supposed wrongs. But I won't be long. Then we'll drink to my son."

An hour later Eugenia gave up the attempt to sleep. She rang the bell at her bedside. It was answered by Mrs. Jarvis.

"Can I get you something, ma'am?"

"Why aren't you in the kitchen? Why didn't Jane answer the bell?"

"I took the liberty of sitting in the linen room, ma'am. I didn't think anyone else would hear if you rang, with all the noise the gentlemen are making."

"What are they doing downstairs?"

"The master has been opening some of his wine. He says everyone must drink to his son. Even Jane and Phoebe and Ellen and I had to go in and take a glass of wine. Now all the ladies have retired, and the gentlemen are having a last bottle. You can't deny them their pleasure, ma'am."

Another loud burst of laughter echoed through the house. A

voice began to declaim. Someone tapped out a one-finger melody on the piano in accompaniment. There was a crash of breaking glass.

Eugenia said in a matter-of-fact voice, "But no one will flog them for being drunk."

"That's a different matter altogether." Mrs. Jarvis moved around quietly, turning up the lamp, straightening the bedclothes, then shaking a white powder into a glass and mixing it with water. She looked a little like Sarah, Eugenia thought. She had the same quiet movements.

This realization produced an intimacy that made Eugenia say, "Was your husband pleased when he knew you were going to have a child?"

There was a little silence. Then, "He never knew. I hadn't told him."

"Oh! But why?"

"It seemed just another thing to put on his shoulders." Mrs. Jarvis stirred the cloudy mixture in the glass. "I would have told him in time."

"Would he have wanted a boy?"

"I expect he would have. All men do. It must be their vanity. They want to reproduce themselves. Aren't you pleased that Mr. Massingham wants a boy? I have no one to care what I have. A child bred by convicts."

The lateness, Eugenia's weakness, the intimacy of the lamp-lit bedroom, had made them neither mistress nor maid, but two women in an elemental situation.

"I didn't know you had this bitterness," Eugenia said in surprise.

"I try to overcome it."

The two women's eyes met. Something passed between them, something Eugenia was too tired and too imperceptive to analyze. She knew only that it was significant. Their lives were becoming tied together, she thought, and she couldn't decide whether this was a good or a bad thing. It simply seemed to be inevitable, though why that should be so, she also could not answer.

And all at once Mrs. Jarvis, as if she too recognized the precarious situation, was back to being a servant.

She held out the glass.

"Drink this, ma'am. It's a sleeping powder Dr. Noakes said I was to give you if you were wakeful. In five minutes you'll be sound asleep and not hear another thing."

Half an hour later Molly Jarvis tiptoed back into the room to see if her mistress slept and stood for several minutes looking at the face on the pillow, the long lashes quiet on the pale cheeks, the tension gone from the too-sensitive mouth.

She was a delicate-looking creature. How would she come through her ordeal? She might have had a soft marriage bed, but her childbed would be exactly the same as any other woman's. Perhaps harder because she was so finely made, so narrow.

Molly ran her hands down her own strong, shapely hips. She had felt her baby move today for the first time. It had given her a moment of exultant pleasure. Bred of convicts, or not, she intended to make a good life for her child, here at Yarrabee.

When she went downstairs, the men were preparing to retire. She walked quickly past the open door of the drawing room, hoping to be unobserved.

But as she went down the passage to cross the courtyard to her quarters, she bumped into a tall figure just coming in out of the darkness. Hands clutched at her. Lips pressed briefly on hers. She heard the master's laugh as he blundered on, pleased with his snatched kiss from whoever it was, but intent only on getting safely upstairs to fall into bed beside his wife.

Molly stood still, tears abruptly streaming down her cheeks.

She hadn't cried—since when? And why now because of something so unimportant as a snatched anonymous kiss?

The answer to that was simple enough—because Gilbert Massingham would never remember it, and she, as her surging blood told her, would never forget it.

"So here I am, and here I must stay," Eugenia wrote to Sarah a few days later. She was referring to the fact that she was

still confined to the sofa in the drawing room. Her words, however, had an underlying meaning that Sarah, who was
extremely perceptive, might guess at. Here she was in the
country to which she had come of her own free will, so in spite
of its many painful aspects and her too frequent homesickness,
she must make the best of it.

She stopped biting her pen, and went on:

> I am utterly delighted about the baby and so is Gilbert—
> he comes to me with a twinkle in his eye saying, "Give Papa
> a kiss." The doctor has ordered bed in the mornings and the
> drawing room sofa in the afternoons for the next two or three
> weeks; then all will be well. I believe our guests enjoyed their
> visit, in spite of having such an inactive hostess. They all left
> on Tuesday morning, but Gilbert has invited Mrs. Ashburton
> to come back and stay at Yarrabee while her son is absent on
> his proposed exploration of the interior. He seems to have
> developed quite a partiality for that garrulous woman, and he
> also thinks that I require vivacious company in my condition.
> As if constantly searching for Mrs. Ashburton's lost belongings
> and listening to her chatter are going to keep me in good
> spirits!
>
> It is almost winter, and the days are getting short. Gilbert
> is very busy clearing more land for vines, digging and trench-
> ing and planting windbreaks. There is also the constant prob-
> lem of keeping our unique brand of laborers working honestly.
> A penal colony is not a happy place, and I often spend useless
> time wishing that this condition did not exist. But I must not
> go on like this. Gilbert does not like me to talk politics . . .

Chapter 13

By midwinter Mrs. Ashburton had settled in. She had brought so many trunks that it looked as if she never intended to leave.

Yarrabee was a haven compared to the noise and bustle of Sydney. It had been a mistake to join her son in Australia. An old woman needed peace and quiet. If Godfrey were to find gold in the interior or there were other pleasant aspects to keep him there, she would stay exactly where she was.

She settled more comfortably in her chair, a plump hen spreading her feathers over a secure and cozy nest.

"At least I promise to stay until your baby is born."

It was the conditions on the *Caroline* all over again, the round figure in the flying shawls trundling after Eugenia, the complaining voice forever saying, "Wait for me, my dear. Why are you in such a hurry? Do you want to be alone? Is that why you shut the door? But being too much alone isn't good for you in your condition. That's what your mother would say. Since you haven't her here, I will take her place." Or, "Really, Eugenia, I can't think why you keep that surly Peabody. He simply grunts in the most unmannerly way when I give him advice. As for Jane, you haven't succeeded in improving her in the least. And I also think you give that housekeeper of yours too much liberty. You have to remember she was a convict. Is that kind ever to be trusted? And how is she to do her work when she has her baby?"

The monologue went on and on until Eugenia lost her temper.

"This is my house and my servants, Mrs. Ashburton. If you find it so disagreeable, you are perfectly free to leave."

The old lady's bosom rose and fell in supreme indignation. But canniness fought with her outrage. She had the grace to say, "I apologize, my dear. I am a nasty, interfering old woman. You must always tell me when I behave badly. I love you and Gilbert, you know. I think of you as my children."

"And behave like a mother-in-law," Eugenia said. "But I suppose there is sometimes a pleasant, lovable mother-in-law."

"You do not find me one?"

"Oh, you silly creature! My husband does, if that is a comfort to you. But he doesn't have to listen all day to your criticisms."

Mrs. Ashburton nodded meekly. "You are perfectly right, Eugenia. I am glad we have had this talk. Now, when I feel impelled to make a critical remark, I will button my lips together. You will see."

Eugenia was fairly certain she would see nothing of the kind. But she did have an affection for the irritating old lady, and it was true that Gilbert was fond of her or said that he was.

So the weeks wore on, filled with quiet occupations. Sewing baby clothes, writing the long weekly letter to Sarah, supervising Peabody as he dug borders and planned the garden that was to burgeon into life in the spring, going for walks, attending church on Sunday, and visiting Mrs. Bourke, the wife of the new governor, Major Bourke. They had only recently arrived, replacing Governor Darling. Mrs. Bourke had taken a great liking to Eugenia and enjoyed inviting her to an informal tea party. In the evenings Mrs. Ashburton and Gilbert talked, and she listened dreamily. There was no need to search for subjects of conversation now that Mrs. Ashburton was there with her unending chatter. But there was also the drawback that the opportunity in the long winter evenings to get to know her husband more intimately had to be postponed.

Their only private conversations took place in their bedroom, and by that time Eugenia was struggling with her familiar inhibitions, although that old haunting nightmare was now less vivid and Gilbert had become very thoughtful of her now that she was pregnant. He was afraid of harming the baby.

Then it was spring and the night of the big frost.

A severe late frost was one of the hazards of vine cultivation. Since he had established his vineyard, Gilbert had had only once before to fight a frost. That one had not been too severe, and by lighting enough fires, he had managed to save most of his vines.

It was the French theory that plenty of smoke coated the vines and rendered them immune to frost. In those early days Gilbert had had only brush and straw, with green leaves and rubble piled on top, to make a smoky fire.

Now he was much better equipped, with hundreds of frost pots filled with crude oil. It was a precaution he had taken as soon as he had enough acres under cultivation and when he knew that the devastation of a year's crop would mean ruin. This was the factor about which shrewd men like Wentworth and Lachlan Macquarie, a former governor, had warned him. A flock of sheep would have provided an insurance against bankruptcy.

But Gilbert Massingham was a stubborn man who seldom listened to advice. There was a danger of his brain being pickled by his wine, people said, for he could think of nothing else. He would not contemplate large flocks of sheep running on his acres. He intended to have one enormous vineyard, and surely it would be bad luck if all the grapes failed in one year.

So he took what practical precautions he could and prayed in church on Sundays for mild nights in winter, not too much rain, which would mean mildew, in spring, and a complete absence of hailstorms.

Hope and prayer and a great deal of vigilance. It was a tense, exciting life exactly suited to his nature.

All the winter he was on the alert for frosts. The slightest increase in cold, and he was sitting up in bed, his sensitive nose sniffing the atmosphere. He frequently rose in the middle of the night and dressed and went to walk around the vineyard, testing the stillness of the air and studying the sparkling stars.

His wife was carrying their child, but this sprawling area of young vines was his personal child, being gently nursed and watched over until maturity.

The night of disaster began innocently enough. At ten o'clock Gilbert looked outdoors. A slight wind and clouds trailing across the moon reassured him. It would be no colder than usual. He could go to bed with an easy mind.

It was three in the morning when Tom Sloan aroused him by throwing pebbles at the window.

"Mr. Massingham, sir," he whispered hoarsely as Gilbert put his head out of the window, "it's freezing hard. Shall I light the pots?"

Rime glittered on the windowsill. The frosty air bit into Gilbert's face. The moon was polished gold in an absolutely clear, frozen sky.

Eugenia stirred in alarm.

"What is it?"

"Frost."

"Oh, is that all?"

Dragging on his trousers, Gilbert had time to say, with an edge to his voice, "It's enough. Go back to sleep."

"I thought it might be trouble with the convicts." The alarm had left her voice. She asked sleepily, "Is there anything I can do?"

"What could you do? Run up and down the furrows with tar pots? This is a man's job."

Gilbert finished dressing in the moonlit darkness and was gone. Eugenia curled up in the warm bed, relief flowing through her as the shadow receded. No desperate fugitive tonight, no fear of bloodshed, no haunted, betrayed eyes. She could sleep.

So she didn't see the hundreds of moving lights, like jack-o'-lanterns, as the men, roused from sleep, carried the flaming, smoking frost pots up and down, letting the tarry smoke pour over the young vines. They themselves were soon black from head to foot and half-choked with smoke. Toward dawn they became so weary that one of them stumbled and dropped his pot. In a flash the master was standing over him, cursing him, but before he could gather up the sticky, still-flaming receptacle, someone else snatched it up. A woman in skirts.

"I'll take a turn," said Mrs. Jarvis.

"What are you doing out here?"

Gilbert's voice was hard with tension and weariness.

It was the last straw that he should have to allow a woman so far gone in pregnancy to help to save his vines.

"I would have been here at the beginning if I had known. I woke up and saw the lights. Tell me what to do."

"Just walk up and down letting the black smoke coat the vines. We're almost finished. Daylight will show us whether we've wasted our time."

"I didn't know about the frost."

There was such distress in her voice that Gilbert slowed down to walk beside her.

"What's it to you?" he asked.

"I would hate to see the crop fail, sir."

"Are you afraid of losing a comfortable home?"

She ignored his sarcasm, saying simply, "I like the vines. I enjoyed vintage last summer. It would be a wicked shame if there wasn't one next summer."

He was surprised and strangely grateful for her concern.

"Watch that flame. You don't want to set the vineyard on fire. That would certainly finish off the frost damage."

"It looks pretty," said Molly Jarvis, watching the flaring lights. "Like a procession." She began to cough. "But the smoke gets down your throat."

"Don't swallow it. Keep it out of your face."

She gave a low laugh. "Perhaps my baby will be born black, after this." She sounded excited, in spite of her distress about the situation. She moved off down the furrow, a strong, upright figure, broad with the child she carried. Gilbert watched until in the darkness she couldn't be distinguished from the men. But he knew she was there. He felt more cheerful and set off briskly to encourage the tired men. It was strange that he had ceased feeling tired.

An hour later the darkness began to lift. There was a faint glow on the horizon. The yellow tongues of flame from the blackened pots became paler.

Gilbert raised his voice. "All right, everybody. Sun's coming up. We'll soon know the worst."

"As soon as that?" Mrs. Jarvis was behind him.

"Yes. The frost is like a black hand. The vines we haven't saved will have withered."

The men gathered around silently. The light grew, and the whites of their eyes showed in their blackened faces. They all shared this moment of suspense.

The light on the horizon deepened to gold. A flame burst through as the sun rose. The mist dissolved, showing the glittering frost rime, the rows of blackened vines.

Like a tattered, diseased army, they drooped in immobile exhaustion.

For a little while no one moved or spoke. Then abruptly Molly Jarvis began to cry, with a small, wailing sound.

Gilbert looked at her impatiently, suddenly wanting to strike her, to vent his impotent anger on somebody.

"That'll do no good," he said curtly.

He strode off to inspect the whole of his vineyard. He couldn't believe that it was all like this. Some of the vines must have survived. His dream could not be collapsing before it had fairly begun.

He walked for an hour. He began counting the vines that remained healthy. A few acres on the lower slopes, the muscatels which he had been inclined to despise since he was more interested in brewing wine than making raisins, were almost untouched by the scorching frost. There was also an area of the more firmly established vines that he had brought from Bordeaux and Portugal in the year in which he had become engaged to Eugenia. But the entire planting of the cuttings which had come out on the ship with Eugenia was lost, as well as a large area of the sauternes.

He could estimate a harvest of a quarter of his crop—if that managed to survive other hazards, such as too much rain or humidity, the pest of the furry caterpillar, a swarm of locusts, a drought.

He would not be able to pay his debts this year. Nor would he be able to replace his lost vines unless the bank advanced him a loan. He had been too extravagant and too optimistic. He had tied up his entire capital in Yarrabee, building a house that was too ambitious, because he was marrying a woman who needed that kind of setting, because that was how he had planned his life. His dreams had leaped ahead of reality. Three good years and a growing market had made him overconfident. He had overspent and been a fool.

Now he would have to go humbly to that sour-faced Andrew Jackson, his bank manager, and admit that his cautions in the past had been justified. "Keep a reserve against a rainy day." The fellow had harped on that theme in his dry, meticulous way. But Gilbert had had a bride arriving and a great deal of necessary spending to do. And anyway, it wasn't rain but frost that had now defeated him.

Defeated? That was not a word in his language. He would write for another consignment of vine cuttings immediately. He would make a trip down the Hunter River and see what replacements he could get from vignerons there. Some of them no doubt would be in financial difficulty and glad to sell part of their stock.

He would replant his stricken acres. He would learn patience. His plans had been set back three years in this one disastrous night. But he was still only thirty. There was plenty of time. Eugenia would have to wait a little for those treasures from the Orient. Yarrabee could not be another Vaucluse for some years.

If next year's crop also failed . . .

Gilbert stuck out his chin pugnaciously. He had always defied fate. He would do so again.

All the same, as the sun rose, he could scarcely bear the sight of his ravished vineyard. Hot moisture trickled out of his eyes. He clenched his fist, rubbing his knuckles fiercely across his cheeks.

Tom Sloan's voice sounded behind him.

"It's cruel, sir. But there's no use brooding over it."

He turned sharply on the man, blackened face looking at blackened face.

"I'm not brooding. I'm planning."

"You can't bring the vines back to life," said Sloan pessimistically. "They're finished."

"Nor have I any intention of trying to."

"Better get in and have some breakfast, sir. Things don't seem so bad on a full stomach."

Gilbert walked away, not answering. He didn't want sympathy. But he suddenly remembered Mrs. Jarvis.

"Have you sent the men down?"

"Yes, sir. They're black as coons. Mrs. Jarvis, too. She's a strong woman, that one. She worked like a slave."

"Yes, yes, she will be duly rewarded. You can give the men an issue of rum. Well, that's how it is, Sloan. But don't imagine I'm beaten."

"I didn't imagine that, sir. Not you."

"Thanks, Tom. You're loyal. And I sent your woman away, too."

"I'm glad you did that. I've lost my taste for the dusky ladies."

"Then you'd better find a white woman and get married."

"I was thinking of that, sir." Sloan had an alert, monkeyish face, tough, hardened. Gilbert would never have paid for his passage from England if he had not been sure of his durability. He was a little slow-thinking, a little too fond of rum, and undiscriminating to the point of folly in his choice of women, but Gilbert liked a man with virility, and in every other way Tom Sloan was reliable, honest, and loyal.

He was pleased to hear that the tough little man, getting near forty now, was going to settle down. He would be glad to improve his living accommodation to include a wife.

"You've picked one out, have you?" Gilbert's voice was a little absent, his mind not fully on the matter. The rising sun had not warmed the atmosphere. The frost was penetrating his bones.

"Yes, sir, I have. When she's got over her present problem."

"Problem?"

"Having a young one, sir. I don't object to being father to another man's child. Not when Molly Jarvis is the mother."

"Molly—you mean Mrs. Jarvis?" Gilbert stopped abruptly in his tracks.

"That's who I mean. She's a fine woman. I don't give two hoots for her past." Sloan sensed something in Gilbert's manner. "Now don't you or Mrs. Massingham be upset, sir. She'll stay on in the big house. She'll only be Molly Sloan, instead of Molly Jarvis."

The fellow was too familiar. It was difficult to control these characteristics in such a raw country. In the great spaces and the loneliness, all men were equal. One got down to the basic fact of survival. Gilbert had treated Sloan as a friend when they had set out together to conquer this corner of the wilderness. They had talked late into the starlit nights, discussed the universe, made plans. They had faced a party of hostile natives with spears and sent the ugly brutes packing; once Gilbert had saved Sloan's life when the little man had been swept down the Hawkesbury River in one of the sudden summer floodings. That fact above all bound them together. But now, suddenly, Sloan was intolerably familiar.

"Do you think she'll have you?" he heard himself saying in a tight, unsympathetic voice.

"I shouldn't think there'd be much doubt. I'm not speaking for my personal charms. I'm only thinking a woman like her wants a home for her child."

"She's got that already."

"In a manner of speaking, sir." The earnest eyes in the blackened face peered up at Gilbert, saw something uneasy, and were immediately repentant. "I oughtn't to be talking about my affairs at a time like this. Don't know how I came to. It was you mentioning Yella."

Gilbert began striding swiftly toward the house.

"You've got a child there whom you might feel an obligation toward. Mrs. Jarvis' is nothing to do with you."

Eugenia was waiting at the door. She was wrapped in a dressing gown and looked distraught.

"Gilbert, please hurry—" She stopped, seeing his sooty face with the white runnels down the cheeks. "Gilbert, is it as bad as that?"

"As bad as what?"

"You have been—you have marks on your cheeks."

"So would you cry if you'd seen what I've been looking at," he said harshly. "What are you doing down here in the cold? You aren't even dressed. Go back to bed. I don't want my son lost, as well as my vineyard."

She had made a movement toward him as if she would have embraced him, in spite of his dirty, disheveled condition. But now she stepped back, and her face went still.

"I was only going to tell you that someone must go to Parramatta for a doctor. Mrs. Jarvis is having her baby."

Mrs. Jarvis, Tom Sloan, the ruined vineyard, his own feeling of terrible exhaustion—that accounted for the strange fact that he hadn't in that moment wanted his wife in his arms, that he had repelled her first truly spontaneous gesture toward him.

It was the timing that was wrong. Everything was wrong. Now Molly Jarvis, through working too strenuously on his account, would probably lose her baby. She would be able to marry Sloan with no impediments.

"Is she far gone yet? Have I time to clean up?" he asked wearily.

"I don't know. Mrs. Ashburton is with her. She won't allow me in the room." Eugenia's face contorted angrily. "I'm not so useless as all that. You all pamper me too much. It's ridiculous!"

"Mrs. Ashburton is perfectly right. Thank heaven she is here," Gilbert said absently and turned to bellow for one of the maids to go tell Murphy to have his horse saddled. "Go upstairs, my love," he said over his shoulder to Eugenia. "I'm just going to wash and change my jacket. I'll be back in no time."

"Gilbert, you didn't tell me—the vineyard—"

"Later."

It gave him a feeling of dull surprise that there was something of more urgency than his ravaged vines.

Underneath his surprise was a sharp sense of shock, a truth he didn't want to face at this particular moment. No other woman in labor except his wife would have had prior importance to his own disaster.

Chapter 14

EUGENIA thought that it had been the most terrible day of her life. The acres of frost-blackened vines were bad enough, and the air of melancholy in the house. Even when the sun rose and streamed through the windows, and the day became crisp, brilliant, and beautiful, nobody made much noise except Erasmus who had recently picked up a phrase of Mrs. Ashburton's, "I declare to goodness," and now had a notion to practice it with exhausting repetitiveness.

Eugenia was haunted by the two worst moments of the day. The first had been when she had encountered her husband in the doorway, looking like a man who had come up from a coal-pit. His wild, haggard appearance would have made her shrink from him if there had not been the telltale white marks down his cheeks where the tears had run. Those had made him so painfully vulnerable that she had wanted to throw her arms around him, to cradle his black-smeared face against her breast. But he hadn't noticed her impulsive gesture, and the shaft of tenderness that had pierced her died away as he curtly told her to go back to bed. Suddenly she saw her marriage as such a meager thing, a body for his use at night, a vessel in which to carry his child, an ornament for his house. It was a paralyzing realization that had made her able neither to embrace him nor to sympathize with him in the loss of his vines. She had watched in a frozen stillness as he had dropped his filthy clothes on the bedroom floor, flung himself into clean

ones, and then hurried downstairs to leap on his horse, which
had been brought to the front door.

Someone else could have ridden for the doctor. But who
else? All the men had toiled all night, and Gilbert was a good
and conscientious master, not asking anyone to do more than '
he could do himself. Also, he would count Mrs. Jarvis his special
responsibility, since her premature labor was due to her hard
work on his behalf.

Everyone, Eugenia thought, was of use except herself. She
was not a useless person, and she refused to be treated as one
on this day of crisis. Instead of going back to bed as Gilbert
had ordered, she went across the courtyard, still glistening with
frost, to the kitchen quarters and then down the passage leading to the maids' bedrooms. Mrs. Jarvis occupied the one at the
end. As housekeeper she was entitled to the best room. It had a
window leading onto its own veranda beside the glass-roofed
potting shed and the kitchen garden. The baby, when it was
born, would be able to sleep in its basket on the veranda on
warm days. The quarters had been planned originally for a
man and wife, so that now they were ideally suitable for a
widow with a child.

Listening outside the closed door, Eugenia heard Mrs. Ashburton's voice, followed by a long, low moan.

Her heart fluttered. She told herself that this was a natural
sound. Childbirth was extremely painful. Her mother had
given her that information, in carefully phrased sentences, just
before she left England.

But none of her mother's judicious words had prepared her
for the shocking scream that suddenly pierced her ears, making
her snatch her fingers from the doorknob as if it had been red-
hot. There was another scream, followed by a shuddering
groan.

"That's the way, deary," said Mrs. Ashburton, unperturbed.
Suddenly Mrs. Ashburton, to Eugenia trembling in the passage,
was a heroine. Somehow she made her stiff fingers turn the
doorknob and push open the door. Then she was within the

room, looking at Mrs. Jarvis' flushed, contorted face on the pillow and the large, comfortable rear of Mrs. Ashburton as she leaned over her patient.

She went forward steadily. "Let me help. What can I do?"

Mrs. Ashburton straightened and turned. Her face was purple, her gray hair hanging in strands, her eyes bright with surprise.

"Good gracious, Eugenia! You can't come in here."

"Why not? Aren't I a woman, too?"

She sat at the bedside and took Mrs. Jarvis' hand. The strong fingers immediately clenched hers painfully. Not wincing, Eugenia looked into the suffused brown eyes and said, "If it helps, I'll stay."

"This is no place for you," Mrs. Ashburton declared.

"If you, why not me?"

"Because I'm sixty-five years old, and I've seen servants in back bedrooms before today. If you faint, I'll have two of you on my hands."

"I won't faint," Eugenia said calmly. "Besides, this is something I need to know more about. Mrs. Jarvis and I are in the same position."

"You don't need to be that curious," Mrs. Ashburton said. "Well, I suppose I can't throw you out bodily, can I?"

Mrs. Jarvis stirred. "It isn't that bad, ma'am," she said, and managed to give Eugenia a reassuring smile before the pain caught her again.

Eugenia was still there two hours later when the doctor, a little red-faced man smelling strongly of rum, burst in. He was rolling up his sleeves before he got to the bedside.

"Out of the way, miss. Is there plenty of hot water?" He looked at Mrs. Ashburton. "You stay. You look as if you know what this is about. Don't want any fainting young girls in here."

Mrs. Ashburton nodded to Eugenia briefly, indicating the door.

"But this is not a fainting young girl, Doctor," she said tartly. "She is the mistress of the house."

*   *   *

Although Molly Jarvis had been touched and comforted, too, by the mistress' presence, she was thankful to see her go, so that she could give way to the agony that rent her. She had had to control herself while that too-sensitive face bent over her; she had had to remember not to frighten the young thing out of her wits.

Now she could scream as much as she pleased. But that slim hand so determinedly holding hers had made another bond between herself and the mistress. She was not sure that she wanted that.

For much later there was the other face bending over her, the ridges of weariness cut into the flesh, and her heart was beating suffocatingly.

"Are you all right, Mrs. Jarvis?"

"Yes, thank you, sir."

"The baby?"

"A girl, sir. She's small, but strong. The doctor said—"

"I know. I saw him. He says you could have lost your child after what you did last night. I came to thank you."

Molly could not bear the quenched look in the blue eyes above her. She had to close her own, to hide her tears.

"That's all right, sir. I wanted to help. Is the vineyard ruined?"

"Don't worry about it. We'll put it right. And I'm very grateful to you."

After he had gone, it seemed as if sleep would never come to ease her aching body.

It had been a long day for everybody. When Eugenia and Mrs. Ashburton and Gilbert sat at dinner that night, they were all too tired to do more than make sporadic conversation.

Gilbert had opened a bottle of his best wine. The occasion was not a celebration, but a need to fortify themselves against brooding on the day's disaster.

Although it would be a nice idea, too, to drink to the new life that had arrived at Yarrabee.

"Will the baby be all right?" he asked Mrs. Ashburton.

"Oh, yes. She's small, but she's tough. Like her mother, I would say."

Mrs. Ashburton sipped her wine and nodded peacefully. She alone had enjoyed the day. It had been full of drama. If she had been born to a lower station in life, she might have been a midwife. She liked handling those wriggling, squalling objects as they made their appearance into the world. She felt powerful and wise and important. That rum-sodden doctor from Parramatta hadn't really been necessary. He had only given a lot of orders and done nothing.

"I hope you will allow me to take care of you, too, Eugenia." The wine was making her tipsy. She hadn't had time for a proper meal all day, and she was accustomed to eating heartily.

Gilbert answered, "I intend to have Dr. Noakes here, but if Eugenia should have a premature birth, we will be at your mercy, Mrs. Ashburton."

"You mean Eugenia and the baby will." Mrs. Ashburton's lace cap was slipping sideways; her many chins were tucked into her neck. "You will make yourself scarce, my lad. No place for men. Your wife did very well today, did you know?"

Gilbert looked surprised.

"I told you not to go in there, Eugenia."

"Why not? Although I wasn't of very much help, I'm afraid. But couldn't we talk of something else?"

"Certainly," said Mrs. Ashburton. "In the first place, I am a rich old woman with only one son, who, if he lives to receive my fortune, will go through it in a year. This pleases me even less than it would have pleased his father, who worked considerably harder than most men nowadays to make his money. He was an agent for the East India Company, and he died of cholera when he should have had a long and peaceful retirement ahead of him. And he'll have no joy in eternity if Godfrey wastes his inheritance."

The tight look in Gilbert's face had relaxed. He was a little flushed. He, too, had had little time to eat that day. Suddenly he began to laugh.

"I believe you're enjoying my wine, Mrs. Ashburton. That's more than my wife does. I wish I could persuade her to like it more."

"Never mind Eugenia, Gilbert. If she doesn't care for wine, it can't be helped. It will leave you so much more to sell, eh?"

Mrs. Ashburton, pleased with her logic, began to rock backward and forward with laughter. "I am a practical woman. I face facts. You should have married me, Gilbert."

"I believe I should have," Gilbert said amiably.

This appeared to be immensely funny to Mrs. Ashburton. Tears of laughter rolled down her cheeks.

"I declare to goodness! I don't know what's the matter with me. I suppose I realized today that I was still of some use in the world. And now I'm a little tipsy. I'm only trying to say that since my son has gone off into the blue, leaving his old mother alone, you two are now my family. And I want to replace your vineyard, Gilbert. I don't want you mortgaging the place or getting yourself into debt with your bank. I am prepared to finance you until you repair last night's damage. Please don't say no. I owe you a great deal. You have given me a room over my head, friendship, company. Where would I be without you?" She was quite serious now. Her big, protuberant eyes stared at Gilbert. "I confess that I wish you were my son. I'd dearly like to be a grandmother in three months' time. When is Godfrey going to make me a grandmother? I should suspect never. Or at least not officially. So there it is. A loan, a gift, whatever you prefer. But enough to save your vineyard. You're not going to reject a lonely old woman, are you?"

Gilbert, refilling her glass, said, "Do you really think this is my best wine, Mrs. Ashburton? It was put down in twenty-six."

"I like it mightily. Will a thousand pounds be enough?"

"Mrs. Ashburton, I hardly know what to say—"

"Say nothing. You have an expensive place to keep; you're ambitious. I like that. Why shouldn't you be? I shall have the greatest pleasure in keeping you out of the hands of the moneylenders. It will be my privilege. Now I can rest." As good as her word, the old lady sank back, closed her eyes, let her chin sink more deeply into her chest, and fell asleep.

Eugenia stared in dismay. Gilbert began to roar with laughter.

"That's Yarrabee wine. It performs miracles."

"Gilbert, I believe you have deliberately made that silly old woman drunk. I believe you're drunk, too."

"Haven't I the right to be?" His eyes were lazy slits. "It's been a long day, and now Yarrabee has a reprieve. I won't have to go begging to a penny-pinching bank manager."

His carefree face was so far removed from the tragic mask of the early morning that Eugenia wondered if she had imagined it or the rejection of her sympathy. For Mrs. Ashburton had been successful in removing Gilbert's pinched look of disaster in as short a time as it took to say a few judicious words.

"Does this mean," she asked thoughtfully, "that we will have Mrs. Ashburton as a permanent guest?"

"If she wants to stay. The house is big enough."

"It couldn't be why you asked her in the first place, because she is rich and could be an insurance against disaster?"

Gilbert shook his head emphatically.

"Never! I give you my word. Is that what you think of me?"

"You're very ambitious."

"And I use the means to my hand. Certainly. But not to the extent of using rich old women as my prey. Good heavens, Eugenia, what a thing to accuse me of. I owe Mrs. Ashburton a debt of gratitude for looking after you on the journey out, and anyway I like her. She's amusing; she's good company. She's a welcome guest. And if it gives her pleasure to help to save my vineyard, why deny her it? Don't be so intense, my love. Don't take everything so seriously. Just bless the old lady, and let's get her to bed."

Fortunately, at that moment, Mrs. Ashburton opened her eyes and stared about her in perplexity.

"Bless my soul!" she exclaimed. "Did I take a nap? I must have overdone myself today. If you will excuse me, Eugenia, I think I would like to retire. I'll be as fresh as a daisy in the morning." She attempted to rise, swayed, clutched at Gilbert's arm. "Thanks, my boy. That's remarkably good wine. Yarrabee wine. I think a small glass by my bedside tonight? It will make me sleep."

She tottered out of the room on Gilbert's arm, a rotund little vessel tacking in a strong wind. Halfway up the stairs, Eugenia heard gales of laughter. She sat staring into her half-finished glass of wine, reflecting on its handsome ruby color, praying she was not always going to find it as hateful as she did at this moment. It was a dreadful thing to wish that the whole vineyard had disappeared overnight, so that Gilbert would be forced to turn to sheep or cattle, which were so much less complicated. Or decide to give up the Australian adventure and return to England.

But that last thought was one she didn't dare to dwell on, or she might begin to weep from the wave of longing and homesickness that swept over her.

Chapter 15

CHRISTOPHER JOHN GILBERT MASSINGHAM was born at Yarrabee in the province of New South Wales on the nineteenth day of November, 1831.

A weak, fretful baby, too small for Gilbert's liking, but fortunately tiny; otherwise either he or his mother might not have survived.

The ordeal was something Eugenia tried to forget. She had clung to the carved headboard of the French bed until the skin on her hands was lacerated. Although Dr. Noakes had arrived several days beforehand and had been with her throughout the birth, and although Mrs. Ashburton, too, had kept appearing above her, and disappearing, a huge, floating balloon, neither could mitigate the intensity of the twenty-four-hour agony. She was ashamed to hear herself screaming in a way Mrs. Jarvis had never done.

But afterward she made amends. She would not allow Gilbert to see her until she had the strength to have her hair brushed and to be changed into one of her prettiest nightgowns.

Then he came in the room on tiptoe, his face full of such anxiety and humility that Eugenia heard a breathy sound that was her own laughter.

"Why are you looking so worried, my dearest? I have given you your son."

He knelt beside the bedside, hiding his face in her breast. Eugenia touched the crisp, springing hair and summoned up all her strength to say, "It was a perfectly normal confinement. You mustn't worry so much the next time. I'm much stronger than you think." The tension was slackening out of his body. She was aware of her own small stirring of tenderness and triumph and intimacy. "Aren't I to be allowed to give Papa a kiss?"

It was a good moment. So was the one when she first held her baby in her arms. They were the things she would remember when so many of her vexations and anxieties were forgotten.

It was fun to wear her pretty gowns again and play at being a matron, although she frequently felt much too young and inexperienced.

It surely must be inexperience on her part that caused her small Christopher to cry so much, when Mrs. Jarvis' baby had always been plump and contented. Nothing would pacify Christopher. Eugenia would walk up and down with him, and when she tired, Mrs. Ashburton trundled him around, crooning to him in her hoarse voice.

He still cried and seemed to grow thinner, his angry blue eyes staring out of his ludicrously small scarlet face. When he did fall into an exhausted sleep, the flush died out of his face, leaving it too pale, almost bluish.

At the end of six weeks Eugenia was in despair. She wrote urgently to Bess Kelly for advice. Bess wrote back briefly, "Is he hungry?"

How could he be hungry? He tugged at her breasts until he fell asleep, exhausted. But only to wake in less than an hour screaming once more.

Mrs. Ashburton gave him a sugar rag to suck, and Mrs. Jarvis suggested that Dr. Noakes should be consulted.

Gilbert wanted an elaborate christening party arranged. Although he had not forgotten his nightmare anxiety during the birth, he was secretly gratified that Eugenia fitted so completely into the pattern of delicate, highly bred women who suffered severely at childbirth. Now that she was up and about and looking remarkably lovely—the lingering frailty suited her—he wanted to show off both her and the baby.

"But I won't have the boy yelling the roof down," he said. "Shouldn't you feed him more often? He looks half-starved."

So Eugenia had to face her secret worry. Her breasts had never grown large and overflowing with milk. In the last day or two the baby had tugged at them with such comical anger that she had suspected he was getting far too little sustenance. Bess Kelly must be right.

"Perhaps I could try him on a little cow's milk," she suggested.

"He doesn't want cow's milk; he wants a foster mother." Eugenia didn't care for the critical look in Gilbert's eyes as he studied the slender outline of her breasts. "Give him to Mrs. Jarvis."

"Mrs. Jarvis has her own baby," Eugenia said stiffly.

"And milk enough for two. You only have to look at her. Do it, my love. I'll speak to her myself."

So that was how it was that the two babies lay side by side in their baskets on the veranda on the warm afternoons and shared the same milk. The pleasure of seeing Christopher thriving at last made Eugenia overcome her resentment.

If she couldn't feed him, she could make an exquisite christening robe for him and have the greatest pleasure and pride in carrying him up the aisle of the church on his christening day.

The occasion was something to write to Sarah about.

We had scarcely got over Christmas when this much more important day arrived. Dr. and Mrs. Noakes had come to us for Christmas. Poor Marion could scarcely be dragged away from the nursery; she loves babies so passionately. Gilbert wanted Philip to be one of the godparents, and Mrs. Bourke has asked to be one. Gilbert was highly delighted because of the honor bestowed, and I because I am genuinely fond of Mrs. Bourke. She is rather shy, rather plain, and, I think, as homesick as I sometimes am. Also, she does not appear to be in the best of health and finds the climate trying.

The christening was a rather grand occasion, since both the governor and Mrs. Bourke were there, and two of the gover-

nor's aides, and other prominent people with whom we have
become acquainted in Parramatta. (I do not suppose they
would be prominent in a city, say, the size of Worcester, but
here the butcher, the baker, the candlestick maker are all
prominent and are just as good, if *dull*, people!) Dear Bess
Kelly could not come. She is expecting another baby herself.
And others of our Sydney friends, such as the Wentworths,
were not there because Gilbert did not want me to have too
large a house party. I have been rather feeble since Christopher's birth but am now recovering rapidly.

The church was filled with all our servants, including a
rather hangdog row of ticket-of-leave men. I cannot describe
my bursting feeling of pride when I walked out, carrying
Christopher in his long christening robe, and all the servants
bobbed or touched their foreheads.

The only person of our household missing was Mrs. Jarvis,
who had remained at home to prepare the luncheon which we
gave to twenty people. Gilbert toasted his son with his best
wine. He is laying down a claret this vintage which is to be
kept until Christopher's coming of age or his marriage, which-
ever happens first. I fear that Mrs. Ashburton, as has been her
habit lately, got a little tipsy.

But I do not blame her. There has not been any news about
her son since he left to cross the Blue Mountains and explore
the interior nine months ago. People are beginning to fear
that he is lost. It really looks as if Mrs. Ashburton's home will
be permanently at Yarrabee, but I have grown accustomed to
her now. I believe I would miss her if she left. And Gilbert is
so much in her debt.

But he has now planted many more new vines, and we hope
to be able to repay Mrs. Ashburton after the following year's
vintage.

My dear waspish Peabody was as pleased as could be when
the visitors admired his garden. It is quite miraculous the way
it has developed. The first roses have been in bloom; the lily
pond has been dug, though not yet filled with water since that
has to be piped from the well; the honeysuckle has already
climbed several feet up the veranda posts. This has taken away
the glaring newness of the house, and it is really beginning
to look most attractive, its white façade against the green vines

growing up the hillside. Peabody has made a trellis of nice crooked knotty stakes, and the climbing roses will be a picture next year. I have chosen white; they are like snowflakes and will look so cool. Needless to say, the native shrubs have grown with abandon and are surprisingly pretty, the scarlet bottle-brush, the heavenly blue jacaranda, the myrtle which has a kind of peach blossom flower, frangipani with its honey sweetness, and the scarlet poinsettia.

I am determined that Yarrabee shall be as famous for its garden as for its wine . . .

Eugenia did not include in her letter the last two events of that day. When the visitors had left, Gilbert came to her when she was resting in their bedroom.

He opened his bureau drawer, took out a small dark-green leather box, pressed the catch, and the lid sprang open to reveal an immense diamond and topaz brooch. At least to Eugenia, used to modest pieces of jewelry, it looked immense.

"It's for you, my darling. I kept it until everyone had gone." Then he couldn't contain his pleasure and excitement. "Take it out. Look at it. Put it on."

Eugenia's fingers hung reluctantly over the box.

"It looks—so expensive!"

"Well, it wasn't exactly nothing, but on the other hand, it was a great bargain. I happened to meet a man who had been an apprentice jeweler in Hatton Garden. He set it from some stones I bought. It is meant to be a rose, do you see? I know they are your favorite flower."

The apprentice would have been a convict, of course. She owed her first real piece of jewelry, just as she owed her house, to convicts.

Oh, for goodness' sake, you silly creature, stop being so imprisoned in that old obsession, she told herself, and in the desire to overcome her scruples, she flung her arms around Gilbert in an extravagant gesture.

His face went soft with delight. "You like it, then? I meant to have it for you when Christopher was born, but to be honest, I hadn't enough cash, and I knew you would want to know whether Mrs. Ashburton had been at the bottom of it."

She laughed, although with faint wryness.

"Do I have such bad manners?"

"You! My little paragon!" He kissed her, though gently— he was getting intuitive, she thought—then pinned the brooch to the ruffles of lace at her neck.

"Now you have something to wear besides your pearls," he said with satisfaction.

As inevitably as night followed day, Gilbert turned to her in bed that night.

She had been so long in recovering from the birth of the baby that he had exercised a patience for which she knew she should be grateful. She also knew that she should have gone gladly into his arms. If she could not do that, she could at least perform her wifely duty acquiescently.

But surely there was more to marriage than this—shouldn't there be love talk, longing satisfied, an intimacy so close that even this act was a pleasure?

Was she just being a romantic?

Or was she one of those cold, pure women unable to feel desire?

She slipped out of bed, put on a wrap, and went out to the balcony. These summer nights were beautiful, the air warm, the moon shining over the quiet landscape. The cicadas kept up their eternal song, but she had grown so used to it now that she scarcely heard it. She would have liked to hear the soft *who-who-oo* of an English owl, but failing that, she did have the scent of roses.

She looked back into the dark room, to the long shape in the bed, and her eyes filled with tears. How ungrateful she was not to be happy, to expect something more, something she couldn't define. An intense, inexpressible longing.

But she had her baby. Whatever was the matter with her?

Chapter 16

IT was vintage again, but lacking completely the gaiety and effervescence of the previous year. The harvest was poor. It was gathered in two days. Fortunately, there were sufficient black grapes for Gilbert to lay down five dozen bottles of claret for Christopher's coming of age. He labeled the bottles YARRABEE CHRISTOPHER 1831 and then had to turn his attention to the sweet sauterne that bored him and that he marketed as quickly as possible.

Next year would be a bumper one.

Vignerons, Eugenia had discovered, lived on optimism.

But thanks to Mrs. Ashburton's generosity, no pinch was felt at Yarrabee.

Soon after the new year the tragic news had come that Godfrey Ashburton, dying of starvation, had staggered into the little town of Adelaide on the southern coast of Australia twelve hundred miles away. By the time his poor skeleton had been identified and the news had reached his mother, he had been buried for several weeks.

Mrs. Ashburton had shut herself in her room for two days, then had emerged, suffering, she said vigorously, not so much from grief as boredom.

She had scarcely known Godfrey since he had run away to sea at the age of sixteen. He had been an incorrigible adventurer, a stranger, and what she had known of him during the last year in Sydney she hadn't cared for.

Eugenia and Gilbert and the darling baby were her family

now. That was what God had decided, and she was happy to accept the direction of a higher will than her own.

She would observe custom by wearing partial mourning, black touched with a little lilac, but she saw no reason for not accompanying Gilbert and Eugenia to the soiree at Government House next week. It did no one any good to sit at home brooding.

The soiree was a surprisingly fashionable affair. There were two ladies recently arrived from England, and Eugenia found it ironic to realize that now she was one of the colonials, listening eagerly to news of the latest fashions. To her satisfaction, she found that her gown of white silk with green velvet ribbons was quite passable. She cared for clothes and did not intend to grow dull and dowdy simply because London and Paris were so far away. Also, she hardly thought the two new arrivals had the best taste. Surely the Bond Street shops were not selling quite such a plethora of ribbons and bows or those exaggeratedly full leg-of-mutton sleeves.

She caught the humorous gleam in Mrs. Bourke's eye and found that that lady was having precisely similar thoughts.

"You have probably observed, Mrs. Massingham, that this is going to be a wonderful country for the flamboyant. What do you think the reason for it? A compensation for being so far from civilization?"

"Or that it attracts people who prefer to be big frogs in little puddles?" Eugenia murmured.

"That is a wicked remark," Mrs. Bourke said enjoyably. "It is probably true. But I think, too, that one feels very small in such vast spaces. So, like all those gaudy parrakeets, we have to put on brighter colors to be noticed."

Mrs. Bourke herself wore the most modest of gray silk gowns. She looked tired and pale, and Eugenia noticed that she frequently sat down to rest a few minutes before moving among her guests again. Her husband, who was tall and lean and looked handsome in evening dress, was engaged in talking to the men. He was interested, to the exclusion of everything else, in the welfare of the country and thought time spent in paying compliments to women was wasted if he could be furthering the colony's affairs.

Eugenia caught snatches of conversation, about grants of land, increased grain production, the growing importance of the wool industry, the necessity for a steady flow of a good hard-working type of emigrant, with the essential leavening, of course, of upper-class settlers. One didn't want the country to be run by a hodgepodge collection of freed convicts and squatters. Major Bourke, more liberal than some of his predecessors, did not have an arrogant contempt for the small man or the freed convict. He might have occasionally remembered that his friend William Wentworth's mother had been a convict, although that, in face of Wentworth's growing affluence, seemed more like myth than reality.

Mrs. Bourke tapped her husband on the arm with her fan and murmured that this was a time for pleasure, not business. He should mingle more with his guests. And look, there were some late arrivals who must be welcomed. Did Eugenia know them? They were a young couple who had obtained a grant of land some miles distant. Nice people, but the wife hadn't a lot of poise. Look at her now, in a great state because of the lateness of their arrival.

But it appeared that Mr. and Mrs. Newman had an excellent reason for their lateness.

Wasn't it a ghastly thing? Young Robert Wardell, a close friend of William Wentworth, had been murdered by three convicts. His body had been found concealed under bushes, and later the convicts had been found hiding in the scrubby, uncleared land that formed part of young Mr. Newman's grant. Dingoes barking constantly had drawn the troopers to the spot.

Young Mrs. Newman was blond with baby blue eyes. She clung first to Mrs. Bourke, then to Eugenia, saying wasn't this a dreadful country for women. What with convicts and snakes and those great repulsive lizards, she never took an easy breath.

"How can you look so calm, Mrs. Massingham? Aren't you ever afraid?"

The murdered body flung into the bush, the ragged shadows

with the eerily hopeless eyes creeping silently away, the barking dogs . . . The eternal nightmare . . .

"One gets used to it," Eugenia said. "One has to. It really
isn't that bad, Mrs. Newman, although I admit I felt as you
did a year ago. What a pretty gown you are wearing! Is it part
of your trousseau?"

The girl smiled ruefully. "It was the latest style when I left
England, but now I suppose it is old-fashioned. Isn't it exasperating that we are always to be behindhand in everything?"

It was wiser to embark on trivial talk about fashions in gowns
and bonnets than to dwell on the loneliness of beginning life in
a small farmhouse miles from civilization.

"You must come visit us at Yarrabee," Eugenia said. She was
suddenly ashamed of her own comfort compared with this
young woman's isolation, but when Mrs. Newman said, "It's no
matter; I can endure it for my husband's sake. I could endure
anything for him," Eugenia lost her sympathy and felt nothing but envy. The two young things must be very much in love.

Mrs. Newman, a pretty new face, was swept away. Eugenia,
fanning herself at the open window—the chandeliers with their
myriad lighted candles were very decorative but made the room
far too hot—heard someone saying, "The beautiful Mrs. Massingham. I have heard so much about you. May I introduce
myself?"

The tall young man bowing before her was slim and dark-
haired, with black eyes in a serious, brooding face. He introduced himself as Colm O'Connor. Marion Noakes, the doctor's
wife, in Sydney, had told him about Eugenia.

"She is always singing your praises. I have been looking forward to meeting you. It isn't often one of your sex speaks so
admiringly of another."

Since this last remark seemed to be a question, Eugenia made
an automatic answer, "A deplorable failing we have, Mr.
O'Connor," while trying to remember where she had heard of
this young man.

"Mrs. Noakes told me that if ever I had the good fortune to
meet you, I would certainly want to paint your portrait."

"Now of course, I know who you are. Mr. Colm O'Connor, the artist. Yes, I do remember someone talking of you. I think it was Mrs. Wentworth. You had painted her children."

"That is correct. And if you are about to ask me what I am doing in Parramatta, I will speak the truth. It is not primarily to meet you, although I hoped this would occur, but to make a sketch of Government House." He smiled with a sparkle in his dark eyes. "You see, I am coming up in the world. I am, temporarily anyway, official artist to the government."

Eugenia raised an eyebrow. "Coming up in the world, Mr. O'Connor? Are you not up already?"

The sparkle remained in his eyes. Eugenia found it very attractive. He had the manners of a gentleman, combined with a pleasant informality and originality that were refreshing.

"Well, I can assure you that I am not a ticket-of-leave man, nor do I have a prison sentence behind me."

"Mr. O'Connor! What an extraordinary statement to make!"

"Not at all, in this country. One meets a miscellaneous variety of people, even at Government House. Do you see that person engaged in conversation with your husband? Twenty years ago he was transported for forgery. Now he is a rich landowner and would like to have a part in running the country."

"And my husband, I have no doubt at all, is attempting to sell him Yarrabee wine," Eugenia murmured, her own eyes twinkling. "But how did you know that was my husband?"

"I made a point of finding out."

"Why?"

"I was interested. I wondered who in this room a woman like you would have married."

"And?"

"And what, Mrs. Massingham?"

"If you make a statement like that, you must complete it. Does my husband have your approval?"

"How can I answer that until I have met him? Not that I will be anything but prejudiced since he owns you."

"Owns?" Eugenia laughed merrily. This was the kind of

light, flirtatious conversation she enjoyed and was accustomed to. For more than a year, she reflected, she had had nothing but tedious Australian comments on the drought, the state of the natives or the sheep or the convicts or, more particularly, the vines. She suddenly felt at home, her wits sharpened, her eyes pleased by the graceful appearance of Colm O'Connor. "Because one is married, is one owned? But that has another aspect. Perhaps I also own my husband."

"Fortunate fellow."

"Mr. O'Connor, you are a flatterer."

He shook his head. "No, no. I speak the strictest truth." He smiled, but Eugenia thought that she detected melancholy or loneliness in his eyes. When he went on to say that it was very hot indoors, couldn't they step out on the veranda, she acquiesced at once.

"What has brought you to this country, Mr. O'Connor? Are you a wanderer?"

"Yes. A confirmed one. But not idle. I am preparing a book on the flora and fauna of the antipodes. Later I intend going to New Zealand, though I hear that is much more primitive than Australia. The natives are inclined to be warlike."

"But at least they don't have dangerous convicts at large," Eugenia said. "Perhaps I am foolish to allow this hazard of Australian life to prey on me so much. I had an alarming experience shortly after I arrived here."

"What was that? Do you care to tell me?"

"Oh, a brush with an escaped prisoner. Ever since then I have felt responsible for his death. A well-deserved death, everyone assured me."

"I can see that you are too sensitive. Are you often homesick?"

In the warm darkness, responding to the sympathetic voice, Eugenia cried, "Oh, yes, yes, sometimes I could die of it," before she could stop herself. "There is so much I miss," she added defensively. "Especially one favorite sister, and my parents, and my old home. I have a very handsome home now, but it's new. It takes a long time to grow accustomed to new things, to belong in them. My husband says we are making our own history, but I still prefer a place that already has a past."

"You don't need to apologize for those feelings, Mrs. Massingham. I sympathize entirely. I come from an old house, too. In Ireland. Galway. It has been in my family for six generations."

"Then you're Irish?"

"On my father's side. My mother was English. She died when I was born. Now I have a stepmother and two half brothers and a sister who is the toast of Galway."

Eugenia turned on him passionately. "But don't you miss it all? How can you be happy in this great crude country?"

"At this moment I am very happy."

"That is just being gallant. You have evaded my question." Eugenia leaned over the veranda rail, sniffing at the still-unfamiliar odors of strange shrubs. "At Yarrabee I have planted honeysuckle to climb up the veranda posts. It flowered this summer, and the scent takes me back to England. I sit outside in the dusk and grow nostalgic. My roses have bloomed, too. And I have sweet peas and stock and marguerite daisies and cherry pie."

"So you are bringing a bit of England to this great crude country, as you call it?"

"Don't we all try to do that? What is your bit of Ireland in Australia, Mr. O'Connor?"

"Meetings like this."

"Do you have—many of these?"

"None at all until this evening."

Eugenia opened and closed her fan. She couldn't stay out here. Gilbert would be looking for her. He expected her to shine at functions like this. She should be talking to the emancipists and cattle breeders, the politicians and get-rich-quick landowners. And to their wives who were shopkeepers' or farmers' daughters and none the worse for it, except that it made them desperately dull in topics of conversation.

She was twenty-three-years old, a married woman and a mother. She wore the badge of her husband's approval, the too-large diamond brooch, in the lace at her bosom. Her days of youthful flirtation were over.

"Would you consider it impertinent of me, Mrs. Massingham, if I asked permission to paint your portrait?"

Eugenia's eyes sparkled with delight.

"I was hoping you would ask me that. I would be immensely flattered. But it would mean sittings?"

"Would that be so tedious? Or don't you have time?"

"Oh, I have plenty of time. Plenty," she repeated, thinking that this would mean Mr. O'Connor's coming to Yarrabee, walking in her garden, beginning to make the history of her house. If, that was, his tall, graceful, slightly melancholy figure made any impact on it.

"I would have to ask my husband," she said.

"Would he have any objections? Surely not. He would be proud to have your picture hanging on the wall. Anyway, I am sure he refuses you nothing."

"With my baby, perhaps. I believe he would like that. Yes, you are perfectly right. He does refuse me very little." Eugenia put her hand impulsively on his arm. "Come ask him now. If you have been commissioned to paint Government House, I am sure that he will be impressed. And another thing, I might persuade you to give me some lessons in watercolors. I am reasonably proficient, but not nearly so much so as my sister Sarah."

Gilbert had been looking for her. She caught his look of inquiry when he saw her companion.

She began to laugh, leaning her hand on Mr. O'Connor's arm, as she said eagerly, "Gilbert, this is Mr. Colm O'Connor, who is an artist. He has asked if he can paint a portrait of me and Baby. Please let him. I think it would be the greatest fun."

Gilbert's eyes were on her flushed cheeks. Why did she have to glow like a schoolgirl when she was excited? Because she was excited and she supposed there was no deceiving Gilbert about that.

"What are your qualifications, Mr. O'Connor?" he asked.

"Various commissions I can tell you about. A book I am preparing. But this is hardly the place to talk business. Perhaps I might bring some of my sketches to Yarrabee, where you will have time to study them and decide on their merits."

"I know nothing about painting. The only artistic knowledge I have is in assessing the merits of a good wine. Are you a wine lover, Mr. O'Connor?"

"I scarcely touch it," Mr. O'Connor replied easily. "But I could do a panoramic scene of your vineyards, also, if you wish. It could be a small record of the history of Australia."

"It could indeed," Gilbert said thoughtfully. "I believe I like the idea."

"But I must insist that portraits are my principal forte."

"Very well, you may do my wife and my son. If I approve of your ability. I won't have a hash made of them."

"Gilbert, Mr. O'Connor has painted the Wentworth children, among others."

"That is still not to say I will approve of what he makes of you." Gilbert tucked his arm in Eugenia's possessively. "My wife has the kind of looks that will not be easily captured on canvas, I fancy."

"My plain face," Eugenia protested.

Mr. O'Connor gave a half-smile.

"I am inclined to agree with your husband's assessment, rather than your own, Mrs. Massingham. Then I take it I may present myself when I have finished my present commission?"

As Mr. O'Connor gave his slight, graceful bow and walked away, Gilbert said, "Don't be taken in by him. He may be a good artist, but it's easy enough to see what else he is."

"What?"

"A remittance man, of course."

Eugenia withdrew her arm from her husband's. The glow was fading from her cheeks. "I have never known exactly what a remittance man is."

"Oh, come, my love. You've been in this country long enough. You must have heard the term. It means a man who represents such an embarrassment to his family that they pay him to live in a foreign country; the farther off, the better. The trouble usually lies with the bottle."

"But Mr. O'Connor said he hardly ever touched wine."

"Perhaps not wine. More likely rum or brandy. He'd be all the better to take a glass of wine now and then. It doesn't intoxicate in the same way."

"I won't have you defaming him before you know him," Eugenia said indignantly. "This can't be true. He is so presentable, so pleasant."

"Then perhaps he has reformed. Let's hope so. And I must say it's a capital idea to have a panoramic view made of t e vineyard, as well as your portrait."

Chapter 17

Dearest Sarah,

We are all much enlivened by the visit of a young Irishman called Colm O'Connor. He is painting a portrait of Baby and me sitting in the garden with the house in the background.

At Mr. O'Connor's request I am wearing my white silk dress with the green velvet sash. I have my hair done in one thick curl over my left shoulder. Baby sits on my lap, and as an original touch, Erasmus perches in his cage at my side.

For the first time since I came to Australia, I feel I am leading the kind of life I enjoy. Dressing and playing with Baby, giving orders about meals, supervising Phoebe and Ellen, who are still lacking in almost every virtue but willingness, walking around the garden with Peabody, since he would be extremely hurt if I neglected this important feature of the day, sitting for an hour or more, if Baby is good, for Mr. O'Connor, doing my own sketching, and my needlework when I sit with Mrs. Ashburton, who also would have hurt feelings if I failed to give her some of my time. The day simply flies. Then it is time to dress for dinner. This is a pleasant meal now that the days are shorter and the lamps are lit and the curtains drawn. Mr. O'Connor is an excellent conversationalist. He even persuades Gilbert to be quite lyrical on various subjects. Gilbert is not an easy talker except about the subject he knows best, viticulture. But Mr. O'Connor has that peculiarly Irish gift of making everyone seem witty, even Mrs. Ashburton. I have not laughed so much since I came to Australia . . .

It could not last, of course. The portrait would be finished, and Colm O'Connor would go on his way.

It was a very good thing that it could not last. For Eugenia was perfectly aware of the fact that she was forming too close an attachment to him. She believed that she had known this would happen from the first moment of their meeting. Her heart had beaten more quickly then, and now it beat faster every time she heard his footsteps or his voice. She found herself taking exaggerated pains with her appearance, scolding Phoebe if her lace caps or her muslin gowns were not immaculately laundered and ironed, her petticoats starched, her shoes shining. She went down to breakfast, instead of having it brought on a tray to her room, took a much more active interest in household matters, and even talked animatedly to Gilbert on vineyard affairs.

When Gilbert wanted to know why she was suddenly converted to the fascination of viticulture, she had a moment of guilt and remorse. She was not converted; she still thought the smell of the cellars nauseating, and the hazards of the industry too agonizing. But how could she confess that she merely wanted their guest to see her in nothing but a favorable light, that she was indulging in vanity and hypocrisy. She looked in the mirror and saw that for the first time in her life she was nearly beautiful. She hid her face in her hands in shame, then looked again, telling herself that it was maternity, the natural fulfillment of a woman, that was making her glow like this.

And congenial companionship. She hadn't talked so much since she had left Lichfield Court. She realized how starved she had been for good conversation. Now words flowed out of her compulsively. She sat half in the sun, half in the shade, with the baby playing on her lap, the cockatoo at her side, her stiff white silk skirts spread gracefully, her wide-brimmed leghorn hat with the green ribbons cast negligently on the grass, and talked and laughed until Mr. O'Connor had to tell her to be still a moment; there was an expression he wanted to catch.

He stood in front of his easel in his working clothes, paint-spattered trousers and a cravat tucked loosely inside the neck of his shirt. The sun struck sparks off his crow-black hair. His face was serious and absorbed as he worked. If the baby clapped his hands and crowed or Eugenia made a witty remark, he would look up and laugh. There was an intimacy about their shared laughter.

"We see things in the same way," Eugenia said. "I suppose it's because we have lived the same kind of life. My husband laughs at different things from me."

It was the first faint criticism she had made of Gilbert. She was ashamed of it and bent her head to kiss the baby's plump neck, adding, "Gilbert had a lonely hard childhood. It has made him very strong, but practical and logical. He doesn't have time to talk nonsense."

"And you like to talk nonsense?"

"Yes, I do. One's imagination should be exercised. I like to be fanciful. But this is a country for logic and hard facts."

"You don't belong in it, you know. Any more than I do."

"Where do we belong?" Eugenia asked, her heart beating fast.

"In England, if you like. But more in Ireland. You could have all the whimsy you wanted there. We live on fairy tales." He looked at her consideringly, his brush poised in his hand. "I can see you there, walking in the ragged garden under the great oaks. Your dress trailing in the long grass. Your eyes the color of the mist. That's where you belong, alannah."

This was not whimsy. This was dangerous fact. Eugenia pressed the baby against her breast until he wriggled in angry protest. She listened with compulsive fascination.

"Who could think you could belong here? It's subtlety you need. Atmosphere. Rain the color of moss against the trees. Old gray houses like ghosts. Not savage sun and dust and birds that cackle like horrible old hags. And snakes as ugly and beautiful as sin." He was painting with swift, sweeping strokes. Eugenia knew that he was talking about his own private nightmare. So he had one, too. Her lips trembled with emotion.

"It's the convicts whom I dream about. The men who have

been in chains." She had thought she would never be able to say this to anyone. "One night I watched Gilbert beat one of them. It was necessary punishment, I know, and Gilbert says I must accept this fact. But I never will. I never will. I never will."

"He built you a grand house," said Colm O'Connor.

"I know. But that was for his own satisfaction, too. His vanity, I suppose."

"And you in the house. He has good taste."

"For the rest of my life," Eugenia whispered. She hadn't realized that fact so clearly before.

Colm O'Connor gave her his long, considering look.

"Well, now, aren't we getting too fanciful? It's those poor fellows in the huts down the hillside who are the prisoners, not the beautiful Mrs. Massingham. And aren't we a little too hard on this country? The sunsets are straight out of heaven—or flaming hell, if you like—and the colors of the birds make me feel as if I'm drunk or crazy. And the Blue Mountains have all the mists you could want. Isn't it possible this will grow on us so that we'll even forget the British Isles?"

Us, he had said.

"You haven't seen the black swans on the lake yet," Eugenia said irrelevantly. "I'm never sure whether I think them beautiful or like mourners at a funeral. We must ride over to see them one day. How much longer will the portrait take, Colm?"

The name had slipped out unconsciously. Color ran into her cheeks.

"One week. Two weeks. Alannah."

She couldn't look at him. The caress in his voice had been too obvious.

"It's time I took the baby in. Will you bring Erasmus?"

The cockatoo suddenly fluttered its wings, screeching. Then it said in a low, intimate voice, "Alannah."

Their looks met in dismay. Colm gave the cage a shake. "Holy heaven, you're too clever!" Then he began to laugh, his face so crinkled in merriment that Eugenia had to join in, though less certainly.

"One small Irish word that means nothing," he said.

"Does it not?"

"Well, perhaps a little more than nothing. But let me guard my tongue in front of that feathered witch."

It seemed to be an accidental gesture that he held her arm to cross the garden.

Looking out the window, Molly Jarvis saw them approach the house. They made a handsome trio, she thought, the baby laughing as his mother swung him in the air, the Irishman all attention.

The mistress didn't get that pink in her cheeks for the master. It was a pity that she didn't seem to recognize the honeyed tongue of the Irish. She appeared to be taking the artist gentleman seriously.

"Well, what do you make of him, Molly?"

Molly spun around, her breath hissing with shock.

"I didn't know you had come in, sir. I was waiting for the mistress to bring in the baby to feed."

"I'm hungry, too. Can you put something out early? I want to take the buggy into Parramatta this afternoon to pick up stores."

"Certainly, sir. There's cold mutton or cold pork pie."

"Some of each, Molly. I'll eat in the kitchen."

He had begun to call her Molly soon after that terrible night of the frost when she had nearly lost her baby. He had given her no more than casual thanks for her help that night, but this calling her by her name had been his recognition.

She had been deeply pleased. She noticed, however, that she was always Mrs. Jarvis, correctly, when the mistress was present. She hadn't let herself wonder if that meant anything in particular. Her self-discipline had been practiced too long for it to betray her now. She went about her work as usual, delighting in her baby and finding it inevitable that the other baby, by tugging at her breast, also crept into her heart. It was hardly surprising. He was Gilbert Massingham's son.

"You didn't answer my question, Molly." The deep line down his forehead that came in moments of stress or anger was very pronounced. He had glanced out the window again, his eyes narrowed in suspicion. "What do you think of our Irish friend?"

"I've seen his kind before," Molly said.

"You mean all charm and no responsibilities?"

"And the drink, sir."

"Ah! But he hasn't touched a drop here except a glass of wine at dinner."

"The need will come over him all at once."

Molly looked at the master with her direct gaze and saw him begin to smile in appreciation of her perceptiveness. She knew very well that he admired her for what she was, capable, observant, discreet. She wondered what he would have thought if he had known how often she remembered, lovingly, a drunken kiss in the dark.

He had always been astonished at her adamant refusal to marry that dull little man Tom Sloan.

In a moment, however, his attention had left her, and the frown was cutting down his forehead again.

"Well, Molly, my wife hasn't had the experience of the world that you have. It's a pity experience has to be painful, isn't it?"

Since it was such a beautiful early winter day, as warm as an English summer, Eugenia had the impulsive idea, after luncheon, to ride over to the lake, to show Mr. O'Connor the black swans of which she had been telling him. Gilbert had gone to Parramatta, Mrs. Ashburton was dozing in the basket chair on the veranda, and Ellen would pick Christopher up after his nap. There was no reason why she and her sketching master should not broaden their horizons.

They rode at a leisurely pace down the dusty track and up the hillside until the house and vineyard were out of sight and there were only the low dipping hills, the lonely gum trees and thornbushes, the thin, sharp cries of pewits, and, in a far hollow, the lake ringed with rushes and waterweeds.

From a distance it was like a jewel, sapphire blue, but Eugenia knew that the water was stagnant and scum-covered and that in a drought it evaporated under the blazing sun, leaving only a cracked crater.

Today, fortunately, it was splendidly full, with small waves blown by the wind. And the black swans were there, a dozen or more, sailing in their funereal splendor across the fretted water. Other smaller water birds fussed around the rushes, filling the air with their cries.

Excited by the sight, Colm kicked his horse into a gallop and was off down the hillside to the water's edge. He was a fine horseman, as was to be expected of a man who had ridden with the Galway blazers. Eugenia had anticipated this, but not that his beautifully upright figure with the high-held black head would make such an impact on her senses.

She began to laugh aloud elatedly as she rode after him.

"This is wonderful," he called, dismounting at the lake's edge. He made a sweep of his arm. "The lake may never be exactly like this again."

Eugenia pulled up her horse at his side. She was still laughing.

"It often is."

"Never. Patterns change. Will the sun be exactly at this brilliance, or the wind make just the right amount of movement on the water, or the swans make such a formal design? Or you"— he looked up at her with his extraordinarily eloquent black eyes —"be sliding off your horse"—he opened his arms—"to lay your head against my heart."

"Colm! No!"

"But you can't stay up there forever." His voice was gently teasing. It was her own wild imagination that had read too much into it.

"You are very poetical all at once, Mr. Colm O'Connor."

"Wouldn't I need to be dumb and blind if I were not? The place and the company. Now your look is reminding me that we came here to work."

She nodded, allowing him to assist her to dismount. If her heightened senses had anything to do with it, she would paint a masterpiece.

But how could she have been so stupid as to come here alone with him? She should have brought Phoebe and Ellen and the babies and had a picnic.

And denied the wild life fluttering in her pulses?

Colm was unpacking the satchel of sketching materials. He found a whitened log and told her to sit on it and begin work. He himself intended to move quietly nearer to the water's edge and attempt to get some close-up sketches of the plump black terns which were skittering so busily among the reeds.

"This is wonderful material for my book."

The danger removed a few paces, she pouted. She had thought he would sit near her and observe her work.

And that, she told herself sternly, was silly, coquettish behavior. She must calm herself and work seriously.

This was less difficult than she had expected. Presently she became absorbed. It was quite an hour later that Colm came to observe her progress and comment on what she had done.

"That's good," he said. "That is your best work yet. I believe you have a gift for painting birds. This one in flight—"

"I felt inspired," Eugenia said, without meaning to, and abruptly he dropped down beside her and said with repressed intensity, "I am dying of love for you."

"Oh! My darling! No."

"My darling, yes. And you are no more blind than I am."

Eugenia sat still.

"We shouldn't have come here."

"Here is just another place. I love you as much in your garden, watching you walk down the stairs, listening to you at the piano, playing with your baby." He laid his hand over hers. "Keep on looking at me like that. Your eyes are full of love."

"No," she whispered.

"There's a lake at Lirrisfall in Ireland, too. No black swans, but a white heron. And old trees covered in moss. You could walk there in your white dress."

"Colm, this is all a dream."

"So it is, and I'm a dreamer."

"You can't imagine me there in reality."

That was a mistake. The quick pain in his eyes was a pain in her heart.

"It's only because I don't dare to."

"No, you mustn't. We're both a little mad. I have a husband and a child. As if I need to tell you."

"And you were only half-alive until I came."

She put her fingers over his lips. "Don't say any more. If things aren't said, perhaps they aren't facts."

"I want you, alannah."

She stood up in a flurry. The purpose in his eyes was so clear that she could not sustain his gaze. "I told you not to speak— not to put things in words. We must go. It's late. Gilbert will be home. Baby will be crying for me. He knows I always put him to bed. There. Those are facts."

"Sure, and they are, too. And the light goes out of your eyes as you tell them to me." He reached up and seized her arms. She laughed, not believing his intention. But when she went to move away, she found she could not break his grip. It was so strong that she lost her balance and tumbled forward and was completely in his arms. As he had meant her to be. Perhaps as she also had meant to be, for, mysteriously, her resistance died, and she could not have struggled if she had wished. When he kissed her, such a soft, limp, pleasurable, swooning feeling came over her that she had to cling to him for fear she would fall. She only wanted to be lowered to the warm grass, as he was doing, and her clothing loosened, as he was also doing in an instinctive way.

When he lifted his lips from hers, she gasped, "Don't go away!"

"Just for a moment, alannah." He was loosening his clothes, flinging off his jacket, untying his cravat, undoing buttons.

Eugenia closed her eyes, feeling the sun golden on her eyelids. It darkened to shadow as it was obscured by the down-bending head above hers. She opened her eyes momentarily. Her voice, deepened beyond recognition, said, "It would be better if you were to take my skirt right off. Otherwise, I might be smothered by my petticoats." A small burst of laughter shook her, then died in the golden dizziness and the warmth and the sun exploding inside her . . .

The day had vanished all at once. The sudden antipodean dusk had never seemed so treacherously rapid. The last mile of the journey home was ridden in a blanketing, moonless dark.

"Don't be in such a hurry," Colm said.

"We're late. It was foolish of me not to notice the time."

"Foolish if you had," Colm corrected.

Eugenia's body felt warm and glowing, as if she were soaked in sunlight. She was languorous and dreamy, yet one sharp rational part of her brain kept hurrying her on. Baby would be overtired and screaming. Gilbert would be striding up and down impatiently, as he always did when she was late to dinner. He liked her to be dressed and waiting for him. Mrs. Ashburton would have had an extra glass of wine, which would have made her flushed and talkative.

The cataclysmic events of the afternoon would not have altered the routine of the evening at Yarrabee in the very least.

"Alannah, we have to talk," Colm urged.

"Not now."

"Then when?"

"Tomorrow morning in the garden, while you work at my portrait." She reached for his hand. "It will be better to have time to reflect."

He reined in his horse, holding her hand so tightly that she had to slow her horse to a walk or be pulled from the saddle.

"That's what I'm afraid of. You'll think of your baby, your husband, your house."

"I have to think of them," Eugenia cried in anguish.

"You married a man you didn't love. You don't have to live all your life with that mistake. This is a big country. We can cross the Blue Mountains and lose ourselves."

"Colm, please! We'll talk tomorrow."

He dropped her hand. "I apologize for being so precipitate."

"Now you're hurt. But you mustn't be. I am simply not a person who can easily overthrow law and order. I must have time to reflect."

"Are you sorry that I gave you no time this afternoon?"

His voice, stiff with hurt, made her turn swiftly seeking his face in the darkness.

"Oh, never! Never, never!"

"Then why, in the name of God, are we being so melancholy?"

She began to laugh shakily, then, as he joined in, merrily and helplessly until her sides ached. Although even in her merriment there was something distraught and hysterical about her laughter.

"Colm," she said at last in a sober, profound voice, "adultery is no laughing matter. I can't think why it should seem like a miracle."

At Yarrabee everything was as she had anticipated. The candles fluttered, striking light in the silver and crystal, lying in pools on the polished wood of the table. Gilbert was carving the leg of lamb in his usual expert manner, only Eugenia noticing that the knife moved a little too quickly, betraying his irritation.

Mrs. Ashburton, as was to be expected, was too inquisitive. She wanted to know if Eugenia had caught the sun; she looked heavy-eyed and flushed. Didn't Gilbert agree?

"I think she looks exceptionally well," Gilbert answered. His tone was unusually mild and so different from the sharp impatience with which he had greeted her on her late return that Eugenia glanced at him uneasily. Did her guilt show? She still felt the honeyed warmth in her veins and scarcely dared look at Colm lest the softness of her eyes betrayed her.

"By the way, Mr. O'Connor," Gilbert went on, "when can we expect this famous portrait to be finished?"

"It's almost done now," Colm answered. "There's a little touching up necessary. The truth is, an artist never wants to let a picture go. It's part of himself, you must understand."

"Yes, I can understand that." Gilbert leaned forward to fill Colm's glass with wine. Eugenia made a protest.

"Gilbert, aren't you forgetting? Mr. O'Connor doesn't care for wine."

"I'm not forgetting, my love. But tonight I insist on his breaking his rules. Good heavens, man, you've been my guest for nearly a month, and you've done no more than take a sip of my wines. It's downright discourtesy. Now swallow that and tell me if it isn't nectar. Eugenia, alannah—"

The wine decanter poised in his hand, he looked up, deliberately waiting for Eugenia's startled glance.

"Did that surprise you, my love? I learned the word from Erasmus. Deuced clever bird."

"It's an Irish word," Eugenia said quickly.

"I use it frequently," said Colm. "It's a habit."

"Yes, I must say you Irish have a poetic way of talking. I'm just a plainspoken Englishman. Anyway, this portrait. I believe I'm the only one not to have had a view of it, which seems unfair since I'm the sitter's husband. I want you to hang it after dinner."

"But wouldn't that be a pity before it's finished?" Eugenia protested. Her heart was beating too quickly. She didn't like that bright look of slightly diabolical mischief in Gilbert's eyes.

"It's very charming," said Mrs. Ashburton. "Very charming. Good enough to be hung in the Royal Academy in London. I can't think why Mr. O'Connor isn't in England making his fortune painting duchesses."

"Today at the lake he painted the black swans," Eugenia said. "You must show your work to Mrs. Ashburton, Mr. O'Connor."

"He can do so later," said Gilbert. "I believe you're enjoying my wine, after all, my dear fellow. Let me refill your glass. I must say I would have been insulted if you had left Yarrabee without being able to talk knowledgeably of its wines. Don't you think this one compares favorably with a French Burgundy?"

"I'm afraid I can't answer that, Mr. Massingham. I'm not a wine drinker, as I've told you."

"Then it's never too soon to begin. That's my motto. And I have a surprise for you later. A bottle of Napoleon Brandy that I've been keeping for a suitable occasion."

"What is suitable about this occasion?" Eugenia asked sharply.

"The hanging of your portrait, my love," said Gilbert, giving her his bright, bland gaze. "Surely one couldn't want for anything more important than that."

Against all protests, Gilbert insisted that the portrait be brought down when they had finished dinner. When it was put in front of him, he looked at it for a long time.

At last he said, "It's a good likeness. I'll pay you your fee, O'Connor, and five guineas over."

"I require nothing but my fee," Colm said stiffly.

"Have it your own way. But at least take another glass of brandy with me."

"Thank you."

"I thought you would. There's only one place for the portrait. Over the fireplace in the drawing room. Let us see how it looks."

"Gilbert, it isn't even framed yet," Eugenia protested.

"That can be done later. I am sure Mr. O'Connor would like to see its effect."

Eugenia noticed that Colm had already swallowed all the brandy in his glass. There was a smoky darkness in his eyes, a look of elation and desperation combined. He was beginning to smile, however, for the first time since they had sat down to dinner. He picked up the portrait and led the procession to the drawing room.

Balancing it on the mantelpiece, he stepped back to study his handiwork. It was embarrassing that he should trip over a footstool and fall backward onto the couch, more embarrassing that he should begin to laugh uproariously.

"From this angle, I believe it looks better. Mrs. Massingham, come sit beside me and look at yourself preserved for posterity. There you are, the beautiful pioneer who braved the wilds, bringing grace and civilization to a country in desperate need of both."

Eugenia took a quick glance at her painted self, thinking that whatever new emotions showed in her eyes after this day, she would never look so serene again.

Mrs. Ashburton gave loud exclamations of praise, and Gilbert, his head cocked critically, declared once more that he was satisfied. It had been an excellent idea to have the portrait done. The workman who had made the elaborately carved mantelpiece with its bunches of grapes and twining leaves could now make a frame for the picture. He was a clever fellow who had made an unfortunate mistake at the beginning of his career. But who didn't sometimes make a mistake of one kind or another? Gilbert asked in his friendly manner, stooping to pick up the brandy bottle.

"Who indeed?" said Colm, holding out his glass. "Glad you're so understanding, my dear fellow. I thought at first you were a bit of a bore with your vineyard. Seemed to love it more than your wife." His voice was now a little slurred. His glass tipped, threatening to spill its contents. "Alannah—Mrs. Massingham, where are you going?"

"Upstairs," said Eugenia. "I'm tired, I hope you will all excuse me."

"Certainly, my love," said Gilbert genially. "I won't be late coming myself. I may leave Mrs. Ashburton to entertain our guest."

Mrs. Ashburton gave her high cackle of laughter. She, too, had collapsed into a chair.

"Mr. O'Connor and I will discuss wine. Isn't it splendid, Gilbert, that we have converted him into thinking it not such a bore?"

Eugenia picked up her skirts and ran upstairs. She couldn't face that terrible scene another moment. Perhaps she was forsaking Colm. But how could she forsake someone who had already forgotten her existence? What could she do by staying, except dash the brandy glass out of his hand, and then he would merely laugh and get another one?

A remittance man, Gilbert had said in his intolerably sure voice. And she would never have believed it. Colm was charming, sensitive, clever, lonely, homesick, all those things. But not this other black one. She thought her heart was breaking.

She hadn't begun to undress when Gilbert came up.

He said, "What, not in bed yet? Hurry up, my love. I'm tired. I want to blow the candles out."

Eugenia went across to the bell rope. Gilbert protested. "No, don't ring for Phoebe. I'll help you undress."

As his fingers fumbled for the pins in her hair, Eugenia moved violently away.

"Don't touch me!"

He pretended surprise.

"Are you angry with me? But I told you the fellow was a drunkard."

"Only because you made him one. You kept filling his glass."

"But I didn't pour the wine down his throat. He did that. Willingly, too. I wasn't as cruel as you think. He would have broken out sooner or later. These drinking fellows always do. I had to show you that before you began taking his poetic language seriously."

He turned her to face him.

"You weren't taking him seriously, were you? Riding off to the lake like that without saying a word. I got into a fine state of jealousy. Do you blame me? Come, don't look so tragic, or I'll begin to think you do care for the fellow. He'll sleep this off by morning. He's had only a half bottle of brandy. I'll warrant a whole one is his usual fare."

"Stop!" shouted Eugenia, her hands pressed to her ears. "Must you go on gloating about it? Do you think I'm content to be here with you while Colm—while poor Colm—"

Gilbert's hands came down to press her arms against her sides in a painful grip.

"You're my wife, Eugenia. For God's sake, you're my wife!"

She nodded, her eyes closed, her whole body trembling.

"Did you think I was blind? Did you think I didn't notice the sheep's eyes, the blarney? I let it pass until this escapade today."

"Gilbert, let me go."

"Am I not to touch you?"

"I only wish you wouldn't."

His hands fell to his sides. "Then let's stop arguing and get to bed." His voice was stiff with anger or hurt; she cared little which it was. She watched him begin to strip off his clothes and, struggling with her own buttons and buttonholes, thought that no one had ever told her marriage could be this sad, ludicrous affair—two persons determined to lie at the farthest possible point from each other all night.

There could be no talk between her and Colm in the morning. A little time would have to elapse before either of them knew what to say.

The talk was only postponed, she told herself, as, in the first light, she tiptoed downstairs.

There was a smell of stale brandy in the drawing room. And a long, inert figure sprawling on the couch deeply asleep. Eugenia pulled back a curtain, letting the pale morning light touch his face.

For the first time she was aware of the marks of dissipation. Gilbert had been right; she had been remarkably innocent and unobservant. But a sleeping face was a betrayal, the slack mouth, the lack of animation. The high, intelligent forehead was still there, the slightly hollowed cheeks, the long dark lashes. She loved him unbearably. Together, she was certain, they could overcome his weakness.

Together . . . What a cruel word for lovers who must part!

For they must part temporarily, at least, to allow him to save his face. She had an unhappy intuition that otherwise he would never forgive her for having seen him like this.

She picked up the empty brandy bottle, thinking to remove the visible proof of his embarrassment. Then she went to her writing desk in her sitting room and wrote:

> COLM, MY DEAREST,
> Write to me. Tell me where we can meet. I love you.
> EUGENIA

He stirred as she slid the note into his breast pocket. She went rigid, afraid that he would awake. But he continued to sleep heavily, and at last she had to tiptoe away.

She knew that he would be gone before she came down again.

She could not even begin to contemplate the frightening thought that she had ruined not only his life, but Gilbert's and her own.

Chapter 18

SOMEHOW the long day passed. Unexpectedly Gilbert came to luncheon. He was disturbed because Eugenia ate almost nothing.

"It isn't you who had too much to drink last night." His tone was kindly enough and might even have held a note of apology if she had allowed herself to listen for it. He could afford to be as charming and tender as he liked, since he had so successfully done what he had set out to do. He wasn't looking beyond the present, of course.

Nor, at the moment, was she, for from tiredness and shock she had felt wretchedly ill all morning. She pushed her plate away, saying that she thought she had a slight fever. She would go upstairs and rest. Perhaps later Mrs. Jarvis would bring Baby up. Could she bear to look at her baby's plump, lively face and consider leaving him? The two people she loved most in the world, Colm and her son—which was to be the dream and which the reality?

Colm had said they could cross the Blue Mountains and disappear. She knew all too well the stigma attached to a woman who left her husband and ran off with another man. No doubt it was just as great in Australia as in England, though here one could escape from society more easily. It might even be possible to live an honest life under an assumed name.

When Colm had found her note and answered it, she would be able to make her decision. She could not plan anything today while her head ached so badly.

One day soon she might ride away from Yarrabee, her garden, Peabody, Mrs. Jarvis holding Christopher and making him wave his fat hand, Gilbert narrowing his eyes against the sun so that that lonely look didn't show . . . The little tableau was sharply behind her eyelids. She stirred and awoke with a start as Mrs. Jarvis came in quietly with a tea tray.

A little later the untouched tray brought Mrs. Ashburton to her bedside.

"Now what is it, Eugenia? Are you sulking? I can't abide sulks."

"No, I am not sulking," Eugenia said faintly, but indignantly. "You don't need to look at me in that way. I have only an upset stomach, which is hardly romantic."

"Aha!"

"Mrs. Ashburton, please! You say aha mysteriously in a loud voice that makes my head ache. What are you suggesting?"

Mrs. Ashburton began to give her hoarse, breathless chuckles.

"Really, my dear, for someone who has been expectant once, you are remarkably unobservant. I have been saying to Mrs. Jarvis for the last week or more that you would be telling us your news in your own good time. I have lived too long not to have an instinct about these things."

Eugenia shot up from her pillows.

"Mrs. Ashburton, I will not have my affairs discussed with the servants!"

It was the only thing she could think of to say. What Mrs. Ashburton was suggesting was so totally unacceptable. Yet a frantic calculation told her that it could be true. She had been in such a happy dream with Colm that she had overlooked certain signs.

The shrewd eyes regarded her.

"When is it to be, deary? How long are you going to keep it a secret? Come, child, why are you looking like that?"

Eugenia pounded the pillow with clenched fists.

"It's too soon after Christopher. I don't want a baby now."

Mrs. Ashburton's face was compassionate.

"Are you still remembering that birth? It was a bad one, I admit. I can still hear you saying, 'Brush my hair; make me decent before my husband comes,' when you had barely the strength to lift a finger. Now those were the words of a woman in love. And you were quite right, because Gilbert does take a most exorbitant pride in you."

His baby had been in her womb when she had lain with Colm.

It was the cruelest irony. Their private miracle was ruined. Now she could never go to him. A woman swelling with another man's child!

"But it won't be so bad the second time," Mrs. Ashburton was saying briskly. "Stop looking so peaky, and come downstairs and tell Gilbert. It isn't fair not to tell him. Besides, he needs cheering up. He was terribly worried last night when you were late. I believe he almost thought you had run off with that Irishman."

From sheer defiance against fate, she did as Mrs. Ashburton suggested and went downstairs that evening. But it wasn't a success. Conversation seemed impossible, and after several attempts Gilbert wanted to know if she would prefer to return to her room; she still looked poorly.

"I am not ill," she said stubbornly. "I have recovered."

"Well, your face is the color of the tablecloth and about as cheerful as a starving cat's. Are you fretting for your drunken Irishman?"

He could not have said anything more calculated to bring the color back to her cheeks. She guessed that he had deliberately tried to provoke her.

"I wish you would not use language like that."

"My language is the simple truth."

"He was only drunk because you kept filling his glass with your wretched wine. I hate your wine. There, that's the simple truth, and I have told you at last."

Gilbert began to laugh. He always looked attractive when he laughed, his face creasing, his eyes very blue.

The days when her blood had stirred at his attractiveness seemed very far-off. She could think of nothing but introspective dark eyes, sensitive and perceptive.

"I like that better," Gilbert said. "I hardly thought you had lost your spirit. And you're not telling me anything I didn't already know. You've always disliked the winery and the vineyard, haven't you? I'm not blaming you for that."

She looked at him in surprise.

"Don't you mind?"

"I expected it, to tell the truth. Any wife would be jealous of a profession that took so much of her husband's time."

Jealousy! So that was his interpretation. She stared at him, astonished.

"I can understand," he went on, "that you thought you could provoke me by indulging in a flirtation. I don't mind telling you you finally succeeded."

"And if it was more than a flirtation?"

"Oh, come, I know you better than that. But I let Mr. O'Connor off much more lightly than he deserved."

He took too much for granted! She had the greatest temptation to enlighten him on that point, but because of the baby, she couldn't do so now. Perhaps she would never be able to do so.

"You really didn't have anything to worry about," she said tiredly. "You had already made sure that I was entirely your possession."

It seemed that this was no secret to him either.

"A baby?" he said, pleased. "To tell the truth, I had my suspicions."

"Why did everyone know but me?" Eugenia cried exasperatedly, and Gilbert laughed again.

"Your moods are fairly readable, my love. That is, to your husband. I don't suppose an outsider would understand them in the same way. It's a good thing the Irishman left. I'm sure he wasn't bargaining for painting a pregnant woman."

When she didn't answer, he gave her a long, steady, inquiring look.

"You want this baby, don't you?"

She bent her head. "You know that I always wanted babies."

"Then don't speak in the past tense. You want to have this baby. Isn't that the way to say it? Looking ahead. I want you to be happy. I built Yarrabee for you."

"I know you did."

"You can't make someone happy who won't be happy," he said with such perplexity that her sense of fairness had to prevail.

"Sometimes I am homesick. I can hardly hold you to blame for that."

The note of appeal in her voice had her in his arms.

"Listen, I'll make you a promise. As soon as I have a good vintage, I'll send you on a voyage home to visit your family. This sister you write all the letters to."

She looked up with widened eyes. "But what about the children?"

"Children, is it?" he said elatedly. "I'd like a dozen, if I were to tell the truth. Shall we face that problem when the time comes? What I do propose doing at this moment is writing to Phil and Marion Noakes. We'll get them down for a few days. Phil can take a look at you, and Marion will give you all the gossip from Sydney. That will stop you brooding."

That night, as was to be expected, she was gathered into his arms. He did nothing but hold her closely, although she could feel the restrained passion in his body. She was thankful for his restraint, although she had a small, irresistible, treacherous stirring of warmth from the pressure of a male body against her. She thought so vividly of Colm that the tears squeezed beneath her closed eyelids.

"Look, my lady! That's an Australian robin. Now what should there be about that innocent wee bird that makes you sad?"

Peabody was not to know that Colm had been the person to make her familiar with the Australian red-capped robin, with its jaunty red crest and bosom, as well as with various gaily colored wrens and the charming, flirtatious fantail.

Marion Noakes was interested only in the fact that Erasmus had been banished to the back veranda.

"But he's getting so amusing, Eugenia. He doesn't leave you with any secrets, though, does he? I've heard him speaking exactly in Gilbert's tone of voice, and even if I hadn't seen that lovely portrait Colm O'Connor has done, I would know he had been here. That bird has picked up an Irish accent."

"He can cry like a baby, too," Eugenia said a little acidly. "Mind you, he has plenty of coaching in that part, what with Christopher and Mrs. Jarvis' baby."

"Are you complaining?" Marion asked.

"No, of course not."

"I believe I'd slap your face if you were. You don't know when you're lucky."

"Sick every morning?"

"I'd be sick every evening, too, gladly."

"Oh, poor Marion. Forgive me."

"Forgive you because I could produce only one sickly child who refused to live? What blame is it of yours? But you might give me a thought when you are queasy in the mornings. It'll probably alleviate your sufferings."

"What was Bess Kelly's new baby?"

"A boy. Ten pounds. He nearly split poor Bess in half, and she thought the ugly little devil was beautiful. So did I, to tell the truth."

"And you pretend not to be sentimental," Eugenia said.

The other woman said in a low, fierce voice, "I can't cry all the time. Can I?"

But she could spend a great deal of time playing with the two babies. Rose Jarvis was toddling now, but her world rotated around Christopher's wooden pen. Marion was endlessly amused to see the babies together.

"What will happen to them when they get bigger?" she asked. "They can't seem to bear to be parted at this stage."

"Gilbert wants to send Christopher to a good boys' school that has begun in Bathurst," Eugenia said. "That will be when he is eight or nine. In the meantime, he will have his own brother or sister to occupy him. Rose? I expect she will learn to help in the house."

"She's a bright little thing."

"She's the daughter of convicts."

Marion gave Eugenia a sharp look.

"Are you always going to remember that? She is also your son's foster sister."

"Yes."

"Sometimes, Eugenia, I declare you not only look but behave like the lady of the manor. Just as haughty and frosty."

"Aren't I the lady of the manor?" Eugenia was nettled by Marion's tone of voice.

Marion gave her short, cynical ejaculation of laughter.

"You're an Australian the same as the rest of us. You might have found that out by now if that husband of yours had allowed you to. But being what he is, the romantic fool, I doubt if you ever will."

Eugenia frowned a little. "I really don't know what you are trying to say."

"I'm trying to say you can't transfer one world to another. Or something like that. But perhaps *you* can. I wouldn't put it beyond your ability. Perhaps we need a few people like you here."

"Marion! Don't you like me?"

"Bless you, I love you, you adorable, fastidious creature. But you belong in a hothouse. Not in the heat and the mess and muck of this beginning of a world."

"Isn't Yarrabee a hothouse?" Eugenia said, smoothing her immaculate muslin skirt. "I'm sure that's what Gilbert intended it to be."

Colm's letter, for which she had waited with deep anxiety for three whole months, arrived at last. It was brought by a young, bearded man, riding a tired horse. He told Ellen who answered the door that he had been required to place the epistle in the hands of no one but the lady of the house.

Ellen came running into the sitting room where Eugenia was busy at her desk.

"Ma'am, there's a wild man at the door with a letter for you. You'll have to come. He won't give it to no one else."

"To anyone else, Ellen," Eugenia corrected mechanically.

Her heart was beating fast. She did not need to open the sealed envelope to find out from whom the letter had come. She gave orders that the young man was to be taken to the kitchen and given a meal. She longed to ask him when he had last seen Colm and how he looked.

Discretion and her desire to get the letter open kept her mouth shut.

She took it upstairs to her bedroom, shut the door, and sank down in a chair at the window to read the precious script.

ALANNAH,

You have asked me to write, and I have done so every evening since I discovered your note in my pocket. But most of my scribbles have to be destroyed, for it is one thing to write and another to get a letter dispatched with any certainty that it will reach your hands and no one else's. Now at last I have that opportunity. The young man who brings you this is on his way to Sydney and has promised to stop at Yarrabee on his way.

I am not going to waste time apologizing for that lamentable last evening. By doing so, I only remind you of it, and I do beg you to forget it, for I have not been like that since and will not be again. I am determined to conquer my weakness, for I feel that only by doing so will I ever see you again.

But I want you to know that you live in my heart forever. I constantly dream of that day beside the lake, and I thank you for it again and again. For the more practical side of life I have been working very hard and diligently since I arrived in Bathurst which is on the other side of the Blue Mountains. I have been painting the children of some French settlers, a

Monsieur Édouard and his wife, nice people, talkative and lively. I am also giving drawing lessons to the elder daughter, Marguerite, and we are good friends. Neither have I neglected my book, and have made sketches of mountain flowers, and become acquainted with several new species of birds. You will see by this that I intend to be famous and make a great deal of money, and then perhaps—dare I mention this wild dream? Of an old gray house, and a green garden, and mossy broken statues, and wild primroses under the trees, and mist with a little bit of sun breaking through, and yourself in that house and that garden.

I beg you to answer this letter and to address it care of the Édouards. And tell me that you believe in dreams.

Your wandering Irishman,
COLM

Eugenia read the letter with mingled relief and disappointment.

It seemed that Colm had never intended to do anything so rash as ask her to run off with him until he had something concrete to offer her. So she was not faced with the immediate and painful task of disillusioning him.

This was a relief, and it was illogical to be disappointed that he had not written a wild urgent letter swearing that he would die without her.

He had, after all, survived for three months, and he was practical enough to know that dreams were pretty thin sustenance.

But they were alluring.

The gray house and the green garden, the white doves circling. Eugenia began to smile.

"I have added doves," she would write to him.

Someone knocked at the door.

"Yes, who is it?" she called absently.

Ellen put her head in.

"The master sent me, ma'am. He says are you all right, luncheon is getting cold."

"I feel a little tired, Ellen. Ask Mrs. Jarvis to send me up a tray, with a little soup and some thin toast. I intend to rest here quietly for the afternoon."

"Very well, ma'am."

"I will come in and see Baby at bedtime, of course."

"Yes, ma'am."

Ellen bobbed and withdrew. She was really learning to curtsy quite well, Eugenia thought, sitting back luxuriously and plunging deep into the dream. *You live in my heart* . . .

Baby was enchanting. He crawled and made funny attempts to stand upright on uncertain fat legs. He clapped his chubby fists together and gave deep gurgles of laughter. He was very handsome and knew already that he had a slavish following, especially his foster sister, who delighted in retrieving his toys and handing them to him solemnly.

"She spoils him," Mrs. Ashburton said darkly. "Starting like this in his cradle, that young man will expect women to wait on him all his life."

"And I expect they will," Mrs. Jarvis answered, thinking that Christopher had his father's eyes, deeply blue, very alive. The kind of eyes a woman couldn't resist.

Little Rosie also took after her father, but in this case not so fortunately. Harry Jarvis had had narrow features and slightly slanted brown eyes. He had been a wisp of a man, and Rosie had inherited his small bones, his straight brown hair and the strange tilted eyes. She was a queer little elf. It was possible she would make an appealing enough young woman, but doubtful, Mrs. Ashburton thought. She hadn't any of her mother's handsomeness.

They were all looking forward to the new baby. Eugenia, poor child, who suffered so much in the early months of pregnancy, seemed to have got over that trouble now and was looking much more cheerful. Although she sat at her writing desk too much, writing those endless letters. She was becoming an obsessed letter writer. But perhaps that was as well. It was an outlet for her, now that her social life had had to be severely curtailed. She did little more than drive to church each Sunday and make an occasional visit to her friend Mrs. Bourke, who was ailing and homesick for England.

The baby was due at the time that the grapes began to ripen. So far the weather had been ideal. The vines that had survived the big frost were bearing in profusion; the new cuttings had flourished. One didn't dare to look more than a day ahead in this sort of life, but it almost seemed that both new baby and new vintage were going to be a profound success.

There was one problem, however. Dr. Noakes had expressed it as his opinion that Eugenia was not the type of woman who would have a free flow of milk. So either another young woman expecting a child at the same time must be found, or Eugenia might prefer to try the more difficult method of rearing her baby on cow's milk.

Mrs. Jarvis expressed her opinion that the latter course was the best. Perhaps she was jealous of another woman having what had been her privilege. Maternity had developed her figure. She was a fine, full-bosomed woman now, and it was strange that she had not married again. There were others besides Tom Sloan who admired her. But she kept her eyes lowered, her mouth prim. No one knew what she thought or hoped for. Perhaps she already had all she wanted.

The sun that was so beneficial to the ripening grapes was torture to Eugenia, in her last weeks of pregnancy. She wandered about the darkened room, limp and exhausted. Only in the early morning or in the evening did she venture outdoors, and then she did no more than walk across the parched lawn, pausing now and then to sniff a wilting rose or admire some new feature of Peabody's genius. For it was genius that kept anything alive and in flower this summer. Except, of course, the hardy native plants that blazed with their outrageous crimsons and purples.

Peabody, carrying endless buckets of water, shared the garden with the mistress in the brilliant mornings and warm golden evenings. He paid special attention to the white climbers because he knew she loved them. She looked like them herself in her pale trailing gowns. A bucket of water around their roots revived the roses, but the mistress quietly dried up in the heat, her eyes becoming larger and her face paler as her stomach grew.

When the sun at last sank and the gum trees stood crow-black and lonely against the paling sky, she would revive a little and make some remarks.

"The night stock smells so sweet, Peabody. Could we have more of it next year? And Mrs. Bourke has promised me some carnation cuttings from the Government House garden. Do you think we can persuade them to grow in this rusty soil?"

"Ain't done bad so far, my lady. All the things you thought couldn't be done—the roses and the sweet Williams and the peonies. All flourishing."

"That's due to your watering, Peabody. Suppose the wells were to run dry. Mr. Massingham says that's a thing that can happen."

"The trees will have grown up by next summer. You'll have more shade. Won't need so much water. And I aim to lay gravel on the paths to keep down the dust. I thought of planting rhododendrons down at the bottom. Make a nice patch of green."

"I'd like some lilacs," Eugenia said. "Purple lilac and red and white rhododendrons. It would be nice if we could persuade wild primroses to grow."

"You can't have everything, my lady. If you're going to be able to pick ripe lemons and oranges in your garden, you'll have to do without such delicate things as primroses. You've got to admit some things in this country has their advantages."

Eugenia sighed. "Yes, Peabody. You're perfectly right. But don't you ever get homesick?"

The old man scowled furiously. "I'll give myself time for a thought or two in that direction when I lie on my dying bed." He picked up his gardening fork to stump off. "Primroses is all right in their place. Pale things. I'd give you them if I could, my lady."

At the end of the summer it was Mrs. Bourke, the governor's wife, who was overcome by the heat. She took to her bed; her thin, sweet face that had been slowly growing more and more waxy and delicate turned the color of candle tallow, and in three short weeks she was dead.

Gilbert wanted to keep the news from Eugenia. Mrs. Ashburton said bluntly, "How?"

So the sad information was imparted, and Eugenia said, "Gilbert, if I die when the baby is born, I would like to be buried near Mrs. Bourke. She was my dearest friend in this wilderness."

"What absolute poppycock!" Gilbert exploded with outrage. He didn't know what else to say. He hated melancholy; he would have protected Eugenia from it if he could. Her white face looked like a pearl in the shaded room. She was entirely too quiet. Why didn't she cry or have the vapors or something and get rid of her grief?

He could only tell her that the second baby would be easier than the first. Hadn't Phil Noakes said so?

And there was to be absolutely no question of her going to Mrs. Bourke's funeral. She could have Peabody pick a sheaf of flowers from the garden and he would take them to Parramatta.

Eugenia stirred at last. "I will choose them myself."

This task, however, was not finished, for before Peabody could complete cutting the lilies and the delphiniums, Eugenia had to tell him apologetically that she would have to go indoors; she had a sudden severe attack of cramp.

Her baby, a fragile little female creature not much bigger than a tadpole, with her mother's enormous smoky-blue eyes, was born that night. She was six weeks too early, but she had a lusty cry. When the tiny head lay in the crook of her arm, Eugenia had a feeling of tenderness so deep that it was almost pain. She had not felt like that about her first baby. She wondered why.

"I want her called Victoria," she said.

"Such a big name for such a shrimp," said Mrs. Ashburton.

"If she is little, she will need an important name."

"Then that's settled," Gilbert said.

Chapter 19

By the time the grapes were ready for picking the baby had overcome the disadvantage of her premature birth and was thriving. To Eugenia's delight, she had been able to feed her for the important first weeks of her life, after which the change to cow's milk was made with reasonably little trouble.

The cow Daisy, a placid brindled creature with a crooked horn, was milked morning and evening by Ellen, who had taken on this task at her own request. She didn't want any of those convicts whose hands might not have been clean touching the milk that was to feed the new baby. Little Victoria was her special charge. After all, Mrs. Jarvis had Rosie, and Christopher, too, by tacit consent, since he screamed when he was separated from Rosie.

Eugenia's strong possessiveness about Victoria still puzzled her. The little, large-eyed creature was ineffably precious. She was almost secretive about her love for the baby and kept all mention of her arrival out of her letters to Colm.

How could she have told a lover that she was having another man's child? How could she inflict such pain on someone who was as sensitive as herself? Better that they should both bury themselves deeper in their dream and write things like:

> Yarrabee has acquired a ghost. I thought only old houses had them, but I can swear I sometimes see a tall, thin Irish shadow on the wall . . .

But how explain that she was aware of the ghost less frequently now that she had the new baby to occupy so much of her time? She thought that the intensity of her feeling for Victoria was due to the fact that she had had to accept her as a substitute for her lover. If she couldn't have Colm and that vividly remembered delight he had given her, she would pour all her emotion into maternal love. It was a defensive device nature had created in her.

She was really surprisingly contented. A return of savage heat as late as the middle of March affected her far less than usual. She was too busy to think too much about it. Baby must be kept as cool as possible, and Christopher, or Kit as he was beginning to call himself, must be taught to use up less energy in the middle of the day when the heat was at its worst; otherwise he was too cantankerous to be endured by evening.

It was fortunate that Sarah's latest box arrived from England at this time. It took everyone's mind off the sweltering weather.

They all clustered around it, Eugenia on her knees on the floor, Mrs. Ashburton poking and prying, the maids giving gasps of excitement as the contents were displayed.

A length of gray taffeta—Eugenia made a mental note to write and tell Sarah that gray was a little insipid in this country. One was outshone by the birds.

An exquisitely fine lacy shawl for Baby. A jack-in-the-box for Kit (he screamed with excitement) and a wooden doll for Rosie. Sarah was always eminently fair.

There were lengths of striped gingham for dresses for the maids and a great assortment of ribbons and colored silk. And books, which Eugenia seized with delight. And at the bottom of the box half a dozen cravats for Gilbert.

Eugenia, flushed with excitement, sat back on her heels.

"Kit, darling, fetch Papa. Show him your new toy. Tell him there's a gift for him."

She clapped her hands with pleasure when the little boy understood and toddled off calling, "Papa, Papa," in his high voice.

Presently he returned, followed by Gilbert.

"What's this? When did this arrive?"

"Not half an hour ago. I'm afraid we have made short work of it. Look, I am to have a new gown, and you have six new cravats."

Gilbert folded one around his neck consideringly.

"Seems I'll be the best-dressed man in Parramatta."

"And about time. You were getting decidedly shabby. Perhaps we might give a dinner party?"

"Papa, Papa, look!" Kit cried, holding up his toy.

Gilbert nodded, but his eyes were on Eugenia.

"You're looking very pretty. I believe you're as excited as the children."

"Indeed I am. I do so love a box from England. Look at these books. They'll last all the winter." She brushed damp curls from her brow. "It's so hot. As usual, I can't believe winter exists in this country."

"But you're getting accustomed to the heat, aren't you? You have quite a color. You used to be so pale when the temperature was this high."

"I admit I can stand it better. That doesn't mean I *like* it any better."

Gilbert laughed and swung her to him. Briefly, his hand lay over one breast. She could not quite prevent her tremor as a shatteringly vivid recollection of Colm's exactly similar action that long-ago day by the lake came to her.

Her face contorted. She had thought she had successfully forgotten that forbidden pleasure. Gilbert dropped his hand. He had seen her look of pain. She was sorry about that. She was afraid she hurt him too often, and she could never tell him why. It was a pity, because at moments like this she could not help thinking what a pleasant family they were and that if her marriage did not hold the rapture that only Colm could have brought to it, it was probably as successful as most.

The idea for a dinner party was discussed again, but Gilbert had had a much more ambitious idea. He wanted to take a consignment of wine to Sydney and proposed doing so by ship and having Eugenia accompany him. The sea air would do her good. So would a little social life in Sydney. She must pack her prettiest gowns.

Eugenia's excitement was spoiled by her reluctance to leave the baby. She wanted to go, of course, but how was she to tear herself away from the cradle?

Gilbert was impatient. Privately he intended this to be a second marriage trip. It was time he and Eugenia grew closer again. She had recovered from the baby's birth, and there was an air of maturity about her. After Kit's birth she had still seemed young and girlish, but now, suddenly, she had this indefinable air of being completely a woman. Gilbert found it exciting, but tantalizing, for there was too often a far-off look in her eyes that he didn't understand. It was her eternal homesickness he supposed. He must make renewed efforts on this journey, to persuade her to fall in love with this entirely wonderful country.

"The baby will thrive just as much without you," he said in answer to her protestations. "You know that Ellen dotes on her. If it comes to that, aren't you worrying about Kit, too?"

She frowned a little.

"No, I don't think I will ever need to worry about him. He's so healthy. And Mrs. Jarvis takes such good care of him. But he has an awfully strong will, Gilbert. He has very naughty tantrums. You will have to take him in charge shortly."

Gilbert laughed. "He's only a baby."

"He's nearly two years old. It's time he learned to obey."

"We'll settle that on our return. Young Christopher shall learn his manners. I must confess I dote on the little fellow."

"He's exactly like you, that's why," she teased him. "You're seeing yourself all over again."

"Am I as vain as that?"

She gave her little curling smile that always delighted him.

"Perhaps. At least you boast enough. About your wine, your home, your family. You quite embarrass me sometimes."

"I'm an honest fellow. I say what is true, no more, no less. With you, I have to guess at all your unsaid thoughts."

Eugenia evaded answering that by saying, "When I come

back I intend to take over Mrs. Bourke's charities. There's a great deal to be done. I shall need to drive to Parramatta at least once a week."

"Well, that's a fine way of not answering me."

She laughed and said mischievously, "I am very proud of my home and my boastful husband and my pretty babies. There. Is that better?"

It was unfortunate that Kit caught a cold just before they were due to leave. It made him fretful, and he screamed loudly when he saw his mother dressed in her traveling clothes.

"Mamma, no! Mamma, no!"

Eugenia gathered him into her arms where he clung to her, sobbing.

"Put the boy down," Gilbert ordered. "You're perfectly right; he is spoiled."

"No, Papa! No, Papa!" The little boy's yells grew to a crescendo as he was taken from his mother's arms.

"Gilbert, he isn't well. His forehead feels hot. I don't think I should leave him."

"There's nothing wrong with him but a sniffle. Christopher, stop that noise at once."

Such an imperious voice from his father struck enough awe in the child to dry up his sobs. He stood hiccuping miserably, his angry blue eyes fixed imploringly on his mother. He was very flushed, but that was probably from his rage.

Eugenia tried to loosen the hot fingers that clung to hers.

"Gilbert, I am a little alarmed. Could we not postpone our trip and catch the next vessel?"

"That's out of the question. I have my wine being loaded on board. I want to see that the barrels are lashed down securely. What sort of wine can I present if it's been tossed all ways on the voyage? It has to be treated carefully, like a baby. I've explained that to you before."

"Your son is a baby, too."

"And I don't want him mollycoddled. Where are the servants? Get Ellen to take him to the nursery."

"Now I wasn't being too hard," Gilbert said as they sat side by side in the buggy. "The child has a cold, and he was shrewd enough to play on it. You told me yourself that I needed to take him in hand. So don't sulk now that I have made a beginning.

"Anyway," he added presently, in a milder voice, "he has Mrs. Jarvis, who has plenty of common sense, and Mrs. Ashburton."

"Mrs. Ashburton!" Eugenia said worriedly. "Haven't you noticed how much wine she drinks? She's practically in a stupor every night."

"What of it? She's an old woman. It comforts her. I like to see her enjoy it."

"And you encourage her, my love."

"Certainly." Suddenly Gilbert was in a good humor again. "I encourage everybody to drink Yarrabee wine. I intend to have it served at the captain's table every evening of the voyage. And I hope you will show the ladies in Sydney that a glass of sauterne or a light Burgundy is a very suitable drink for the fair sex."

The firm conviction that she should not have come clung to Eugenia until they were on board the *Tasman Star*. Then the cool sea breezes and the lift of the deck beneath her feet exhilarated her, and her anxiety began to fade. Gilbert was perfectly right. She was a too anxious mother. The babies would do very well without her. She needed the stimulation of a sea voyage. It was so wonderful to get away from the parching dusty heat and to be surrounded by sparkling blue water. She was a good sailor. She enjoyed the dip and swell of the waves. There was room in the little cabin to unpack and hang her gowns. She would wear her prettiest one tonight and drink Gilbert's wine to please him. She would even try not to think too much about her children.

It was possible that she could also escape from her dream about Colm O'Connor and the letter that came every two or three months, by whatever means Colm could find to send it. Her own replies were a long, satisfying outpouring of her spirit.

She sometimes wondered if she could exist without this mental communication. It had become a necessary release.

She had moments of despising Gilbert for being so entirely unaware of her secret life.

And moments of deep remorse, when she determined to make greater efforts to please him.

The trip was a great success. They stayed with the Kellys, who now had five children, visited other old friends, talked around dinner tables until the early hours. Everything was growing so rapidly. The country was being opened up, and men such as Sturt and Hume were beginning to explore. There was talk of the possibility of finding gold. The future was unknowable.

Anticipating its riches produced a constant state of frenetic excitement. It seemed that there were valleys thousands of miles away to the south where grapes might be grown even more successfully than in the Hunter River area. But in the meantime there was nothing to stop the enjoyment of Yarrabee wines. Gilbert had tremendous pleasure in persuading even the hardened rum and whiskey drinkers to pronounce favorably on his claret.

On their last evening in Sydney, Gilbert presented Eugenia with diamond earrings to match her brooch. She made herself shut out the thought of the unpaid debt to Mrs. Ashburton and thanked Gilbert warmly. The earrings were beautiful. She would have the greatest pride in wearing them.

She also made a private resolution to be less critical of Gilbert—for instance, it had been mean-minded of her to think of Mrs. Ashburton's debt. Gilbert was impulsively generous and deserved a generous response. She must also be practical and philosophical about the more intimate aspect of this gift. Gilbert would expect a loving wife in his arms tonight, and there was no use in allowing her whole body to stiffen with the knowledge of her disloyalty to Colm. This was how her life was, and she must now decide to make the best of it.

Besides, she had lately formed the surprising notion that if Colm were not so vividly in her mind, she might be able to turn to Gilbert wholeheartedly. That old nightmare was no longer so irrevocably associated with him. It was strange how it was slipping away. All the same, she was desperately eager to get home to her children. And to her writing desk.

Her thoughts were pleasurably occupied with the possibility of there being a letter awaiting her at Yarrabee as the *Tasman Star* dropped anchor in the little harbor at Parramatta. Ellen had instructions that if any traveler arrived, as one had done several times previously, carrying a communication from "a friend in Bathurst," she was to take personal charge of the letter until the mistress returned.

Unexpectedly, Ellen was one of the little group waving from the jetty.

Eugenia saw her at once and clutched at Gilbert's arm.

"Gilbert, there's Ellen! Who can have given her permission to leave Baby? I wish they would hurry with the gangway. I can't wait to hear about the children. It's been so long. Not a word for three weeks."

"You knew that had to be, my love. Be careful! Don't fall overboard."

Gilbert pulled her back as she leaned too far, struck by a stabbing fear. For she had suddenly noticed that Ellen's round face was wet with tears. And Mrs. Ashburton, dressed in black, stood beside her.

"There's something wrong," she said. "It must be Kit! You remember he had a cold. Oh, please don't let it be—" She was biting her gloved fingers, her mind filled with all the small graves that were talked about so much, with Marion Noakes' empty face, with Bess Kelly stoically filling a too suddenly vacated cradle.

Gilbert leaned forward, calling vigorously, "Mrs. Ashburton! Everything all right?" He put an arm around Eugenia. "You jump to conclusions too quickly." But his grip was unnaturally hard. He had felt the tension, too. There wasn't a smile among the small waiting group of people.

He called again, attempting a joke. "Don't tell me that Yarrabee has burned to the ground."

Mrs. Ashburton started to say something, but her voice came out in an unintelligible croak. She was a great plump crow in her black garments in the brilliant sunshine.

The gangway was secured. The passengers began to press down it. A hand held Eugenia back.

"Mrs. Massingham." It was the captain. His round red-bearded face was suddenly different, seared with compassion. "Will you step into my cabin? I have some news for you."

"Tell us here," Eugenia said tightly. "It's our little boy, isn't it?"

"Not your little boy, ma'am. He's recovering. It's your baby. Your friends have sent a message asking me to break the news."

Eugenia put her face in her hands. The blackness surged up inside her. Behind her closed eyelids a picture was printed so vividly that she might have been standing in the dried cracked bed of the creek, reading the inscription burned into the crooked cross. The child's grave. And the letters now read VICTORIA . . .

She had always known that grave lay there waiting for one of her babies . . .

"My love! Come sit down. The captain's sending for some brandy. Come."

She knew at once that Gilbert was intensely relieved that the victim was not his son. She could hear the relief in his voice.

It was natural. He loved his son, and he hadn't yet got to know the ineffable sweetness of his daughter. She had been like one of Peabody's white rosebuds.

Had been!

A storm of violent rage swept over Eugenia. All her old prejudices were back; nothing had altered. She tore herself away from her husband's protecting arms.

"I told you Kit was ill. But you couldn't stay; you said your wines would be spoiled. They were the most precious thing. We had to think of them first. So we sacrificed our baby instead!"

Her voice was so wild that everyone was staring. Gilbert tried to take her hands, telling her to hush, but she snatched them away and, pushing her way through the curious knots of passengers, fled down the gangway and ashore.

"Hush, little one, hush!" Mrs. Ashburton's voice was infinitely loving and soothing. "It was the scarlet fever. She didn't suffer long. And Kit is almost himself again."

Mrs. Ashburton's black bosom smelled of stuffiness and lavender water. Her purpled face had aged shockingly. Eugenia had to lift her heavy eyes and contemplate that change.

She turned to Ellen.

"You cared for her, Ellen?"

"I held her in my arms, ma'am."

"You might have caught the disease yourself."

"As if I cared!"

Gilbert had joined them.

"Let us all go home as quickly as possible. Has Sloan brought the buggy?"

Eugenia said with automatic courtesy, "Mrs. Ashburton and Ellen must have had a dreadful time. While we were—" Her voice trembled uncontrollably.

"Now don't you blame yourselves for anything," Mrs. Ashburton said vigorously. "We would have sent for you if we could. But since we couldn't, we had the doctor stay three days until Kit was out of danger. That Rose, that charity child," she added vindictively, "didn't even get a spot on her. And if the Lord in heaven thinks that is fair, I don't."

Chapter 20

WITH some of the proceeds of the sales of his wine in Sydney, Gilbert had an expensive tombstone in the form of an angel with folded wings erected over the baby's grave. He was unhappy that Eugenia would never go to see it.

She preferred to walk down to the creek instead, holding her parasol at its habitual elegant angle over her head, and sit for a long time beside the poor grave of the unknown child with its nailed sticks for a headstone. When she came back to the house, her face was sad and empty, her manner vague. Dr. Noakes had come from Sydney. His advice to Gilbert was to give Eugenia time to recover. Women took these things hard at any time, but especially when they were in exile.

But Eugenia would be all right. After all, she still had the boy, and she would have more children. Just give her time. The excessive antipathy she had toward the vineyard would also lessen. At the present time she had to fix the blame on something.

Actually, Eugenia had made a difficult apology to Gilbert for her thoughtless and unfair remarks. It was not his wine but her own deep love for the baby that was to blame. It gave her a feeling of guilt that she had dared to love anything so much.

She would grow out of that morbid notion, Gilbert was sure. All the same he was deeply uneasy about her. He had gone wrong somewhere with her. How? He had been a good husband, generous, more tolerant than most. He had had to stop that nonsense with the Irishman, but that was over long ago. And he understood that he had a wife of excessive sensibility, but he had been long-suffering enough about that. Occasionally, after the baby's birth, he had sensed her almost within his reach. If she didn't fly into his arms, at least she didn't shrink from him. There was often a warm, laughing gaiety in her eyes. Then this damnable tragedy had happened, and she had removed herself so far from him that she might have been perched on some chilly star.

Patience, Phil Noakes had advised. But he was getting sick and tired of patience.

It was 1833, and the convicts continued to arrive in greater numbers than ever. The ships, with their strange assortment of living creatures, convicts in fetters, sheep, goats, pigs, turkeys, ducks, pigeons, as well as their unofficial cargo of rats and cockroaches, set sail from Portsmouth and three or four months later came up Sydney Harbour, a pleasant sight with their billowing sails. Closer inspection was not to be recommended. Their cargoes had deteriorated appallingly. The surviving human population was skin and bone with vermin-filled hair, rotting teeth, diseased bodies. It was difficult to find an able-bodied man or woman who would be capable of a reasonable day's work.

But conditions had improved in the colony. There was ample food now that the sheep and the grain industry were established. A few weeks ashore, and prisoners whose crimes did not warrant their being sent to the coal mines at Newcastle were available for hire.

From the last ship arriving, Gilbert, who needed more labor at Yarrabee, chose a fourteen-year-old boy because the lad's look of stubborn courage pleased him. A few weeks of good food would make that emaciated adolescent body fill out. The breadth of bone was there, if not the flesh. The boy's name was Jemmie McDougal. He spoke well because, he said, his mother had had schooling. She had taught him to read and write. But his father had liked the bottle and had taken the money his mother earned as a laundress and also the miserable pittance Jemmie and his sister brought home from the cotton mill where they worked. So there was never enough to eat, and one day he began to steal. Not much. A loaf of bread, a bun, apples, a bit of fish, once a whole chicken. It was only food to keep them all alive. He became adept and had been doing it for six months before he was caught.

They didn't hang him. They said he was too young. They transported him instead. And now he didn't know what had happened to his family. He supposed he would never know.

But he was too young for misery to last. Gilbert had seen the spark in the lad's eyes when he contemplated the vast horizons. He realized the boy was feeling as he had himself on his first sight of the country, awed and dazed and tremendously excited.

So he took him to Yarrabee and told Tom Sloan to keep a fatherly eye on him. They could make something of him, perhaps. At least the boy would be given a chance.

One day soon after Jemmie's arrival, Gilbert, in the winery racking off ten gallons of claret, felt himself being watched. He turned sharply and saw the boy standing in the shadow. Realizing he was discovered, Jem moved like a cat.

"Stop," said Gilbert peremptorily.

Cautiously the boy turned.

"It's all right. I'm not going to beat you. Why have you come here? To steal?"

The boy winced. The stubborn chin went up.

"No, sir!"

"Then what?"

"I was watching. I want to learn."

"To make wine?"

"Yes, sir."

"You're interested, eh?"

The boy took an impulsive step toward Gilbert.

"I was watching you filling the bottles. You don't fill them right to the top."

"That's to allow ullage. Air space. There must be just the right amount. Too much, and the wine will go sour; too little, and it can't breathe. The cork must be sound and bottles laid on their sides. Come and I'll show you. The thin weak wines I market immediately, but a good vintage like last season's, when the color is a good ruby red, and there's a broad, earthy flavor with just a hint of acid tang—those are the wines for keeping."

"How long do you keep them casked, sir?"

"This one has been casked for two years. Now it has a bouquet. Like to smell it?"

"Yes, sir."

Gilbert poured a little wine into a glass, nosed it, then handed it to Jem, amused and pleased to see that the boy exactly imitated his action.

"It's fine, sir."

"How do you know?"

"It smells good."

"You're right, it is good. This is Yarrabee Claret. It will be on the governor's table in four or five years' time. Well, now you're down here, you can give me a hand. I want all those bottles and corks washed. No soap in the water. When the wine's in the bottle, I put the cork in with a mallet. Like this. Always hold the bottle with a gloved hand. Then dip the neck in melted sealing wax and stamp the Yarrabee crest on it. Do you follow?"

"Yes, sir."

"Then get on with washing those bottles. And when you want to come here again, ask permission."

"I'm sorry if I did wrong, sir."

"No, no, you might be useful if you're interested. Not everyone cares for the smell of a winery. My wife finds it nauseating."

The boy stared in disbelief. Gilbert had to laugh again, but with tolerant amusement. The lad spoke well. It might be a good idea to train an apprentice, someone who could take over if he were unable for any reason to do things as the strict routine demanded. The boy said he could write, so he would teach him to keep the record book. He could begin today by writing,

"Ten gallons claret made 1832 racked off. Thirty gallons muscat made 30th April turned . . ."

If Jem McDougal, aged fourteen and a convicted criminal, was as interested as he seemed, it looked as if he might be at Yarrabee long after he got his freedom.

Eugenia kept Kit at her side a great deal. For some time after his illness he had been pale and peevish, and she had watched him with constant anxiety. But now he had recovered all his chubbiness and was restless when he was shut in the little sitting room with Mamma.

"Rosie!" he would shout imperiously, banging the closed door with his fists. "Kit wants Rosie."

Eugenia had tried hard not to share Mrs. Ashburton's prejudice against Mrs. Jarvis' little girl, simply because the child had contrived to escape the deadly scarlet fever. But she was growing increasingly impatient of Kit's devotion to the plain child with the slanting topaz eyes. She was like a little pale fox with her triangular face and wispy brown hair. She had a way of appearing in places where she should not be and then disappearing, always silently. One couldn't complain to her mother that she was a nuisance because she had always vanished before the complaint could be made.

In any case it would have been of little use because Kit would have burst into loud sobs and demanded that her banishment end. He wanted her with him wherever he was. Finally, it was easier to let him go to the kitchen quarters, rather than endure the poking silent little girl in the drawing room or Eugenia's sitting room.

It would have been different if Victoria had lived, to provide a playmate for her brother.

So usually Eugenia's only company at her writing desk was Erasmus in his cage. She could then write in her secret letters to Colm, "When Erasmus says 'alannah' in exactly your tone of voice, it seems as if you had never gone away . . ."

She believed that if she had not had her letters to Colm and to Sarah she would have died of grief and loneliness.

DEAREST SARAH,

I know you must be getting weary of hearing about my sorrow, but I still miss my little Victoria every hour of the day. I constantly blame myself for having left her when she was so young. If I have another child, it shall not leave my sight for the whole of its first year . . .

But would she ever have another child? Because since the baby's death she had not been able to endure Gilbert near her. She did not attempt to rationalize her feelings, nor was she moved by the look of hurt and pity in Gilbert's eyes.

Without any embarrassment she allowed him to ask the servants to have another room prepared for him. Nor did she wonder or care what the servants thought. She had the big French bed to herself at last. She sank into its comfort mindlessly.

You ask me to tell you about Christopher's little ways. I am sorry to say that he became very spoiled when Baby left us, and he has still to overcome his naughtiness. His father has temporarily forgotten his intention to take the child in hand because he is engaged in teaching a new employee the secrets of winemaking. He is, of course, one of the convicts whom the English government will persist in sending out here.

All the same, I must be fair, and say that this lad seems better than most. Gilbert declares that he is honest, and that even if he were not, his flair for viticulture would compensate for a lot of sins. I do not know how his father will take it if Kit grows up to share my present strong aversion for wine . . .

The winter was exceptionally mild. It seemed as if the frosts had scarcely begun before they were over, the duckling-yellow wattle was in bloom, and the first daffodils to grow in the red Yarrabee soil were sending up their green spears. The fresh brilliant mornings were a riot of birdsong. The willows down at the creek were bursting into leaf. One hot afternoon when the first lizard appeared, sunning itself on the veranda, Eugenia knew it was time to get out her parasol again.

But the days were still miserably long. Eugenia made little jackets for Kit, since he would soon be out of petticoats, and then, relenting her hostility, took great pains over embroidering a sprigged muslin dress for Rosie. More and more merchandise was arriving by the now regular fleet of ships from England. It was possible to buy a great many varied goods in the drapers' and haberdashers' shops in Parramatta. Eugenia drove into town in the buggy and shopped, buying skeins of colored silks for her tapestry, ribbons to refurbish an old bonnet, buttoned boots and sailor hats for Kit, and a length of lilac lawn for a new gown.

When she had shopped, she paid calls or attended a meeting of her charity, the Parramatta Women's Benevolent Society. She became a familiar figure driving down the dusty street, sitting very erect, her bonnet ribbons tied securely beneath her chin, her gloved hands lightly holding the reins. Her maid Jane had never stopped fretting for England and had finally decided to return home, accompanying a family en route for London. So it was Phoebe or Ellen who accompanied the mistress, sitting in the back seat. Sometimes her little boy perched at her side, a handsome little fellow clutching his straw hat.

The young women newly arrived off ships and in need of positions were at first intimidated by Mrs. Massingham's dignity and her probing, serious eyes. But her soft, sympathetic voice eventually lured them into blurting out all their terror and unhappiness. It became the ambition of most of them to work in the big house at Yarrabee. The one or two who heard the gossip that things were not as they should be, that the master was shut out of the mistress' bedroom, refused to believe it.

Or if it were so, it must be Mr. Massingham's fault. Mrs. Massingham was so sweet, so kind, so gentle.

And spent so many hours at her writing desk . . . And the spring days grew longer and warmer, and no one's patience could last forever. Certainly not that of an impatient man like Gilbert Massingham.

He chose an evening when Eugenia had seemed happier and more friendly. He didn't want to risk another rebuff, but she had laughed at dinner, and her eyes had been bright and lively.

He had never been faithful to one woman for so long with so little reward. He had not expected to have to practice celibacy when he had a healthy wife.

Give her time, Phil Noakes had said. Now he had done so. It was spring, and he had no intention of being patient any longer.

"You haven't sung for a long time, my love," he said.

"I haven't felt in the mood."

"You would if you began. I've missed your singing."

"So have I," mumbled Mrs. Ashburton, sunk deep in an armchair. She had, as usual, dined and drunk fully, and now was dozy, her puce satin exactly matching her complexion.

"You can't grieve forever," Gilbert said.

"The only way to stop grieving is to fill the cradle again," Mrs. Ashburton observed. "I wonder you've waited so long."

Eugenia had made an indecisive move toward the piano. At Mrs. Ashburton's remark she stopped, and in the dreamy way that had become habitual to her she said that she was sorry, she could not sing tonight, she had some letters she must finish to catch the next English mail.

The door of the sitting room closed behind her.

"Oh, dear me! In the end she'll have nothing but writer's cramp," Mrs. Ashburton remarked to the ceiling.

Gilbert paced up and down for a few moments, then, coming to a decision, went to the sitting-room door and flung it open. He was not drunk, but he had taken a little more than usual to make his tongue persuasive.

Eugenia, absorbed in her letter, did not hear him come. She had a clear, flowing script. The words, "My beloved," at the top of the sheet of notepaper were all too visible.

Gilbert put his hand out and snatched up the notepaper. Eugenia stiffened, giving a startled exclamation.

"My beloved," Gilbert read out. "Now whom, I wonder, do you address in such intimate terms?"

"Gilbert, this is unforgivable! My private correspondence."

"So private?"

"All correspondence is private. I would never dream of reading your letters."

Gilbert was holding the letter close to the candlelight, frowning over the contents.

"If I had written one like this, you would have every right to read it." He began to read aloud, his voice full of outrage. " 'My beloved, It is now nearly three months since I last heard from you. As usual, you see, I am counting every week, every day. Your letters are such a source of life; without them I sometimes think—' "

"Gilbert, stop!" Eugenia said with intensity.

"You sometimes think what?" Gilbert asked curiously. "Tell me."

Eugenia sprang up. Her chair fell over with a clatter behind her. The candle flames dipped wildly.

"I find this an intolerable intrusion."

"But you can't go on locking yourself away, can you? First in your bedroom, and now in your sitting room. Am I soon to be locked out of my own house? Now tell me"—his voice was short and hard—"who is this letter to?"

"To my sister, of course. You know I write regularly to Sarah."

"Regularly seems to be an understatement. You sit at this damned desk pouring out your life to her. Or to someone. And I do find it extraordinarily difficult to believe that you address your sister as 'my beloved.' Isn't that a little extreme, even taking into consideration family affection? You never address me by that term."

"Gilbert, please lower your voice. Mrs. Ashburton will hear."

"The whole world can hear as far as I'm concerned. I believe you are hoodwinking me. This letter is to a man. Isn't it?"

Eugenia lifted her chin, suddenly reckless.

"Yes, it is. I admit it. And if you hadn't been so complacent and blind all these months, you would know who the man is."

"Complacent!" Gilbert echoed in disbelief. "Complacent!"

"Yes, that is the word. I haven't misused it. Because if you think I can forget my deeper feelings simply because Mr.

O'Connor was banished in that very summary way, you are not only blind and complacent, but stupid as well."

"You're telling me that you've been conducting a correspondence with that drunken Irishman all this time!"

"Yes. I have."

If he had not been so outraged, Gilbert would have noticed how well she looked, with her eyes flashing and her head high. But all he wanted to do was to slap her face hard, making the mark of his palm on her cheek. He had to clench his hands.

"Eugenia, you're not in love with him. That's impossible. You had a flirtation. But that's more than a year ago."

"How long is a year?"

"Long enough," he shouted. "You've had my child in that time. Are you mad?"

"Your child died," she said. "And I'm not mad."

"Then what? Have you an obsession for living in letters? You wrote enough to me once upon a time. Don't you remember?"

"I remember."

"Then didn't I live up to your dreams? Do you think your drunken Irishman would live up to them if you had him falling into your bed every night? Do you?"

She winced. Suddenly she covered her face with her hands. Gilbert pulled them away, making her look at him.

"Well, drunk or sober, I intend to come to your bed tonight. I've had enough of this farce. Being patient because I thought you were grieving for the baby, and all the time I find you writing sentimental rubbish to another man! Is that a fair way to behave? Aren't you ashamed of yourself?"

"You're being horrible," she whispered.

Abruptly he vented his anger on her desk, kicking at it until the delicate wood splintered. When Eugenia gave a cry of pain, he said furiously, "I'd like to knock it to pieces! You sit here all the day living in your damned dream. Wake up, for God's sake! That black Irishman had no substance even when he was with you. You both only lived in the past. I've listened to you.

Mourning for Irish rain and English mist and snowdrops and God knows what. Let me tell you something. If you went back to your beloved English mists, you'd hate them. You'd fret for the sun. You think you have too much of it, but wait until you lose it. You'll find you can't live without it."

"No, it's the other way," Eugenia cried. "I can't live with it. It's burning me up!"

"Why are you two making such a lot of noise?" came Mrs. Ashburton's querulous voice from the doorway. "You've ruined my nap. Are you quarreling? I declare to goodness!" Her eyes protruded with surprise, as she saw their stiff hostility. "I don't suppose you want to listen to an old woman's advice, but if you do, I can tell you the best place to make up a quarrel. And high time, too, if I may say so."

"You may not say so," Eugenia said icily. With deliberation she took the piece of notepaper Gilbert had been holding, tore it to shreds, then, with the same deliberation, lifted up her skirts and walked from the room. She went straight upstairs. A little later there came the distant but distinct bang of her bedroom door.

"I declare to goodness," said Mrs. Ashburton again, "it's time that young woman had another baby."

"And so she shall," Gilbert promised.

But no one could make love through a locked door. And it seemed that Eugenia had no intention of opening it.

Her voice was far-off, chilly with distaste.

"I would like to be alone. It would be a good thing if you could refrain from waking the whole house."

"Eugenia! Damn you!"

Gilbert had thought he had lost his temper pretty thoroughly when he had nearly kicked her writing desk to pieces, but this was worse. He never remembered being in such a rage. He stamped down the stairs and out of the house. At the stables he shouted until someone came running. It was young Jem McDougal.

"Can you saddle a horse in the dark? Then give me a hand."

"Yes, sir. Is there trouble, sir?"

"None of your damned business. Keep your mouth shut."

He leaped on the saddled horse and rode to Parramatta, galloping all the way. At the first hotel he came to he dismounted, strode in, and ordered rum.

The barkeeper recognized him.

"Mr. Massingham! I heard as you never drank anything but your wines."

"Then you heard wrongly."

There had been occasions in the past, before Eugenia had come to Australia, when Gilbert had looked for and found a woman in one of these small shabby places. The two of them had wandered down to the river and lain on the hard dry earth, and it had been good, swift, relieving, temporary. He was telling himself, as he drank the now-unaccustomed fiery rum, that it could be good again. It would ease the hot anger and resentment that throbbed through the whole of his body. He had been faithful to one woman for three whole years, and she a pretty cool woman, too, who at the best of times had done no more than tolerate him.

Now she had had the effrontery to lock him out of his own bedroom, and yet here he was, brooding over his drink, realizing that he no longer had any taste for a blowsy barmaid. He must have become addicted to his wife's fastidious elegance.

But surely not to chastity!

Even the drink, fuddling his brain and relaxing his knotted nerves, couldn't make him accept this incredible fact.

Nevertheless, before midnight he was on his horse and riding home. It was a still, soft night, the warmth of early summer in the air. The ride cooled his brain slightly but still left him tense and restless, his mind full of images of soft breasts and slender legs. Hair spread over a white pillow, lips seeking. Damn it, damn it, damn it!

And there, as he rode slowly up the drive toward the house, was one of his images in reality. Surely that white form walking in the garden was Eugenia.

Eugenia, anxious, and looking for him?

He sprang off the horse, dropped the bridle over the

gatepost, and walked across the lawn a little unsteadily, the rum getting at his legs.

The figure had moved behind the bushes and disappeared. No, there it was going softly, along the veranda in the shadow.

"Wait!" Gilbert hissed, and the figure abruptly stopped. He saw the pale blur of the back-turned face.

Someone in a long wrap, her long blond hair falling over her shoulders.

"It was warm. I couldn't sleep," whispered Molly Jarvis.

"Neither could I," said he.

They stood absolutely still, a few paces separating them.

"I heard you riding off," Molly said.

"And that was why you couldn't sleep." It was a statement, not a question.

"No. No, I was hot. It's going to be an early summer."

Gilbert made one quick, instinctive, inevitable movement.

"It's summer now," he said, holding her warm, soft, ample body in his arms, seeking for her lips amid her thick, falling hair.

"Your room?" he said a little later. "We can't stay here."

"Rosie!" she protested.

"She won't wake."

He thought dazedly that if she had let go of his hand, he might have been able to come to his senses. But their fingers were locked together, hers as tight as his. He could hear her fast breathing.

The French doors to the little room at the end of the veranda were open. A small cautious part of his brain registered that the next room was the dairy. They would not be overheard.

It only remained for them to tear off their clothes, he his shirt and trousers, she her loose wrap and nightgown, which she let fall to her feet.

And it seemed as if he had never been with a woman before. It was fresh and amazing and miraculous, and he had forgotten how triumphant it was to hear that female cry of pleasure.

Afterward she was silent for so long that he thought she must have fallen asleep.

"Molly!"

"Yes, love."

"I've always wanted you. I tried not to believe it."

"And I the same," she said simply. "What are we going to do?"

"Love each other."

She moved her head.

"Stop doing that with your fingers in my hair. It makes me daft. I mean, what about the mistress?"

"She has locked me out tonight. I expect you knew."

"I heard something. I feared."

"You feared right."

"I can't be disloyal to her in her own house."

"Too late," he said, without irony.

He kissed her forehead, the tip of her nose, her throat. His head moved down toward her breast. She could not prevent a sigh of pleasure.

"We must talk, love."

"Not now. We'll wake the baby. You said so yourself."

She gave a little gurgle of amusement, not denying it.

"Tomorrow she can be moved to another room," Gilbert said. "She's big enough. Kit sleeps alone."

"Tomorrow? But, sir—"

"Shut up with your sirs. You're a beautiful woman, Molly. You're as starved as I am."

She nodded in simple acquiescence.

"Eugenia—I love Eugenia. But she doesn't starve, Molly."

"Oh, sir! Oh, love."

"Talk later," he muttered, his lips coming down fiercely on hers.

Chapter 21

Eugenia surprised Gilbert by coming down to breakfast the next morning.

She was dressed in one of her immaculate muslins; her hair was arranged in glossy ringlets. She was pale and had dark stains beneath her eyes, suggesting a sleepless night. But her manner was composed and gentle. She was perfectly in control of herself again, even when she began a difficult, but charmingly humble, apology.

"Gilbert, I lost my temper and behaved very badly last night. It was wrong of me to lock the bedroom door. I promise never to do so again."

He looked at her, not speaking, his own feelings a mixture of guilt and elation. Both of them! he was thinking irrepressibly.

"And I also promise"—a look of pain was fleetingly in her eyes—"not to write any more letters to Mr. O'Connor, since this displeases you. Except a short one of explanation, of course. You must permit me that."

When he still didn't speak, she said in alarm, "Gilbert, you are going to forgive me, aren't you?"

The faint imperiousness in her voice amused and pleased him. He wanted an amenable, but not a servile, wife.

"I had good reason to be displeased," he said. "Love letters to another man."

"But only letters," she pleaded.

"I should hope so." His voice was gruff, his own guilt trou-

bling him. But only slightly, for guilt seemed no part of last
night's lovemaking, rich and inevitable as it had been.

"Are you doing this from what you conceive to be your
duty?" he asked.

"Naturally. What else? If we are to live all our lives together,
we must make up quarrels. You told me that I was living in a
dream, and I realize that this was true."

"You must have done quite a lot of thinking in the night."

"Yes. I heard you come home."

He looked at her sharply.

"But I didn't hear you come upstairs."

"I slept on the sofa." He had not intended to remind her of
another sleeper on that sofa, but his chance explanation was
fortuitous, for she winced and said no more.

Then, by another chance, Molly Jarvis came in carrying a
coffeepot. She hesitated when she saw Eugenia. She must have
expected Gilbert to be breakfasting alone, as usual, and had
not been able to resist the chance of words with him.

They would have to be clever about that sort of thing, he
thought with the ruthless logic the circumstances required.

But the rest?

The contrasting images of the two women were printed on
his mind, his wife cool, elegant, graceful even in her humility,
and the big-bosomed, quietly moving Molly with her smooth
cheeks and downcast eyes.

There they were, the vintage and the *vin ordinaire*. Each, he
realized, an absolutely essential part of his vineyard and his
life.

In a stabbing moment of perception he knew that he could
part with neither.

Without intending it to be, his voice was sharp.

"Where's Ellen, Mrs. Jarvis? Why are you waiting on table?"

She didn't raise her eyes. She put the coffeepot in front of
Eugenia, saying quietly, "Ellen is giving Master Kit his breakfast. He slept late this morning. Will that be all, ma'am?"

"Yes, thank you, Mrs. Jarvis. There's nothing wrong with
Kit, is there?"

"No, ma'am, he's perfectly well."

"I'll come up to the nursery presently. Gilbert, we must begin to think of lessons for Kit. He's so lively; he must have something serious to occupy his brain."

Mrs. Jarvis had withdrawn, and Gilbert was thinking irresistibly of the tumbled bed in her room and the smell of honeysuckle coming in from the veranda.

"Gilbert!"

"Yes, my love? Oh, Kit? He's a little young for a governess, isn't he? But do what you please. And why talk of this now?"

"To make conversation," she said, and that was the only time that there was a hint of despair in her voice. "I don't care for the servants to know that we have quarreled."

"You're perfectly right, as always." He stood up. "I'll send in a carpenter to mend your desk. I'm sorry about the damage."

Eugenia abruptly bent her head. He was afraid she was hiding tears. He was embarrassed. The logical thing would have been to kiss and embrace her, but his mind was too full of the memory of another woman in his arms. He wanted to leave her, cool and dignified, on her pedestal for a little while.

With immense care and discretion it should not be impossible to make two women happy. Or content, at least, and who could reasonably hope for more than contentment?

He dropped a swift kiss on the bowed neck. Sanity, today, lay in his vineyard. Yesterday he had noticed signs of furry caterpillar on the Malaga vines. He would want them gone over leaf by leaf. The day looked promising, fine and sunny.

He had given enough time to women and their problems for the moment. He walked out, whistling, crossing the courtyard outside the kitchen without turning his head.

Eugenia, left alone, bit her lips furiously. What had she expected? The scene had gone off very well, hadn't it? Gilbert had been generous—though not overgenerous—in forgiving her. Anything more would have been false to a man of his pride. False to a woman like her, too, if she had admitted that after locking her door last night, she had suddenly and most inexplicably wanted him to break it down.

She had crouched against it, feeling strange shivers of fearful delight go over her. He had looked magnificent in his rage. When he had kicked her desk, a violent pain had clenched her stomach. And when he had ceased to pound on her door, she had sat for hours in the dark, telling herself that violence was horrible. There must never be such a scene again.

But some strange metamorphosis had come over her. She kept wondering what it would have been like to feel the taut anger go out of his body and tenderness take its place. A tenderness she knew that she could coax into being. If only he would give her the opportunity.

It seemed that he had no intention at present of parting with his righteous anger. She would have to be patient.

Very well, she could be that. There was plenty of time. All their lives.

Not that she had any high esteem of herself. The letter she must write to Colm, cruelly honest, was still a complete betrayal.

She wept with shame and sadness as she wrote it.

> I find I cannot be two people after all. Forgive me, dear Colm. Can you ever forgive me? But something has happened that has made me realize that I must make an attempt to be one single wholehearted person. It is my duty to my husband and my child. Our continued liaison is quite impractical. We are allowing ourselves to turn into figments of a dream . . .

"I don't like this room," Rosie said in her self-contained voice. "Why must I have a bed in this room, Mammie?"

"Because you're a big girl now," Molly replied calmly. "You'll be next door to Phoebe. You like Phoebe, don't you?"

"Will I always have to sleep here?"

Molly looked at her daughter's sharply intelligent face. What the child lacked in looks, she had been compensated for in wits. Molly hadn't cared for Rosie's looking so much like poor Harry; it had seemed a pity that being a girl, she wasn't bonnier. But now she was thinking that wits might be a more useful thing than beauty. Otherwise, Rosie might indeed always sleep in this narrow bit of a room in the servants' wing. Australia was a great country with boundless horizons. The lowest could rise to be the highest.

"No, you won't always have to sleep here, love."

"Kit won't know where I is."

"You can tell him, can't you?"

The child's mouth tightened in a grimace, a mannerism she used when tears were repressed. She seldom cried. She withdrew into some private world where tears were not necessary. Molly found her a strange, unknowable, elderly little person. She loved the child deeply and was passionately determined to make amends to her for her inauspicious conception and birth. She was hurt now because she was banished from her mother's room, but that had had to come soon enough. It was difficult to be single-minded about protecting Rosie's feelings today. She had too many of her own.

All the same, looking at her daughter in her neat cotton dress and apron, she did wonder what characteristics Harry Jarvis had had that she had not known about and what he may have passed on to his daughter.

In the end, moving the two or three rag books bestowed on Rosie by Kit in a generous mood and the wooden doll with the gummed-on tow hair that had come in the English parcel, it was Molly who had to wipe away tears.

But that was because she was in such a trembling emotional state today. She had been so happy last night that she knew soberly she could never reach such a state of ecstasy again. For one thing, daylight had brought guilt and remorse. What a terrible thing she had done to the mistress she liked and admired. How could she remain at Yarrabee and be so treacherous? She had intended to give in her notice immediately, before she weakened.

It was for that reason that she had taken in the breakfast coffee, thinking to find Mr. Massingham alone.

Instead, there at the table had been the mistress, too. And looking delicious in her frilled muslin gown. And taking all her husband's attention.

Molly had been shocked by the intensity of her jealousy. When Mr. Massingham frowned at her and spoke sharply, she had almost flung the tray to the ground in a passion. She heard herself answering questions with apparently the right words, while all the time in her mind she was cradling that splendid redhead on her breast. She was trembling. Her arms actually ached with longing.

She knew that she had come to the point in her life when all her painfully learned discipline meant nothing. She could not leave Yarrabee. Even if she lay night after night, alone, she must be there, waiting. For one night he would come again. She knew that as surely as that there would be another vintage, and another and another.

She was in a thrall, and there was no answer for someone like her. Only waiting and snatching at crumbs.

So she shifted Rosie to the narrow little room that was meant for the newest and lowest servant and recognized one crumb that she could already ask for. Or demand.

Eugenia no longer found her writing desk such a haven. She had hardly been able to read the strange, incoherent note that had come from Colm, her eyes had been so blurred with tears.

It was written in sprawling, unsteady writing.

> Duty, duty, duty! Is that all that's in your mind, alannah? I am returning to Sydney, where I have a bit of a shack at Double Bay. But don't be soiling your feet in its dust.
> All the same, you could have made a man of me. Alas.

Eugenia tore the letter up, which was not much use, for the painful, accusing words were burned into her mind.

But there would be no more letters like this. And life would never be quite the same again. For Gilbert had decided that for the sake of convenience they would continue to have separate bedrooms. It had been thoughtless of him to disturb her, with his early rising and late retiring. On the hot nights, also, it would be more comfortable to sleep apart. After all, the house was big enough.

He didn't quite look at her as he said these eminently sensible things. If he had looked at her, she might have flung herself into his arms and confessed that in spite of what he imagined, she didn't really care about sleeping alone.

But he wouldn't meet her eyes, and she knew that she had offended him so deeply that he had stopped loving her.

It was what she deserved. She had made two men unhappy with her vagaries. Why should she expect to be cherished?

"So get the servants to fit up my room properly, will you, Genia?"

"But now I will never know when you come in."

"That's the idea." He dropped a light kiss on her brow, lifting a curl out of the way to do so. "Your beauty sleep won't need to be interrupted by crises in the vineyard."

After the new order was established, he did occasionally come to her room. She had thought he might have meant to stop that practice, too, and was sure he would have done so had his flesh allowed it. He no longer made a pretense of wooing her but took possession of her briskly and unemotionally, as if merely establishing a relationship.

She tried to tell him once that she had got over her nightmare, but he had looked at her blankly. What nightmare was she talking about?

"Hold me in your arms," she whispered.

"You are a funny creature! You said you had got over this mysterious nightmare."

He obeyed, however, and held her indulgently, like a child. He had made love with as little fuss as possible, since he knew she didn't much care for that sort of thing. Now he wanted to sleep.

She could read his thoughts perfectly. She lay in the dark, in the circle of his arms, letting the slow humiliated tears slide

down her cheeks. How soon would he return to his own bed?
When would he come to her again?

Eugenia had to force herself to pick up her pen to write her
weekly letter to Sarah. Even when at last she had some real
news.

MY DEAR SARAH,

It is midsummer again and, as always, tediously, exhaust-
ingly hot. We have been leading a very uneventful life, although I must drive into Parramatta later today as I am to
interview some young women in order to find a suitable governess for Kit. I do not think he is too young to begin learning
his letters. I remember that you and I could read words at
that age.

Mrs. Jarvis has asked if her little girl can share in the lessons.
She is a silent, though I am sure very clever, child, but I am
not entirely sure that I like her being Kit's constant companion. However, living in this isolation, there is no alternative,
and Gilbert favors the proposal. He is more enthusiastic than
I. Indeed, I confess that Mrs. Jarvis asked in such a strange
way, as if it were her due. I hope she is not going to get above
herself. I must be charitable and sympathize with her desire
for the best for little Rosie.

I wish you could see my garden this summer. Peabody is as
proud as a peacock. He has had great success with almost all
the new plantings. We now have a lavender border, and the
white rose has simply flown up the trellis and is a mass of
bloom. What is more, miracle of miracles, the lily pond now
holds real water, though not as yet lilies. We have had enough
rain this season to permit us to be extravagant with water.
The children dabble their fingers in it, scarcely able to believe
it. The fig tree is now big enough for me to sit in its shade.
I am having a table and chairs made to put under it, and we
will have tea out there. Also, Peabody found an old sundial
in a shop full of discarded junk in Parramatta. He has erected
it in the center of the lawn. I confess I have a liking for the
inscription, EVERY HOUR SHORTENS LIFE, but Gilbert finds it
morbid and stands indignantly beside it, looking quite im-
mortal himself.

When I talk to Kit about Lichfield Court, he listens with big eyes, but he can never understand that there is another house where Mamma once lived. He asks endless questions about Grandmamma and Grandpapa and his aunts, but how he sees them in his little mind, I can't guess. He will be four and a half years old when the new baby is born.

There! I have kept my news until the end. Gilbert, as usual, is delighted, and so am I, for I have not been able to bear the empty cradle since little Victoria left us. I hope you will not think it too tiresome of me if I ask you to send me some more of that delightful soft white wool, and I would dearly like some Nottingham lace and materials for baby gowns. They will not arrive before Baby does, but that isn't important. I will make them up later.

Mrs. Ashburton had an unfortunate accident the other evening, tripping on her skirts and falling down the stairs. She was shaken, but luckily not badly hurt. I fear she was in a condition which made her feet unsteady and accounted for her fall. But my husband says this was a mercy, as people in that condition fall in too relaxed a manner to break bones.

All the same, I would *much* prefer her sober. She is something of a trial. But she must remain here. We are so much in her debt.

It was not until after vintage that Molly's bedroom was invaded again. She had lain night after night, sometimes calm, sometimes in despair. Sometimes she wondered if he had forgotten he had ever been with her. Or if he treated his occasional women like this, with a deliberate loss of memory.

He had his conscience to deal with, she told herself. He was reconciled with his wife; he was as honorable as most men.

All the same, deep in her consciousness, she knew he would come.

When he did, slipping into her bed in the early hours one morning, smelling strongly of wine after the celebration following a successful vintage, he had no time to speak.

He simply took her, hungrily, and then fell soundly asleep. She had to rouse him at first light, whispering that he must go before any of the servants were stirring.

He was still half-asleep as he dressed.

"The devil take it," he complained. Her fingers found the buttons for him and did them up. She wound her arms around his neck and kissed him passionately on the lips.

"Molly, what if we have a child?"

"Then I would go away."

"No!"

She smiled but was half in tears at his violence.

"It isn't likely. There was something went a bit wrong at Rose's birth. The doctor said I'd be lucky if I had another. Lucky!" She managed to laugh a little.

He kissed the back of her neck, tenderly now.

"My poor Molly. And you had no one to tell."

"It didn't matter."

"It did. It did. Molly—I've been fighting this."

"I know."

"You've never said a word."

"How could I?"

"You're a rare woman, aren't you?"

"Never mind it now. You must go quick."

In the dim light she could see the quizzical gleam in his eyes.

"You know I'll come back, don't you?"

"Yes. I know."

"Is that enough for you?"

"It's all I can have, isn't it?"

He began to laugh. "You put Rosie out of the room, I see. You're a treasure. Would you die for me, Molly?"

"I think you're jesting."

"Not in the least. I've always wanted to hear a woman say that to me. Not to carry it out, of course." He patted her shoulder swiftly, pushed her away. "Must be off."

As the door closed softly behind him, she leaned against it, laying her forehead on the cool wood.

"Yes, I would die for you," she whispered.

Chapter 22

THE young women sat in an uneasy row on the hard bench. They had been told that Mrs. Massingham was expected at any moment. She was in need of a nursery governess for her little boy. Any girl who was given a position at Yarrabee could consider herself fortunate. It was the grandest house—apart from Government House—in the district, and Mrs. Massingham was the kindest of mistresses. Though strict, of course. She expected a high standard of morals and behavior.

The girls whispered among themselves. Two of them, Emmy Dawson and Minnie Higgins, had arrived only a week previously, sailing as emigrants under a scheme arranged for the purpose of bringing decent young women to the colony to work and to provide wives for the many unmarried settlers. The remainder of the young women had unfortunately arrived against their will. One was a freed convict; two were on ticket-of-leave.

It stood to reason that Emmy Dawson or Minnie Higgins was the logical choice for Yarrabee. It was widely known that Mrs. Massingham, for all her benevolence, did not like convicts, in spite of the fact that her housekeeper had been one.

There were vague whispers about that, too. Something about Mr. Massingham admiring her looks, although that scarcely seemed likely since he was said to worship his wife.

And who would doubt that? For Mrs. Massingham, when she arrived at last, had the wholehearted admiration of Emmy and Minnie. She wasn't impressively beautiful, as they had

been told, but she looked so graceful in her cool sprigged muslin and large leghorn hat tied beneath her chin with green
ribbons. Her face was so delicately pale, her large sensitive eyes
so gentle, it would have been very surprising if her husband
wasn't crazy about her. The firmness of her chin was not apparent at first, at least not when she was smiling with genuine
warmth at the row of doleful young women.

She knew who they were. She spoke to each by her name.
Emmy Dawson, the freckle-faced Cockney born within sound
of Bow Bells, had been taught needlework in the orphanage in
which she had lived for fifteen of her twenty years. She could
have become apprenticed to a milliner and worked soul-de-
stroying hours for her food and lodging. But something had
stirred in her blood, she said. She didn't think God had put
her on earth to live such a dull life.

Minnie Higgins spoke with a good accent. Her father had
been a schoolmaster who had died of consumption. So had her
mother and one of her sisters. Another sister was governess to
the children of one of the new cotton magnates in Manchester.
She was comfortable and happy, although she thought the family vulgar. Minnie had wanted a similar position, but her appearance had been against her. She was short and squat with
rounded shoulders, her growth stunted by rickets as a child.
She knew no man would be likely to want her; she was too
ugly. So she had created her own enormous adventure by coming to Australia. She had mild eyes and a pleasant smile, and
her accomplishments were impressive. She could speak French,
draw moderately well, play the piano, and had a good knowledge of literature.

She was really far too accomplished for the humble post of
nursery governess, but if she settled down happily at Yarrabee
and they all liked her, and the next baby was a girl, she could
become a permanent member of the household.

As for Emmy Dawson, she was too good to lose. Since
Phoebe, Mrs. Massingham's personal maid, was walking out
with a blacksmith and likely to be married soon, Emmy could
take over her duties, and also do the household sewing and

mending, and make baby clothes and shirts and trousers for Kit. It would be a very convenient arrangement.

For those who would not be going to Yarrabee, Mrs. Massingham had suggestions for suitable positions where they would be given an opportunity to live honest lives. She had all their names written down in a little leather-bound book.

She would not be losing sight of them, she assured the anxious, homesick young women. She had organized a system whereby either she or one of her helpers kept in touch with them and gave them advice, money, or shelter as deserved.

Any of them genuinely desirous of living a respectable life would be given the opportunity. But she did not accept backsliding.

She drove back to Yarrabee at a spanking pace, Minnie and Emmy in the back of the buggy, clutching their boxes and their bonnets and admiring their mistress' straight back and her expert handling of the reins.

So what people said of Mrs. Massingham was all true. She was beautiful and generous and kind—and ever so slightly alarming.

On her second day at her new post, Minnie Higgins asked permission to speak to Eugenia. Was it true that she was expected to include the housekeeper's child in the morning lessons?

"She just came in and sat down, Mrs. Massingham," Minnie said nervously. "She said she wanted to learn her alphabet and that she and Master Kit always did everything together. She seems a very forward child, if you'll excuse me saying so."

"Yes, she's a bright child," Eugenia agreed. "I overlooked speaking to you about her. I had thought we would get Master Kit established in his routine first, but if Rosie is so eager to learn, she had better begin at once. It certainly wouldn't be fair to deny the child an education. Anyway, it's better for Kit to have company. They're foster brother and sister, and they're devoted to each other."

The sooner Kit's own brother or sister was born, the better, Eugenia thought.

But did it matter, really? Gilbert said it didn't. He was quite diverted by the children's attachment to each other. He was very modern in his thoughts. He wanted equality insofar as it was practicable. It was certainly practicable that his son have a playmate.

Until he went away to school, Eugenia decided privately. And until Rosie was old enough to wear a cap and apron. She herself was certain that equality among the classes would never work.

Some months later, on a midsummer morning in the comparative coolness of her darkened sitting room, Eugenia wrote to Sarah.

> The baby is a girl, and I am delighted. So, I think, is Gilbert, although I suspect that he would have preferred another son. However, there is plenty of time for that, and in the meantime I am taking the greatest pleasure in my new daughter. We have decided to call her Adelaide, which is a name I have always admired. She has Gilbert's reddish hair, and I think she will be very pretty. She is also a strong baby, much stronger than either Christopher or Victoria, so I do not feel as anxious about her as I did about the other two. She has taken to the bottle immediately, and in her three short weeks of life she has thrived.
>
> Now you can picture Yarrabee as a family home, with Kit in the schoolroom and Baby in the nursery. The schoolroom is reigned over by Miss Higgins, or Higgie as Kit calls her, a plain little creature who looks like a pleasant frog. Ellen is in the nursery, very important now she has the new baby, and Phoebe having left me to be married, I have an immigrant called Emmy Dawson, who sews exquisitely and who is learning to be a good personal maid. Of course we still have our treasure, Mrs. Jarvis, who takes such a genuine pride in the house, and her little girl, Rose, who is as sharp as a needle. She will be given small household duties as soon as she is old enough, to keep her out of mischief. I fear she is already jealous

of the new baby or jealous of the interest Kit takes in it. You may say this is remarkable for such a young child, but Rose has always had an elderly face, and she also regards Kit as her brother and no one else's. A curious situation.

But I do enjoy having the house full of children's voices. It is no longer lonely . . .

The heat was bad this summer. Even Gilbert admitted that he had not experienced such a long period of extreme temperatures. He had boasted that the wells at Yarrabee would never run dry, but they were coming perilously near to it.

Eugenia's garden had to be sacrificed. She could hardly bear to look at the wilting, shriveling plants. Her early-morning and late-evening walks were given up. For one thing, it was too hot even at those hours. The heat, close and suffocating, lasted all night and turned to a furnace at midday. Sometimes a strong wind blew dust, the precious topsoil from the paddocks, through every smallest crevice. All the windows had to be kept tightly shut, and even then the filter of red powder hung in the air.

The hardy Australian shrubs, the thornbushes and spinifexes and the gum trees, haggard and stark against the burning sky, survived. So did the lizards and the flies, and the noisy shouting birds, the parrots, the kookaburras, the crows. Although one day a small cloud of tiny green parrots, gasping and dying, settled in the wattle tree like shriveling green figs.

Kit caught one of them, and it died in his hot hand. He was extremely distressed. He had not known that birds died.

The great danger was a bush fire. Gilbert watched every day for the significant stain of smoke on the heat-blanched horizon.

This was still only a threat. A reality was the way the bunches of grapes on the vines were shriveling. When the wells were dangerously low, Gilbert organized a clumsy, but continual, conveyance system from the lake by means of buckets and bullock wagons. The lake, too, was in danger of drying up, the remaining water brackish and crowded with water birds, who were forced farther and farther from the reedy shores.

Eugenia wanted to beg an occasional bucket of water for her white climbing roses, but did not dare. The greedy vines demanded every drop.

She felt as limp as her drooping roses. Even Gilbert lost his look of ruddy health and grew almost emaciated, his blue eyes blazing in his deeply sunburned face. There was no longer water for bathing. A few cupfuls in a china basin had to suffice. The baby, fretful with the heat, had a damp sponge squeezed over her body at intervals. Eugenia contrived a meager toilette in the same way, but Gilbert, frantically preserving every drop of water for his vines, fell into his bed at nights lean, sweaty, exhausted. His wife was the last thing in his mind.

Lying in the warm darkness in her own room, listening to the everlasting hoarse harping of the cicadas, Eugenia conjured up in her mind all the cool green things she could remember. Streams trickling over mossy stones, rain on a summer garden, cool flagstones beneath bare feet, the smell of roses when the dew still lay on them . . .

Sometimes the power of her imagination failed, and she could think of nothing but her discomfort. She was being dried up, parched, made prematurely old, a prisoner in this old, old land that was lying waiting outside for the brief darkness to be over so that it could smolder and burn again in the triumphant sun.

Then abruptly the rain came, streaming out of the low clouds in a waterfall, creating lakes in every hollow, running over the sunbaked earth too quickly for absorption so that every creek was swollen to a miniature river, and the river itself burst its banks.

Sheep and cattle, weakened by starvation, were swept into the rising floods and drowned. Kangaroos, wallabies, dingoes, foxes, shared the horrible gray odorous debris along the banks of the receding river. But the earth was growing green again; the immaculate blue days suggested a serenity that was profoundly welcome, if no longer believable.

There would be no vintage, Gilbert reported bleakly.

His vines had survived, but not their harvest. The grapes

hung in shriveled, rotting bunches. News drifted through that every vigneron in the Hunter River Valley had suffered a similar disaster. Some had sufficient means to carry on. Others intended abandoning such a precarious way of life, either turning their landholdings to ordinary farms or giving up altogether and returning to town life.

One family was actually planning to catch the next ship to England. When Eugenia heard of this, a wild hope leaped within her. She dared to speak of it only in the most devious way.

Gilbert was so haggard, so remote, so sunk in his disappointment that ordinary conversation was almost impossible.

The night after he had made his announcement about the ruined harvest, he had not come upstairs until dawn, and then only to wash and change his clothes. Eugenia thought he must have sat up drinking alone or perhaps with Tom Sloan. But he showed no signs of having been drinking when he did come up in the early dawn. He saw her in the doorway and apologized for disturbing her.

"Where have you been?" she asked.

"Talking. Discussing ways and means."

"But not all night!"

"Seems like it." He was busy at the wardrobe, looking for a clean shirt, fingering his growth of beard. "We didn't realize until we saw it getting daylight. Young Jemmie cried. A big lad like that. He had been looking forward to his first vintage."

Miserably, Eugenia was aware that she also should have cried. That might have been one way of getting closer to a husband who had grown too remote.

"Aren't you going to rest now?"

"No time. Don't worry yourself, love. Go back to sleep."

But she was wide-awake, tense, puzzled by something in his manner. There was something subtly different about him. She realized what it was. His look of strain had gone. He was gaunt and hollow-cheeked, but strangely relaxed. And this, after a night sitting up, talking. Some remarkable conclusions must have been reached.

She couldn't help saying, "Gilbert, this profession is too hazardous. Wouldn't it be wiser to turn to something else? Before you get deeper into debt—" She faltered, not quite able to meet his gaze.

"Is there anything you want you haven't got?"

"No, no, I have too much. But your debt to Mrs. Ashburton —when will it be paid?"

"This is hardly the time to remind me of that. Mrs. Ashburton certainly didn't. Indeed, she has already offered me a further loan."

"And you've accepted?"

"Of course I have," he said in surprise. "How can I let myself be beaten at this stage? You don't seem to understand."

"I only understand that it's all so intensely worrying. Next year it will happen again. We'll go through these weeks and months of anxiety. I don't think I can stand it. I haven't the temperament."

"That's only because you have no liking for wine or wine-making." Now he was indulgent. She hated his indulgent manner. "But you must try to have patience with it. Go back to bed and get some sleep."

Mrs. Ashburton was smugly pleased about the turn of events. She liked to be indispensable, even if the reason was only her fortune. But such an unpleasant necessity as money must not come between her and dear Eugenia. She was growing more devoted day by day to the children, Gilbert and Eugenia, Yarrabee. She would like very much to be little Adelaide's godmother. She adored that baby. So vigorous and demanding, so like her father with her imperious blue eyes.

"I wish I could live to see her grow up. I'll make a prediction that she'll leave her brother miles behind."

"I should hope not," said Eugenia. "And of course, you will live to see her grow up."

Mrs. Ashburton shook her head. She was growing untidy in her clothes, her cap was always awry, her gray locks straggling.

"I think not. My legs swell. Philip Noakes tells me I'm dropsical."

"You drink too much wine."

Mrs. Ashburton chuckled, not at herself and her self-indul-
gence, but at Eugenia.

"You're getting to be a real Australian, my dear. I believe
you'll make your mark on this country. And on your husband,
in spite of himself."

"What do you mean, in spite of himself?" The uneasiness
and unhappiness touched her again as she remembered Gilbert's strange manner that morning.

"He has an obsessive nature," Mrs. Ashburton replied enig-
matically.

"Oh, you mean his passion for his vineyard. I have accepted
that. I realize it will always come first with him."

"It doesn't need to, my dear."

"But it will," Eugenia said hopelessly. Her eyes filled with
tears. "And I so long to go home."

Mrs. Ashburton patted her hand. Eugenia noticed how the
rings cut into the old lady's swollen flesh.

"I know, child, I know. Although sometimes I suspect you
confuse homesickness with another thing altogether. But don't
blame me for this state of affairs. If I didn't help Gilbert, he
would find other means. Much better to be in debt to me. And
it's time you realized that you didn't only marry a man, you
married a country. For better or for worse. Eh, my dear?"

Chapter 23

EUGENIA had not been to Sydney since that ill-fated journey when little Victoria had died in her absence. Before that tragedy there had been the terrifying events of her wedding journey. She could not help associating the trip with disaster.

Now, however, the recently knighted governor, Sir Richard Bourke, was returning to England, and a farewell ball was being given in his honor. It was unthinkable, Gilbert said, that they should not attend.

"We'll leave on Saturday and return a week later. You can buy yourself some new clothes in Sydney. A ball gown in the latest fashion."

His assumption that the untidy colonial town would have the latest fashions, as well as his irresponsibility about money, jerked her out of her worry about leaving the children and also about the possibility of meeting Colm again, a prospect that both elated and alarmed her. She turned on him, scolding.

"How can you suggest such a thing? We have no money except Mrs. Ashburton's. I imagined that was for more important things than clothes."

Gilbert shook his head impatiently.

"You're too honest for this catch-as-catch-can country. You say that your new maid is a good needlewoman. Then see what she can do with your clothes if you won't agree to buy new ones."

Once he would have said that he wanted to show her off. He was growing out of those small courtesies.

But he did want her to shine, even if he didn't say so, for he supervised her packing and insisted on studying every detail of the gown which she and Emmy concocted from a length of French brocade, bought at a bargain price in Parramatta.

Finally, he said, as she revolved before him, "I think you were right after all, Genia. You don't need to worry about fashion. You can make your own."

"You may think so, but the Sydney ladies won't," Eugenia said worriedly, fingering the low-cut neck. Was it too low? It was exactly as in the fashions in the English journals sent by Sarah.

"Who cares about the Sydney ladies?" Gilbert's eyes were approving. He called her Genia only when he was pleased. "You look fine to me. Don't forget your diamonds."

Three days later Mrs. Jarvis watched them drive off, Eugenia laying her gloved hand on her husband's arm as the buggy swayed around a curve, Emmy and Tom Sloan in the back to mind the baggage and the crates of Yarrabee 1830 Claret, a vintage that had so far not been surpassed.

Her eyes narrowed as the equipage was lost in a cloud of dust. She stood a few moments longer, a pleasant figure with her well-rounded bosom, her luxuriant fair hair parted in smooth curves over each side of the forehead. There was a far-off look in her eyes, as if she were wondering what it would be like to be driving off to Sydney to a week of gaiety, to be wearing elegant clothes, and to being, as Mrs. Massingham always was, the center of attention.

But she didn't linger long to watch the dispersing cloud of dust. No one need think that discipline would be relaxed because the master and mistress were away.

A flicker of pink caught her eye in the acacia tree.

"Rosie! Why aren't you in the schoolroom?"

Her daughter was still a moment, then guiltily slid out of the tree.

"Mammie, Kit said—"

"Kit needn't think, because his mother's away, that he can

do as he pleases. It's half past nine, and Miss Higgins will be waiting for you both."

"But Kit's mother said he could have a holiday today."

"That doesn't mean that you can."

The child pouted rebelliously. "It isn't fair. I don't like to learn to read *all* the time."

"But you're going to, my lamb. To please your Mammie."

It was pleasant, after all, to be in Sydney again. The changes were enormous. There were many more streets built with small neat brick or sandstone houses. In the center of the town some fine public buildings had been erected. The harbor was full of vessels of all sizes from four-masted schooners to the little rowing boats that took people on pleasure expeditions. Carriages rattled down the dusty streets. There was a constant hubbub that was exhilarating after living so long in the country. Eugenia noticed the many new and thriving shops, the improved quality and variety of merchandise, and the modish clothes the women wore.

She was agreeably surprised by the comfort of the hotel. The bedroom reserved for Gilbert and herself was large and cool, the linen immaculate; the washstand and dressing table contained everything she could need. When she pulled the bell rope, a polite, cheerful chambermaid came and indicated her willingness to do anything required. Water for a bath in the flowered tub behind the screen, a tea tray with freshly brewed tea and freshly baked cakes, travel-soiled clothes removed for laundering and ironing. Anything for Eugenia's comfort seemed possible.

"Happy, my love?" Gilbert inquired in the pleasant, unemotional voice that he all too frequently used to her. They scarcely even quarreled now, for he would not be drawn. She supposed, unhappily, that there was no zest to quarreling with someone for whom he no longer had any passion.

The old guilt nagged at her.

And alarmingly it wasn't yet finished with. Or so she learned from Bess Kelly.

Bess had got comfortably fat. Edmund had prospered, and they now lived in a larger house in a more fashionable part of the town. Tom was away at school. The girls were cheerful and plain, with colonial accents. (Adelaide should never be permitted to speak like that.)

"Well, I declare, Eugenia. We were all discussing whether you would have got countrified, but we might have known better."

"Nonsense! I can't pretend to keep up with the latest fashions."

"Yes, there'll be some showy dressing at the ball. But I don't imagine you'll pass unnoticed. Gilbert wouldn't allow you to. Is he just as proud of you as ever?"

"Well, yes, I believe I come somewhere between Yarrabee and his wine, and his children."

"Was that a cynical tone in your voice, Eugenia? Have you and Gilbert quarreled?" Bess looked uneasy. There was something distrait in her manner. She had curtly told the children to leave the room.

"Naturally we have, now and then," Eugenia answered. "Don't all husbands and wives? Why do you ask?"

"Only—there are rumors—people have evil tongues."

"Dear Bess! What are you trying to tell me?"

"That Irishman who painted your portrait. He talks when he's had too much brandy. I'm sure he doesn't mean to. He's perfectly charming when he's sober."

Eugenia flushed, then went pale.

"He's in Sydney?"

"Yes. They say his book's to be published soon and that it's a valuable record of Australian flora and fauna. But he won't be at the ball, so you don't need to worry about that embarrassment."

"He wasn't invited?"

"Not with his—unpredictable behavior."

Eugenia gave a faint sad smile. "That's a charitable way of putting it, Bess. But I imagine there will be plenty of Australian or English or Irish gentlemen at the ball whose behavior won't be entirely predictable. I haven't noticed a marked tendency to sobriety in this country, not even excluding my own husband."

"So long as you don't still care for him," Bess murmured.

"Care for whom?" Eugenia's chin was in the air. "Mr. O'Connor?"

"He's supposed to have said something about letters he has," Bess said uneasily. "I just hope they won't get exhibited around."

Eugenia hid her shock, although she couldn't speak for a moment.

"Then they mustn't be allowed to, must they?"

"I thought I should warn you. You might hear it from a less charitable source. This town's a dreadful place for gossip."

Eugenia straightened her shoulders. She found that she was very tired from the long journey, after all. Her heart was throbbing uncomfortably.

"I expect all towns are full of gossip. It will be all right. Colm is a gentleman."

"When he's sober," Bess said. "Which isn't often." Reluctantly she added, "I must say this to you, Eugenia. You'll have to do more than depend on his being a gentleman."

Eugenia's eyes widened. "Are you telling me I ought to ask him for my letters back?"

"It would be wisest, love."

"See him!"

"I'd come with you if you want me to. We could take the carriage and drive around the bays. You ought to see them. They're very pretty. Rose Bay, Double Bay, Rushcutters Bay."

"Colm told me he lived in a shack."

"Yes, I've seen it from a distance. It's not much of a place. Lonely. Sam can look after the horses while we walk down to the beach for half an hour."

"Sam?"

"We have a coachman now," Bess said with pride. "He's a surly old fellow, but he doesn't gossip. Anyway, he'll only think we want to get a breath of sea air."

"You have this all arranged!"

"Edmund told me to," Bess confessed. "He said it would be an awful pity if this gossip flared up while you and Gilbert are in Sydney. You're such an innocent, Eugenia. You've been too sheltered all your life. You don't know how mean people can be, especially if they're jealous. And I can assure you the ladies here—if you can call them ladies—will be jealous. The men, too. I know Gilbert's having trouble with his vineyards, but he cuts such a figure. You're both such assets to the colony, and I love you. I won't let you be in the middle of a wicked scandal, especially one caused by a drunken Irishman."

"That's what Gilbert called him. You're on Gilbert's side, Bess."

"Oh, you silly little innocent, I'm on both your sides. Marriage is for a lifetime, you know. So you ought to give it a chance to be happy. If you have to have a lover, wait until you're older, at least."

Eugenia tried to laugh.

"Bess! You so worldly!"

"Well, worldly is a thing you are not, my dear. It's time you woke up."

"I have. Can't you see I'm no longer young and naïve? It was only because I was homesick for so long." Her eyes were anguished. "Colm understood. I took refuge in those letters, not thinking what I was doing to him. It preys on me that I've driven him back to drinking."

Bess shook her head, her eyes cynical.

"You don't know much about the curse of strong drink either, do you?"

"Don't despise me, Bess."

"I don't despise you. I despise Colm O'Connor for taking advantage of an innocent."

"I think he's an innocent, too."

"Then it's time he also woke up. I'll call for you at your hotel tomorrow afternoon at three o'clock. Tell Gilbert I'm taking you driving."

"Must *I* do it?" Eugenia asked painfully.

"No one else can. Can they?"

Though Eugenia tensely and nervously kept her ears alert, she heard no other whisper of this scandal. There was a dinner at Vaucluse that night. Eugenia and Gilbert were welcomed warmly and given flattering attention. Eugenia thought that Marion Noakes kept rather persistently and protectively at her side, making her tart, amusing comments, and that Mrs. Wentworth sometimes darted her an anxious glance. But the conversation remained on safe general topics, the state of the colony, unsubstantiated rumors of a gold strike, the type of emigrants who were arriving in constantly increasing numbers, the possibility of the cessation of convict transportation. And children and schools and servants and fashions.

The dream that had kept her at her writing desk was far away and insubstantial, the necessity of a meeting with Colm O'Connor a fact she had to face.

For once she was glad that the gentlemen spent so much time commiserating with Gilbert on the ruin of his harvest and expressing their admiration for his stubborn determination to continue when so many vignerons were giving up. They appreciated his wine, sniffing it, holding it up to the candlelight, rolling it over their tongues. It was exactly the kind of evening Gilbert enjoyed. He was in the greatest of good humors when they returned to the hotel, but the rather substantial amount of wine he had consumed had made him lethargic. He undressed and fell into bed and was instantly asleep. Weariness made Eugenia sleep, too. Although she woke once in the night, crying from a sad dream that she couldn't remember.

But the next day shock and pity had taken the place of tears.

The shack was truly a shack. It must have been one of the earliest dwellings erected in Botany Bay, its earthern walls sagging and cracking, its roof a piece of rusty iron.

Eugenia lost courage and could not knock at the door, and it was Bess who rapped briskly for her.

After a long interval a blurred voice called, "Who is it? Who's there?"

Bess nudged Eugenia sharply.

"Tell him."

There was no need, for a moment later the door opened, and a scarecrow figure stood blinking in the light. Haggard, unkempt, distressingly thin, aged beyond belief.

Eugenia cried, "Colm!" in a shocked whisper.

Colm straightened himself, with a shadow of his old dignity, then sketched a bow.

"Mrs. Massingham! To what do I owe the honor?"

"Colm, you look so ill."

"Not ill, ma'am. Just dissipated."

"Let me come in."

He stood across the doorway, swaying a little.

"Not fit for a lady in here."

"Oh, hush that nonsense. I'm coming in."

Bess protested, taking her arm, but Eugenia impatiently shook it off.

"You stay outside, Bess. I won't be long."

She swept into the small dark room, trying not to notice that it was desperately untidy and full of the smell of sour spirits.

"What's happened to you, alannah? You didn't used to be like this. Behaving like a duchess."

"You didn't used to be like this either."

"The old demon drink," he said, grinning.

She couldn't allow herself to think, or she would be unable to endure this dreadful scene. She said quietly, "I've come for my letters. You must give them to me."

Behind his drunken bravado, the merest hint of desolation showed.

"What, my only treasures!"

"I've heard that you boast about them. I can't allow that."

"My God, you've become a respectable matron."

"Colm, please. I must have them. Or at least I must see them destroyed. Can't we burn them here and now?"

"A funeral pyre?"

"Oh, Colm!" She laid her hand on his arm. She could feel
the bone through the thin flesh. "Why did you let this happen
to you?"

"Because I'm a weak fellow. You might have saved me. I don't
know. I should have carried you off that day at the lake." He
took his arm away from her, quite gently. "Don't touch me. I
know I'm disgusting. All right, you can have the letters. Did
you really believe I would make a scandal?"

"Not when you are in possession of your senses."

"Which isn't often, as you've probably heard."

He was fumbling in a box. Presently he produced the small
bundle of letters and, throwing them in the ashes on the hearth,
stirred them with a poker into a thin blaze. Then he crouched,
holding his outspread fingers over the warmth. He seemed to
have forgotten that she was there.

Bess was tapping tentatively at the door. Eugenia called to
her to wait. She wanted to see the last sheet curl into flame. She
felt old. Grown-up at last, she thought. A matron, as he had said.

"Not quite devoid of honor," he said, getting to his feet. "I
didn't know I'd boasted. Though it was something to boast
about."

"Yes," Eugenia said pitifully. And added in a whisper, "It
was."

He prodded at the curling ashes with his toe, then turned on
her fiercely. "You've got what you came for. Why don't you go?
The world's waiting for you."

"It could be waiting for you, too. They say your book is
beautifully done. You have so much talent, Colm."

"For the bottle, my dear. Immense talent for the bottle. It's
all right; don't look upset like that. I was a weak fellow long before you met me. A failing of the Irish. Most of us drink.
Some of us do it more thoroughly than others and finish up in
an early grave. A short life and a merry one." He had picked up
a bottle that showed only the dregs of some liquor. "I'm a desperate case. Even you couldn't have saved me, alannah, and
that's the real truth I'm speaking."

There was nothing to do but go. Bess' nose was wrinkled in

disgust; she took Eugenia's arm and hurried her away across the sand dunes to the waiting carriage.

"What were you so long about? Did you get the letters? That dreadful man! So drunken and rude. What was he saying as you left?"

"Nothing. Nothing that made sense."

But it had made sense. It had been a brave attempt to relieve her of her guilt and remorse, to tell her that even with her faithful love he would have become that ragged travesty.

She wanted to cry from the sadness of it. But the tears gathered into a hard ache in her throat and refused to be shed. All the way back to the town she sat with a rigid body and frozen face, ignoring Bess' attempts at reassurance.

But the letters were destroyed. Her reputation had been saved. She would have to live an important, a valuable life to justify what she had just done. At this moment she didn't know how to live at all.

The next night the ball was a brilliant affair. Eugenia would not have believed there could be so many fine clothes and jewels in a colonial city. She thought she looked a modest figure compared to most of the women who had a distinct tendency to overdress. But someone said behind her, "The beautiful Mrs. Massingham," and she flashed around, hearing echoes of Colm's voice from another long-ago night. The portly gentleman who had spoken looked surprised at her reaction.

"Did I startle you, Mrs. Massingham? May I have the honor of this dance?"

Her lips trembled uncontrollably as she allowed him to take her arm.

It was after midnight when a small stir ran through the assembly. "The Irish artist," someone said.

"That drunken O'Connor," someone answered. "Fancy him daring to come! He actually looks sober."

Her breath caught, her heart pounding, Eugenia stood rigid looking across the room at the tall figure in the doorway. Well groomed, correctly dressed, an elegant wraith who must have been waiting to catch her eye, he bowed to her with grave deliberation and walked on out of sight.

He must have made a tremendous effort to give her this respectable glimpse of himself. It was his farewell. She knew, with certainty, that she would never see him again.

Chapter 24

THE situation was becoming repetitive.

Eugenia wrote:

> DEAR SARAH,
> Will you be interested to hear that Kit and little Adelaide are to have a brother or a sister early next year? I am quite delighted. I feel now that the more children there are to fill this big house, the better.
> Since our visit to Sydney I have been more than content to resume my quiet life at Yarrabee. We were the victims of too much gaiety, being drawn into a frenzied social life which I found artificial and empty. We enjoyed renewing old acquaintances, however. Bess Kelly has grown very stout, and Marion Noakes looked old and yellow in complexion. It does not suit a woman who so longs for children to be barren. But she had lost nothing of her caustic tongue, and I grow to like her honesty more and more. So much better than the simpering of all those newly arrived middle- and low-class creatures with their latest fashions which they hoped would make us pioneers look dowdy . . .

She hoped the new baby would be a boy, since that was what Gilbert wished. And the next might be a girl for her own pleasure. She thought that she preferred girls to boys. Kit was a handsome child, but difficult and subject to screaming fits. Eugenia sometimes had the notion that he had never recovered from his attack of scarlet fever and the shock of little Victoria's death, in his mother's absence, although it seemed strange that so young a child could have been so affected.

Whatever it was, she now had little control over him. He seemed to love her passionately, but if he was rebuked in the smallest way, he screamed for Mrs. Jarvis. That Mrs. Jarvis could manage him when she, his mother, could not rankled.

Gilbert, however, seemed amused and unconcerned.

"The little scamp knows you have a tender heart, my love. He plays on it. Mrs. Jarvis gives him a good thumping when he needs it."

"Is it something to do with her being his foster mother?" Eugenia brooded. "Holding him to her breast as a baby?"

"That's advanced thinking." Gilbert didn't seem to want to pursue that subject. "Wait until he goes to school. He'll get out of his baby ways then."

"Rosie leads him on," Eugenia persisted. "That child, in her quiet way, is extraordinarily naughty. All the worst pranks are her idea."

"Better get them both out picking grapes at vintage. That'll take the mischief out of them."

"Oh, Gilbert! Child labor! You can't mean it."

"Of course, I mean it. The boy can't start taking an interest in his future too soon."

"Don't you think you might develop a dislike in him for it if he's forced into it too young?"

"Nonsense! It will only be a game to him."

"It isn't Rosie's future."

"I know that, of course. You can take charge of that. Get the child trained in whatever you like. Whatever her mother agrees to, naturally."

"She's very bright. She's much quicker than Kit at reading. I have vague ideas—but it's looking a long way ahead."

"Yes, my love? What are those?" Gilbert asked politely, without interest.

"I want to begin organizing a school in Parramatta for the

children of the working classes. I know it isn't usual to educate children of this kind, but I do think, in a new country, we could begin setting a standard that even England might follow."

Gilbert stifled a yawn. "Yes, love. A splendid idea. What has it to do with Rosie?"

"I thought that she might be able to teach in it. I'm sure Miss Higgins can give her a good enough education to do this. It will be an interesting experiment."

"Do whatever amuses you, my love."

"It's not for my amusement," Eugenia said strenuously.

As it happened, her plans almost came to nothing. Her new baby, another girl, was born prematurely, and she came within a mere breath of dying.

After it was all over, she found she had only a hazy memory of pain that had seemed to go on forever, then of deadly, swooning weakness. Once she remembered the lamplight fading, and she herself crying for the wick to be turned up; she was suddenly so afraid of the dark. Didn't anyone realize that she had always found the dark in this country full of terror?

Someone must have heard her, for later the light had grown brighter, and Gilbert's face was bending over her. It looked so anxious and sad that she had groped for his hand. His strong clasp seemed to stir a little life in her.

She whispered, "The baby?" and saw that he was crying.

"It—didn't—live!" she managed to say in terror.

"It's fine. A girl. Looks like you."

Then he kissed her very gently on the brow, and afterward she could feel the damp of his tears remaining. She understood the next day or perhaps the next week, for time had lost meaning, that that had been the moment when they had known she would live.

But there must be no more children for a long time.

That was a piece of news they refrained from telling her until she was able to leave her bed and sit in a chair on her balcony. The new baby lay in its basket at her side. She had already begun to feel a great attachment to this tiny, fragile creature, and

Dr. Noakes' careful explanation about the danger of having another child made the little one inexpressibly precious.

"I've told Gilbert, Eugenia. It can't be risked for a couple of years, at least."

"What does he say?"

"He'll talk to you. He agrees, of course. Now don't take this badly, Eugenia. You have three children already."

"Just when I began to want a houseful." She was full of pain.

"Life is full of compromises."

"I know. I must be grateful. But after little Victoria I can't help being nervous. The new baby reminds me so much of Victoria. If she doesn't thrive, I'll insist on taking her to England."

Dr. Noakes patted her shoulder.

"They have a high child mortality in England, too, you know. We're no worse off here. Better, if the truth be known. I don't suppose you ever saw a London or a Liverpool slum."

"I'm not speaking of slums," Eugenia said. "I'm speaking of my own home."

"Of course. I was only generalizing. I have to talk to my wife in this way. She blames Australia, too."

"I ought to be ashamed of myself," Eugenia exclaimed in remorse. "Here I have three children, and I'm complaining."

"Complain as much as you like, my dear. This has been a shock. You've taken it very well. We simply can't do without you, you know. You add a very great deal to the place."

"I do?"

"Haven't you any vanity either?"

"I see my faults. Too many of them."

"Then start seeing your virtues. We do, I assure you."

Did Gilbert see them, too? It seemed that he did, for he came to her with a lugubrious face.

"You have given me the devil of a fright, Genia. We simply can't risk anything like this again."

She could only say that she was sorry to have been so stupid. Was it certain that it would happen again?

"We're not going to risk finding out." He knelt beside her, taking her hands. "Look at these. So thin. A puff of wind would blow you away at present."

She had to blink back her tears.

"Do you find me too delicate?"

"To tell the truth I'm afraid of breaking you. And admit it, my love"—his voice was blunt—"you have never cared much for that part of marriage, have you? I didn't expect you to. Women of your kind don't."

"That is a generalization." She tried to speak lightly, but the resentful words burst out. "I hate this bed alone."

"My dearest!" He looked startled. "Are you still nervous of the dark?"

"No. I am not nervous. But neither do I want to feel like a widow."

He laughed, pressing her head against him.

"We're neither widow nor widower, thank God. But for a few months—" She remembered how once he had always forced her to look at him. Now he contented himself with stroking her hair. An aching tenderness dissolved her at his touch. She found she could not ask him how the new austerity would suit him. She was too afraid that the prospect suited him too well.

Once again she turned to her baby who had been called Lucy. Since she took a long time to grow strong, she liked to linger in bed in the mornings and have Ellen bring all the children to her.

Kit was growing out of his infant plumpness. He had a wiry, thin body and a mop of blond curls. Adelaide was learning to walk and was fiercely independent. She would make her own way to Mamma's bedside and clamber onto the bed to play with the carved cupids.

Sometimes another small figure appeared at the door. It was Rosie. She knew she was forbidden to come up here. But at times the temptation was irresistible. She stood with her finger in her mouth, staring until Ellen rounded on her and sent her packing. Downstairs, where she belonged.

Eugenia felt unkind, but the child was doing very well. She must realize that some things were forbidden.

For some reason the house was happier. Perhaps it was because of Lucy's arrival. She was an enchanting baby, as pretty as a picture. Perhaps it was because Mrs. Ashburton, sinking into a sleepy old age, had lost her querulous faultfinding tongue and had become a great favorite of the children. She was a perfect subject for their pranks, for she never guessed that the hat that mysteriously moved across the floor had a kitten beneath it or that the masked face at her doorway was not that of an ogre. She could never win the games they played or guess their riddles. She amiably accepted their laughter at her stupidity and produced sweetmeats from her pockets and told them the fairy tales she had been told as a child. Had she *ever* been a child? they wondered. Fortunately, they were not awake to see her uncertain progress up the stairs to bed after her customary half bottle of claret with her dinner, and another later to help her to sleep.

Or perhaps another reason for the relaxed atmosphere was that Mrs. Jarvis had taken to singing softly as she worked. She was in her middle thirties now, a plump, handsome woman with her smoothed fair hair and her warm brown eyes. Eugenia sometimes reflected that she had never seen Mrs. Jarvis out of temper or other than quietly capable. Though she was strict with the maids and even stricter with her daughter. Rosie had been banished from her mother's room to sleep alone at a very tender age. That, Mrs. Jarvis said, was necessary since the child had to learn to stand on her own feet. She would not have a nurse and a governess at her beck and call as had Miss Adelaide and Miss Lucy. Certainly she shared the schoolroom lessons with Master Kit, but these would end when Master Kit went to school and the schoolroom was occupied by the two little girls.

Not necessarily, Eugenia said, and asked Mrs. Jarvis to sit down while she told her her plan. When Kit had gone to boarding school, Rosie should stay on in the schoolroom to be educated to the extent of Miss Higgins' ability. Then she herself could go out into the world as a teacher. It was fairly certain that for many years there would be a great shortage of teachers in the colony.

But why was Mrs. Jarvis crying? Eugenia had never before seen her in tears.

"You're too good, ma'am. I so dearly longed to learn things when I was a child. I never thought the day would come when people like us got a chance."

"Oh, that day will come, I'm certain. We're already making a beginning. I'm going to form a committee in Parramatta. We'll get a piece of land and build a school. I intend talking to the governor about it at the first opportunity. I think the native children should be taught, too, if we can persuade them to come to school. Though Mr. Massingham thinks that very ambitious and unwise of me. But you remember Yella. Her child shouldn't grow up completely ignorant."

"You're a good woman, ma'am," Mrs. Jarvis said again, earnestly.

"No, no, far from it, Mrs. Jarvis. I have enough shortcomings. But since it seems that I'm to spend my life in this country, I feel I must do what I can for it. If that's being good—I'm afraid Mr. Massingham simply thinks it's making me a blue stocking." Eugenia paused, studying the pleasant face before her. Fifty years later in Australia's history, they might have been friends. For if one were to judge by a lot of the people arriving to settle here, there would not be too much reverence for the class system. But she was what she had been brought up to be, the mistress of a house, and this pleasant woman with the damp cheeks and downcast eyes was her servant, in spite of what they had been through together.

There were changes taking place in the colony. It was rumored that the English government was not going to send any more convicts to the land they still called Botany Bay. It would mean the end of cheap labor. Gilbert was too honest to hide his dismay. He believed that he was one of the best employers the con-

victs had. During the years he had lived at Yarrabee, he had
helped rehabilitate many men. He fed and clothed them decently, saw that they attended church, seldom used the lash.
He also attempted to cure them of their rum-drinking habits, his most notable success being young Jem McDougal. But
then the lad had been too young to have acquired bad habits.

Eugenia, however, made no attempt to conceal her relief.

"I'm so thankful. Now we can have decent, honest men on
the place and sleep safe at nights."

Gilbert's eyebrows rose.

"Since when have you not slept safe?"

"I have to confess I have always been nervous. I have always
felt half fear and half pity. Some of the men have looked so desperate."

"Only because they hadn't trimmed their hair and beards.
Cut all that fungus off, and they look as tame as anyone else."

"But are not always. You know that they can murder and
steal and terrify people."

"Not ours on Yarrabee."

"Perhaps not, but even sitting in church, I've felt their eyes
full of resentment like needles in my back. I've wondered if
they would lie in wait for our buggy on the drive home."

"Now where could they lie in wait on a perfectly flat plain,
without even a thornbush to conceal them? You're being fanciful, Eugenia. You should have told me about this long ago,"
he added.

"And you would simply have told me I was being fanciful,
as you just have."

"I expect you have never forgotten that night at the inn. I
should understand that. Only it seems so long ago. Well, we
have three long-termers here, and the rest have sentences of up
to four or five years to complete. By that time the vineyard will
be doing well enough for me to afford high wages. It looks like
a record vintage this year by the way the vines are bearing. But
there's still time for hailstorms or blight or a plague of locusts."

"You make it sound Biblical."

Gilbert's eyes got their intense, almost fanatical light. "It is. They were making wine when Christ sat at the Last Supper. And centuries before that."

"And getting drunk," Eugenia said.

"Easing their cares."

"That's merely an excuse. What cares does Mrs. Ashburton have, for instance?"

"A fear of dying, perhaps?"

"The way she's behaving she's hastening her death."

Gilbert said with impatience, "Don't be so logical. And don't tell the old lady that. Let her enjoy her remaining years."

"If the vintage is going to be so good, you will be able to repay her the money you borrowed, won't you? I find it so humiliating being in debt."

"Mrs. Ashburton doesn't look on it that way, my love. She regards herself as being in our debt. What is money or hospitality among friends? Must we argue about that?"

The fine weather continued; the grapes hung in abundant green clusters, waiting for the long, warm days to swell and color them. Anticipating a record harvest, Gilbert intended to hire all the extra help he could. But once again his unlucky star was shining. Without warning the price of wool dropped disastrously. In Cornhill in London where the traditional bidding took place by the measure of a lit candle—when it had burned down an inch, bidding was closed—almost no voices were raised, and the wool, the wealth of the colony, went for so low a price as to be ridiculous.

The impact of this disaster shuddered across the world to the enormous sheep runs and the laden bullock drays with their suddenly unwanted cargo. Thousands of hopeful settlers were faced with ruin. Banks began to fail; sheep were being sold for sixpence; farmers, with the panic of despair, gave away their runs and moved into the towns. If this sort of thing went on, few were going to have the price of a mug of beer, let alone a bottle of wine.

Gilbert found himself besieged by gaunt-faced men begging

for work. This, he realized, was only the beginning. If the slump continued, the colony would be bankrupt. He could store his wine and market it at a more propitious time. He was fortunate in that, unlike livestock, wine cost nothing to keep and improved with keeping.

But as always, he was dogged by the lack of ready cash. Yarrabee was an expensive place to run. There were too many servants to be fed and paid; he had no intention of allowing his wife and children to grow shabby and the greatest reluctance to reduce his comfortable style of living.

Fortunately he still had cheap convict labor.

And Yarrabee's permanent guest, Mrs. Ashburton.

He was genuinely fond of the bibulous old lady. They had spent many evenings sitting over their Burgundy or claret, talking while Eugenia played the piano or stitched at her embroidery. It was an irony that Mrs. Ashburton, listening to his reminiscences, knew him better than his wife did. There were so many things that he could not or would not tell a sensitive, fastidious woman like Eugenia. It wouldn't be right.

But Mrs. Ashburton had an honesty and a touch of bawdy humor that came out as the wine relaxed what few inhibitions she had. She understood a man's world. He told her he would erect a magnificent tombstone in grateful memory over her grave, and she rocked with appreciative laughter.

It was only to be expected that when the disaster of the slump hit him, she should come to his rescue once more.

"Say nothing," she commanded him when he tried to thank her. "I'm leaving you and Eugenia my fortune, anyway. You're only getting some of it in advance, and I enjoy being here to see you do it. I won't see anything when I'm under that grand tombstone, will I?" Her bleary eyes moistened. "Now keep this from Eugenia. She's a proud creature, a rare delicate thing for this raw country, and you must reassure her."

The old lady was getting a bit maudlin. Gilbert patted her hand, sharing her sentiments entirely.

"I do that already."

"Then go on doing so. D'ye hear me?"

In spite of the slump and the pessimism, the vintage that year was a merry one. For a week there was singing and dancing and riotous behavior. Everyone was well fed, well paid. Many got drunk on raw wine and forgot the troubles that lay ahead. The vats, scrupulously cleaned by Jem McDougal, who was intensely proud of the trust put in him by the master, were bubbling with fermenting wine. What the impoverished market could not absorb would be kept in casks or bottled and laid in racks. For the first time the cellars were filled to capacity. It was a sight Gilbert had dreamed about. This was his wealth. He was almost happy that he did not need to part with it at present. He would enjoy gloating over it when he turned the bottles at suitable intervals and made records.

His children growing, his wife losing her look of excessive fragility, Molly Jarvis warm, voluptuous, discreet, undemanding, a paragon of a woman, his vines healthy and his cellars full. Yarrabee was going to ride out the economic storm, and other storms, too, please God. Life still appeared hopeful and felicitous.

Until Mrs. Ashburton turned against him.

But that was a long time later.

Chapter 25

SUDDENLY time was running away so fast. Kit was eight years old, and it was time for him to go to school. Just as well, too, for he had had a passion lately for digging holes wherever he could find sandy soil. He was prospecting for gold, he said, but instead, he nearly died from snakebite. If Peabody hadn't been near to hear his scream and then, with long-acquired knowledge, to suck out the venom, they would have lost the boy. As it was, he was dangerously ill for several days, and his mother developed a nervous horror of anything that moved in the grass.

"Dearest Sarah," Eugenia wrote when this crisis was over:

> We have just returned from taking Kit to school. It was my first visit to Bathurst, and now I look forward to many more as I found it a most attractive place. It is an arduous journey over the Blue Mountains. We took three days on the road, camping at nights, which Kit thought the greatest fun. The air was so sharp and clear and frosty that I quite thought myself in the Welsh mountains.
>
> Kit behaved very well until the moment of departure came, and then his lips trembled, and the tears could not be controlled. He suddenly looked so young, and I felt what monsters we were abandoning our baby like that. Gilbert was strong, of course, but I believe he had painful feelings, too. He was silent for a long time on our journey home, and his face had the preoccupied look which I know better than to disturb. However, the school is very good, and Gilbert insists that it

will make Kit a man. His playmate, Rosie, is disconsolate, but she will have to grow accustomed to his absence. She is getting to be a big girl and must begin doing tasks in the house.

The little ones are bonny. Gilbert dotes on Adelaide, and I, to be honest, do the same with my darling Lucy. She has so completely taken my little lost Victoria's place in my heart. How I wish you could see her, for none of my sketches does justice to her, the way her hair curls around her little face, and her big eyes are so solemn. She is very shy. Her tender feelings are all too easily hurt. I keep her at my side a great deal. Whatever happens, I will not allow her to be sent away to school, not even the one for the daughters of gentlefolk which has been opened in Parramatta by the Misses Chisholm.

They teach music and drawing and dancing and other refinements and are filling a need in this cultureless country. I have every intention of sending Adelaide there when she is old enough, as she is the sort of child who will benefit from this kind of establishment.

We are hoping that at last the dreadful slump is over. Poor Sir George Gipps, who is the governor now, has been blamed for everything, from his method of allotting land, to his reputed convict sympathies. Even the droughts are blamed on the poor man. And he is very incensed about the way some squatters shoot down natives. It is barbarous. But I think this country will always be barbarous to some extent. It is much too big to be tidily civilized.

Eugenia bit her pen, pausing at the end of the closely written page. It was sad that for so long now she had had to have secrets from Sarah. It would have been unbelievable when they were girls together. But Sarah continued to live her sheltered spinster life with no anxieties except the care of aging parents. And she, in the years since leaving England, had experienced so much.

Her pride forbade her to tell Sarah that Yarrabee had weathered the slump and she had not been deprived of comforts solely because of Mrs. Ashburton's continued financial help.

And that although her health had now been restored, she

still, except for very occasional nights, slept alone in her charming bedroom.

Eugenia was secretly perplexed by Gilbert's behavior. He had never been an austere man. She did not think he could become one overnight. He seemed too cheerful and relaxed to be practicing self-discipline. His noisy games with the children when Lucy had to fly and bury her face in Mamma's skirts because Papa was too rough didn't suggest an unhappy man. His voice could be heard all over the house when he shouted for one of the maids or when he embarked on one of his long, reminiscent conversations with Mrs. Ashburton, who had grown deaf. His face had the brick-red, healthy color of days spent in the burning glass of the sun; his eyes were merry and sparkling.

All this suggested a man with desires that could scarcely be satisfied by the occasional visit to her bed, and his now-careful, inhibited handling of her. He had not been at ease with her since Lucy's birth—or even before that. There had been something in his eyes, an uneasiness that communicated itself to her, and left her frustrated and often in tears.

She thought he might have a woman in Parramatta and dreaded finding out, for then she would have to take some action. And what could she do about a husband who had formed an image of his wife that he would not have altered? She was a delicate creature who must be fondly and ridiculously spoiled and pampered, so that everyone must envy them as a remarkable couple, and no one must guess that they had lost each other.

There were so many things to do. Eugenia picked up her pen and wrote vigorously to Sarah.

I am planning to have a garden party when the roses are at their best. Poor Peabody has become very lame with rheumatism, so I have begged for Jem McDougal when he can be spared from the winery. He is a decent, honest young man, and although he now has his freedom, he wishes to remain at Yarrabee as he is so interested in the vineyard. He has an ambition to have one of his own someday, and perhaps he may realize it. At least this country does give the ex-criminal a chance of making something of his life.

Anyway, he is a good strong young man for digging and planting shrubs. Peabody behaves like an autocrat, giving orders and stumping about, his voice as shrill as a peacock's. Adelaide has developed a devotion for Jem and trots behind him, gathering up leaves and dead flower heads in her pinafore and thinking she is helping. Peabody and I have realized our dream of having lilacs in the hollow. This spring they flowered for the first time, and I can't tell you how nostalgic the scent made me. I felt transported to that little heavenly green dell where we used to play. Oh, Sarah, if only I could have a trip home!

Gilbert promised me one last year, but the wretched slump has ruined everything. Perhaps next year, he says. But it is perfectly clear I will have to travel without him, as he will not leave his beloved vineyard. I would bring Lucy for you to dote on . . .

It really seemed as if this might happen. Until the dreadful morning of Mrs. Ashburton's accident.

Afterward Molly Jarvis realized that she and Gilbert had been getting too careless. Happiness was an emotion that made one reckless.

Or perhaps it was the long-established routine that made them careless. Emmy took the mistress' breakfast tray upstairs at eight o'clock every morning. After she had breakfasted, Ellen took the children in to spend half an hour with their Mamma before returning with them to the schoolroom.

When Emmy had attended to the mistress' breakfast, she prepared a tray for Mrs. Ashburton. With some grumbling, for she said the old lady never thanked her and was also inclined to spill coffee on the sheets, which Emmy then had to launder.

Mrs. Ashburton, increasingly slow and with hands that had developed a permanent tremor, rose at about half past ten. She rang for Emmy to help her dress, a task the girl found distasteful. She had an old, fusty smell. She didn't wash her hair often enough or bathe enough, if it came to that. Emmy hadn't bargained for being a part nurse to a drunken old woman when she had come to Yarrabee.

When Mrs. Ashburton was successfully dressed in her black silk dress, her cap on her gray hair and her lorgnette dangling around her neck, she made her slow way downstairs. She had a favorite chair under the fig tree in the garden. She sat there dozing in the shade on a hot day, looking like a giant black mushroom, scarcely stirring when the children shouted and played around her. She came to life only in the evenings, when dinner was served. Then she began her long, rambling monologues, while the master filled her glass too often and the mistress frowned at him. But let her be happy, the master said. People should not be deprived of their particular pleasure in their old age.

It was unknown for the old lady to come downstairs before ten thirty.

So how could either Molly or Gilbert expect her at the door of the dining room when Molly, serving the master's breakfast herself, as had become her habit, was caught playfully by him and pulled onto his lap?

He wanted to kiss her warm brown throat where her collar unbuttoned. It had a pulse he could feel beneath his lips.

She resisted for a moment, but he laughed.

"What's the matter? Running away from me?"

"Someone might come in."

"Let them."

She did not find the risks they ran stimulating, giving an edge to their illicit love. She lost her feeling of guilt only when they were safely closeted in her room, the door locked, their clothes discarded, and their passion as impossible to stop as a bush fire in a raging wind.

But Gilbert enjoyed these snatched kisses and caresses. He had a mischievous habit of coming silently behind her in the kitchen, lifting her coiled hair and laying his lips on the nape of her neck, when at any moment one of the maids might come in. Or he would grasp her around the waist and whirl her around, laughing as the color rose in her face.

She lived in perpetual apprehension. She knew that she would have to leave Yarrabee if ever the mistress discovered her treachery. Her code of honor, which was all she had had to live by for so long, would demand that. But it would be annihilating. If Gilbert, by his recklessness, allowed it to happen, she would want to kill him.

Watch the life flow out of this vital, strong body that pulsed against hers? The vivid picture flashing through her mind made her wince. She sighed in despair, her body going limp in his arms.

"What is it, love?"

"I suddenly thought of you dead."

"Dead! What a morbid notion. I'm far from it, I assure you. Let me demonstrate."

And then Mrs. Ashburton's voice came from the doorway. Hoarse, shocked, but strangely unsurprised.

"Aren't you both ashamed of yourselves?"

Gilbert sprang up so abruptly that Molly nearly fell to the floor. She had steadied herself in a moment and hastily smoothed her skirts and fumbled with the betraying buttons of her bodice.

"Good morning, Mrs. Ashburton. Aren't you down early?" Gilbert said.

"A little too early for you, eh?" Mrs. Ashburton was an undignified picture herself, with her hair straggling, her eyes bloodshot, her bed gown sagging across her vast bosom.

"What is it you want?"

Gilbert had regained enough of his usual superb confidence to allow himself some impatience with this doddering, bulbous-eyed old creature. What business had she to wander in so unexpectedly?

"Hasn't Emmy taken you your breakfast?"

"Oh, yes, I've not been neglected. I must say that for you, you've always looked after me well enough. Treated me like your own mother. Gilbert Massingham, you fool!"

"Fool?" Gilbert's eyes glinted dangerously.

"I could call you worse than that. Insensitive. Uncouth. Have your mistresses if you must, and I suppose you must. But not under the same roof as your wife."

Molly moved. Mrs. Ashburton's quivering finger was pointed at her.

"Get back to the kitchen, where you belong. Mr. Massingham will send for you later, if he has any sense, and tell you to pack your bags."

Molly allowed herself an alarmed look at Gilbert. He managed to give her the smallest nod of reassurance. His color was high. He was about to lose his temper. And it would be the old lady, for all her belligerence, who came off the worse.

But he was still controlling himself as Molly left, lingering at the door to hear him say with a calm reasonableness, "Now, Mrs. Ashburton, what's this wild talk about mistresses, because you find me snatching a kiss from my housekeeper? I had always regarded you as a woman of the world. Even if you're as shockable as an old maid, I question your right to tell me what to do in my own house."

"My house, if you please," Mrs. Ashburton said.

"Yours!"

"It could hardly be yours still without my support. Could it? And if I withdraw that support, if I demand to be repaid the amount I have lent you, which is now ten thousand pounds, where will you be, my fine gallant?"

"You can't expect me to take this threat seriously."

"I don't make idle threats, my boy. Just as you, I imagine, don't make idle love. That was no snatched kiss in passing. You're having a liaison with Mrs. Jarvis, and I regard it as being in the worst possible taste. I love Eugenia. Her mother made me responsible for her when we left England together. She's still just about as innocent as the day she was born, bless her, and I won't allow that innocence to be destroyed."

"So?" said Gilbert with ominous quiet.

"So I suggest you find a mistress at least as far off as Parra-

matta. Sydney would be better. And I also suggest you
send Mrs. Jarvis and her child packing."

"You can't expect me to do this!"

"I do. No more, no less."

"And if I refuse?"

"That would be a pity, Gilbert. Then I would have to make
that tiresome journey to Sydney to see my solicitor. I would
require to make a new will and place a warrant of distraint
on Yarrabee. I believe that's what the nasty thing is called."

"You're mad," said Gilbert bluntly. "How dare you dictate
to me like this?"

"Eugenia could take the children and return to England,"
Mrs. Ashburton reflected. "She's always longed to, poor child.
I don't suppose you even realize that; you're so wrapped up in
your own affairs."

"Be quiet, you old witch!" Gilbert exploded. Presently he
said in a calmer voice, "Come now, Mrs. Ashburton, you're
having a brainstorm. We're friends. We can't turn against each
other like this."

"Can't we?" muttered the old lady hoarsely. "Can't we? I
tell you, when I saw that woman in your arms in that indecent
way, something turned black inside me."

"Why, Mrs. Ashburton, I believe you're jealous!"

There was a rustling as Mrs. Ashburton came toward the
door. Molly had to slip away quickly.

She couldn't hear the next words, but she did hear the old
lady saying in a smothered, virulent voice, "And I'm not senile
either. I mean every word I said. You can make up your mind
by tomorrow at the latest. Twenty-four hours, my boy. That's
what you've got."

Molly found Rosie crying in the kitchen.

"Now what are you sniffling about?" she demanded, venting
her distress on the child.

Rosie flung herself at her mother.

"Mammie, we won't have to go away, will we? What would
Kit do when he came home if I wasn't here?"

"What are you talking about?"

"I don't know. I heard Mrs. Ashburton saying someone had to pack their bags. It wasn't us, was it, Mammie? Mammie, was it? Was it?"

"For goodness' sake, hush, child. Why do you always get so excited? You must control yourself. Ladies don't make scenes like this."

"Is it true; is it true?" Rosie demanded, beating at Molly with her bony fists.

"Of course, it isn't true. Do you think Mr. Massingham would hear of any such thing?"

Rosie drew away, her tears arrested, her face suddenly still.

"Why wouldn't he?" she muttered.

"Because he's a good man. Now off up to the schoolroom with you. Don't keep Miss Higgins waiting. Have you got on a clean pinafore? Have you brushed your hair properly? If you want to be a lady—"

Rosie suddenly stamped her foot. Her face was crimson. "I don't want to be a lady!"

"Of course you do." Molly kept her voice calm. Rosie was such a funny secretive child, saying little until she would burst out in one of these tantrums. But there was an unfailing cure for her storms. Molly used it now, deliberately. "How would Kit like you if you weren't?"

Rosie's head went down, her hair falling over her eyes. Then she slid out of the room without saying another word.

At luncheon Eugenia said to Gilbert, "I can't think what has upset Mrs. Ashburton. She refuses to leave her room. She says she's perfectly well but would like her meals sent upstairs today. I do hope she isn't going to begin habits like this. It will be very tiresome for the maids."

"She's only sulking with me," Gilbert said. "We had some words. She'll get over it."

"Words about what?"

"One thing and another. I told her to mind her own business. She pokes her nose into too many things."

"But what things, Gilbert?"

"Only a trifling matter. The old lady's getting senile."

Eugenia frowned uneasily.

"But I always thought you were such devoted friends. You mustn't quarrel with her. You owe her too much."

"There's no need to remind me of that." Gilbert's voice was testy; the taut look that heralded his quick, explosive temper had come to his face.

"I'll go up and talk to her," Eugenia said placatingly. She hated it when Gilbert did lose his temper.

"Leave her alone!"

"But, Gilbert! Is this difference you've had with her serious?"

Gilbert obviously regretted the sharpness of his voice and made himself speak more quietly. "She's only indulging in a fit of jealous pique."

"Jealous pique? At her age?"

"A woman can be jealous at any age. Didn't you know that? I hadn't taken her into my confidence, that's all."

"But what about?"

"Leave it! Leave it, can't you? Since when have you been so deeply interested in my vineyard?"

"Oh, it's about your vineyard." Eugenia sighed, obscurely relieved. The strange notion that Mrs. Ashburton should nourish some personal jealousy about Gilbert was as distasteful as it was incredible. Though it was obvious enough that she doted on him.

"She'll be down to dinner," Gilbert said. "She won't miss her dinner."

She was down that evening. But not to dinner. There was a commotion just after Ellen had lit the lamps in the hall and the sitting room. No one saw what happened. There was only that half-smothered cry and then the terrible slithering, bumping sound on the stairs, and when Ellen and Mrs. Jarvis rushed out, it was to see Mrs. Ashburton at the bottom of the stairs, her petticoats over her head, her dropsical legs immodestly displayed.

Ellen screamed, and presently Emmy and Miss Higgins screamed, too. Mrs. Jarvis, as was to be expected, kept her head. She turned the poor lady onto her back and put a pillow under her head and felt for her pulse. When Eugenia came hurrying down the stairs to see what all the noise was about, she was met by the terrible fixed stare of the old lady's bulbous eyes. She had to cover her eyes for a moment, unable to continue looking at the dreadful face.

"I fear she's killed herself, ma'am," came Mrs. Jarvis' voice from a long distance.

Eugenia forced herself to open her eyes.

"The children," she said faintly. "Ellen! Keep them away. Emmy, run for the master." The strength that had once made her hold Mrs. Jarvis' hand in childbirth now enabled her to kneel beside this other prostrate figure. She took one of the plump, beringed hands and began massaging it feverishly.

"Get some smelling salts, Mrs. Jarvis."

"It's too late, ma'am. The poor lady's broken her neck. Look how her head lies."

Eugenia managed to control her sickness. Words erupted from her instead.

"I always knew she would fall again one day. I'm afraid it's the wine. She drank too much wine, Mrs. Jarvis. Did you know? Night after night she and my husband would sit finishing a bottle. Or two bottles. And today when she was upset after some quarrel they had—she must have been drinking in her room. Can you smell wine on her breath?"

Hard fingers jerked Eugenia back from the grotesque face.

"Don't, ma'am!"

"How silly of me! Of course, there's no breath. She's not breathing." Hysteria was rising in Eugenia. "But I know it will be because of the wine. This dreadful fall. It's one more reason to hate it. Yarrabee Burgundy, Yarrabee Claret, Yarrabee Port. All of them." She couldn't stop talking. The words pouring out of her seemed to ease not only her shock but the weeks and months of strain she had been living through. It was only when Gilbert stood over her and the body of the old lady, whose skirts had been decently straightened by Mrs. Jarvis, that she fell silent.

He jerked her to her feet, not ungently.

"Eugenia, go in the sitting room. I've sent Sloan for the doctor. I think she'd better not be moved."

"She can't lie on the hard floor," Eugenia protested, a sob rising in her throat.

"That won't make any difference to her now."

Gilbert's face had become a stranger's. Bleak, frozen, tight-lipped, a hard look of tragedy in his eyes. He must be thinking that now he would never be able to make up his quarrel. Poor Gilbert. Remorse was terrible. She had realized that all too well when, a little time ago, the news of Colm's death had reached her.

The doctor, dusty and disheveled after the ten-mile journey, expressed it as his opinion that Mrs. Ashburton might have had an apoplectic seizure, causing her to fall. But of course, there was the sad evidence in her room of two empty claret bottles, a chair tipped over, and other signs of disorderly behavior.

He begged Gilbert and Eugenia not to be too grieved about the accident, for, from the dropsical swellings of the ankles and the gross overweight, he feared that the poor lady could not have lasted long. She had been spared a distressing slow illness that could only have ended in death. In his opinion, she had been taken mercifully.

Gilbert, Tom Sloan, and two men sent for from the convicts' huts carried her into the library and laid her on the table there. The doctor said he would send a woman to do the necessary things. She could drive out with the undertaker. In the meantime, Mrs. Ashburton lay beneath the fringed tablecloth, a vast, still mound, and already the house seemed empty without her.

Eugenia kept the little girls with her. She took them in the garden, keeping them outdoors until the sudden dusk fell and then upstairs, where she bathed them herself, and they were allowed the treat of having their supper in bed.

Adelaide seemed unconcerned by the silent, haunted state of downstairs. She prattled on as usual about her own affairs. She was a self-important little creature with a mind as direct and unswervable as her father's. Lucy, however, was completely silent, her eyes unnaturally large, her round cheeks pale, her lips inclined to tremble.

When Eugenia kissed her good night, she clung wildly to her mother, begging her not to go.

"She's afraid," Adelaide said with contempt. "She really shouldn't be such a baby, should she, Mamma?"

"What are you afraid of, my darling?" Eugenia asked.

The little girl buried her face against her mother's breast. At last she managed to whisper in anguish, "Why doesn't God take Grandmamma Ashburton away?"

"But He has taken her away. I told you."

The little fingers dug into her flesh.

"He hasn't. She's downstairs. Ellen said so. She's on a table. Why must she lie on a t-table, Mamma?"

"She's happy, little one. She has no more pain, no more cares."

"She's singing with the angels," Adelaide said. "Surely you know that, Lucy. She's probably holding our baby sister Victoria in her arms."

"On the table!" Lucy whispered, horrified.

"No, you silly, in heaven."

Eugenia rocked the child in her arms.

"Yes, darling, Adelaide is telling you the truth. Grandmamma Ashburton is in heaven."

That irreverent old creature, who Eugenia was sure had not said a prayer for the last thirty years, whose voice, if she tried to sing, was as croaking and hoarse as a crow's. What were God and His angels to do with her in heaven?

If she laughed at the impossible vision, hysteria would rise in her again. If she cried, Lucy would be doubly distressed. If she began to dwell on the fact that Mrs. Ashburton's death was fortuitous for Gilbert since now he could forget their quarrel and her inconvenient demands, she would begin to have dreadful suspicions.

The old lady's death was an accident, of course. But if the question had arisen about who was to be sacrificed, she or the vineyards, which would Gilbert have chosen? Had he deliberately encouraged her to drink herself into this state of ill health and incompetence? Who had seen that she had been supplied with two bottles of claret in her room to be consumed greedily in her state of anger and hurt?

Eugenia, again refusing to dwell on questions that were too worrying, thought only that the evenings were going to be very silent. The voices and the hoarse shouts of laughter coming from the dining table after Eugenia had retired to her sitting room would return like ghosts to the air for a long time to come.

The surprising thing was that although Adelaide and Lucy had been distressed, it was Rosie, that seemingly unemotional child, who was the most profoundly affected by Mrs. Ashburton's death.

It was not until dark that Mrs. Jarvis discovered she was missing. When she didn't appear, Tom Sloan and Jem McDougal went looking for her. She would be hiding up in her favorite tree, they surmised. She was a regular tomboy for climbing trees, especially when Master Kit was home.

By midnight she still had not been found, and the search widened. The master joined it. The maids were told to search every room and cupboard in the house. Mrs. Jarvis came as near to breaking down as anyone had seen her. She was always calm on the surface, her feelings locked deep inside her. Emmy said she had no deep feelings, but Ellen, older and wiser, said that her self-discipline came from her years of dreadful experiences.

"Who knows what's inside the poor creature? Anyway, she

doesn't deserve a little scamp like that Rosie for a daughter."

It was dawn before the child was discovered, and then of her own volition. She came across the courtyard, a skinny little scarecrow, dragging her feet, straws in her hair and a furtive, wild look in her eyes. She said she had slept in a haystack.

When her mother demanded, "Why did you do it, you naughty girl? Don't you know we've been up all night looking for you?" she hung her head, scuffed her feet, and said nothing.

"Rosie! Were you frightened of the poor dead lady? Tell Mammie." Mrs. Jarvis held out her arms and drew the rigid little body into them. But Rosie still remained silent.

It wasn't until she had been persuaded to drink some hot milk and a bit of color had come back to her cheeks that she confessed she had been more frightened of the flying foxes than dead Mrs. Ashburton. They had squeaked in a branch above her head. There had been possums, too. She had been afraid one would drop on her and sniff at her with its bulbous pink nose.

She wouldn't sleep outdoors again, she promised. Or not, at least, until Kit came home. She was recovering her bravado. She didn't need to confide in anybody.

Chapter 26

THIS story was sad telling for Sarah in England. Eugenia wrote:

> Gilbert has been deeply distressed by Mrs. Ashburton's death. He seems to have felt it more sharply than anyone. He says he once promised her a fine tombstone, so this has been ordered, and it is intended to recount all her virtues. To be a little cynical, one of her greatest virtues was her financial help, as she literally has saved the vineyard for Gilbert. Now she has also made him the sole beneficiary in her will. She describes him as the person in this world of whom she was most fond, and this was true. I am even suspicious that her regard for Gilbert was not just maternal, although that sounds a strange thing to say of someone of her age. She had become very possessive and was jealous of their evenings together.
>
> Now, however, it appears that her estate was not nearly as large as she had given us to expect. I never did want Mrs. Ashburton's money and was painfully embarrassed by our debt to her, but I must admit I am now suffering a great disappointment. Gilbert had promised that I could at last have my long-awaited trip home, leaving in the early summer, so as to escape the heat, and taking Adelaide and Lucy with me. Now, however, it appears that Yarrabee, that hungry monster, needs all this shrunken windfall, as Gilbert terms it. So once again I must postpone my trip.

But I must not complain. We have had the enormous benefit of Mrs. Ashburton's help, and Gilbert tells me that the
market for wine is improving at last after the disastrous depres-
sion. So let us be optimistic . . .

It was sad that there were always secrets to be kept from
Sarah, indeed from everyone. For whom could she tell that she
now suspected Gilbert's kindness to Mrs. Ashburton had never
been for any other purpose than getting her money, that his
obsession for his vineyard would drive him to any immorality?

With suspicion nagging at her, Eugenia sat across the table
from him in the evenings, studying his face for signs of the
corruption that this business of viticulture was producing in
him. His face was imperceptibly changing. There were lines
grooved on each side of his mouth and between his eyes. The
sun and wind had bitten into his flesh, leaving it a permanent
brick color, so that the blaze of his blue eyes was startling. His
face was even more the map of Australia, Eugenia thought—
the blue sky, the stony, cracked red earth.

When he sat at the table, he had a tense, restless look as if
he could not wait to get back to his own affairs. Was it because
he had a nagging conscience and constantly saw a bloated, ge-
nial, tipsy ghost in the empty chair beween them?

It was obvious that he genuinely missed Mrs. Ashburton. He
scarcely touched wine. It wasn't worth opening a bottle just for
himself, he said. But the abstention or his conscience made him
irritable and explosive. Eugenia thought miserably that they
had never been further apart. She began to allow the little girls
to stay up later so that they could sit at the table with Papa for
the first course. They nibbled sweet biscuits while the soup
was served. Adelaide prattled happily. She adored her father.
But Lucy was nervous of his loud voice and his sudden jovial
jokes. She hung her head and could scarcely be persuaded to
speak.

Gilbert refrained from showing his impatience with her because she was such a perfect miniature of her mother. But he

THE VINES OF YARRABEE 290

didn't admire timidity and shyness. He liked his children to speak up for themselves, as Kit and Adelaide did. They were bold and forward and had to be punished frequently, but tantrums were much preferable to timidity.

Kit had written from school:

> DEAREST MAMMA AND PAPA,
>   This is a fritful place. I am fritfully unhappy. Mr. Jenkins says my spelling is apalling but my sums better. My friend is James Burton. His father has a sheeprun in Victoria. He is fritfully unhappy, too.
>   Only Rosie may play with my things. Not Addie or Lucy. They are too yung. How is old Erasmus? And old Higgie? James and I are going seeking for gold when we are grown up. I am sorry about Grandmamma Ashburton, but you always said she would fall downstairs one day.
>
> Your loving son,
> CHRISTOPHER

Gilbert roared with laughter at the letter. Eugenia answered it lovingly:

> My darling, you must work hard at your spelling. And I must ask you not to refer to Miss Higgins so disrespectfully. Erasmus is well and talking as much as ever. But I wish he would forget the things poor Grandmamma Ashburton said, as it gives me quite a turn to hear what seems to be her voice coming from the veranda . . .

Then suddenly news arrived from London that at a gathering of wine connoisseurs, Gilbert's 1834 Claret had won special mention. In addition, some bottles of the same vintage sent to that most critical of vignerons, Eugenia's Uncle Henri in France, had elicited guarded approval from the old man. One couldn't expect high enthusiasm from France, the vain queen of the wine industry. Uncle Henri's grudging praise was enough.

This was the turning point, Gilbert said exultantly. Now

Australian wines would begin to be recognized in Europe. It made all the anxieties and difficulties worthwhile. Wouldn't life be dull without this challenging, exciting profession? Could Eugenia truthfully say she would prefer him to be a sheep breeder?

Gloom was dispatched. It was impossible not to catch Gilbert's enthusiasm when he suggested a celebration. They had never had a ball at Yarrabee. Money had always been too short. But now he had a credit with the bank and an assured future. They could spend a hundred pounds or so on furbishing up the house and hiring musicians and extra servants. The rugs could be taken up in the drawing room and the floor polished. The room was big enough for thirty couples. Those who sat out could use the library or Eugenia's writing room or the veranda. It would probably be a warm night, so people would want to stroll in the garden.

Yarrabee's first ball . . .

"I had always imagined it," Eugenia said, her eyes shining.

"So had I, but I was afraid we might have to wait until the children were grown-up. I didn't get rich quickly, did I, my love?"

Gilbert pulled her to him and kissed her warmly. She felt a sharp throb of her heart. But his mind was full of the gaiety ahead. He let her go, talking rapidly.

"You and the girls must get new party dresses. Kit must be home, of course. He's old enough to take a turn on the dance floor. He'll want to learn that new dance everyone is talking about. The polka. You'll want your garden at its best."

"Yes, when the roses are out. I'll tell Peabody. And you must let me have Jem permanently until then. Poor Peabody has got dreadfully slow, but he can still give orders. He will enjoy having his garden admired."

"Your garden, my love. Peabody might have planted it, but you've added the touch of genius."

She was back on her pedestal, she recognized. But perhaps after all, it was better than the guilt-ridden unhappiness of the last few weeks.

"Dearest Sarah," she wrote three weeks later:

> The ball is over and it was the greatest success. Everyone
> came. There were no less than ten carriages driving up to the
> front door at one juncture. You can imagine the scene with
> the horses fidgeting and the ladies in their ball dresses alight-
> ing. Some of the guests brought their children, who were put
> to sleep in the nursery. Ellen had a very busy, happy evening
> with all her charges. The Kellys and the Noakeses came from
> Sydney and stayed over the weekend. They left this morning,
> so I have some time to myself again. Bess brought her three
> girls, who are old enough to go to balls. Alice is just the right
> age for Kit, but she is a dumpy, plain girl and I fear Kit was
> rather rude to her. At least not rude, but neglectful of her.

Eugenia paused, sighing. It was hot, and she was very tired.
And as usual, there were things she couldn't tell Sarah. She
looked around the room, still filled with flowers from the gaiety of the weekend, although the wattle was wilting. It went a
dirty mustard color when its blooms shriveled. Some people
said it was unlucky to have indoors. All she had noticed was
that it had made one of the governor's aides sneeze violently.

Everyone had admired the decorations, the refreshments,
the house, the furniture, the portrait of herself and her baby
son hanging over the fireplace. (What a look of dreamy innocence her face had had!) The house had come to life as it never
had before. This was the kind of occasion Gilbert had had in
mind when he had insisted that the drawing room be large
enough to hold a ball.

It had been a triumphant night. Except for that one thing
which she didn't intend discussing with Sarah.

> Kit wore his first grown-up suit. He looked so handsome. He
> is very tall for his age, and he knows how to charm people
> already. He danced with his mother very prettily. I discovered
> that there was no need for me to guide him. He knew the
> steps already. He quite enslaved Alice Kelly, who looked at
> him with cow eyes, but, as I said, did not get much attention
> from the object of her devotion . . .

How could she have. Because Eugenia, taking a turn in the garden with the young man who had been so much afflicted by the pollen in the wattle, had seen a flicker of white in the shrubbery.

Peabody's rhododendrons had done well after a slow start. They now made a dense green hedge that enclosed the bottom of the garden and provided not only a dim, shady walk, but also, it seemed, protection for lovers.

The young aide, also glimpsing the movement in the dimness, wanted to turn back tactfully. But Eugenia had a sudden suspicion too strong to be ignored. She had been trying to keep an eye on Kit, hoping that he was enjoying his first ball, anxious that his father would not encourage him to drink too much wine. Gilbert had so much enthusiasm and so little sense where his wine was concerned.

But her duties as a hostess took all her time.

She realized that she hadn't seen Kit for the last hour. She was almost certain that he was concerned with the flickering white dress in the shrubbery.

"Kit, is that you?" she called.

For a moment there was complete stillness in the dark screen of bushes.

Then, slowly, Kit emerged, dragging by the hand a slim scrap of a girl in a white dress.

Rosie!

"It's all right, Mamma," he said easily. "We came down to feed the opossums in the tree." He did, in truth, have some scraps of food wrapped in a linen napkin. Eugenia, striving against alarm, remembered that as a little boy Kit had liked to feed the nocturnal animals that came slithering down the branches in the dark. But she could not help observing the possessive way in which Rosie clung to him. Perhaps the girl thought that in the dark of the moonlit garden Eugenia would not notice the handclasp or jump to the conclusion that the two had been kissing. She recognized the defiant lift of Kit's chin, a sure sign that he intended to defy any accusation of misbehavior.

How could she accuse him now? The matter must wait until the morning.

But Rosie! That little vixen with her slanting eyes.

Eugenia knew that Mrs. Jarvis had made her a new dress for the occasion. It hadn't seemed fair that Adelaide and Lucy should be elaborately dressed in their bows and sashes without Rosie also having a pretty dress. But it had been understood, naturally, that the girl would be in the background. She could watch the arrivals from the stairs, just as Adelaide and Lucy did. She could even linger on to catch glimpses of the dancing after the younger girls had gone to bed.

But to lure Kit into the garden! That was unforgivable. She was his foster sister. It was highly indecent that she should be clinging to him like this. A childhood affection was one thing, but this was becoming too significant. Something would have to be done about Rosie Jarvis.

"Now don't get in a state, Mamma," Kit said the next morning when she had called him into her sitting room. "I told you that Rosie and I were only feeding the possums."

"You were absent from the ballroom for more than an hour," Eugenia said. "As it happens, Adelaide saw you and Rosie go out."

"That little telltale!" Kit said furiously.

"We are speaking of you and Rosie. You can't have been feeding the opossums for more than an hour. Anyway, you know your father has forbidden you to encourage them. They're pests. They get into the vines. Apart from that, where were your manners? Leaving your guests for so long."

"They were yours and Papa's guests, Mamma."

"Kit, don't contradict me, please. You were hiding in the dark with a servant girl. It was in the worst possible taste."

Kit's fair skin showed too vividly his change of color. His mouth went sullen.

"Rosie isn't a servant girl."

"Then what is she, pray?"

"They might talk like that in England, but not in Australia."

"You're not suggesting it's I who have bad manners!"

"No, Mamma, your manners are perfect, but old-fashioned. Rosie's my friend. She's not a servant; she's an equal."

Eugenia held her back a little straighter. "I don't pretend to make the laws in Australia, but I do in my own house. I shall be speaking to Rosie's mother about her future. Now you may go."

He had failed to make the defense she had hoped he would. He had not insisted that Rosie was only his foster sister, and therefore, their meeting in the dark was harmless. Instead, he made an appeal to his father. Gilbert sought Eugenia out in her sitting room.

"Eugenia, what's this about sending Rosie away?"

"Is that what Kit has been telling you?"

"Something to that effect. The boy was upset. Thought you wanted to punish Rosie for something. Has she been offending you?"

"Yes," said Eugenia briefly.

"Then have it out with the girl."

"Since Kit thinks I'm being so harsh, he might have told you the whole story. Didn't he?"

Gilbert said cagily, "Oh, something about the pair of them sneaking out to feed the possums the night of the ball. I told him he'd do better to take a gun and shoot the pests. He could knock down a few roos at the same time."

"At midnight by moonlight? I thought that was much more a time for lovers."

"Are you suggesting Kit and Rosie—but good Lord, they're practically brother and sister." Gilbert laughed heartily, then stopped. A flicker of uneasiness crossed his face. "And still children," he added.

"Did you think yourself a child at fourteen?" Eugenia asked.

"No, but I—"

"But what?"

"Well, I'd had to get out and fend for myself. I had to grow up young. I wasn't pampered like Kit. Now look here, Eugenia, forget this escapade. The boy must have had a glass too many of wine. He hasn't a head for it yet."

Eugenia stood up, not attempting to control the temper flaring through her. For once she would forget the good manners with which Kit had taunted her.

"In one breath you say Kit is a child, and in the next you admit you have been encouraging him to drink too much wine. It's your wretched wine all the time! You helped both Colm O'Connor and Mrs. Ashburton to their deaths. No, don't deny it. Indirectly you did so. Perhaps not so indirectly with poor old Mrs. Ashburton. And now you laugh because your son is fumbling with servant girls in the shrubbery because he has had too much to drink. Kit! Only fourteen! For heaven's sake, Gilbert, teach him discipline and discrimination. Don't allow him to ruin himself because you think you can brew a good wine and, therefore, everyone must drink it. Don't you *see?*"

"I see you've got yourself in a state."

"Gilbert! Listen to me!"

"I've listened." Gilbert ran his hand wearily over his forehead. "Everything always comes back to my wine, doesn't it? Every disaster. You must forgive me for saying you are a little fanatical on that point."

"But you admitted yourself that Kit must have had a glass too many."

"Oh, very well. I concede that. But I do *not* concede the comment on Mrs. Ashburton's death."

"I meant every word of it."

"My God! You can be an implacable woman, can't you?"

"When necessary. I intend speaking to Mrs. Jarvis today. I'll have Rosie placed in a position. She's quite old enough. I've been thinking for some time that she should go. Miss Higgins has given her a reasonable education. She has us to thank for that. But I don't think she has much gratitude. She neglects the duties she was given in the house. The maids say she always disappears when she's wanted, and they find her sitting in the tree at the bottom of the garden. The same tree where the opossums were supposed to be the other night. It's her favorite spot. Of course, she must have lured Kit down there. There's no question about that. So I won't have her in the house any longer."

"You speak as if you hate her."

"And why do you defend her?" Eugenia asked, and was puzzled to see the uneasiness flicker in Gilbert's eyes again. Surely that sly girl hadn't been using her wiles on him, too.

"Because she is only a bit of a thing, I suppose. You wouldn't want to turn Adelaide out at that tender age."

"Adelaide!" Eugenia exclaimed. "But how can you make a comparison between her and Rosie?"

She would like to have sent Rosie farther away than Parramatta. She had discovered that being a mother could bring out a ruthless side to her nature, which she hadn't known she possessed. Since Gilbert did not seem to realize the danger of Kit's and Rosie's continued friendship (or alternatively did not object to it), she must take control of the situation herself.

If only Rosie had inherited her mother's honest character and her gift for knowing her place, it would have been a different matter. Eugenia supposed servants like Mrs. Jarvis were a vanishing race. Certainly in this country they were. She and this woman had gone through so much together, illness, disaster, childbirth, yet Mrs. Jarvis had never been guilty of a word or an action that could be criticized.

Mrs. Jarvis made no protest about Eugenia's decision. But she looked pale and tired, Eugenia thought. Aging, too. There was gray in the soft blond hair. And her hands, clasped in front of her, were worn with hard work. She kept her eyes lowered too much, as if she were afraid of Eugenia seeing the trouble in them.

"Now don't be so worried, Mrs. Jarvis. You must see that it's time Rosie began work. Idleness isn't good for her."

"Has she been up to some mischief, ma'am? You would tell me, wouldn't you?"

Eugenia prevaricated. "Ellen and Emmy tell me that she's lazy. She won't do her work properly. But that's understandable. She hasn't been trained for housework. She has quite enough education to take a position as a governess or in a school, which was what I had always intended for her. I can easily find a nice family in the country who would like a governess. There are all too few girls available. Or if she prefers to remain in Parramatta, where she can come here on her day off, then she is at liberty to do so. Will you speak to her yourself?"

"Yes, ma'am. I will. And you're right in what you say about her. She has a bit of wildness. But she'll grow out of it, I'm sure."

"Yes, I'm sure, too," Eugenia said kindly.

"It was not knowing her father's nature well enough. Who knows what he had in him?"

"Who knows what tendencies any of us inherit? We won't blame Rosie for what she can't help. I expect she'll find herself a good young husband soon enough. Then that's settled, Mrs. Jarvis."

Kit went back to school, and without protest Rosie packed the wicker bag that her mother had brought from Sydney fifteen years ago. She was happy to leave Yarrabee. She didn't much mind where she went, for the next two or three years. She bent over the small mirror on the table beside her bed studying her reflection. Straight brown hair, a nondescript face, those strange slanting eyes. Not much there to attract anyone's attention. Except Kit's, and she had always known how to have him in her spell . . .

With the candle blown out and Molly's face only a dark shape on the pillow beside him, Gilbert said, "I hope you're not fretting about Rosie going off. My wife has a bee in her bonnet."

"Not a bee. Common sense," Molly replied tranquilly.

"Then you don't mind?"

"No. It's the best thing. Rosie has to make her way. It's time she began." She added, probing delicately, "Did you agree with the mistress?"

"About separating Kit and Rosie? That's what it amounts to, you know. It's probably best at present. They're pretty young."

"And later?"

"Anyone belonging to you is always welcome at Yarrabee. Does that answer you? Witch woman."

Molly sighed in his arms.

"You're not getting tired of me?"

"Now what are you wanting? Compliments? I never thought you were vain." He kissed her, holding her close. "I still love you, Molly. I love two women, in different ways. Does that make me a wicked fellow? Or just unique?"

"Just lucky, perhaps," Molly murmured, with a gurgle of laughter. Then she gave a faint shiver. "When I'm with the mistress, I feel guilty. I admire her so much. Ever since that first night at that nasty inn when she was so scared."

"Scared? Eugenia? Not of me?"

"Of that escaped convict. Of you, too. She was very young and a bride. I hope you were kind to her." Molly suddenly rolled over, gripping him hard. "All the same, I can't bear to think of it. I shut my thoughts to it. The nights you go to her."

"I *am* kind to her," Gilbert said, detaching himself from Molly's grip. "Knowing you has made me much more understanding, if that eases your mind. I treat her like porcelain. I should have from the start, I suppose. You've taught me that. No two women could be less alike than you and she. But she's the kind of wife I wanted, Molly. It's some vanity in me."

"You're a good man!" Molly said in a stifled voice. "Don't let anyone ever tell you you're not."

Gilbert snatched her to him violently.

"But what would I have done without you—are you happy? You never ask for anything. You just wait. You're always here."

"And always will be. Don't you fret, love."

Of course, she waited; of course, she was always there. These hours were her heaven. No one could have heaven all the time. No one would be foolish enough to spoil it by making impossible demands. She had suffered too much in her life to risk losing this unexpected beneficence.

But she was human enough to want more for her daughter.

Chapter 27

As the leaves began to fall that autumn, there was nobody to sweep them up. Peabody had died. He was found in his bed in his hut, his face turned up to the ceiling, his wide-open eyes lightless. No pain showed on his face. He had gone as easily as a leaf falling off a tree.

No one had ever known much about him. He had romanced about the great gardens he had worked in England, but that might have been all fantasy. He had never mentioned a family or even what his first name was.

All that could be put on his tombstone was PEABODY—A GARDENER.

Eugenia thought he would like that as much as Mrs. Ashburton would have liked her long panegyric. She missed the old man grievously. His spare, crooked figure pottering around was as much a part of the garden as her white roses. The garden was his true memorial. He had lived long enough to see the honeysuckle grow to the tops of the veranda posts, for the rhododendrons to shut out the view of bare, dusty paddocks, as they had been meant to do, and for the lilacs and laburnums to flower as prolifically as tropical plants. The herbaceous border was flourishing. Clumps of irises were reflected in the lily pool. Flocks of brilliantly colored finches frolicked in the birdbath and were Lucy's special delight. Frangipani smelled sweetly; flame trees made permanent rags of color in the background.

But the roses had been Peabody's pride. He used to stump

up and down beside the trellises, declaring that there was none better in the whole of New South Wales.

"When you catch the scent of them tea roses, you'll remember me, my lady," he had been saying lately. That had been his only hint of an awareness of approaching death.

There was no one to take his place. Eugenia tentatively suggested Jem McDougal and was promptly refused.

"I've been training that lad for ten years to be a vigneron. Turn him into a gardener! Nonsense!"

Although he enjoyed the growing fame of Yarrabee's garden, Gilbert would let nothing interfere with his vineyard.

"Find a good lad in Parramatta. It shouldn't be difficult."

There was really no one to replace Peabody, although Eugenia found a respectable, inarticulate young man who had arrived on a recent emigrant ship. His name was Obadiah White, and he hadn't been at Yarrabee a week before he was making sheep's eyes at Emmy. Emmy began to find an astonishing number of errands which took her through the garden. However, that was nothing to worry about. It had been Eugenia's suggestion that as the convicts departed (and now there were only two long-term men left), their huts should be refurbished and made into decent living quarters for married couples or the single men who wished to stay at Yarrabee permanently, such as Tom Sloan and Jem McDougal.

If Emmy's blushes meant impending matrimony, she could simply move from her room in the servants' wing to a comfortable hut. Some of the convicts had made small gardens and neat paths around their living quarters. Time had softened everything at Yarrabee. Now the buildings belonged to their background.

And it seemed half a century since that dreadful night when Gilbert had come in with his shirt spotted with human blood.

Kit was in his last year at school. Adelaide, Eugenia regretfully admitted in her letters to Sarah, was a hoyden. Her father spoiled her. He liked her better riding astride her pony than sidesaddle in a ladylike way. The next thing, Eugenia said, he would be letting her wear trousers! And he encouraged her to walk up and down the terraces of vines with him or to join him in the cellar when he was casking or bottling wine. She would come in with her frock stained with red grape juice, her face sunburned and freckled because she would let her hat fall back on her neck as soon as she was out of sight of the house.

Let her be, Gilbert said. She was the new kind of woman that Australia was going to produce. Healthy, outdoor, capable. What nonsense to sit indoors all morning sewing or sketching or struggling with her French grammar when the weather was so good! Besides, one didn't need to be a man to learn viticulture. Eugenia would be surprised if she saw how skillful Adelaide was at drawing off wine from casks into bottles. She and Jem had bottled the entire season's sauterne, and now it was ready for marketing.

Eugenia was horrified.

"Whatever do you want? An Amazon for a daughter? I won't allow it. Adelaide must attend to her studies. Miss Higgins says her French is deplorable, and she has never yet had the patience to read a book from cover to cover. I can endorse that her music leaves a great deal to be desired. She may indeed know a great deal about viticulture, but how is that going to help her in fashionable drawing rooms?"

Gilbert looked at Eugenia wonderingly.

"Do you know, sometimes I wonder if you have ever actually left England?"

"There is no need to criticize me because I mention Adelaide's shortcomings. She's my daughter, as well as yours, and I insist on her having a decent, cultured upbringing. I won't allow her to be an ignorant hoyden. Anyway, it isn't right that she should be alone with Jem so much."

"Good heavens, she's only a child."

"She's nearly thirteen years old—and precocious. After the summer holidays I intend making inquiries about placing her at the Misses Chisholm's College of Arts and learning to be a young lady. A thing I am afraid she will never become while she stays at Yarrabee."

"Very well," said Gilbert, after a pause. "I have no objection. But after vintage. I've promised her she can help this year."

"Gilbert! With all those rough people!"

Gilbert became impatient, as he always did nowadays when Eugenia attempted to have a sensible discussion with him.

"You're too fastidious! Once it was those terrible convicts. Now it's that rough riffraff from Parramatta."

"Once you wanted me to be fastidious," Eugenia pointed out.

"Yes, I did. And I still want you to be. It's right for you." It never worried Gilbert that he contradicted himself. "But Adelaide's an Australian. That's different."

"I hope you won't have these ideas about Lucy, too."

"No, no, you have my permission to give Lucy all the lady-like education you want to. But try to make her less scared of things. She won't even go near that bumbling old pony that wouldn't hurt a fly. I can't have a daughter who can't ride."

"Does it matter? She can stay with me in the house. She sketches beautifully, and she has a very pretty singing voice. She already dances very gracefully and can sew better than I can. Do those things mean that she isn't suitable for life in this country?"

"I told you—you can do what you like with Lucy. But leave Adelaide to me."

Lucy was delighted when Adelaide went to school. Now she had her beloved Mamma all to herself. After the morning lessons with Miss Higgins, she and Mamma could spend the long afternoons together. If it was too hot to go outdoors, they sat in the relatively cool drawing room sewing or making pictures of dried flowers and listening to Erasmus screeching on the veranda in reply to the thousand swooping, shrieking galahs in the gum trees. When it was cooler, they would walk in the garden, Lucy clinging to her mother's arm so as to share the shade of the parasol. Her skin burned painfully in the sun. She was supremely happy that she had inherited her mother's delicacy.

Adelaide had departed with her boxes, to join the thirty or so pupils at the Misses Chisholm's establishment. The brochure said that the Misses Chisholm specialized in singing and music, languages (French, German, Italian, and Latin), drawing, enamel or china painting, oil painting in figures, landscapes or flowers, and watercolors on paper, satin, silk, or wood, and dancing.

It was to be hoped that Adelaide would now apply herself to her studies and prove that she could become a cultured young lady. This was the end of galloping around the countryside astride Poacher or mingling among all those noisy rough people at vintage.

Kit wrote:

DEAR ADDIE,

So you are being packed off, too. Sometimes I think Mamma's ideas for us are too lofty altogether. I had a letter from Rosie. She is now governess to a family at Darling Downs, as I expect you know. There are four children. She says she doesn't mind it, and she doesn't miss old Higgie and the schoolroom, but she always misses Yarrabee. She isn't coming back for a while because she says she wouldn't be welcome. I know that Mamma has been a bit hard on her, but I don't know why she has always thought her own mother doesn't care about her. She says when she was only four years old, she was put to sleep in a room by herself, and she knew then that her mother didn't want her. This is all a bit deep for me. I have always thought Mrs. Jarvis was a pretty good sort, but I expect Yarrabee could manage without her even if Mamma and Papa think it couldn't. Don't let anyone else see this letter. Mamma would be furious if she knew Rosie wrote to me.

Adelaide was writing her own private letters.

DEAR JEM,

I am writing to you because I don't trust anyone else to look after Poacher. Will you see that he is exercised enough and rubbed down properly? I want your solemn promise to this. And can you keep an absolute secret? The girls here don't believe I am allowed to drink wine and have never tasted it themselves. I wonder if you could smuggle me a bottle of sauterne (too sweet, ugh! But these girls are quite ignorant about wine and wouldn't like a dry to begin with). If you let me know when you are going to be in Parramatta and could put a bottle under the bottlebrush just inside the gate, I could get it when we have recreation in the afternoon. *Don't seal the cork*, or I won't be able to get it out. We will have a midnight party. *Please burn this letter after reading it.*

Your friend,

ADELAIDE MASSINGHAM

To Adelaide's disappointment, however, when the bottle was hidden under the bush at the gates, it contained not wine but a note written in Jem's large awkward script.

DEAR MISS ADELAIDE,

Not a drop of wine in this bottle, ha ha. Do you want to get expelled and me lose my job? When you are two years older, I will oblige. I gave Poacher a good gallop this morning. The vines on the south terrace have got some blight. Your father is worried, but we are cutting them down and burning them to stop it spreading. I miss you around.

Your friend,

JEM

The letter almost made up for the hoax of the empty bottle. Adelaide had been boasting to her two closest friends. She would have to climb down now. She didn't enjoy that prospect. But—"I miss you around . . ." Dear silly Jem. And if he thought she was staying in this prim and proper school, with the devastatingly tedious drawing and piano lessons, for two years, he was mistaken.

It seemed, however, that she might have to, for Eugenia was delighted with the improvement in Adelaide's deportment and manners. Within three months her hoydenish daughter was showing signs of being a lady. She held herself straighter ("How can I not, Mamma, when we have to sit for hours with a board tied to our backs?"), spoke more politely, and was beginning to take an interest in clothes. Her best friend, Jane Thompson, had a crinoline and six starched petticoats. Couldn't Adelaide have one, also? And Jane had been allowed to put her hair up for a party. Adelaide was literally dying of longing for the day when she could stop wearing hair ribbons and those two thick, tiresome plaits down her back.

But the lessons were infinitely boring, and she had no gift for music or painting or needlework. The Misses Chisholm said they had never seen such clumsy fingers.

"It's Lucy who should be at school, not me," Adelaide sighed. "She would come first in everything."

"That's because she takes pains with her work," Eugenia said. "But she isn't strong enough to go to school, I'm afraid."

"She'd be teacher's pet if she did go," Adelaide said under her breath, and got a critical look from her mother.

"Do speak up, Adelaide. No one enjoys muttering. And if you're going out, pray put on a hat. You've been home for only a week, and already I can see freckles on your nose. Where are you going, anyway?"

"Just to the stables, Mamma."

"You spend too much time at the stables. Why don't you sit quietly in the garden with Lucy and me? It's much too hot to rush about."

"I have to exercise Poacher, Mamma."

"Jem seems to manage that very well when you're at school."

"But he's my horse, Mamma. When I'm home, I have to do it."

"Very well, then. But don't get overheated. And I want you back in time for tea. Mrs. Bishop and Mrs. Stevenson are driving out from Parramatta. They have expressed a special wish to see you."

So there would be no time to stop at the winery, was virtually what Mamma was saying She was well aware that Adelaide had a habit of doing that and that if a cask was in the process of being bottled, Papa or Jem permitted her to taste the contents. What she didn't know was that Adelaide already had quite a palate. She could pronounce almost as accurately as her father which wine would improve with keeping, which would go sour and thin.

Gilbert would roar with delighted laughter as Adelaide rolled the wine around her mouth, reflected, then spit it out. Jem watched with intensity, his expression suggesting that the spectacle was more interesting than the verdict. Jem was getting near thirty now, and whether or not he had a girl in Parramata was not known. He had never shown any interest in the maids at Yarrabee, to the chagrin of Ellen in particular. She had been kind to Jem ever since he had arrived, as a skinny, starved lad straight off a convict ship. She was older than he, of course, but that didn't seem to matter since the master had singled out Jem to be his assistant. He was as important as or more important than Tom Sloan, and it wouldn't have been a bit like marrying someone beneath her if he had shown a fancy for Ellen.

But he didn't. His serious face, neither handsome nor plain, became young and animated only when the children were around. Particularly Miss Adelaide. And she was a spoiled, precocious miss in Ellen's view. It was Kit's business to learn the wine, not Adelaide's. So it had been the wisest thing the mistress had done to send Adelaide off to school. As she grew to be a fashionable young lady, Jem would realize his place.

Lucy had never set foot in the winery. She had paused timidly at the door one day, caught the waft of sour wine, and been nauseated in exactly the same way as her mother. Her father had told her gruffly to keep away. To stay with her mother and keep out of the hot sun.

She was very much in awe of her father. She never knew what to say to him and believed that he found her stupid and too timid. She knew that she was much prettier than Adelaide, yet it was always Adelaide who got the hearty greeting and the admiring glance. Even when she was dressed for church on Sundays, and Mamma and Ellen and Miss Higgins had all admired her immaculate little person, telling her she was as pretty as a picture, Papa scarcely gave her a look. He would bundle her into the buggy beside Mamma, paying no heed to whether or not he rumpled her frock, and if she cried, as she often did, silently and in furious shame, he would say impatiently, "What's she blubbering about now?"

She would really have been blissfully happy if she had only needed to see Papa, say, once a week. She didn't think she liked men very much. They had such loud voices. Even Kit shouted at her when he came home from school, expecting her to fetch and carry for him. He had had slaves at school, he said. Now he was home, she would have to do instead. On the whole his demands were innocent enough, but there was one thing that worried her intensely. Every now and then he would slip a letter into her reticule and ask her to post it when she was in Parramatta. The letter was always addressed to Miss Rose Jarvis.

There didn't seem to be much harm in Kit's writing to Rosie, so why did it need to be so secret? Kit had impressed on her that she must never let Mamma see her posting the letters. She must make an excuse to go into the little post office, where the postmistress also sold haberdashery and sweets. Surely she always needed a reel of cotton or something.

It was easy enough to do this, but the deception kept Lucy awake at nights. She had never had secrets from Mamma. She had an uneasy feeling that Kit was using her in this way because he enjoyed his power over her.

Men really could be beastly.

The ball had been a milestone in Yarrabee's history, but late that autumn a much more important event was to happen.

Eugenia wrote to Sarah:

> What do you think, we are to have a viceregal visit! You will remember my telling you that our governor, Sir George Gipps, had returned to England, and that his place had been taken by Sir Charles Fitzroy and his wife, Lady Mary. Well, they have expressed a wish to come here not only to inspect the vineyard (which Gilbert, by his dedicated endeavors, is making famous), but to spend an entire weekend. Lady Mary says flatteringly that she has heard about my garden and

confesses she will find that more interesting than grape vines and wineries.

Gilbert is extremely pleased, he is walking about like a dog with two tails, and I admit that I find the prospect exciting and challenging. In Australia entertaining the governor and his lady is comparable to entertaining the Queen and Prince Albert at home. Though rather less formal.

So you can imagine the flurry we are in. As well as Sir Charles and Lady Mary, there will be their son, George Fitzroy, and Colonel Mundy, adjutant general. And Lady Mary's maid and a valet and a coachman. We have enough bedrooms and are hastily having the largest of these refurbished for the vice-regal pair. It fortunately has its own dressing room. Kit is moving out of his room to allow George Fitzroy to occupy it, and Colonel Mundy will be accommodated in one of the small west rooms. I will make my sitting room available for Lady Mary's use, and the men may play billiards or read the newspapers in the library.

Adelaide has permission to come home from school that weekend. Although she is only fifteen, she is very mature in many ways, and it will do her good to meet a sophisticated and, I hear, good-looking young Englishman like George Fitzroy. My little Lucy is still too young for these excitements. She has remained a child much longer than Adelaide did, rather to my selfish pleasure. I have no desire to lose her to a young man, no matter how eligible, for a long time.

We will be sitting at least nine to breakfast and more to luncheon and dinner, according to how many other people we invite. Gilbert wants to plan a shoot, and we will all ride to the lake for a picnic if the weather is fine. That is, provided Lady Mary feels able to. She is very large and stout (as also is Sir Charles) and is something of an invalid. Gilbert says we must have at least one large dinner party and music and dancing afterward.

Mrs. Jarvis and I have been discussing menus. She is quite unflustered by all this, indeed seems to enjoy it. She has requested that I hire two extra girls for the weekend, but only to help in the kitchen. And she insists on doing the waiting on table herself, with the assistance of Ellen and Emmy. She wouldn't trust untrained girls, she says.

So that burden is off my shoulders. All I will have to do is entertain my guests and see that they are comfortable. Lucy has asked to do the flowers in all the rooms. She is very artistic. I do not need to add that Gilbert is getting out his best wines . . .

It was true that Molly Jarvis was enjoying the occasion. Her abilities had never been tested to this point, but she was supremely confident. The larder, built of thick stone to keep out the heat, was stocked with provisions. The maids had their instructions down to the last detail. It was a pity that Emmy Dawson was so lovesick about Obadiah White. She had been forbidden to see him or think of him while the great visit was in progress. In any case, he was too busy putting the garden in perfect order to be bothered with Emmy mooning over him. He had enough to do seeing that Miss Lucy didn't steal his best blooms for the house. And he worried that there would be a strong wind at the last minute, so that he would have to sweep up leaves and comb the precious green patch of lawn back into order.

No one got to bed early on the last evening. Molly was the latest of all. But she had at last finished plucking and stuffing the chickens; the big, rich, dark fruitcake was out of the oven and cooling; the kitchen was set to rights. She stood for a moment surveying, with pleasure, the well-stocked larder. She had not forgotten the terrible half-starved years following her arrival in Australia. The sight of food aroused an almost sensuous pleasure in her.

"Looks famous," came Gilbert's voice behind her, startling her. "Are we really going to get through all that?"

"A good deal of it, I should think. Have I overestimated?"

"Better too much than too little. I'll never be known for parsimony." He lifted the heavy coil of hair from her neck and laid his lips on the warm exposed skin. "Nor will you."

She sprang away. "I've told you, not here! Someone may come in."

He laughed softly. "I like seeing you jump like that."

"Ah, don't risk it. We've been too lucky. I get scared."

"Then go to your room. I'll be with you in a few minutes."

"Tonight!"

"I can't tomorrow night. I'll be drinking port with His Excellency. Besides, I have a gift for you."

"A gift?"

"You never ask for anything, do you?"

"I have no right. I'm guilty enough."

"Don't talk like that. Off with you."

The gift was an amethyst and pearl locket, which Gilbert hung around Molly's neck as she sat half-undressed. It hung between her breasts, and he said that that was where he would always like to see it, against her bare skin. She wanted to refuse it, to say she wasn't that sort of mistress.

Instead, she said scoffingly, "Whenever will I wear a thing like that?"

"When we're together. I know you can't wear it in public. But I wanted to give you something. Can't you gloat over it in private?"

"Gloat?" Her eyes flashed.

"I've used the wrong word, I suppose. I'm not clever enough. But I'll be disappointed and hurt if you refuse it. You will keep it, won't you?"

She half-nodded. She was thinking against her will that although this was a very pretty thing, it was only an amethyst. The mistress got diamonds. No, she wouldn't refuse it, much as she wanted to. She would keep it for Rosie.

Chapter 28

LUCY couldn't believe her eyes.

"Addie, you're not putting your hair up!"

"What else do I appear to be doing?" Adelaide asked, inserting more pins expertly into the heavy red-gold coils over her ears.

"But did you ask permission? You're not sixteen yet."

"Life would be very dull if one always asked permission." Adelaide turned her head this way and that, critically studying her reflection in the mirror. "Especially when it wouldn't be likely to be granted. There! How do I look?"

"Practically grown-up," Lucy had to admit.

"This is the latest fashion in London. We had some fashion journals at school."

"Were you allowed to put your hair up at school?"

"If we liked," Adelaide said airily. "At least, Miss Annabel Chisholm would let us, but Miss Hester is an old stick." She pulled at the neckline of her white muslin dress. "This is a *child's* dress," she said. "I have half a mind to cut the neck lower. If I did"—her eyes were suddenly sparkling—"you could sew it for me, couldn't you? Everyone is always praising your needlework."

Lucy backed away, her eyes widening.

"You wouldn't dare!"

"Oh, you are a milksop, Lucy. Always scared of everything. The great George isn't going to take much notice of you if you behave like that."

"Do you mean George Fitzroy? But I'm not expecting him even to look at me."

"And he won't either, in that case. It's a great pity, because you're really very pretty."

Lucy was fighting the too easy, always shameful tears.

"Why is it a great pity? I'm not out of the schoolroom yet."

"But you will be one day. And I suppose he has a memory."

"Don't be silly, Addie. It's you who is to fascinate him. Mamma said so."

Adelaide shrugged. Her poise was quite alarming.

"Perhaps. However, it just happens I don't want my husband chosen for me."

"But if you fell in love with George Fitzroy, it would be all right, wouldn't it? They say he's very good-looking."

"And probably as vain as a peacock. If he behaves condescendingly to us, I shall very quickly put him in his place."

"Addie, you wouldn't!"

"Indeed I would—" Adelaide broke off to give a squeal. "I can hear a carriage." She rushed to the window. "Here they come! Look! That must be George riding beside them. And Colonel Mundy on the other side."

"Don't hang out so far. They'll see you," Lucy said nervously. But she was hanging a modest way out herself, for she thought the young man on the chestnut mare very handsome. Tall and slight and elegant, the sun shining on his glossy brown hair. She hadn't expected him to be quite so good-looking. Surely now Addie wouldn't be so contemptuous of him. She patted her carefully arranged ringlets, wishing suddenly that she herself were old enough or bold enough to do her hair in the latest London fashion. As it was, George Fitzroy would think her just a little girl and hardly notice her. If only she could overcome her painful shyness and converse with him. But what about? How could he possibly be interested in anything she had to say?

At least one thing was certain, and that was that Mamma would not lose her poise. Confronted unexpectedly with Adelaide with her hair up, she smiled serenely, looking quite beautiful in her lavender-blue gown.

"Lady Mary, may I present my daughters to you? This is Adelaide, and this"—her hand rested lightly and reassuringly on Lucy's shoulder—"is Lucy."

They both curtsied to the large, very stout lady in the bottle-green traveling clothes. Lady Mary Fitzroy said, in a jolly voice, "Good gracious me, Mrs. Massingham, you look much too young to have such grown-up daughters."

"They're really not very grown-up, Lady Mary. Adelaide goes to Miss Chisholm's school, and Lucy has a governess. Now I am sure you would like to see your room before the gentlemen come in. It's on the cool side of the house, although even that isn't very cool at times. Lucy has done the flowers. She's very clever . . ."

The voices died around the turn of the staircase. Adelaide was overtaken with a fit of giggles.

"Can you hear her huffing and puffing? I hope she doesn't fall down the stairs like Grandmamma Ashburton. She is very nearly as fat. I wonder where the men are. Surely Papa hasn't taken them to the winery already. I will be furious if he has, because I want to go, too."

Adelaide darted away before Lucy could beg not to be left alone. And so it was that she was standing nervously in the hall when George Fitzroy strolled in.

"Hello," he said, and sketched her a small bow. "Are you the elder daughter or the younger? I'm George Fitzroy."

Lucy murmured breathlessly that she was the younger. The warm brown eyes smiled at her briefly and impersonally.

"I thought you must be. I saw you both looking out of the window."

Lucy colored in embarrassment.

"Addie—has her hair up."

"Oh! Has she really?"

Lucy was trembling with nervousness. Where *was* everybody?

"Won't you c-come into the drawing room?"

"Thank you. The others are on my heels, I think. Ah, there you are, Mr. Massingham. I took the liberty of coming in."

Papa had on his jolly company face, his eyes sparkling, his lips smiling. He would tell amusing stories and laugh a lot and not once raise his voice in anger this weekend. But Lucy would still try to be invisible if his bright, fierce glance shot her way. Otherwise, she might be expected to say something clever or informative in the way that Kit and Addie found so easy and that was utterly beyond her.

"You've met my younger daughter, I see," Papa was saying, and the stout gentleman behind him said in a loud jovial voice, "My son may have, but I haven't. Well, this is a pretty sprite, Massingham."

"Yes. She's like her mother. Where's Adelaide, Lucy?"

"Who has her hair up," murmured George Fitzroy in a voice Lucy prayed no one else heard.

"She was here a moment ago, Papa. Oh, here she is."

Adelaide came bursting back, saw the company, and turned her boisterous rush into a graceful curtsy.

"Sir Charles, may I present my elder daughter—good God, girl, what have you been doing to yourself?"

Adelaide's poise was not so complete after all. She went crimson.

"I have only put up my hair." She stared defiantly. "It was time."

Papa, despite the fact that he was in the presence of the governor, began to roar with laughter.

"Well, there's a minx for you, Sir Charles. It was done for your benefit, I haven't a doubt."

"But I have," said Sir Charles, beginning to smile broadly. "Why should a young lady dress herself up for me?"

He turned pointedly to his son, who was also smiling in the most admiring way, his eyes fixed on Adelaide's scarlet face.

"Whoever it's for, I must say that it suits her," George said.

"Well, come in, gentlemen, come in." Papa waved toward

the drawing room. "Addie, since you consider yourself old enough, you must help entertain the guests."

"Don't make it sound like a penalty for the young lady," Sir Charles said.

They filed into the drawing room, Addie leading the way. No one seemed to notice that Lucy was left behind. No one had asked her to come in. She clenched her fingers into the palms of her hands, praying not to have to cry. Wasn't she used to this? Addie always stole the show. Usually Lucy was glad for her to. She preferred to sit silent and unnoticed.

But not today. Not after looking into those warm brown eyes. Suddenly she desperately wanted to be noticed. And how could she be? A little girl with her hair in ringlets.

"Lucy, my love, what are you doing?" came Mamma's voice. "Have they gone in without you? Then come in and sit beside Mamma. Lady Mary thought your flowers were most artistic."

She was only fourteen, much too young to be in love. But she began to make up fantasies about George Fitzroy, imagining he walked in the garden with her at dusk, said he admired her, held her hand. As she sat at Lady Mary's feet on the veranda, holding wool for Lady Mary to wind or threading needles for her, she dreamed impossible, rich, beautiful dreams.

"Bless me, Mrs. Massingham, this is a quiet mouse," said Lady Mary.

"Yes, but such peaceful company," replied Mamma. "I like her to be with me. I'm afraid Adelaide is much too restless and impatient."

"H'm. Well, my son doesn't seem to think so."

"He does seem to admire her," Mamma said in her polite voice, which didn't quite hide her gratification. "She's much too young, of course. She put up her hair without permission, but it will have to come down when she goes back to school on Monday."

"She seems to know a great deal about viticulture."

"Yes, it's quite unsuitable knowledge for a girl. She's too precocious."

"So is George," said Lady Mary placidly. "You must bring your girls to the next garden party at Government House. I suppose I shall have to give one soon. But I find it very exhausting in the hot weather." Lady Mary mopped at her scarlet face. "How long did it take you to get accustomed to the Australian summer?"

"I still am not. My husband forbids me to go out without a parasol."

"Well, you've kept your complexion, I must say. Most of the women I meet have faces like leather. Very unbecoming."

The voices prattled on, and Lucy dreamed. At the Government House garden party she would wear her organdy hat with the wide frilled brim. George wouldn't be able to take his eyes off her. The beautiful Miss Lucy Massingham . . .

But she scarcely said another word to him during the whole weekend. There wasn't an opportunity.

Adelaide would have said, "Make one." But how could she when he was much too busy talking and laughing with Kit, with whom he got on famously, or Adelaide, or the three of them were saddling their horses and going off on a long ride, or everyone took part in a picnic at the lake, or people came to dinner, and music and dancing followed. She could at least have sung at the piano, as Mamma pressed her to, but the very thought of singing before such a large company made her tremble with fright. Her imploring eyes made Mamma desist. So there was really nothing left to do but be a schoolgirl, well mannered but virtually invisible.

George was an expert dancer. He taught Adelaide the polka. They whirled up and down the room until they were both out of breath and Adelaide's hair had begun to tumble down. Then at least he could see that she was almost as much a schoolgirl as Lucy was. This, however, did not make him turn his attention to Lucy.

Perhaps he would come again when she was older. But she knew he never would.

Everyone except Lucy pronounced the important visit a great success. Kit was pleased that George Fitzroy was as infected by gold fever as he was. George, when he could escape from duties with his father, was planning to go to the state of Victoria to try his luck. Kit had determined to accompany him, although he was keeping quiet about that at present. There would be an almighty row with Papa, who could never see farther than his last row of vines. Privately Kit thought everything about growing grapes and making wine, except the drinking of it, a great bore. At least his father was pleased that he was rapidly becoming a connoisseur. But the silly old man never could refrain from pointing out that a great deal of hard work must be done before one reached the ineffably pleasant state of pouring the rich red stream from the bottle.

The reprimands became monotonous. There were plenty of people on Yarrabee to do the hard work. Laying the odorous farm manure in the autumn after the vines had been stripped of fruit and had dropped their leaves, piling up the soil to protect the roots from frosts, pruning away the unnecessary wood, leaving the vines in strange primeval shapes. That was only the beginning of the preparation for the next harvest. In the spring, when the shoots began to grow, another pruning must be made, and after the flowering an unceasing watch must be kept for fungoid, pests, barrenness. And plenty of prayers needed to be said for rain in the right quantity, sunshine of the right quality, and an absence of hailstorms.

Kit did not believe too much in prayers. Nor did he like piddling about in the winery. Besides, Jem McDougal had charge there, and Kit was damned if he was going to take orders from an ex-convict.

The whole thing was not his choice of occupation, and he intended to be off on an exploration trip even if he had to wait another eighteen months until he was of age.

Sir Charles Fitzroy had proved to be a great winebibber. He said that he intended to spread the fame of Yarrabee wines far and wide. This put Gilbert into the greatest good humor. As the departing carriages were lost in a cloud of dust, he turned and swept Eugenia into his arms, kissing her soundly in full view of everybody.

"You did famously, my love. No one could have managed better. Lady Mary admired you, and Sir Charles was ready to eat out of your hands. You know, you look exactly as I had anticipated."

"I look as I always do," Eugenia said in some perplexity.

"I mean, I knew when I married you that you would look like this today. Yarrabee, too. And our children."

"It was what you wanted?"

"Exactly. Why do you look at me with that little frown?"

"I don't know. We seem to be at odds too often."

"That gives marriage a spice. Can't have it getting dull. I think we ought to get that Irish painter fellow back and have him do a family portrait. The Massinghams in middle age with their children. I'm sure—what was his name?—would be glad to earn some money."

"It would scarcely be any use to him since he is dead."

"Dead! When?"

The sudden angry color stained Eugenia's cheeks.

"How can you be so surprised? It was you who said he would drink himself to death. How could he still be alive a dozen years later?"

"Is it as long ago as that? By George, how time flies. Well, don't get in a fuss, my love. I meant no harm."

Eugenia lifted her skirts to return indoors. She was suddenly tired. The weekend, for all its pleasure, had been a strain. "There, you see what I meant about always being at odds," she paused to say. "But your remark about middle age is right. You have some gray hairs, did you know? I noticed them last night, at dinner. And how did you hurt your hand?"

"My hand? Oh, that sore. I knocked it, and it hasn't healed. It's nothing."

"It needs some embrocation on it. Ask one of the maids for some. Now I must go speak to Adelaide."

"I don't care for that tone of voice," Gilbert called after her. "What's Addie been up to?"

"Didn't you notice she had her hair up? Without my permission, I assure you. She's behaved in a most forward way during the whole weekend."

"Well, young George liked her. Doesn't that please you?"

"Dancing with her petticoats flying over her head. And riding astride, I daresay, as soon as she was out of my sight."

Gilbert's hearty laughter followed her up the stairs.

"She's got plenty of spirit. Don't dampen her down too much."

Dampen her down? How was it possible? For there was more trouble immediately after Adelaide returned to school. Miss Hester Chisholm drove out especially to see Eugenia.

It seemed that three girls in Adelaide's dormitory had been found in an intoxicated state.

"We were intensely worried, Mrs. Massingham. We simply didn't know what was wrong with them and called the doctor. He asked bluntly what they had been drinking. Imagine it, Mrs. Massingham. The scandal in our school!"

"And what had they been drinking?" Eugenia asked as calmly as possible.

"Wine, of course. It seems that someone from Yarrabee—and I can't prevail on Adelaide to give his name—had hidden a bottle under the bush at the gate on her request. The three girls in question were then persuaded to drink it out of mugs in their dormitory that night. With young girls, unaccustomed to intoxicating liquor, the result was predictable."

"Was Adelaide also in this condition?"

Miss Chisholm lifted her chin in as contemptuous a gesture as she dared.

"Naturally not, Mrs. Massingham."

"If you are suggesting that wine is my daughter's habitual beverage, Miss Chisholm, I can assure you that you are mistaken. What action do you propose to take?"

Miss Chisholm looked uncertain. She had shot her big gun, and that had taken all the temerity she had.

"I had hoped you would make a suggestion, Mrs. Massing-ham."

"It's your school. Naturally Adelaide must obey your rules. Do you wish to expel her?"

"Why, *no,* that would never do!" Miss Chisholm was horri-fied. "We couldn't afford the talk that would cause. We must keep it quiet. Adelaide will be punished by having all privileges withdrawn for a certain time. But I would like your assurance that this can never happen again. In other words, the person who delivered the wine is as much to blame."

Kit, Eugenia thought wearily.

"I understand, Miss Chisholm. You can safely leave that side of the deplorable affair to me."

"Your daughter is a very bright, very advanced girl, Mrs. Massingham."

"Yes," Eugenia agreed. "She is both those things."

Kit swore he had had nothing to do with the affair.

"Honestly, Mamma. Anyway, I haven't been in to Parra-matta for a week."

Gilbert, whose mouth was twitching irrepressibly, agreed that this was true. Kit hadn't been off the place.

"Then who has?"

"I have. Jem and I took a shipment for the coastal towns. But if Addie wanted a bottle of wine, I would give it to her and make no bones about it. I wouldn't be hiding it under a bush. A bottlebrush, I believe. Aptly named, eh?" And then Gilbert's suppressed laughter did escape. He put back his head and roared until the tears rolled down his cheeks. "The minx, eh! I'm sorry, Genia, it's just so deuced funny."

"So it was Jem," said Eugenia.

"Jem?"

"It wasn't you, and it wasn't Kit. Who else could it have been?"

"Old Jem, of course," Kit said gleefully. "He and Addie have always been friends."

"Friends?" Eugenia said. "I should hope not."

"You know that Addie always tailed him about when she was little. And now she talks to him about winemaking. She's interested in it. Much more so than me."

"Then why can't she discuss it with her father if she must discuss it with someone? Anyway, it's not a suitable subject for a girl. Gilbert, Jem will have to be dismissed."

Gilbert stopped chuckling.

"Hardly, my love."

"Isn't this a dismissable offense? If Miss Chisholm hadn't been too scared of me or you, Adelaide would have been expelled."

"But she isn't going to be, and neither is Jem going to be dismissed. Quite frankly, apart from any other consideration, I can't do without him."

"So he is to escape scot-free?" Eugenia demanded incredulously.

Gilbert eyed her narrowly. A faint cynical smile touched his lips.

"If he were still serving a sentence, I would give him a dozen lashes. Would that satisfy you?"

"Gilbert! How can you!"

Eugenia, seeing a long-forgotten glint in his eyes, was overwhelmingly conscious of a memory she thought had grown too dim to bother her.

"If you asked Jem to make a choice, I could predict he would take the lashes, rather than dismissal. He has the makings of an outstanding vigneron. I refuse to lose him because of a schoolgirl prank. But I'll speak to him. I promise you that."

"Only speak to him! Is that all?"

"Yes," said Gilbert curtly. "That is all."

Chapter 29

DEAREST SARAH,

First, we are not so old-fashioned as you think. We are all now wearing bustles and six petticoats, *quite* unsuitable for this climate, and we have been learning to dance the polka. I should qualify that last assertion by saying that Kit and Adelaide are the polka enthusiasts. We had Sir Charles and Lady Mary Fitzroy staying here, together with their son, George, who took quite a fancy to Adelaide. But I daresay that was only a harmless flirtation. Adelaide is very headstrong. So different from Lucy. Although I fear for Lucy. She has such tender feelings. She has been pale and *triste* since the governor's visit, but when I ask her what is the matter, she says nothing. It is growing pains, I suppose, though Adelaide never suffered in this way.

I wish I could bring both my girls to England. Gilbert has been hinting that if next year's vintage is as good as this one was, we may really go. This journey now seems as unreal to me as a journey to the moon.

Now for some servants' hall gossip. We have given Obadiah White and Emmy Dawson permission to marry. Then I hope they will work properly again, as they are hopeless in their present lovesick state. I still miss Peabody dreadfully. Obadiah is a diligent worker (when not gazing hopefully toward the house to see if Emmy will appear), but he has not Peabody's touch of genius. It must be my imagination that none of the flowers has been so brilliant, or if it is not imagination, the fault is due to the long, dry summer.

As for the rest of the servants, Mrs. Jarvis and Ellen are not on such good terms as they used to be. At least Ellen is inclined to sniff or avert her eyes when Mrs. Jarvis appears, although she assures me they have not quarreled. I suppose women living together for so long must sometimes get on each other's nerves.

Gilbert, I am sorry to say, has been looking fatigued. He works such long hours among his vines, not seeming to realize that he is no longer young. He has had a nasty little ulcer on the back of his hand which refuses to heal. The doctor says he has seen afflictions of this nature, and he thinks they are caused by the hot sun. Gilbert must keep his hand covered when he is in the sun until the sore heals. He scorned going to a doctor until Mrs. Jarvis added her persuasions to mine. She once saw this type of persistent ulcer in her early days in Sydney, and it had become quite serious. But of course, the sufferer was an unfortunate convict who would have had no medical attention.

Our next important festivity at Yarrabee will be Kit's coming of age ball. Gilbert wants to make it a very magnificent affair. Part of his reason for this is, as usual, his wine. He will be opening the claret laid down at Kit's birth. So I really don't know which will be being toasted, our son or the Yarrabee vineyard. I wish, for my husband's sake, that I could have grown more enthusiastic about wine growing, but it is a profession so full of anxieties one can never be at ease. And I regret to say that I have now seen enough of the effect of wine to have an obsessive dislike of drunkenness.

I have left my own small piece of news to the last. Not that it is much to relate, but I cannot help feeling ridiculously proud of it. I have been asked to lay the foundation stone of a school the government is building in Parramatta. At last they are taking education seriously, and it seems as if my own efforts have helped slightly toward this. Hence the honor. My name will be inscribed on the stone. So whether I like it or not, I will have a small permanent record in the history of the colonization of this country.

I really have tried to help all the forlorn and homesick new arrivals, especially the young women. I identify myself so much with them. No one who had not experienced it can imagine the enormity of cutting off one's home ties and beginning life in a strange and often harsh country.

That spring Gilbert found the oldest section of his vineyard suffering from oidium. It was a disease of old age, he told Eugenia. "Something we all have in common," he said, looking at the small itching ulcer on his hand, which still refused to heal. The vines would have to be rooted out and burned.

"Perhaps the same should be done to me." He laughed, the myriad wrinkles around his eyes deepening. But his eyes were still a brilliant blue, still sunny and charming when he was in an amiable mood. He had grown thinner, and this suited him. There was a shadow of austerity in his face which Eugenia found moving. She could not tell him this because she had repressed her feelings for too long. She had become what he had wanted her to be, a poised, composed woman in control of her emotions. He never knew how often her heart ached. For too many years he had been quite unobservant of her more subtle shades of feeling. He admired her but didn't *see* her, she would fume inwardly, and when her repressed emotions had to find an outlet, it was in an argument about the children or the vineyard.

Even when he began looking tired and she urged him to work shorter hours—after all, he now had Kit to take over some of his duties—there had to be an argument.

"The boy doesn't show enough interest," Gilbert grumbled. "I can't even trust him to bottle a cask of Burgundy. I found he'd sealed all the corks without leaving enough air room. Jem had to do the job all over again. Jem makes ten of Kit, I'm sorry to say."

"He's young. He doesn't take life seriously yet," Eugenia said.

"Then it's time he did. At his age I had sailed around the world and begun to clear my own land."

"Perhaps you should let him go off exploring for a year.

That's what he wants to do. Then I'm sure he would be glad to come home and settle down."

The familiar obstinacy came to Gilbert's face.

"This is his place, and here he will stay. I haven't worked all my life to establish something that won't be carried on. If I had more than one son, that would have been a different matter. But this is how it is, and this is the way it will remain."

It was a worrying spring. A blight called black spot, or, more officially, anthracnose, appeared among the sauternes. Gilbert identified it with dismay. It had been a curse to viticulturists since the beginning of grape growing, but until this season he had not encountered it. Sores and punctures appeared on the newly sprung leaves, making it certain that the vines would not bear fruit. The remedy, so the French said, was to puff sulfur over the afflicted area. Once again a tense, exhausting fight took place.

The blight was contained in a relatively small area, by which time a herd of kangaroos had trampled through the southern corner of the vineyard and completed their journey of destruction in Eugenia's garden. She was awakened in the early morning by the great smoky gray creatures. She rushed onto the balcony and screamed at them. One, holding a pulled-up rosebush in his paws, stared at her blandly. Others took small leaps that landed them in the center of the daffodil and hyacinth beds or the newly planted borders.

At last the appearance of Emmy and Ellen on the veranda flapping aprons at them made them leave, sailing with effortless leaps over the shrubbery.

The garden was sadly wrecked. A flight of kookaburras settled in the fig tree and cackled with what seemed like macabre mirth. Erasmus screeched from his perch at the open window of Eugenia's sitting room. The morning was shattered with the raucous sounds. And Gilbert, coming in from inspecting the vineyard damage, had no sympathy to spare for the garden.

"A few flowers! Grow some more."

Then there was another disaster to relate to Sarah, a most

distressing one. Lady Mary Fitzroy was killed in a carriage accident. The horses had run away, upsetting the carriage at a sharp bend in the road. Her husband, who had been driving, escaped serious hurt by clinging to the reins, but the ADC seated beside him later died of his injuries. Lady Mary, that nice, stout, kindly lady, had been killed instantaneously.

It was a great tragedy. Eugenia did not wish Lucy to go to the funeral, but the child begged not to be left at home alone. She would keep seeing dear Lady Mary seated in the rocking chair on the veranda with her wool and her knitting needles, she said. Please not to leave her at home with a ghost!

Eventually it was decided that Adelaide and Lucy should wait at the cemetery gates, while Eugenia, Gilbert, and Kit followed the sad procession to the vault where Lady Mary and the poor young ADC were laid side by side.

They were not far from the ornate tombstone marking Mrs. Ashburton's grave. Peabody lay at the farther side of the burying ground.

"Our baby sister's grave is under the palm tree," Adelaide said, as if the blowing sand and the small gray angel in the shade of the shaggy palm tree hadn't been known to Lucy from the beginning of her life.

One day, she thought, everybody at Yarrabee will lie here.

More and more people were arriving in the colony. Laborers, craftsmen, rich men in search of adventure, a considerable number of rogues who had fled before Newgate got them, and a few dissolute sons of great English or Irish families who found it more comfortable to have their embarrassing offspring on the other side of the world.

There were also professional men, scientists, engineers, botanists, geologists, who saw romance in participating in the birth of what one day must be a great country.

The white-sailed ships sailed into Sydney Harbour; the travelers disembarked amid the usual chaos of baggage, lost children, and fearful wives. Some remained in the towns because they were growing so fast and were full of opportunities.

Or their wives were nervous of the immense heat-blanched spaces, of which they had heard too much for their small reserves of courage. Others, more adventurous, wanted to start exploring at once. Most of them, especially the Irish, were hungry for land.

The most desirable types of new arrival were the ones who regarded the great continent, still largely unexplored, with its blazing sun and dust storms, its everlasting gum trees, and strange primeval animals, its noisy birds, kookaburras, currawongs, and fantastically hued parrots, its sudden clouds of galahs like a pink feathered sunset, its endless stretches, mile after sun-bleached mile, its great rivers and mangrove swamps, its sheer fabulous immensity, as the biggest challenge in their lives. This was a land, they were told, that went back to an unbelievable antiquity. It was older than Egypt, older than Greece, older than Crete of the Minotaur. Old and new at the same time. And already there was a new race in the world who had never seen England or the continent of Europe.

The young Massinghams of Yarrabee, for instance. Yarrabee was becoming a known stopping place, whether the traveler was interested in vineyards or not. He would receive warm hospitality, drink Yarrabee wine, meet that charming and now-famous hostess the elegant Mrs. Massingham and, with luck, her good-looking daughters. Miss Adelaide, who was friendly, freckle-nosed, bouncing, and Miss Lucy, much the prettier, but extremely elusive. And dull, the young men who had contrived a conversation with her reported. She had nothing to say for herself. She might have the looks, but Addie had the vitality.

So what with old and new acquaintances, there was a long list of guests for Kit's coming of age ball.

All the same, Kit and Adelaide were exasperating. Kit showed no interest in the very suitable young women Eugenia proposed inviting. Maud Kendall, daughter of Judge Kendall, was a charming young lady. So was Millicent Lyon, whose maternal grandfather was an earl. Bess Kelly's daughter Alice had not yet found a husband. Kit laughed about her. "You wouldn't marry me to dumb Alice, Mamma. A wife requires to speak sometimes." It seemed he didn't want to be married to anyone. At least, not yet.

Adelaide was even more feckless. Her careless indifference had driven away that pleasant, eminently suitable young man George Fitzroy. News had just come of his interest in a young lady in Sydney. He would be unable to attend the Yarrabee ball.

Adelaide found that information diverting. Lucy, however, went pale, and Adelaide cried cruelly, "Why, I do believe Lucy cherishes secret feelings for him. Are you in love with him, Lucy?"

"Don't be absurd! She's far too young," Eugenia said. But the child's face went red, then pale again, and the too-ready tears filled her eyes.

"Adelaide, don't be a tease. You know how sensitive your sister is."

"If she's old enough to fall in love," said Adelaide with logic, "she's old enough not to blub like a baby."

Kit came to Lucy's defense. "Leave her alone, Addie. Wait until you know what it's like to be in love."

"You sound as if you know a lot about it yourself, Christopher Massingham."

"Perhaps I do."

"Then pray," said Eugenia, "stop quarreling and tell us who the young lady is, so that we can include her among our guests."

Kit raised blue eyes to look steadily at his mother.

"Suppose I told you it was Rosie."

"Rosie Jarvis?"

"There's only one Rosie, Mamma."

"Then I would say that you are teasing your mother, which isn't a very polite thing to do. Besides, Rosie is your sister, virtually, and you haven't seen her for five years."

"If she's my sister, why doesn't she live at Yarrabee?"

"Now, Kit, don't be tiresome. You know why Rosie was sent away. And your father and I absolutely forbid any tree-climbing episodes at this ball."

Kit had his father's way of throwing back his head and laughing. But none of his father's look of strength and determination. He was very slender, with a narrow, fair-skinned face and a sulky mouth. He looked younger than he was. The quick temper and willfulness that had been his failings as a child had not left him. He also had a tendency toward being a dandy, which his father scorned. The boy would have to grow up and have that knocked out of him.

"You forget, Mamma, that Rosie is of age, too. She's not likely to want to shin up trees now."

"I hope not, but I also have no intention of finding out. Rosie is happily settled at Darling Downs."

"How do you know, Mamma? Have you ever inquired?"

"She writes regularly to her mother, who informs me. Now, can we get back to the business in hand? I would like a little seriousness."

"Did you think I wasn't being serious?"

"I could scarcely believe that you were. Unless you meant Rosie to help her mother and Ellen. Even that wouldn't be suitable since she hasn't been trained as a maid."

"My God, Mamma, that must be exactly the way Queen Victoria speaks. As if servants aren't human beings."

"Kit, I won't have you swearing like that. And I don't know why the Queen is being brought into this conversation. We may be a long way from England, but we still have conventions. One is that I do not ask my housekeeper's daughter to a ball. Now, where have we got to with our list, Lucy? How many people will need to stay the night? That's an important factor. I don't think we can manage too many extra beds, with the house guests we will have already."

"Who wants a bed?" said Kit. "The party won't be over until daylight."

"It will be for the older people. Lucy dear, place a tick against the names of those who will require to stay the night. Write clearly because Papa will want to see the list."

That was another anxiety. Gilbert's eyes were growing weak. Their brilliant blue was fading slightly, but remorselessly, al-

most as if at last the sun were draining their color. That annoy-
ing sore on his hand had not healed, and two others had appeared on his forearm, nasty, hard, blanched spots that were
just as obstinate as the first one. The doctor had given them
a name now. They were skin cancers, he said. Troublesome,
but not serious. They appeared on skins that had been exposed too much to the sun.

Gilbert kept them hidden from Eugenia but allowed Mrs.
Jarvis to apply ointments. She had had a great deal of practical
experience of illness, he explained, when Eugenia came unexpectedly upon the dressing operation on the veranda outside
Mrs. Jarvis' room.

Mrs. Jarvis nodded, saying nothing. But she looked troubled,
Eugenia thought. She was a curious woman, so calm, always
keeping her own counsel. They had lived together for more
than twenty years, and except for occasions of great stress, they
had kept their mistress and maid status. Eugenia was perfectly certain Mrs. Jarvis would not have had it any other way.
She knew what was right and what was wrong. So much for Kit
and his talk of equality.

But perhaps, as a recognition of Mrs. Jarvis' long service
and loyalty, she should have invited Rosie to the ball. No. The
thought was dismissed instantly. It would be an embarrassing
situation for everybody, for Rosie herself most of all.

Anyway, Kit had only been teasing. He liked to hint that his
mother was too much of a *grande dame.* He was going through
the rebellious stage. He would be as conventional as anyone
when he was a little older.

A dressmaker came from Parramatta to make Adelaide's
and Lucy's dresses. Much to Adelaide's disgust, she was to wear
white satin with a blue sash. She would have liked something
much more dashing, like striped taffeta with a very low bodice.
Lucy's dress was identical, except that the sash was pink.
Mamma had been adamant about this. She said that she and
her favorite sister, Sarah, had been dressed alike for their first
ball. The effect had been charming.

But that was *years* ago, Adelaide complained, and begged the dressmaker to cut her bodice much lower. She was seventeen. She utterly refused to look like a little girl.

Lucy, it seemed, preferred to look like a child. She even protested about having her hair up for the first time. It made her look much too grown-up. She would be expected to converse like an adult, and she simply didn't know how to. She never knew what to say to anybody.

"Then it's time you learned," Adelaide said. "I can tell you this, men don't care for girls who can't open their mouths. They find them inexpressibly dull. No wonder your passion for George Fitzroy wasn't returned. Of course, you're so pretty, you might just manage, but you'll have to smile and look pleasant. As for me, if I were not vivacious, absolutely no one would look at me."

This was scarcely the truth, for Adelaide was handsome in a breezy way that might well become flamboyant. Although the Misses Chisholm had loyally hushed up the scandal of the wine episode, it had somehow got about and the redheaded Miss Massingham of Yarrabee was getting a reputation for being fast. She had a man's taste for wine, it was said. Both she and her brother knew altogether too much about the drinking of it. Kit had had to be assisted home from a night out in Parramatta often enough. But that was hushed up, too. The knowledge would distress his mother too much. It was a good thing for her sake that her youngest daughter was so quiet and good.

"Who are you going to talk to especially?" Lucy asked Adelaide.

"I don't know. Certainly not all those eligible young men Mamma is asking. Actually, I prefer older men."

"Older? How much older?"

"Well—about thirty, I suppose."

"But they would all be married!"

"Not all," said Adelaide carelessly. Then she changed the subject abruptly by wondering if Kit had been serious when he had talked about Rosie.

"But he couldn't be. She was only a sort of elder sister to him."

"Yes," said Lucy uneasily. It must have been nearly a year since Kit had stopped forcing her to post his letters for him. The amusement seemed to have fallen flat. This did not mean, however, that he was not still communicating with Rosie.

"I don't believe he's interested in girls at all," Adelaide decided. "He really has nothing in his head except going off on an exploration trip. I believe if Papa doesn't allow him to, he'll go, anyway."

"Surely he wouldn't," Lucy said, shocked.

"Lucy, you are a milksop. Are you meekly going to obey Mamma and Papa all your life? If you are, you'll never be a person. I mean, a real person."

"Oh, Addie, how can you say that? I'm sure Mamma never disobeyed her parents."

Adelaide brushed her hair vigorously before saying thoughtfully, "*Is* Mamma a real person? Sometimes I think she isn't. She always looks beautiful; she never gets in a rage; she does everything properly. You'd never find her making blots on a letter, for instance. Or getting her needlework grubby. Or saying the wrong thing to somebody. Or being caught with her hair falling down or her dress mussed up. She's really too perfect to be real. That's what Kit says, anyway."

"I don't," said Lucy indignantly. "Neither does Papa."

"Papa?" Adelaide gave her a sidelong look. "I wonder. Oh, I know he adores her. But when I'm married, I don't intend having separate rooms. My husband is going to share my bed. All the time, until we're grandparents and great-grandparents. It won't bother us getting old."

"Mamma and Papa aren't old," Lucy said confusedly.

"That's what I mean, stupid."

As it happened, something apart from Kit's and Adelaide's exasperating behavior nearly wrecked the ball. Tremendous news arrived. Gold had been discovered at Bathurst. The Noakes, traveling from Sydney, were full of the news. Everyone was leaving the city. The roads were choked with bullock wagons, drays, every kind of transport. Shops and businesses were being abandoned as their owners joined the hysterical rush to the goldfields. There were nuggets as large as ostrich eggs, it was rumored. A man could get rich in a day.

Parramatta was swept by the same fever. Laborers were dropping their tools and begging any kind of ride or, failing that, walking on their two feet, knapsacks on their backs, in the direction of the Blue Mountains.

Mr. Wentworth's voice was heard from Sydney. "The discovery of gold," he said, "must precipitate us from a colony into a nation."

Even old men were joining in the mad rush. But not so at Yarrabee. Gilbert said, "Our gold is here." He was speaking to his vineyard laborers, who had been ordered to gather in the courtyard. He stood on a chair in order to dominate them. Any threatened danger to his vineyard still aroused intense feelings in him. His eyes glittered; his voice rang with authority and conviction. He was a burly figure, his hair and side-whiskers sprinkled with gray, his skin an ocher color that had lost its healthy red. Few of his workmen would defy his quick temper, his hardness. One at least remembered the savage pain of the lash on his bare back. But he was a fair man, a good employer, so they listened to him in spite of their restless excitement. Gold. One listener, at least, had the fever shining in his eyes. The boss' son, no less.

"This year," Gilbert said in his strong, confident voice, "the prospects for a good vintage have never been better. With luck it will be a record one. We have had no severe frosts, favorable weather at pruning time, sufficient rain since. There's no sign of blight. With luck there won't be a hailstorm. The sun is filling the grapes with sweetness. I make a prediction that the claret and Burgundy laid down this year will be drunk with pleasure twenty and thirty years hence. Let others have their creeks and their pans of dirt. This"—he waved his arm toward the terraces of green vines—"is our goldfield. To every man who stays with me until after vintage I promise a bonus of a half year's pay. Gold sovereigns in his hand, rather than a panful of yellow dirt that may turn out to be nothing but clay. I don't ask you to make up your minds now. Think it over. Talk about it. But I want each man who decides to stay to come to me at nine o'clock tomorrow morning and sign his name in the wage book. And after that I expect him to keep his word, as I will keep mine. So there it is, lads. Yarrabee and a good vintage. Or a lot of thirsty work for no wages on a goldfield that may turn out to be a myth."

"Did I get them?" Gilbert said to Molly afterward.

"I don't know. You should have. The older ones, I think, but I'm not so sure about the younger ones."

"No. I'd have been the same myself at that age if I hadn't had my head full of viticulture. That was my gold fever. I hope to heaven Kit doesn't get it into his head to rush off. Anything to escape a day's work, that boy. He was born lazy. Or Eugenia and I made him so. Did he have life made too easy?" Gilbert sighed. He was tired again. His impassioned appeal had drained him of energy. He was just past fifty. Too young to be so tired.

"Anyway, he can hardly go off with this ball in the offing, can he?"

"No, love, no," Molly said soothingly.

"I just wish he'd be more enthusiastic about what I've made for him. Yarrabee. It is something, isn't it, Molly?"

"It is something."

"Yes. Well, I expect all parents try to run the world for their children. I wonder what a son of ours would have been like."

"Crazy like you, I expect."

"Loyal to the very soul," Gilbert murmured, his mouth against hers.

Eugenia hadn't heard the appeal, but she listened sympathetically to Gilbert's account of it and said that she was sure he must have convinced the men. A half year's wages as a bonus were extremely generous. Could he afford it?

"I anticipate being able to do so. I also anticipate doing something else."

"Not my trip home at last!"

He looked disappointed that she had guessed his surprise.

"I know I have promised it to you often enough. But this time it is really going to happen. I'm buying a passage to England for you and the girls."

"The girls, too!" Eugenia was daring to be excited.

"Isn't that what you want? To present them at court? I'm snobbish enough to like the idea myself. Mind you, I'll miss Addie, and I don't expect you to keep her away too long or turn her into a fashionable, useless creature. Lucy may be best suited to an English husband. But Addie I want back."

"Gilbert, I may write to Sarah about this?"

He smiled. The brief rare tenderness that she so much longed for showed momentarily in his eyes.

"If you trust me to keep my word."

"I believe I do this time." Spontaneously Eugenia went to kiss him.

"Are you so glad to get away from us all?" he grumbled.

"It's only the sun, Gilbert. I have always hated that glaring sun and the dust. And the constant anxiety about the vineyard."

"And your husband sometimes, too. He gets included with the worst of Australia."

"No. No, you are wrong about that."

He looked at her quizzically, and she said unhappily, "You have been wrong about that for a long time."

He stared at her, not believing her quiet, obstinate words. Or was it that he didn't want to believe them, for he dropped his eyes and said a shade too heartily, "Well, I am glad not to be too much of an outcast."

"Outcast? I thought that was me. Or should I say misfit."

He had to look at her again, puzzled.

"Outcast! Misfit! I don't know what you're talking about. You know you have been the wife I wanted. I've told you so often enough."

"But not the wife I wanted to be."

"And what was that?" He was humoring her now, but the strange uneasiness lay just beneath his jolly manner.

"If you're referring to—well, you know, that was doctor's orders and so on. And as for these arguments we have, the truth is, I like you most when you complain about the vines and are righteous about the children. It shows how you're involved in it all. I don't know what I'll do when you're away. You're the life of this house. When I look up and see you coming down the stairs, my heart lifts up. Believe what I'm telling you. None of this nonsense of wanting to be different. You are you, and I am me, and we've had the good sense not to try to change each other. Though I must say, you've had a good attempt now and then."

He laughed, expecting her to do the same. But she couldn't, and he exclaimed, "All the same, I don't care for you when you get intense. I hope we are not to have too many of these moods before your departure."

How was it possible for two people to live together for so long and know so little about each other? Or so much, but not the truly vital things.

Chapter 30

STARLIGHT and the carriages rolling up to the front door. Ellen and Emmy in crackling white aprons peering down the stairs. Miss Higgins in her best black bombazine nervously clasping her hands and wondering who would talk to her if she went downstairs. The mistress had insisted on her coming down. She must see her pupils in their finery, Master Kit a handsome gentleman with his fair side-whiskers and air of assurance that he copied from his father. Miss Adelaide with crushed red geranium petals rubbed on her cheeks and lips and all the assurance in the world. Miss Lucy as sweet as an angel with her downcast eyes and little hands gripping her fan so tightly it would probably break. Funny timid little thing that she was. You'd think she must have seen a ghost when she was born.

The three of them were handsome enough, but they couldn't touch their parents for looks if the truth were to be told.

Miss Higgins' adoring eyes took in every detail of the mistress' appearance, and thought she had never looked more beautiful. Her piled-up hair was graying, it was true, but that added to her distinction. She wore a cream brocade gown cut low over her slender shoulders. She looked like a lighted candle. So Miss Higgins remarked fancifully to Emmy, who for once didn't laugh at her friend's romantic flights.

She whispered back, "Don't she and the master make a lovely pair?"

Then the first guests began coming in, and Emmy and Ellen had to hurry down to take wraps and show the ladies upstairs. Mrs. Jarvis was somewhere in the background. She never craned her head over the banisters. She was much too superior.

The musicians had come from Sydney. They knew all the latest dance tunes. In no time at all the first quadrille had been formed. Marion Noakes was saying to Eugenia, "Is it true you are really getting your trip home at last?"

"How did you know?"

"Gilbert has written to the shipping company. The manager is a friend of ours. Good gracious, Eugenia, this country is still a village for gossip."

"When is Philip going to let you have a trip?" Eugenia asked.

"Never. I don't want it. Look at me. Dried up. An old hag. It's different for you. You've kept your complexion. Heaven knows how, but you have. You really are the most pampered woman in Australia, Eugenia."

"Me! Pampered!"

"From the moment you arrived. And if you don't know it, then I'm sorry for Gilbert."

"Oh, tush! I've had as many troubles as anyone else."

"Well, I can only say they've sat very lightly on your shoulders. You have a look still—I can only call it innocent—and laugh at me if you like."

Eugenia did laugh as merrily as possible.

"And me the mother of three great children. I'll be a grandmother before too long, I have no doubt."

Marion's eyes sharpened with curiosity. She was joined by Bess Kelly, fatter than ever, looking the way Marion obviously thought a mother of grown children should look.

"Has Kit someone in view, Eugenia? Is he in love?"

Eugenia shrugged. "Now don't ask me. You know that mothers are the last to be told these things. But I don't think so. He wants nothing more than to rush off to the goldfields. Gilbert won't allow it, naturally."

"After tonight, can he stop him?" said Bess. "He'll be of age. When are we to sample this famous claret?"

"At supper. Gilbert and Jem have tasted it and pronounced it excellent."

"Jem?"

"Jem McDougal. He helps in the winery."

"Oh, I remember. He's the lad who was a convict."

Eugenia frowned slightly.

"He got his freedom long ago, but he wanted to stay at Yarrabee. He has a natural instinct as a vigneron, Gilbert says. He's over thirty now." She sighed. "Everything seems so long ago."

"He hasn't married?" Bess was overcurious about eligible bachelors. She had three daughters to marry.

"Not yet," said Eugenia. "I doubt if he ever will. He's even more obsessed with the making of wine than my husband is. Here are some more guests arriving. You must excuse me."

Yarrabee at its peak, its crowning. The scent from Eugenia's lovely garden drifting through the open doors, the lighted candles in the sparkling chandeliers shining on the gay scene. The chink of glasses, the music, the faster and faster swirling of the women's skirts. They were so much wider this year. The fashion of the crinoline had arrived from England. Everyone who still wore those ridiculous bustles was hopelessly old-fashioned. One needed several stiffened petticoats to make the skirt stand out in a circle, and it was all much too hot in this climate. Not that the women were any hotter than the men in their high, starched collars and embroidered waistcoats. Faces grew redder and damper, and it was with some relief that a temporary cessation of dancing was announced. It was eleven o'clock and time to drink Kit's health.

"At this precise time twenty-one years ago," Gilbert announced solemnly, "Christopher Massingham was born. The next day I bottled the wine with which I now ask you to drink my son's health. Yarrabee Claret, eighteen thirty-one."

Ellen was tugging at Eugenia's sleeve.

"Ma'am, there's a late arrival."

"*S-s-sh!*" whispered Eugenia, watching the red stream Gilbert was pouring into a glass. This was Kit's own wine. For once she had to enjoy drinking it. "Who is it?"

"A young lady, ma'am. Alone."

The repressed outrage in Ellen's voice communicated itself to Eugenia. She looked around and saw the girl standing in the doorway.

Ostentatiously alone, in the dramatic black cape that covered her from chin to feet. Changed, but familiar. One could never forget that three-cornered face with the slanting eyes, the winged eyebrows, the sallow skin. Rosie!

How dare she come uninvited! The impertinence of her! Eugenia's first reaction was rage. She didn't know how to conceal it, but somehow she must do so, for Kit, who clearly must have been expecting the girl, had crossed over to her and welcomed her ardently.

"Mamma, look who's here!" he called, taking Rosie's hand and drawing her across the room. "Papa, another glass. We have one more guest."

"How do you do, Mrs. Massingham," Rosie said curtsying primly. Her eyes were anything but prim. They gleamed with the most outrageous mischief. "I'm sorry to be so late. I came by mail coach to Parramatta, and then I had the greatest trouble in finding someone who would drive me here."

Before Eugenia could speak, Gilbert's hearty voice cut across the babble.

"Rosie! Well, that's extraordinarily nice of you to come to drink Kit's health. And right, too, since this claret was laid down in the year of your birth. Where's your mother? She must drink with us."

"Yes, go to the kitchen and get your mother, Rosie," Eugenia said clearly, and was totally unprepared for the shaft of fury and hostility from Kit's eyes.

"Stay here, Rosie. You're my guest. Ellen will go." With deliberate care he divested Rosie of her wrap and handed it to the still-outraged Ellen.

The ball was ruined, of course. It was the second ball that Rosie Jarvis had ruined.

Not only Rosie, Eugenia had to admit. Gilbert had something to do with it by insisting on Mrs. Jarvis' coming to the ball-room so that mother and daughter looked like honored guests.

Mrs. Jarvis had appeared to come reluctantly, hesitating in the doorway, but Gilbert had gone forward and taken her arm, and Kit had promptly taken Rosie's, and there they were, the men of her family, with those two servants.

Not that they didn't look extraordinarily handsome. Rosie, wasp-waisted, in a green gown of very good taste, her narrow, angular head held high, Mrs. Jarvis in neat black silk with an amethyst pendant Eugenia had never before seen around her neck.

It must have been a gift from Rosie.

It was clear that most of the men present had plenty of ad-miration for the two women and were pleasantly titillated by the situation. Only Gilbert Massingham would do a thing like this. Though why shouldn't a toast be drunk to a loyal servant, that handsome woman, Molly Jarvis, and why shouldn't young Kit have a fancy for the daughter? This was Australia, and vari-ous of the guests could look back to their own lowly beginnings.

Eugenia's face ached from smiling, and her neck ached from holding her head that necessary inch higher than usual.

She drank the toast to Mrs. Jarvis with genuine goodwill. But Rosie—that was too galling. How dare she come, making that deliberate late entrance, behaving as if she were the guest of honor, no less?

And how dare Kit play this trick on his mother, knowing how it would upset her? He was looking across the room at her now, an audacious twinkle in his eyes. He was like his father tonight. She had often wished he had shown more of his father's arrogance and audacity, but not because of a situation like this. She had a deeply uneasy feeling that this was much more serious than an adolescent escapade in the shrubbery.

Mrs. Jarvis had drunk her wine and, with her impeccable manners, turned to go. Kit, however, laid his hand on her arm, stopping her.

"No, don't go yet, Mrs. Jarvis. I have something to say." In a perfectly natural way he tucked one arm in Mrs. Jarvis', the other in Rosie's, and, flanked by the two women, announced in a loud voice, "This is my birthday, and I intend to commemorate it in a more important way than drinking my father's claret. Rosie and I are announcing our engagement." He flushed deeply, lost his formality, and cried jubilantly, "We're going to be married. Mamma! Papa! Young Addie, where are you? You've all got to come kiss the bride."

He was drunk, Eugenia thought dazedly. He must be. Otherwise, how would he have the impudence to play a trick like that?

Gilbert had come across to her and taken her arm.

"Buck up, my love!" he whispered. "You must say something."

"It's a joke!" Eugenia burst out, but felt herself propelled across the floor. All eyes were on her. There was nothing for it but to hold up her head and behave as well as she could. She and Mrs. Jarvis with their dedication to good manners, she thought ironically.

She could even look into Rosie's eyes, brilliant with triumph, and say, "My dear. I am much too surprised to take in such momentous news now. We must talk in the morning."

Gilbert, however, had to kiss the girl heartily on each cheek and then wring Mrs. Jarvis' hand as if he were highly delighted about the whole thing. Perhaps he was.

"Well, Mamma?" said Kit.

"I think you are a very impetuous young man. The extraordinary thing is that I hadn't realized you had grown up. Isn't that ridiculous?"

"Tonight, as ever was," Kit said gaily, and added in a low voice, "Bravo, Mamma." His eyes had exactly the same look of critical admiration that Gilbert's frequently had.

For a disastrous evening, it remained very noisy and merry. No one seemed to want to stop dancing or to go home.

"Why are you so against it, Eugenia?" Philip Noakes asked as they became partners in a dance. "Rosie seems a nice enough girl. Smart. Good-looking. Educated, thanks to you."

"And both her mother and father convicts," Eugenia said bitterly.

"Heavens, that's a quarter of a century ago. Rosie's an Australian. Like Kit."

"She's also Kit's foster sister."

"They're not exactly committing incest. You're a snob, Eugenia."

"Am I? I just can't bear the convict taint. It represents everything I have so hated and dreaded in this country. I sent one of those poor wretches to his death, do you remember? How can I let the memory of those unhappy times be perpetuated in my own family?"

"Have you hated it so much?"

"More than anyone knows."

"Yet you've made such a success of living here."

Eugenia raised her aching eyelids. He really believed that. Dear Dr. Noakes, who knew so much about her body, knew nothing whatever about her mind.

"Have I?"

"You have, indeed. You're one of our great pioneer women. History books will have your name in them."

Eugenia suddenly pulled away from him, crying painfully, "Then I'm a fraud. Let that be recorded as well."

But of course, Kit was only joking. He had played this prank to punish his mother for refusing to invite Rosie to the ball. He would tell them so in the morning. Rosie would go back to her governessing, and Kit would set himself to finding a suitable wife.

That was the frail hope Eugenia clung to. It was soon to be dashed.

Kit was not joking, but he did not stay to tell his parents so. After his outrageous gesture last night he lost courage, for he had another blow to administer. He took the cowardly way of writing a letter for them to find when they came downstairs.

DEAR MAMMA AND PAPA,

Rosie and I are just leaving. We are borrowing the buggy but will leave it in Parramatta, where I have horses waiting for us. We are going to the goldfields and will find a parson to marry us there. This will save Mamma the embarrassment of thinking she has to arrange a big church wedding for us.

I am sorry, Papa, about the vineyard, but you must have realized by now that I am not interested in the wine business. I have no talent for it. I have always only wanted to explore, and I am convinced I will make my fortune. Even if I don't, Rosie is quite happy to be the wife of a workingman. We have always loved each other. Please, Mamma, try to understand.

Your devoted son,
KIT

P.S. Actually, I confess to liking rum better than wine, so how could I be a success as a vigneron?

It was a blow too deep for words. Gilbert, it seemed, had no objection whatever to Kit's marrying Rosie. She would be too good for the young rascal if she took after her mother. But that his son did not intend to carry on the vineyard he found unbelievable and completely shattering.

His eyes were bleak and hard. When Eugenia suggested that surely Kit would come to his senses, that when he found what life on the goldfields was like, he would want to come hurrying home, Gilbert shook his head.

"No. I won't have him back. I've put up with his laziness and disobedience and indifference for long enough. I'm finished with him as far as the vineyard is concerned. When a vine gets a blight, it is cut out. It is a painful, but necessary, operation. And when something attacks it at the roots, it begins to wither." He abruptly straightened himself, as if realizing the too personal truth of his allegory. "I'll run my vineyard myself until I drop. Then Jem can take over. Tom Sloan, too, only Tom's older than me. My God, Eugenia, I feel old today."

"Surely Kit will come back," Eugenia said again. But Gilbert didn't hear her or pretended not to.

"Yarrabee will always be here for you and the girls. Perhaps Adelaide will have a son. My own son a rum drinker!" He shook his head incredulously. "It's beyond belief."

At least Eugenia had the diversion of planning for the long-awaited trip to England. There were wardrobes for herself and the two girls to be made. She wouldn't have them arriving looking dowdy and out of fashion. Emmy and the dressmaker from Parramatta were kept constantly sewing and cutting out, while the sun shone and the grapes ripened and the record vintage Gilbert had hoped for looked as if it would be a reality.

Kit's name was seldom mentioned. Mrs. Jarvis had expressed remorse for her daughter's high-handed behavior, but it had seemed to Eugenia that there was triumph in her eyes. She wouldn't be human if she weren't pleased to have Rosie make such a catch. However, she could not be held to blame. Eugenia struggled hard to be fair.

But she could hardly bear to see Gilbert without the optimism in his face. It had so long been a part of him that this quiet, quenched face was almost that of a stranger. Even the ripening grapes, swollen with sweetness, did not cheer him this autumn.

He said he was tired. When vintage was over, he intended to have a rest. He would escort Eugenia and the girls to Sydney, see them aboard their ship, and then have three or four weeks of relaxation. Jem and Tom Sloan could attend to the pruning of the stripped vines and the manuring. After all, one day Yarrabee would have to manage without him. He had never before made such an admission.

On a clear, brilliant morning that gave promise of being a

hot day, the first of the pickers began arriving from Parramatta. There were more women than usual and a number of
children, the result of the man of the family having gone off to
the goldfields, leaving his wife and children to get along as
well as possible until he returned with a fortune in his knap-
sack.

Gilbert cast an experienced eye over the gathering in the
courtyard. He knew at once which women would work well,
which would easily tire, which of the children, ranging in ages
from six to sixteen years, would be of help and which nothing
but a hindrance.

It was a pity that there was a lack of labor this particular
year, when the vines were so heavily laden with such luscious
sugar-filled fruit.

But they would manage. There had been worse problems.

Gilbert called for volunteers in his own household. Ellen,
Emmy (although Eugenia was reluctant to spare her from her
sewing), and Mrs. Jarvis offered their services. Emmy would be
working beside Obadiah, her husband. Miss Higgins said she
would like to help, but she couldn't stand the sun. She was like
the mistress; too much heat made her feel faint. Lucy, also, was
too fair-skinned and fragile.

But Adelaide, a scarf knotted over her head, an apron over
her cotton dress, stood beside Jem McDougal, waiting eagerly
to begin.

"Adelaide, you must put gloves on," Eugenia cried. "Your
hands will be ruined."

"Oh, Mamma, don't fuss." Adelaide's quick, impatient
frown was her father's. So were her dazzling blue eyes. Gilbert
grinned with pleasure. He looked happy for the first time since
Kit's departure.

"Let's be off," he ordered.

The little procession set off, carrying wicker baskets or pull-
ing handcarts, followed by Tom Sloan with the drayload of
provisions, gallons of oatmeal water, hunks of bread and
cheese, baskets of scones and biscuits, which Mrs. Jarvis had
been up long before dawn to bake.

Everything about vintage Adelaide found exciting and stimulating. She loved the hot sun on her head and her bare arms as she cut the bunches of bloomy black grapes. When the wicker baskets were full, they were emptied into the handcarts, which were pushed to the winery, where their load was tossed onto the presses, and the rich juice and skin (bearing the precious yeast pores) run off into the great vats.

The morning's picking, the cold lunch in the shade of a clump of gum trees, and then picking again until the sudden fiery sunset was the greatest fun, the physical exhaustion a pleasure. But much more exciting was the winery, where, after three or four days, the vats began their mysterious bubbling and seething.

It was the first time Adelaide had been allowed to watch this process from start to finish. Jem was the master here. In the dim, low-ceilinged, odorous room he moved about silently, watching, testing, sniffing. It had got that Papa relied on him absolutely to predict the result of each vat of seething liquid. Almost by tasting the grapes beforehand, he could say whether the wine would be sweet enough or too bitter with tannin or thin and vinegary.

If Adelaide wanted to remain in here, she mustn't prattle in her usual way. She must be silent, observant, intelligent. She could help work a press, if she wished, seeing the juice squirt from the lush bunches of grapes. She could make a guess which vats had fermented long enough and were ready for running off into casks. And which casks should be rolled away to stand for six months, a year, five years, before bottling.

She was even allowed to sip a little of the raw wine, rolling it around her mouth, deciding how good it would be on maturity.

But all the time Jem was the maestro, the wizard. Even Papa admitted that.

"He has a better nose than me, Addie. Or perhaps I'm getting too old. Losing my sense of smell. My palate, too. Jem says this year's claret will be a great wine in thirty years' time. I'm sorry I won't be here to prove him right."

"Oh, you will, Papa."

"No. But you and Jem will."

Color suddenly rose in Adelaide's cheeks. Her eyes followed the stocky figure of Jem, the broad shoulders and muscular arms, the tightly curled black hair over the sunburned forehead. Her childhood friend. There had never been a time when he wasn't there. Papa had said she must go on this silly trip to England to please Mamma, but she regarded it as a complete waste of time. A whole year out of her life at Yarrabee, and what for? That nonsense of being presented at court, of making inane conversation with a lot of sissy, pale-faced Englishmen. Couldn't Mamma just take Lucy, who would love the languid English drawing rooms?

It was a promise that she should be back by next vintage, but imagine not knowing what was happening to the vines during the winter and spring. Or to Papa, left alone with the servants. Or to Jem, who, not having her to talk to, might well begin riding into Parramatta to find other female company. He had always had her. He was bound to miss her. At least, he had better dare to say he wouldn't!

"You will miss me, won't you, Jem?" she said over the noise of the cellar.

He looked at her with his bright brown eyes.

"You don't need to remind me of that, Miss Addie."

He went to pass her, and accidentally his bare forearm brushed against hers. He stopped, and his gaze went back to her, burning suddenly right down into the depths of her heart. For a moment neither of them could speak. Then Jem gave a laugh and said, "There'll be no more bottles hidden inside the school gates. I promise you that."

They both began to laugh hilariously, something released in them.

Adelaide deliberately let herself touch his bare arm again.

"Jem, if you don't dance with me on vintage night, I won't come back from England. I swear it."

"I'll dance with you, Miss Addie. From first to last."

"Dearest Sarah," Eugenia wrote:

> I can scarcely believe that for once nothing threatens our trip. The vintage, as Gilbert expected, has been a splendid one, and I am so happy for his sake, as well as my own. He has been more deeply hurt by Kit's departure than he has admitted, and this good harvest of grapes seems like a compensation to him.
>
> We have had a letter from Kit saying that he and Rosie were married by a Scots minister in Bathurst. Very correctly, he said, although to me it still sounds like a runaway Gretna Green marriage.
>
> Gilbert says I must be tolerant, but something hard and unforgiving rises in me whenever I think of that girl. I admit that I have never been fond of her. She was a sly child, always lurking in passages. Perhaps she felt shut out, and perhaps it was my fault. I don't know.
>
> Anyway, that is past history, and I must accept the unhappy present as best I can. But I grieve for Gilbert's crushing disappointment. There is, after all, nothing to replace a son.
>
> The dance after vintage was pronounced the merriest Yarrabee has yet seen. A young Irishman played the fiddle, and the couples danced in the courtyard and drank a great deal of raw wine. Lucy and I watched from the veranda. Lucy could not be persuaded to join in, though Adelaide, I scarcely need to tell you, danced with untiring enthusiasm. Everyone loves her because she puts on no airs. But she is still far too much of a hoyden in spite of her expensive school. The trip to England comes at a very important time in her life . . .

Much more important than she could tell Sarah, Eugenia thought sadly, laying down her pen. It was true that Adelaide had danced untiringly on vintage night, but almost exclusively with one person. The burly vigorous figure of Jem McDougal.

"What of it?" said Gilbert, flinging himself into a chair beside Eugenia and mopping his brow. "She's doing what's expected of her. Her sister should be doing the same."

Lucy crouched back, trying to make herself invisible. Nothing would have induced her to mingle with that noisy, sweaty mob. Eugenia said, "But not all the time with one man."

"Jem? He's a good chap. She's only teaching him the polka. Deuced amusing, really. Jem's talent is for winemaking, not dancing."

And for kissing. When Adelaide at last came upstairs, she unceremoniously shook the drowsy Lucy awake.

"I'm sorry, but I've got to talk to someone, or I'll burst. Lucy, I've been kissed!"

Lucy eyed Adelaide's flushed face and brilliant eyes half with envy, half with shocked disapproval.

"Not by Jem?"

"How did you guess?"

"I would need to be pretty stupid not to. Even Mamma and Papa talked about how often you danced with him. You were making a spectacle of yourself, Mamma said."

"Mamma will say that about me until her dying day. I shall never be able to please her. But Papa?"

Adelaide's eyes were suddenly so anxious that Lucy could not bear to hurt her.

"He didn't mind. He likes Jem. As a workman, of course."

"What's wrong with being a workman? It's better than being a waster like our dear brother. Rosie will have got more than she bargained for with him."

Lucy shot up.

"Addie! You say that as if you're serious about Jem!"

"Well, he kissed me," said Adelaide, dropping her eyes. A small soft smile curved her lips. "In the vegetable garden, among the cabbages. It doesn't sound very romantic, does it? But it was. We'd only walked away to get cool. And then he kissed me, unexpectedly."

"It can't be the first time you've been kissed," Lucy said, trying to sound cynical.

"No, it isn't, but I've only had pecks before." The smile deepened on Adelaide's lips, which seemed mysteriously to have grown fuller and redder. "This wasn't a peck. Lucy, I think I'm in love."

Lucy lay back, gathering the sheets around her face.

"With Jem?" she whispered. Now she was not only shocked, but afraid. Mamma would never allow this. Never! There would be endless rows and unpleasantness, and Addie was headstrong enough to do—goodness knew what.

"I think I always have been. Like Kit with Rosie. Aren't we funny loyal people, we Massinghams? Very permanent in our affections. Except you, of course. Or are you still dreaming of George Fitzroy?"

Adelaide's voice was not scathing any longer. It was gentle, kind, full of wonder. As if she had discovered another dimension to life, which made her tolerant of everybody, even her silly timid sister.

"Oh, Addie," Lucy said, tears spilling over her eyelids.

Adelaide let her dress fall to the floor and stood in her bodice, stretching her arms, sighing deeply.

"But keep it a secret, Lu. I want time to think."

"You mean—he's asked you?"

"No. And I don't suppose he will. He knows his place, darling good Jem. I expect it will end in my asking him."

"You wouldn't dare!"

Adelaide sighed again, still smiling that infuriating smile.

"Oh, it's been a wonderful vintage. Every minute of it. I've felt as if I've been bubbling like the must. I never wanted it to end." Suddenly she leaped across the room, landing with one spring on her bed. "Of course, I will ask him if I have to."

"He didn't know his place enough not to kiss you," Lucy said, and Adelaide began to giggle.

"No. Thank heaven for that."

In the morning it seemed as if Adelaide had forgotten her late-night confidences. She was a little too quiet, however. Mamma thought she had been working too hard and dancing too much and had perhaps drunk more than was good for her of the sour new wine which Papa foolishly permitted on vintage night. Lucy watched her with intense anxiety, but her decorum was perfect and, for Addie, quite unfamiliar.

She allowed herself to be fitted for the ball gown she was to take to London, and when this was done, she consented to sit sewing lace on her new petticoats, instead of fretting to be out of doors.

Lucy hoped and prayed that her impulsive confidences had arisen from the excitement and the wine and that with sober daylight she was having second thoughts. There were just four weeks until they sailed. If only Addie could keep this quiet, sensible mood until then.

It was the lull before the storm. A lull that lasted three whole weeks.

The house was in a continual upheaval, with gowns and bonnets to be finished, boxes to be packed, decisions to be made about gifts for the English aunts and cousins. Lucy began to sigh about leaving Erasmus. He had an endearing habit of hanging by one claw from the top of his cage when she approached him. He would always respond to her "Good morning, Erasmus," when he frequently squawked rudely or was entirely silent with other people. "Good morning, Erasmus," he would say in exactly her soft, gentle tone. Would he still remember his tricks after a whole year?

Adelaide was much more concerned about Poacher, although she had no need to worry; Jem would exercise the animal. But Poacher was getting old, and Adelaide suddenly was stricken with the fear that he might die in her absence.

She worried all one night about that and came down to breakfast red-eyed.

"Papa, if Poacher should die, you would write and tell me, wouldn't you? You wouldn't keep the dreadful news from me?"

Lucy expected her father to give his roar of amused laughter. Instead, he said quietly, "Yes, Addie, I would write and tell you. I'll also write and tell you if any other animal or person on Yarrabee passes away. I'll even arrange for you to be informed if it happens to be myself."

He was meaning to be facetious, of course. For some reason

Adelaide, in her emotional state of mind, took him seriously.

"Papa, what do you mean? Have you something the matter with you?"

"Only middle age. A serious disease, but not fatal."

"Papa, don't joke about such things!" Adelaide, to everyone's surprise, flung down her knife and fork and burst into tears. Eugenia, coming in at that moment, exclaimed in surprise.

"Adelaide in tears! Whatever is the matter?"

"She seems to have suddenly had the morbid notion that I or Poacher or someone may die while you are all away," Gilbert said. "I have merely pointed out that you will be kept informed."

"Adelaide! What nonsense, child! We are only to be away a year. Do you think we will come back and find everybody gray-beards?"

Eugenia laughed softly at the notion and was quite unprepared for Adelaide's lifting her scarlet, tearstained face and declaring vehemently, "I can't go. It has come over me at this moment. I will stay and marry Jem this year, instead of next, as we had arranged. Forgive me, Mamma." She was babbling now. "I really thought I could go for your sake. I knew how hurt you would be if I didn't. But suddenly I know it to be impossible. I can't leave Yarrabee, and Papa, and Jem. The ship might sink in a gale or strike a rock, or we all might catch cholera in England. I have read that it is rife. It is a very unpleasant d-dis-ease—"

Her voice died away as she became aware of her mother's alarmed face.

"Adelaide, my dear child, I think you are having a brain-storm. It comes from too much excitement. Go to your room, and rest quietly. Ellen will bring you some hot milk to calm you."

"Wait!" Gilbert's hand was raised. "Wait, my love. Adelaide's brainstorm, as you call it, seems to contain some interesting information. Did I understand you to say, Addie, that you and Jem have arranged to marry?"

"Oh, *yes,* Papa! It was to be a secret until we returned from England. We talked about it for hours only yesterday. *I* had to propose to Jem in the most unladylike manner. He was too conscious of its not being his place to do so, as if I were royalty or something. But you should have seen his face. He accepted me with the greatest happiness, and I want you to know that we have no intention of behaving in such a cowardly way as Kit and running off with only a letter left to tell you. I meant to tell you like this, plainly, when we had returned from England. But suddenly I realized I can't go. I simply can't. It would be like tearing my heart out. Supposing there are bad frosts or blight or caterpillars—"

"Or Jem dies," Gilbert echoed, in a strange, mild voice. "I completely understand your anxieties, Addie, my dear. But you must know your mother has set her heart on this trip for longer than either of us cares to remember. And you are not yet eighteen. You can well afford to wait a year before you marry Jem."

"Gilbert—" Eugenia began to say, but was again stopped by his imperious hand.

"Wait, we must hear Addie out. Now, Addie."

Adelaide's tears had dried, and now, with an impulsive change of mood, her face was literally shining.

"Then you will not object, Papa, to my marrying Jem?"

"On the contrary, it has been an event I didn't dare to hope for, for fear it wouldn't happen."

"Oh, Papa! How wonderful you are. I told Jem you would be. But Mamma—" Adelaide dared to glance at her mother's face, and what she saw made her bite her lips.

"Jem is a fine man," Gilbert said. "In my opinion you couldn't have a better husband. What's more, he will want to carry on the vineyard—"

"The vineyard!" Eugenia cried at last in a shaking voice. "I believe you two have made this up between you to protect the vineyard now that Kit has gone." She flung down her napkin and rose. "This is the very last, unendurable straw. Our trip to England is not only ruined on the very eve of departure, but

I am now to have a convict as a son-in-law. It is exactly what I might have expected from the moment I set foot in this country."

"M-Mamma!" Lucy stuttered as Eugenia, stiff-backed, walked to the door.

She could scarcely believe her ears when her mother, unkind for the first time in her life, said curtly, "You may well cry, Lucy, since this is the country where you are to remain for the rest of your life."

Chapter 31

BUT it seemed that Lucy actually wanted to remain here. She had been secretly reluctant to go on such a long journey and meet so many strange people. She would no doubt have been thought exceedingly dull. The idea of curtsying to the Queen had petrified her.

To Eugenia, this was the hardest blow of all.

"But, Lucy, my darling, England would have been like home to you. Your cousins are not strangers. You've heard so much about Lichfield Court. What is there for you here? Will you be content to marry like Adelaide and Kit?"

"Rosie and Jem are just Australians, Mamma. The same as Kit and Addie and me." Seeing the pain in her mother's beloved face, she went on quickly, "I don't mind if I never marry."

"And what will you do instead?"

"I'll stay with you and Papa. I'll have the garden. I thought Obadiah and I might plant snowdrops and lilies of the valley for next spring. English snowdrops, Mamma."

"In this dried-up red dust?"

"It isn't dried up in the spring. You know that we have plenty of rain then. After all, you made a garden here, Mamma. I don't really see how you can bear to leave it."

That thought had sometimes come to Eugenia. She had wondered whether in England, she would have longed for her antipodean garden and perhaps boasted about the brilliant colors of the native flowers. And wondered whether Gilbert ever walked in it at dusk, as he frequently did now, in her company.

Her voice was softer when she answered Lucy. "You should have told us long ago that you preferred to stay at home. It would have saved us all a great deal of trouble."

And there had to be another letter of apology to Sarah.

It seems that my headstrong elder daughter has been dying of love and concealed the fact only for fear of disappointing me too much in my plans. But the truth had to come out, and now a wedding is much more imperative to Adelaide than a visit to England. Jem, to Gilbert's great satisfaction, is a most promising vigneron. So Yarrabee and the vineyard will be kept in the family after all, even though Kit will not be the heir. But I must tell you that Kit has had the good luck to find a gold nugget for which the bank has paid him five hundred pounds. He and Rosie are going to travel through Victoria and perhaps continue all the way to South Australia, where there is a flourishing colony. It is true that this country is full of adventure for the young . . .

"If you're going to stay home, you must begin to look happier." It was no use trying to resist Gilbert when he wheedled.

"Adelaide is the person who has to look happy. At least we don't need to have clothes made for the wedding. So all is not lost. Adelaide can wear the gown she was intended to wear to court, and Lucy as her attendant can do the same. And I shall be in difficulty to decide which of several gowns is best suited for myself as the bride's mother."

"My darling, you will look charming, as always, in any of them."

His words were spoken automatically. She had caught the sudden look of pain that had crossed his face.

"Why did you wince as you said that?"

"Did I? My back hurts. I must have strained it."

"When?"

"I don't know. A few weeks ago, perhaps."

"A few weeks ago, and it hasn't got better! You must see a doctor."

"Nonsense. A bit of rheumatism. I'm getting old."

"So am I, but I don't wince when I move. I'll call on Dr. Wilson when I'm in town this afternoon and ask him to come out."

She was looking at him clearly for the first time since her great disappointment. She wondered how she could not have noticed sooner the look of quenched tiredness in his eyes. His allegory about the withering vine came back to her mind. A pain twisted in her heart.

"You will let the doctor examine you, Gilbert? What about those ulcers on your arm? Have they improved?"

"They're nothing."

Something in his voice made her heart jump.

"Are there more?"

"One or two. For goodness' sake, I've had them for years. I'm not sick. I've never been sick in my life."

"And you would have let me leave you for a whole year without telling me this?"

"That I had a backache? You're surely not turning that into something important as well."

"But you will see Dr. Wilson?"

"That old woman! Oh, very well, if it pleases you." He held out his hand to her. "Don't mind too much about Addie. She and Jem will be happy. They're much better matched than you think. They're members of the same new race. They'll make their own social conventions. How could this polyglot lot of people live with one another if they allowed themselves to be weighed down by all those stuffy English traditions? Who's going to care in a hundred years, in fifty years even, that Jem McDougal came out in a convict ship?"

"I, for one, care now," Eugenia said stubbornly.

"Well, don't go on brooding about it."

"Oh, I shall hold up my head at the wedding. You don't need to be afraid of that."

But it was not to be a grand wedding after all.

Dr. Wilson drove out in his buggy behind his smart gray

mare to see Gilbert. After being closeted with his patient for a long time, he emerged from the bedroom with Gilbert, buttoning his jacket, following him and shouting in a highly irascible voice.

"Get Phil Noakes to come down, Eugenia."

Eugenia was alarmed.

"But why? You're not seriously ill, are you? What is the matter with my husband, Doctor?"

The doctor, with his little pointed beard in the air, walked down the stairs, leaving Eugenia to follow. He was too mannered and foppish for an Australian town. She might have known Gilbert would have little patience with him.

In the hall he answered Eugenia's question.

"I can't be sure yet. I'd welcome Dr. Noakes' opinion. Make your husband rest more, Mrs. Massingham."

"But is that all you can say?"

"My dear lady, don't look so anxious. It may be something perfectly simple. A touch of lumbago. I don't fancy it has anything to do with the skin condition, though I can't be certain."

The chill settled around Eugenia's heart.

"Doctor, what are you afraid of?"

The little beard lowered itself an inch or two. The man was human after all. His eyes were kind.

"Loss of weight, lack of appetite, severe pain in the lumbar region—classic symptoms of a tumor, Mrs. Massingham. But the diagnosis is by no means confirmed. Your husband has been a fairly heavy wine drinker for a long time. This may merely be some aspect of liver trouble. Give him a nourishing light diet, and make him rest. You might do me the goodness to inform me of Dr. Noakes' diagnosis. Good day to you, Mrs. Massingham."

"Old fool," was all Gilbert would say. "Why didn't he stay in London and prey on rich women? I'll take my oath there's a shady story in his past."

"You have to rest more," Eugenia said. "Please, Gilbert. For my sake."

"Are you turning me into an old man?"

"Don't be absurd. You're tired. And tired people rest. If they're not quite lunatic."

"Well, I am lunatic. You know that already." He shook her hand off his arm. "Don't fuss. Oh, very well, for the sake of peace I'll rest until Phil Noakes comes. Not a day longer."

Actually, after that protest, he seemed to enjoy sitting in the rocking chair on the veranda in the sparkling autumn sun. He even displayed an interest in Eugenia's garden.

"What's the name of those fiery red things?"

"Salvia bonfire."

The name pleased him. He nodded his head in a considering way.

"And they flower in the autumn. A brave flame before the frosts. Where are you going?"

"Just indoors to get my needlework."

"Bring it out here."

He didn't like to be left alone. He was resting to please her, so she could oblige by giving him her company. He liked to have Addie at his side, too. But Lucy had always been too nervous of him. He preferred her at a distance, working in the garden. Her slender figure kneeling over the colorful borders looked like her mother's.

The other person who appeared more frequently than was necessary was Mrs. Jarvis. Her movements and her face were quiet, as always, but she was beginning to look old. The servants knew that she was anxious about the master. "And no wonder," Ellen muttered spitefully. But Ellen had had a mysterious grudge against Mrs. Jarvis for some time.

None of these faithful attendants to the sick man knew about his most recent visit to the isolated bedroom beyond the kitchen.

It was midafternoon, and Molly had not expected to see him. She sprang up agitatedly from the armchair where she had been taking a brief rest.

"What are you doing here at this time of day?"

His eyes had the quizzical look she loved.

"It seems a perfectly good time of day to me. A good time to say thank you."

"For what?" she cried.

"Don't look so forbidding. Can't I thank you civilly for all these years? I don't believe I've ever had the decency to do so before."

She couldn't hide the desolation in her eyes.

"You won't be coming again." It was a statement, not a question.

He evaded answering. "There's no time like the present for paying a compliment."

She flung herself into his arms, her own flung tightly around him. She was not crying, although her deep, hard breaths sounded like sobs.

"Bless you, Molly. I'll never know what I would have done without you."

"Nor me without you."

He raised her face, which now showed its marks of age so clearly.

"You're a strange creature. Have you never wanted anything more?"

"Only your child. And then I would have had to leave Yarrabee. So, no, love, I've never wanted anything more."

"Your daughter has my son. That's something."

"I never encouraged it!"

"No, but it pleased you. To tell the truth, it pleased me, too. It's a kind of permanence for us, in its way. If anyone wants permanence. Molly, don't turn your head away. I'm not dying, you know. Me! I'm as strong as an old man kangaroo." He gave her his straight, aggressive look. "Do you think I'm dying?"

She made herself sustain his gaze without flinching.

"I only remember that you once asked me if I'd die for you. Well, I still would. Gladly."

His face tightened. He pushed her away roughly.

"Get on with you. I'll do my own dying. When the time comes. And that's a long way off. And Molly—"

"Yes, love?"

"It's true I won't be coming again."

She looked up in anguish. He rubbed his hand over his eyes.

"I believe I was too optimistic when I thought I could keep two women happy. It wasn't the simple thing I thought it was. I couldn't go to Eugenia after you. That was the trouble. And it seems she minded. And never said so."

"Has she said so now?"

"Of course she hasn't. Eugenia! She's much too subtle. I have to guess what she's thinking. I haven't been trying very hard for a long time."

"Gilbert, you're a good man!" Molly cried, as she had once before.

He smiled faintly.

"What a wonderful, direct, uncomplicated nature you have! If Eugenia had one like that—but then I wouldn't find her so fascinating. I have to make amends a little, Molly. Can you understand?"

She nodded. She understood all too well.

This was a familiar situation, being the one on the outside, the one with nothing . . .

Eugenia looked into Philip Noakes' face and winced away from the compassion in it.

"How long?" she managed to say.

"Six months. Nine. Perhaps a year. He's such a devil of a fighter."

"Let him have one more vintage," she begged, her throat aching.

"We'll see. But don't pray for it, Eugenia. Don't try to keep him alive. It wouldn't be kind."

"What a blessing you didn't go to England, Eugenia!" said Marion. Marion with her yellow face, like seamed pigskin, her tragic eyes.

"I know. How can I help him now? He won't give in, you know. He'll pretend until the end."

"I'd say, be with him as much as you can. For all his ranting and roaring, he's just as much in love with you now as he was the day you arrived. I'll never forget that day. He couldn't wait to sight your ship coming through the heads. He was out with a telescope from dawn."

Eugenia's face had twisted in pain.

"I wish you were speaking the truth. But you're not. Gilbert hasn't loved me for a long time."

"I don't believe it!" Marion exclaimed. "He worships the ground you walk on. You only have to see his eyes following you."

"Oh, he admires me," Eugenia admitted. "I am a sort of perfect doll woman. At the beginning I didn't know how to be a satisfactory wife. I was young and much too virginal. Then—something happened—and Gilbert didn't care for me in that way anymore."

"Couldn't you have overcome it?" Marion asked softly.

"Could you?" Now Eugenia had to finish her bleak confession. "With a husband who suddenly preferred separate bedrooms, who only came to you from duty or necessity or courtesy or whatever word he liked to use, who was relieved when he was told that there mustn't be another child, because that gave him an excuse to stay away! Could you have overcome that situation? I couldn't. It froze me, inside. I could never go where I was not wanted," she added miserably.

Marion, not wanting Eugenia to read her thoughts, lowered her eyes. Gilbert Massingham, the sensual devil! Whom had he been visiting secretly? She supposed that this was the inevitable way a marriage of this kind must turn out.

Yet it was far from being unsuccessful, so long as Gilbert found his satisfaction elsewhere and Eugenia hadn't any volcanoes of passion beneath her coolness.

Marion, looking into those beautiful, haunted eyes, was, all at once, not so sure about Eugenia's legendary coolness. What was the mysterious happening which she insisted had turned Gilbert from her? Surely it couldn't have been that old gossip about the Irish artist. But that hadn't been a real scandal. Or had it? Had Eugenia, with her morbidly acute sensitivity, been pining away for years with a guilty conscience?

"I lost him," Eugenia was confessing sadly. "And it was my own fault."

"Lost him be damned." Marion had picked up too much colonial coarseness in her language. "He's always loved you. There are plenty of ways to love. Why don't you try showing him yours? It isn't too late."

But how did one express that long-held-back emotion to a man who was permanently angry? Gilbert's blue eyes burned with bitter resentment against the fate that he wouldn't admit. He could not endure sympathetic looks or thoughtfulness for his growing weakness. He insisted on supervising work in the vineyard and swore without apology at anyone who tried to prevent him. He even swore at Jem, accusing him of neglect in the cellar. Jem hadn't turned the bottles in the bins frequently enough or kept records up to date. He went about declaring that if he were not there, Yarrabee would fall to pieces. But thank God that day had not yet come.

"It's God he's angry with, not me," Jem said to a bitterly weeping Adelaide.

"So am I," Adelaide sobbed. "I've stopped saying my prayers."

"Now, love. You must say them for the master."

Even with Eugenia, Gilbert had moments of intense irritability, although he constantly wanted her company.

"Why don't you answer me back when I'm rude? Why must you be so saintly?"

"I'll be far from saintly if I find you getting up in the middle of the night again to look for frost."

"But surely you've been the wife of a vigneron long enough to realize the danger of frost at this time of year."

"I only realize that if there is one, Jem and Tom will attend to it. From tonight you're coming back into our bed."

He gave her a quick look.

"You said our bed."

"So I did, and so it is. Or have you forgotten?"

He shook his head slowly.

"No. But I'm afraid I'll keep you awake, Genia. I haven't slept very well lately."

"Neither have I. We can talk."

That was the beginning of another phase in their lives, the whispered confidences that came easily in the dark.

"I've wondered lately—was I too clumsy with you at the beginning, Genia?"

The question gave Eugenia an almost overpowering compulsion to confess her long-kept secret. She had to bite her tongue to stop herself easing her conscience at the expense of destroying Gilbert's treasured image of her.

"I know sensitive women don't much care for that side of marriage," Gilbert went on, misinterpreting her silence. "But I was a strong, tough fellow in those days. I had to be, to manage the convicts."

"It was the convicts who were always on my mind. Especially after that terrible experience on our wedding night." She could make this confession safely. "I think I was the victim of my upbringing. It was perfectly suitable for a young lady in England, but in this country I needed much more practical knowledge and much less refinement."

His arm lay heavily across her breast.

"It was your refinement I wanted. Haven't you realized that yet?" He began to swear quietly to himself. "I'll get over this damned crippled back. It won't beat me."

All night, after that conversation, he held her in his arms. Whether he was aware of her completely loving compliant body, she didn't know, but she thought it was the most poignantly beautiful night she had ever spent.

In the late spring Adelaide and Jem were married. They had wanted a quiet ceremony at Yarrabee, but Gilbert was having none of that. People would think he disapproved of Jem as a son-in-law. Besides, Addie was his favorite child. She should have a church wedding, and he, naturally, would walk up the aisle and give her away. Proudly.

Kit wrote a long letter setting out all his reasons for not coming. It would be an impossible journey over crude roads with deserts to be crossed, rivers forded, and Rosie was expecting a child.

But Kit was an explorer, Adelaide said disappointedly. And Rosie was not someone to be afraid of a long, hard journey, even if she was pregnant.

It was Lucy who thought she guessed the real reason for Kit's failing to come. He had been told that Papa was dying, and he had a horror of death. He had once related to Lucy how he had been taken by Ellen to kiss the cold cheek of his baby sister Victoria after she was dead. Ever since then he had been haunted in his sleep by candle-colored faces and half-closed eyes.

"What a rotten coward he is!" Adelaide declared unsympathetically. "He runs away from everything. Oh, I do pray Jem and I have a son for Papa to see. So he'll know Yarrabee is safe."

"Then you will have to hurry," Lucy said sadly.

The wedding, if poignant, was a happy one. Eugenia was able to write to Sarah:

> I do believe I am going to grow fond of my new son. He has a very appealing gentleness, in spite of his strong appearance, and Addie adores him to distraction. Gilbert tells me that if he has not all the polish I could desire, he has the necessary qualities to be a success in this country. They are rather different qualities from those required in England, physical strength being one of them, and a doggedness of character another. I could go on, but I know you would prefer to hear about the wedding.
>
> It was very quiet, and only a dozen or so friends came out to Yarrabee afterward. My poor Gilbert did what was required of him perfectly, but to see him walking up the aisle, so thin, his fine, straight shoulders beginning to be stooped, his hair almost gray, was anguish to me—I could hear one or two weeping, and I hoped it was only for the reason that some women always weep at a wedding.

Anyway, my dear one had his wish and gave Addie into the arms of the man whom he wanted to be her husband. Now, I foresee that we will have discussions about wine at dinner every night. It will be like the old days of Mrs. Ashburton.

Lucy, of course, attended her sister as bridesmaid and looked very charming. I am glad that she is becoming so wrapped up in the garden. It gives her an occupation and, as I once knew myself when I was a young and homesick bride, a great interest. She has asked if a potting shed could not be built so that she and Obadiah can raise their own seedlings. I am only worried that she does not ruin her pretty hands . . .

Somehow the letter was filled up and dispatched. It was becoming increasingly difficult to write even to so beloved a correspondent as Sarah. Thoughts flew out of her head. She was always listening. Gilbert would be calling for her to go out onto the veranda. Or his slow steps would be coming in from his latest tour of the vineyard, and she would need to see if he required anything.

Christmas came and went. One day, after a long lapse, Eugenia had the notion to walk down to the creek and look at the small grave. She found that the crude cross had fallen over. It lay beside the almost flattened mound of the grave, its lettering only faintly visible. PRUDENCE.

Had her parents long ago forgotten her? Eugenia scratched at the earth and succeeded in putting the cross erect. Three black swans swam on the shallow water, their red feet a strange gaiety beneath their somber plumage. It was very hot. The pale trunks of the gum trees shimmered; their leaves were black against the heat-blanched sky. Eugenia opened her parasol. Gilbert would scold her if he saw her without it.

One morning a week later Gilbert said quite quietly, "I believe I'll have a day in bed. I'm tired."

Eugenia agreed with brisk cheerfulness.

"What a good idea! Ellen will bring your breakfast up."

"Tell Molly to."

Molly?

Once, two or three months ago, Ellen, distressed and embarrassed, had begun to say something about Mrs. Jarvis, but Eugenia had stopped her.

"Not servants' hall gossip at a time like this, please."

And Ellen had flung her apron over her head and blundered out of the room. She had been quite upset. But Eugenia had forgotten the episode until this moment when she heard that intimate, unmistakable note in Gilbert's voice. His guard was relaxed by weakness and a sleepless night.

The truth struck her like a blow.

She paced up and down her sitting room, struggling with her emotions. Anger about the deceit, and a furious impatience with herself for being so easily deceived and so naïve as to imagine that a man like Gilbert, who had always looked admiringly at Mrs. Jarvis, would not one day go further than admiration. All the time in her own house, this had been going on! It was humiliating, mortifying, unforgivable. She was astonished by the strength of her jealousy. She had lived for twenty years with her own guilt, but Gilbert could have felt no guilt whatever about his behavior. From the beginning he must have accepted the bizarre situation as eminently satisfactory and so begun the long deception.

Could he have ever loved her?

But yes, she told herself, determined not to give way to despair. For what about their shared nights now? They were as precious to him as to her. She had no need to be told that this was so. He held her in his arms, or his hand lay on some part of her body, as if he were reassuring himself all the night that she was there.

He did love her. And there were not enough nights left.

All the same, this situation could not be ignored. There would have to be a highly unpleasant interview.

Eugenia rang the bell and sent for Mrs. Jarvis. She waited for ten minutes, tapping her foot with impatience, the color high in her cheeks. At last Mrs. Jarvis appeared, apologizing in her quiet manner.

"I'm sorry to be so long coming, ma'am. The master fancied a lightly boiled egg for his breakfast, and I was just taking it upstairs. He isn't eating enough to keep an infant alive. What is to be done?"

Eugenia closed and unclosed her hands, knowing that, for all her anger, she was a coward. For anxiety had relaxed Mrs. Jarvis' guard. The pain was naked in her eyes. There was no need to cross-examine her. Her very pain betrayed her. To add to it would be an act of unnecessary cruelty, of which Eugenia knew herself to be incapable. She might as easily have tried to wield the lash on a naked back.

Yet something must be said.

"Dr. Noakes has said that we must do all we can to keep him happy. Perhaps you are more successful at that than I am."

The steady gaze of the anguished brown eyes did not flinch.

"Is that why you sent for me, ma'am?"

"Yes. It is. You must have thought me very blind and very stupid for a long time."

"No, ma'am. You nice women"—there was a touch of irresistible contempt in her voice—"don't know much about life." Then she got back her iron discipline and added, "If you will pardon me for saying so."

"You're telling me you kept my husband out of worse hands!"

"No, I wasn't saying that. But it's true, all the same. Others would have made demands. I had no need to ask for anything. Conveniently, I expect you think. I don't suppose you can forgive me. I always felt very badly about deceiving you."

"I should think that, at least!"

Mrs. Jarvis bent her head. "I couldn't help myself, ma'am. If it was to do over again, I would behave in the same way. I loved him too much."

Eugenia abruptly turned away, unable to contemplate the unassailable dignity of this wretched guilty woman who was contriving to look innocent.

"You will wish me to leave, ma'am?" Mrs. Jarvis was asking stonily.

Yarrabee without Mrs. Jarvis? How ever would she explain that to Gilbert? It was an impossibility.

"I don't think you understood me, Mrs. Jarvis. Dr. Noakes has left instructions that his patient is to be kept happy. We must do the best we can between us. For one thing, he must never know about this talk."

She had never seen Mrs. Jarvis cry. Even now the welling tears were sternly disciplined.

"Perhaps, for a nice woman, I know more about life than you suspect," Eugenia added wryly. So now she must live with the eroding pain of jealousy, as well as with the pain of Gilbert's slow, inexorable illness.

He had already lived longer than Philip Noakes had expected him to. When the pain became unbearable, Eugenia remembered Dr. Noakes' advice. "Let him drink, Eugenia. Wine, whiskey, brandy. Anything so long as it's intoxicating. Keep him in a stupor, if you can."

She who had always hated drunkenness. It was the final irony.

Gilbert was not unaware of the irony, either.

"You used to be against this, Genia. You said I helped kill that Irishman. I believe you really thought I killed Mrs. Ashburton, too. That wasn't true, although I admit I encouraged her to enjoy my wine. And I gave her the tombstone I promised her, even though she deceived me about her fortune. The crafty old witch. But she saved Yarrabee. Blessings on her gray head."

Saving Yarrabee was the highest deed anybody could do, in Gilbert's mind.

It was surely fate that arranged the heat wave the night the Frenchman was expected to dinner.

Jacques Sellier was an eminent wine connoisseur, from Paris. Traveling in the antipodes, he had heard of the young Australian wines and was greatly interested. Could he propose himself one evening for the purpose of sampling some of the Yarrabee wine? If it met with his approval, he would be only too willing to take some bottles back to Paris and also to London with his personal recommendation.

When the Frenchman's letter arrived, Gilbert was revitalized. He must be entertained royally. Eugenia and Mrs. Jarvis must work out a menu that would complement the wines which Gilbert was already discussing with Jem. The Yarrabee Christopher Claret, of which there were a few dozen bottles left and which was still Yarrabee's finest wine. The 1850 Riesling and the 1840 Port. Did Jem agree?

"Now don't say yes because you think you have to humor me. I'm still able to listen to another opinion."

"I do agree with you, sir. But Addie thinks the Riesling we drank at our wedding superior to the eighteen fifty. I tell her she's being sentimental."

"What's wrong with sentimentality? Anyway, she may be right. You wouldn't have married a wife without a palate, would you? So let us have Addie's Riesling."

"Thank you, Papa," said Adelaide later. "Did Jem tell you we'll be drinking to something more important than your Frenchman's visit?"

"What's that?"

"Can't you guess? Jem and I are going to have a baby."

Gilbert's sunken eyes gleamed.

"Does your mother know?"

"No. You're the first to be told."

"Make it a boy, Addie."

"For Yarrabee, I suppose. That's what Jem said, too. It's a good thing I like wine, or I would be as cynical as Mamma."

"Don't say a word against your mother," Gilbert said sharply.

It was a miracle how well the master of Yarrabee looked on that final important night. Candlelight softened his gauntness. Excitement brought a flush to his hollow cheeks and the old burning sparkle to his eyes. Nothing was to be said to the Frenchman about his illness. Nothing was to cast a blight over this evening. For the past week he had been getting up and walking in order to get the strength back into his legs.

So that M. Sellier found himself greeted by a tall, overthin, but erect figure, full of animation and enthusiasm. His hostess was as elegant as a Frenchwoman, which was the highest compliment M. Sellier could pay. The younger daughter was enchantingly pretty, though unfortunately too self-effacing. The older daughter had plenty of assurance, and her husband looked to be of sound peasant stock, which, in his opinion, was just what this country needed.

All the same it was a pity that the heat was so fierce on this particular night. There was every sign that another of the colony's disastrous droughts was beginning. The sun had shone unclouded for weeks. The land was crackling with dryness. In addition, a strong wind was blowing, stirring up dust storms and making traveling hellishly unpleasant.

Yarrabee was a surprisingly civilized oasis, the house handsomely furnished, the dinner table with its polished silver and crystal, a pleasant surprise. As for the wine, M. Sellier declared himself to be astonished and delighted.

"But it is excellent, my dear sir. It has a good nose. It is light, fragrant, altogether palatable."

"Ah, I thought you'd be surprised," Gilbert said complacently. "But wait until you taste the claret." He indicated to Jem to pour the wine. Then, as Mrs. Jarvis carried in the roast ducklings, he called to her to wait a moment. Before she served the food, he wanted to drink a toast.

Slowly he stood up, and as he held himself completely erect, he seemed immensely tall, dominating the table. The flickering candlelight even gave an illusion of the old vigorous red to his hair. He raised his glass, and Eugenia saw that he was looking down the table to her. For a long moment his blue eyes burned into hers. She remembered vividly when she had encountered that look across the space that had separated the bobbing boat from the shore, the brilliant blue eyes, the burnt umber head against the burnt umber of the Australian soil.

She clenched her hands to stop them trembling. Her eyes were filling with tears.

"I give you a toast," said the familiar, strong, resonant voice. "To Eugenia, my wife, my partner of twenty-three years."

The room dissolved into mist as the tears ran helplessly down Eugenia's cheeks. She began to rise but was waved down by Adelaide.

"No, Mamma. You must sit. We're drinking to you."

Eugenia fumbled for her handkerchief. "But this—can you think of anything more undeserved, M. Sellier?" She was half-laughing, half-crying. "To be quite honest, I don't even care for wine."

"Then, madame"—she had forgotten how gallant Frenchmen were—"I drink to you again for your loyalty, whether it was to the vineyard or its master."

Loyalty? Was that the word? The blue eyes burning down the table signaled affirmation.

But we were not loyal to each other, she was saying silently. Yet we were, we are, for there are different kinds of loyalty.

"Later Eugenia will sing you some French songs," Gilbert said. "You see, we are far from uncivilized. I remember when—" He stopped suddenly, lifting his head to sniff the air.

The windows had had to be closed because of the strong wind, but a flow of cool air came in through the hall doorway.

It was this that Gilbert was sniffing in such a curious way.

"Smoke!" he ejaculated.

Jem sprang up, knocking his chair backward.

"It's the candles, Papa," Lucy said nervously. "They keep guttering."

Jem was already out on the veranda, Addie close on his heels. "You're right, sir," he called back. "Smells stronger out here."

Already there were far-off shouts. Abruptly the memory of that other ruined dinner party long ago came to Eugenia. But this shouting did not come from mutinous convicts. This must be the other terror. A bush fire.

From the bottom of the garden, where they all had hastened, it was possible to get a clear view of the dark vineyards and the great luminous night sky shot, on the horizon, with patches of orange.

The aromatic smell of burning gum trees was tinged with another smell of singed hair and roasting flesh.

The wind was blowing strongly in their faces, which meant that presently swarms of panic-stricken animals, the ones not already caught in the flames, wallabies, foxes, kangaroos, sheep and cattle, wild pigs, emus, the lethargic wombats, which had not been shaped for speed, would be swarming in this direction in their desperate attempt to reach safety.

What was worse, to the petrified little group in Eugenia's sweet-smelling garden, was that the vineyards lay in the direct line of the advancing fire.

"*Mon Dieu!*" exclaimed the Frenchman.

Jem was already hurrying off. Gilbert's suddenly strong, commanding voice stopped him.

"I've fought fires before. You haven't, lad. I'll take charge. Fetch Sloan. He is probably on his way up by now. We'll want every vehicle there is loaded with barrels of water, all the sacks available, every kind of fire-fighting weapon. Garden tools, brooms, anything that will beat out flames."

Adelaide had fled after Jem, kicking off her high-heeled shoes and unbuttoning her crinoline as she ran. Lucy was immobile, her hands wrung together. M. Sellier was still staring in fascination at the flames on the horizon, exclaiming as they leaped about.

"They're like torches!"

"It's the intense heat," Gilbert answered briefly. "One tree ignites another even from a considerable distance." The thickening smoke was making him cough. Eugenia took his arm. He thrust it off and walked briskly up the path, imitating Addie by stripping off his collar and jacket as he went.

"Gilbert, you can't go to the vineyards!" Eugenia cried in dismay.

He didn't hear or pretended not to. He joined the crowd of

men assembling at the front door. Tom Sloan had brought up a dray. His grizzled head showed in the light from the veranda. Addie and Jem were already aboard. It was Jem who reached out to help Gilbert up.

"No!" Eugenia shrieked. "Don't let him go."

"Mamma, don't you see he *has* to?" Addie cried.

The dray was already rumbling away. Another one, driven by Obadiah White, was coming up. Suddenly M. Sellier exclaimed, "*Voila!*" and sprang nimbly aboard. It was either his action or the first dray rattling into the darkness that caused Eugenia to follow his example. They perched side by side on the uncomfortable wooden seat, too concerned with the flickering sky to think of the spectacle they made in their evening clothes.

Eugenia remembered that she had heard Lucy's horrified "Mamma!" as she had clambered into the dray. Lucy was not fitted for this kind of thing. She would do well to take refuge in the garden, where it would remain comparatively cool. Unless the fire could not be checked. Unless the vineyards and then the house itself were consumed.

Water splish-sploshed in the barrels. It was required to dip the sacks in, Eugenia explained to the Frenchman. They must try not to let it spill. Every drop would be precious.

A straggling line of people followed the drays. Eugenia thought she recognized Mrs. Jarvis' gray-blond head. But it was difficult to see now. The smoke, growing thicker by the minute, was hot and suffocating, and made her eyes water. It seemed that the fire had already reached the northeast corner of the vineyard. And suddenly the darkness was alive with the leaping shapes of kangaroos. Somewhere a dingo was yelping on a high note of pain. Its anguish was lost in the bleating, woolly rush of a flock of sheep unable to soar through the air as the kangaroos did, crashing violently through the vines.

The dray came to a bumping halt. Everyone tumbled out. Something struck Eugenia's head, a bird, half-stupefied in the smoke and darkness. It fell to the ground, a small green parrot which she could not stop to succor. For now the flames were not just torches on the horizon. They were sizzling and crackling a hundred yards away. The fight had begun.

Eugenia found the wet sacks awkwardly heavy to handle. She had to get too near the flames and was in danger of setting herself on fire. Obadiah silently took the sack from her and handed her a garden rake. With this she could beat at the small flames, running like an incoming tide, across the grass. When a row of vines burst into flames, the sight was awesome. The row of fire fighters, with their sooty, heat-reddened faces, was illuminated in a sudden all-enveloping orange glow, like some improbable scene from the Old Testament.

It was on these occasions that Eugenia paused in her backbreaking work and looked toward Gilbert. He was there in the distance, leaning on a stick, but directing the campaign tirelessly, his hoarse voice easily audible above the sinister crackling of the advancing fire.

They must concentrate on the plowed land dividing the muscatels from the Rieslings, he shouted. The muscatels would have to be sacrificed, but if the fire could be prevented from leaping across the intervening space, half the vineyard could be saved. It all depended on the wind, which fortunately seemed to be dropping.

Gigantic columns flamed against the sky as gum trees caught fire. The heat was overpowering. Eugenia had a moment of horror when her swirling silk skirt dragged in smoldering ashes. Why hadn't she had Addie's good sense to throw off her dinner gown and her petticoats? Addie was working like a man in a pair of Jem's trousers.

It was too late for her to put on trousers, but at least she could discard her dangerous skirts.

She dropped the charred and filthy dress and petticoats where she stood and, in only her laced bodice and pantaloons, continued beating at the small yellow tongues of fire. Presently a gust of wind blew a flame onto her discarded gown and turned it to a balloon of flame.

Gilbert caught sight of this phenomenon and exclaimed. He

thought for a moment that someone had been burned alive. Eugenia gave an irrepressible peal of laughter. Gilbert's face was so comical as he turned from what he had thought to be a tragedy to see his wife standing in her underclothing.

"Eugenia! What are you doing here?"

"What everybody else is doing. Trying to save the vineyard."

"Good God!" he whispered. She heard the tortured frustration in his voice, as he realized their reversed positions, he the helpless watcher while she toiled. There was no time to be sorry for him. The flames were taking another direction, frizzling the dried grass in their path. It would be utterly tragic if the Rieslings were burned. Someone was watching to see that no sparks floated in the direction of the house and stables. The stable doors had been opened and the horses left to run free.

Another rivulet of flames was quenched. Some soaring sparks winked out and fell harmlessly. The vines through which the holocaust had swept stood blackened and shriveling, the thin red veins of fire ebbing in the tough stems.

Tom Sloan arrived with a fresh supply of water. The overpowering smoke had given way to a wet, charred smell. Strangely the smoke seemed to be drifting away, and the fierce heat diminishing. A pause came in the intense activity. Eugenia saw Gilbert straighten himself with something of his old vigor.

"The wind has turned," he called out in a strong, excited voice. "By God, we've won!"

His blackened, emaciated figure had a curious affinity with the shriveled vines. But where they were dead and would have to be dug out, he was alive to see the miracle of the wind turning and the saving of his most cherished grapes.

Mrs. Jarvis, Tom Sloan, Addie and Jem, and the Frenchman, whose suave appearance had suffered severely—all came hastening to him, dropping their tools, sighing with exhausted relief.

"Papa, it's going to be all right now," Addie was crying. "We've lost only the sauternes, and we can replant—*Mamma!*

Where are your clothes?" She went into shrieks of hysterical laughter, only to be slapped lightly on the cheek by her father. "Don't you dare laugh at your mother! You saucy hussy! Genia, we've spoiled that girl. All the same"—he held out his hand to Eugenia—"it would be a good idea to go home and freshen up and rest for a bit."

No one would ever know how he had stood on his feet for so long.

But now that the fight was over, he was content to sprawl on the floor of the dray, his head on his wife's shoulder, and she with her little smudged face and her great eyes and her wonderful lack of embarrassment over her state of undress. She sat there, cradling him in her arms, and Tom Sloan tried to avoid the bumps on the track, while hurrying the horse as much as possible.

When they reached the house, Sloan turned anxiously to see how his passengers had fared.

"Wait there while I get some help, ma'am."

"There's no need to hurry, Sloan," the mistress answered in her courteous manner. "We have all the time in the world."

"He's not gone, ma'am!"

She moved her head in a bare acknowledgment. "Just as we left the vineyard. He was looking toward his vines as he drew his last breath. We mustn't grieve. It was merciful." She lifted large, brilliant eyes. Sloan was afraid she was a little deranged. But her voice was perfectly calm, even if her words were strange. "Go indoors and leave us for a few minutes, Sloan. Until the others come. Just now he belongs only to me."

Even the nights that seemed endless did come to an end. The stars moved in their courses, and people died, and morning came. All the same, that night had seemed to Lucy as if it were going on forever. She hadn't slept at all, and she was sure no one else had. It had all been such a nightmare, the terrible fire, Papa's death, and then Mamma in her bizarre, shaming state of undress, of which she hadn't seemed to be aware until

Addie had persuaded her to go take a bath and change before the doctor arrived.

To Lucy, Mamma's strange behavior had been the most unnerving thing of all. But now, at last, it was dawn, and it was a relief to get out of bed and go to the window for some cool air.

As Lucy leaned out, she saw, to her surprise, someone already walking in the garden. It was Mrs. Jarvis, wearing her usual dark dress, even a white starched apron. Was she dressed for the new day, or had she not ended the old one?

Lucy was about to call to her when she heard a footstep on the veranda. A moment later Mamma appeared. She, too, was in the gown into which she had changed last night. It had been one of Papa's favorites. Its flowing pearl-colored chiffon made her look like a slender ghost as she crossed the lawn.

Mrs. Jarvis saw her coming and paused in her walk, her head tilted inquiringly. Mamma said something that was inaudible to Lucy; then surprisingly, but in the most natural way imaginable, she linked her arm in Mrs. Jarvis'.

Together, the two women began pacing up and down, their steps in unison.